TO MY DAUGH
IN FRANCE . . .

Barbara and Stephanie Keating grew up in Kenya. One
sister now lives in France and the other in Dublin. This
novel – a seamless collaboration – is their first.

Barbara and Stephanie Keating

TO MY DAUGHTER
IN FRANCE ...

VINTAGE BOOKS
London

Published by Vintage 2003

15 17 19 20 18 16

First published in Great Britain in 2002 by
The Harvill Press

Vintage
Random House, 20 Vauxhall Bridge Road,
London SW1V 2SA

www.vintage-books.co.uk

Addresses for companies within The Random House Group Limited
can be found at:
www.randomhouse.co.uk/offices.htm

The Random House Group Limited Reg. No. 954009

A CIP catalogue record for this book
is available from the British Library

ISBN 9780099449935

The Random House Group Limited supports The Forest Stewardship
Council® (FSC®), the leading international forest certification organisation.
All our titles that are printed on Greenpeace approved FSC® certified paper
carry the FSC® logo. Our paper procurement policy can be found at:
www.randomhouse.co.uk/environment

Printed and bound in Great Britain by
CPI Cox & Wyman, Reading, RG1 8EX

For Rory and for Norman

Chapter 1

Dublin, 1970

Glenveigh Lodge,
Killiney,
Dublin

20th February 1970

Dear Solange de Valnay,

We have never met and I find myself at a loss as to how I should address you but I feel that I must contact you personally. I am Eleanor Kirwan, the eldest daughter of Richard and Helena Kirwan. Does this mean anything to you?

My father died this week, after a long illness. It was a strange experience to sit at the reading of his will, and to discover, along with the expected bequests to his widow, his two daughters and his son, that a codicil had been added two weeks before his death:

"To my daughter in France, Solange de Valnay, of Domaine de Valnay, St Joseph de Caune, Languedoc, I bequeath the remainder of my Estate." Just that. "To my daughter in France..."

Forgive me, Solange, for revealing this in such a blunt way. The truth is, until today none of us was aware of your existence. We are still in shock. I do not know if you knew that your father — our father — was ill, or that he had died: whether you knew him well or at all. At first we had thought to notify you through our legal representatives, but it seemed cruel to forward this news to you in such an impersonal manner.

My twin brother James discussed with us the legal implications of contesting the will. He is a lawyer, so that was his first response to the situation. Elizabeth, my younger sister, is devastated. She cannot accept that Father had kept this from us. It will take time before the hurt becomes bearable. She is only nineteen.

How long has he kept this secret? In his will he gave no indication of your age, nor did he mention your mother. But when I heard your name read out, I had an odd sense of recognition, as if in some part of me I already knew you. Does that sound strange? I try to imagine all sorts of things about you — who you are, what you might be like.

At first, I admit, I was as shocked as the others. We all looked at Mother, afraid of her reaction, but she is an extraordinary person who never ceases to surprise us. She is an artist, well known here and abroad. Without any indication of her feelings, she thanked the solicitor and waited for him to leave. It was her suggestion that I should write to you. Did she know about this already? Does she know you? I have no way of telling. She has withdrawn to her studio and does not wish to be disturbed.

All evening I have been sitting at Father's desk, in his study, thinking of what I might say to you. I do not yet know if I should even send this letter. Or if, having sent it, you would prefer that it had not come. You may not even be able to read English. I can only hope you do not have to ask someone to translate these pages. I suppose what I really want to do is to reach out, past all the grief and confusion, and discover a world I did not know existed. My father was a complex man, hard to fathom at times. But I loved him deeply and perhaps you did too.

So, Solange de Valnay, I will post this letter, and I hope it will forge a link with that part of his life that you did not share until now. If you decide not to reply, I will have to accept your decision. But you are my unknown sister – my half-sister at any rate – and that has meaning.

I enclose a copy of the will. With every good wish and my sympathy also.

Yours sincerely,
Eleanor Kirwan

*

Eleanor read the letter again. This was her fifth attempt. Was it too familiar? Was Solange de Valnay a grown woman or a child? And why had there been no mention of her mother? She sat back in the leather chair at her father's walnut desk. She had always loved the grain of this wood, the warm, golden glow of it, pitted in places with his history, their history. The earlier scene in the study was etched sharp in her mind. Mr McCann, the family solicitor, tense and frowning, reading the additional bequest; Elizabeth, white and trembling, James leaping to his feet, all bluster, trying to hide his sense of betrayal.

"This is preposterous! It's unreal!" he was shouting. "There can't be another child we've never heard of! What proof is there? This can be challenged in the courts!"

In the awkward silence that followed, Mr McCann had stared down at the desk, the stiff pages of the will crackling under his fingers. Helena Kirwan sat very still, her head bowed. When she raised her eyes her expression was one of painful compassion, and something else unfathomable. "You must write to her, dear."

3

Then she had turned her back on them, relying on Eleanor to restore calm and reason. From the refuge of her studio they heard Beethoven playing. Was she working? Or just remembering?

Realisation made Eleanor jerk forward. Her mother had been pained but not shocked. She already knew! Eleanor was sure of it now. Helena had known of the existence of this child, this "daughter in France", even if she had not been aware of the codicil. But why had she not prepared them for the news? And afterwards – just to walk out and leave her children, floundering in the swamp of their father's hidden life?

Now Eleanor had accomplished the unimaginable task of contacting Solange. The most difficult words had been the first ones – "Dear Solange de Valnay". Eleanor opened the drawer, took out an envelope, and searched for a stamp. The letter would have to go as it was – no point in altering it now. Solange would know them all soon enough. She placed the letter and a copy of the will in the envelope and rose, leaving it on the desk. At the window, she opened the curtains and rested her head against the cold glass. Car lights crawled along the narrow cliff road below her, and the street lights gleamed in pinpricks from Howth Head to the dark cone of the Sugar Loaf Mountain. The night was frosty and the moon hung low over the sea, creaming the waves with silver as the tide churned on the shingle beach. She remembered walking over those smooth, rounded stones with her father, on just such a night, not so long ago.

"Where have you really been all these years, Father?" she whispered. "Who were you? Did any of us truly know you?"

A spasm of grief hit her. She found herself running her nails down the glass. She longed for the solid comfort of Seamus, her mother's twin brother. He could have guided them through this quagmire. But he was away in the mountains of Nepal. He didn't even know that Richard was dead.

"Oh Father! Father! Why did you do this to us? Why? How could you?"

4

Chapter 2

St Joseph de Caune, 1970

Solange de Valnay moved softly across the hall and opened the door of the library. Her father dozed in a chair, his face warmed by the winter sunshine. She smiled and stole away, out into the brightness of the afternoon. The dogs appeared and rushed ahead of her, hunting for trophies in the hedges and along the river bank. An ancient line of plane trees defined the long driveway, their thick trunks emphasising the spidery bareness of winter branches. Brown, leafless vineyards stretched away in all directions, bordered by the surrounding mountains. Solange breathed in the cold air, the scent of wood smoke and pines. She stopped to admire the twisted sculptures of the vines and the dogs halted too, looking back at her with impatience. The iron gates were open, the blue afternoon impossible to resist. Solange passed the letterbox and walked on along the river. In the vineyards a few workers pruned and tied the branches.

She sat down on a tree trunk beside the waterfall, simple contentment making her feel slightly guilty. Soon Guy would be home, and a date would have to be set for their wedding. It was not that she did not miss him – they shared a deep affection for the old house that had been privy to their first declarations of love. But in truth she was perfectly happy being here alone with her father, helping him with correspondence, tending the vines with Joel, walking the dogs.

There was a gentle rhythm to her life that did not seem to require improvement. Solange tried to understand how she could miss her fiancé and still feel content in his absence. She looked down into the fast flowing water, and sensed her childhood rushing away, downstream and out of reach for all time. All at once the afternoon seemed to have turned cold. She shivered and stood up, drawing her jacket around her and calling for the dogs. At the gate to the old house she opened the letterbox and took out the day's offerings.

*

Domaine de Valnay,
St Joseph de Caune,
France

15th March 1970

Dear Eleanor,
    Your letter of 20th February reached me some time ago, followed by a formal advice from your lawyer. This bequest has brought sadness and confusion, and left me with a sense of complete isolation from the people I love the most. Since then, I have been trying to come to terms with the idea that a stranger named Richard Kirwan could be my father.
    My first reaction was to wonder how a man could be so selfish as to disrupt, and even destroy, the lives of two families, knowing that he would escape the consequences. Until that February afternoon my knowledge of Richard Kirwan was minimal, although my mother had mentioned him as someone she had known during her wartime years in Paris. She said that her determination for me to study English was the result of his influence, and that he had inspired her to read widely in both English and French. Throughout my childhood, she read to me in both languages.

It was not easy to find someone in our area who could teach me, but my mother located an English writer living nearby, and persuaded him to become my tutor. He was not enthused by the idea of taking an unwilling child into his home as a pupil. But in the company of Cedric Swann I learned to read and write in this second language.

In your letter you ask about my mother. I will try to tell you a little about her and about the man I have always believed to be my father. But it seems ironic that I am writing about my parents, at the very moment when I realise I know very little of them myself.

My mother was born Celine Marie France de Savoie, in Paris, April 1916. My grandfather was a physician and lecturer in medicine until his death in 1941. After her school years, my mother studied medicine at the Sorbonne. Celine de Savoie married Henri de Valnay in Paris at the end of 1945, and they moved to the Languedoc during the following year. The marriage was looked upon as a brilliant match – a beautiful and intelligent bride, a distinguished groom from a respected family, with property in Paris and large vineyards in the south. I was born prematurely after a difficult pregnancy. I am an only child, and you can calculate that I am now twenty-four years of age. My mother practised medicine in the village here, and she was much loved. Perhaps she was not mentioned in Richard Kirwan's will because he knew that she had died last year. My father misses her desperately. He has been blind, you see, for some years.

You will now understand the unwelcome situation in which I find myself. I have no idea whether my father knows anything of Richard Kirwan. I cannot conceive of any way in which I could approach this subject with him. He adored my mother and this could destroy his memory of her. If he was aware

7

that I am not his natural child, he kept his knowledge hidden and he has always been a most loving parent. My grandmother, Charlotte de Savoie, still lives in Paris. I cannot say whether or not my mother's secret lay with her all these years. As for my own feelings about my mother, these have become a kind of torment.

I am unclear as to what is now expected of me. I remain thankful that I was alone when I received this news. But that does not diminish my anger, the sickness with which I awaken each morning. My life has always been secure, but it is now torn apart. I am soon to be married, but my fiancé is at present overseas and I do not know how I will be able to discuss this situation with him. I have no wish to come face to face with your family, and I do not feel that it would serve any purpose.

I appreciate the courage and the kindness you have shown in writing to me, an unknown and, I am sure, unwanted half-sister. I doubt there is any purpose in our continuing to write to one another, but I cannot deny that there is a connection between us. I may decide to visit my grandmother in Paris and talk to her about this. But for now my strongest instinct is to leave this unfortunate mystery buried with my mother. Thank you again for your letter. Please accept my good wishes to you and your family at this sad time. He was fortunate to have been so much loved.

Solange de Valnay

*

Solange closed her eyes, tired and drained. She had read the letter so many times that she could almost recite it by heart. There were ways to improve upon it but she no longer had the courage or the desire to dwell on them. Her response seemed like an act of disloyalty,

8

recognition of her mother's betrayal. Several times she had torn up the scribbled pages but then she had thought of the courage Eleanor had shown in writing the first letter, and of the Irish family's suffering. Initially Solange had tried to minimise the description of her own circumstances. But pride had overtaken any attempt at a few brief lines of acknowledgement, and she had realised that part of her purpose was to make the Kirwan family understand that she did not need this crude, monetary gift.

It was a long time since she had thought about her lessons with Cedric Swann and now she wondered whether he had been her mother's confidant. Had he known the true purpose behind the English lessons? Solange recalled his pain at her mother's funeral, remembered his hands clasped together in silent grief as the coffin had sunk into the dark hole of eternity, tears flowing unchecked down his thin face.

She returned to the questions uppermost in her mind. Was her very existence an accident? Had Henri de Valnay always known that she was not his natural daughter? During the long months of her mother's illness, when they had sat for hours together talking about every aspect of their lives, why had she not been prepared for Richard Kirwan's dying gesture? It was inconceivable that Celine had been ignorant of his wishes. Solange rubbed away the threat of tears and stood up, determined to rid herself of helpless resentment, to stop brooding, to do something positive. She ran down the main staircase and grabbed her car keys. In the village she mailed the letter to Eleanor Kirwan, stuffing it through the narrow opening of the post box with a mixture of resolution and panic.

Immediately after a dinner with Henri that seemed endless she escaped to her bedroom, pleading fatigue from the day's work in the vineyards. In the safe seclusion of her bed she remained awake for hours, angry at the scalding tears sliding down on to the pillowcase, until finally she drifted into a fitful sleep disturbed by anxiety and fearful dreams.

Chapter 3

Dublin, 1970

Eleanor handed the letter to James. He read it, then walked to the long window overlooking the garden. The trees were still grey and bare and there was no sign of spring. He stood with his hands behind his back, staring out at the lawn and the gravel drive. Memory stirred in Eleanor as she looked at him: the image of their father – same stance, same angle of the head.

"You see Jamie! She's not some gold-digger after the Kirwan fortunes, such as they are. It doesn't sound as though she needs money. She's just as hurt and upset as we are."

James's voice was muffled and she realised why he had moved away from the table. He took out an immaculate linen handkerchief and blew loudly. "It might not be true," he said. "She doesn't know. We don't know either. It could be –"

"A mistake? Oh, I don't think so. Why would he –"

"She's never even met him! She never knew him."

"So what do I do now? None of us knows any more than she does."

"Oh there's someone who knows. Why doesn't she say something? Why does she spend every day in that damned studio? Can't you make her talk to us? Make her explain."

"Why do I always get the bloody awful things to do?" Eleanor scraped her chair back and stood up. "Why don't you ask her? You're just as much her child as I am. Why the hell does it have to be me?"

His arm was round her now, and he was holding out his handkerchief. "Because you're the best at it, El, you know that. I get all, oh you know, high-horseish. And Lizzie would freeze up if she had to say anything sensitive or diplomatic. Mother depends on you. She talks to you, trusts you. Oh I'm sorry – I really am. I'm not just trying to run out on a sticky job."

"All right." She was too weary to argue. "I'll try and talk to her. I'm bringing her a breakfast tray anyway, before I go to work. Will you call Lizzie? She has a ten o'clock lecture. Maybe you could give her a lift?"

"Well, I can't be late and it takes her an age to get sufficiently glamorous to hit the lecture halls. All those panting undergrads!" He leered at her and then laughed.

"Oh go on. Do your duty. You know how she loves being in your MG. She'll make it in time, just for that!" She left him grumbling, glad that he had made her smile.

Climbing the stairs with the tray, Eleanor wondered how to broach the subject of the letter. She had been begging her mother to see the family doctor, but Helena had flatly refused. She needed time to think, she said, and painting was the best way. Her face was pinched with dark circles beneath her eyes, and her slight form had become even thinner. It seemed to Eleanor that there was a lot more grey in the russet hair than before. Could shock and grief do that so suddenly? She knocked on the bedroom door. Helena was curled up on the bed, still in the clothes she had worn the day before, Richard Kirwan's old dressing gown covering her feet. A window was open and a blast of cold air slammed the door shut.

"Mother! The bed's still made up. Have you not slept at all? This just won't do." Eleanor put the tray on the bedside table. She closed the window and sat down beside the bed, stroking her mother's cold hands. "You're frozen! Look, I have orange juice, coffee and toast. I'm going to sit here until you eat it. Come on . . ." She placed a cashmere shawl round Helena's shoulders and handed her a cup of coffee. Her mother stared into the black liquid, her face blank.

"Mother, we have to talk. You can't go on like this. We can't go on like this. I've had a letter. From Solange de Valnay."

"You'll be late for work." The voice was forced, cracked.

"I don't care. I want you to look at this." Eleanor took the letter from her pocket. Helena shook her head, silent. "Well then, I'm going to read it to you."

Helena sipped the coffee, not looking up. When Eleanor had finished the letter she sat quietly, hoping that now the dam would break, and all the things that were paralysing her mother would be released in healing tears. Instead Helena hunched over and drew her dead husband's dressing gown towards her, holding it up to her face. The silence lengthened. Then she spoke. "The first time I met your father was in April of 1939. It was outside the Ecole de Louvre in Paris."

*

Glenveigh Lodge,
Killiney,
Dublin

30th March 1970

Dear Solange,
    How glad I was to receive your letter yesterday, in spite of the situation in which we find ourselves. I truly regret the shock and the pain you have suffered all alone, since you heard from me first. But by continuing to correspond we can at least

try to help each other. Somehow I had assumed that you knew my father, even if it had been only to meet or speak with him occasionally. But never to have ever seen him at all – never to have had any inkling! And yet, his will was so clear. No room for doubt here. "To my daughter in France . . ."

Richard Kirwan was a careful man, Solange. I know he would never have written those words unless he was utterly certain. I have tried to talk to my mother about all this, but she is filled with grief from her bereavement, and perhaps from other things she has not yet disclosed. It has always been difficult for her to communicate. She speaks with her eyes, and through her paintings. She is very small, with a great cloud of unruly Titian hair, and huge brown eyes. Not beautiful, but striking certainly – someone you will always remember having seen. Her hands draw things in the air when she speaks, and she dresses with an artist's disdain for order or chic, yet her clothes always look right on her.

I know she loved Father passionately, and his illness was borne as much by her as by himself. He suffered a great deal towards the end, but she insisted on taking him home from the hospital and nursing him herself, right through to his last breath. He always hated hospitals – something to do with the war, she said. We knew that he had been very ill during that period, and that he was not with our mother when James and I were born. That time in their lives was never spoken about, and even as children we knew that neither of them wished to be reminded of it. My mother was the one who could really soothe his pain – well, she and my younger sister Elizabeth, whom he loved so much. I suppose I can admit that she was his favourite, perhaps because she looks just like our mother.

Yesterday James and I decided to show Mother your letter and to find out what, if anything, she knew. After some hours, she told me something that may explain how my father and your mother met.

Richard Kirwan was born in Dublin into an influential publishing family with substantial property interests. He studied in Dublin, earning a first-class degree in French and History. Every year he went to France where he had many friends, especially in Paris. After his degree he continued his studies at Cambridge University. When a post became vacant in his old college in Dublin three years later, he went home and accepted a Professorship there. He was a striking man, my father, and very charming, but scholarship was his first love, and he was ambitious. In 1938 he was invited to France for a series of guest lectures at the Sorbonne and he took a two-year sabbatical from Dublin. He was thirty-six.

Helena, my mother, comes from the west of Ireland, where she was born Helena O'Riordan. She was an only daughter, but she has three brothers, one of whom is her twin. Her family were fishermen and ship's chandlers and they did not have much money. As a child Helena spent all her time with her brothers, especially with her twin, Seamus. They were considered very wild. Eventually she was sent away to a convent boarding school. Music and art became her passions and she was accepted into the National Art College at the age of eighteen. After graduating with honours, she determined to study painting in Paris. She worked at various jobs, saved her money, taught herself French, and applied for a two-year course in the Ecole de Louvre in 1937.

It was there, on an afternoon in the spring of 1939 that she met Richard Kirwan. She was waiting outside for a bus, with a large portfolio and all her materials in various boxes. A sudden downpour sent everybody scurrying for shelter. In the rush she dropped some of her belongings. Richard Kirwan was passing and he stopped to help her. The funny part was that each thought the other was French. It was only later, in a local café over a cup of coffee, that they discovered their common nationality. The coffee lasted two hours, then drifted on to dinner, the discovery of a shared love of opera, tickets to *La Bohème* on the following evening, and a late-night walk along the Seine. Helena was twenty-five, Richard eleven years her senior.

All this took my mother a long time to tell. As the days go on, she may be willing to reveal more, but I cannot press her too much right now. This does, however, place my father in Paris at the same time as Celine de Valnay, and my mother too. Perhaps they all knew each other. So far as anyone could tell, my parents' marriage was a strong one, and my father was a man of integrity and high principle. However extraordinary or bizarre our present circumstances may be, I truly believe that Father would have tried to do what was right.

I would like to congratulate you on your engagement. I myself am not married or even engaged, although I am twenty-eight years old. But I would like to add "not yet"! I thought I had met my soul mate once, and I shared more than a year with him. I do not regret a single moment of it, except the last. But I suppose even that sort of pain is a growing experience. His wife has made him very happy. He asked me to his wedding, you know, and I went. We had, after all, been friends as well as lovers.

I may have given a bad impression of my brother and sister in my last letter. They are not always as I depicted them. James, my twin brother, is something of an enigma. On the outside he is cold and confident, an efficient and successful barrister — competitive, as all lawyers have to be. But he is also a romantic, and a sensitive man. We have that closeness that is peculiar to twins. My sister Elizabeth trails admirers like a comet's tail. She has my mother's striking red hair and hazel eyes, and her petite frame. But there, I think, the likeness ends. There is much of our father in her – she has his drive, ambition, and force. She is reading history and philosophy and will be a formidable academic like Father. When she finally meets the man of her life, he will want to be very strong.

I believe I have inherited some of my mother's creativity, though it finds expression in the written word rather than in painting. I read English and philosophy at university and I have made a small impression on the Dublin literary scene. Now I work for the family publishing firm to finance my writing, and I find my work deeply satisfying.

I have always been close to my mother – we understand one another well. My father, for some reason I could never explain, kept me at a distance, though he cared for me, I am sure, and he wanted the best for me. Perhaps that distancing was caused by his absence when I was born. I often wondered if I represented some painful memory from that time that he could not confront. During the early part of my childhood he still had serious health problems that made him almost an invalid. Sometimes, when I was little, I would look up and see him watching me with intense sadness in his eyes. I would run to him and hug him, trying to touch the hurt part of him inside. Later I realised it was not me he was looking at, but something far beyond my reach. Now, perhaps, an explanation begins to emerge.

I wonder if you have discovered anything about Richard Kirwan's life in France? If so, you may wish to share the knowledge with me, since you are without a confidante. I hope the information I have given you will be of some use. You may find it strange, Solange, that I have written to you in such detail. I cannot explain it myself – I have always experienced considerable difficulty in expressing my emotions to others. If, however, you would prefer only to exchange information, you must tell me.

I must go now, but I remain yours affectionately,

Eleanor Kirwan

Chapter 4

St Joseph de Caune, 1970

Solange lay watching the cool drift of morning mist vanish beyond the muslin curtains. Beneath her window the river rushed away over the rocks, dim and solid below the water's glittering surface. Her body was still half-suspended in sleep, warm within her bed. The freedom of those first floating moments was brief. Then came the jolt in her stomach, the jarring sensation of dull distress, as the slow sickness of Eleanor Kirwan's letter pervaded the first moments of her day, hanging over her in a silent pall.

She rose and went to the window, resting her head against the old stone wall. All around her the mountains of the Haut Languedoc slept in the dim light, an occasional sliver of pale sunshine banding the folded slopes. A tap on her door brought Lorette, the family housekeeper who had been her childhood nanny. On the small tray with her coffee lay two envelopes. The top one bore Guy St Jorre's neat, sloping hand. Solange picked it up and immediately recognised the Irish postmark on the letter lying underneath. A sense of dread invaded her as she waited, edgy and fidgeting, until Lorette's footsteps faded on the stairs. Then she put her fiancé's envelope aside and opened the second letter from Eleanor. Her initial reaction was one of sympathy, but as she re-read the words, her better instincts were eroded, first by a sense of irritation and finally by a deep anger. Why did this girl so desperately want to submerge herself in the past, force an investigation into circumstances long gone and best consigned to history? Eleanor Kirwan was in Ireland surrounded by her family. She could share her shock, draw on the comfort of her brother and sister.

"My father was a careful man," Eleanor had written. Not so careful, it seemed to Solange. Already married, he had indulged in an affair and fathered a child. How could her mother have become ensnared in such a classically stupid situation? Had it been a last fling before settling down with Henri de Valnay? Could Richard Kirwan have omitted to say that he was married, or promised to leave his wife for Celine? Solange recoiled from the thought of the accidental pregnancy, the unwanted child. Eleanor sounded like the well meaning, martyred type who had probably never broken away from the rigid, religious education to which Irish girls were apparently subjected, almost from infancy. She sounded as though she was still living in the previous century although she seemed to have had some kind of love affair. The brother sounded pompous, and the younger girl vain and spoilt, but Solange felt sorry for Helena Kirwan. Rage filled her at the thought of them discussing her mother about whom they knew nothing. About whom she herself knew nothing.

"Could all this be true?" Solange asked herself, working out the date of her mother's marriage and her own birthdate. "Did she really marry my father while carrying the child of another man? And had they kept up this affair for years afterwards? Did Papa know? Oh God, Papa, did you always know?"

She recalled those last terrible weeks, seeing again her mother's gaunt face, her eyes sunken and faded. Celine's body had shrunk and the once smooth skin had stretched, yellowing and shrivelled, across her protruding bones as the disease ate relentlessly into her. When Solange had bent to lift or turn her into a less painful position, she was afraid the brittle frame might shatter in her hands. Had Celine known then, what her lover would do to them all?

"Oh, Mama," Solange muttered. "This doesn't happen to ordinary people like us. What kind of a man would do this, after all those years? You should have told me – if only to help me protect Papa. How could you leave me to deal with this all on my own?"

Perhaps her mother had always continued to love Richard Kirwan. Solange was glad she had never met the man, never laid eyes on him. These Irish people were so sure he was her father. Could they have additional information they were keeping to themselves? She knew that men and women from every walk of life concealed illicit love affairs every day. But still she wept at night, tears of loss and of baffled rage, as resentment filled her mouth with a bitter taste.

The Irish girl probably thought of French women as casually cynical in their attitudes to love affairs, but Solange knew this to be a foolish generalisation. All human beings reacted in some deeply emotional way to betrayal, and she had seen several of her mother's friends weeping over a partner's discovered dalliance. Celine had encouraged them either to go on alone, to begin a new stage of their lives, or to stay and fight their corner with resolution. But now the wise, compassionate doctor was not here to explain the enormity of her own deceit. Solange could think of no one in whom she might confide the secret of her illegitimate birth, her unwelcome inheritance.

She placed Eleanor's letter in the drawer of her desk and turned away, close to tears. How would she explain to her fiancé what had happened in his absence? His family, with their ancient lineage, would certainly never understand. To Solange, Guy's father had always seemed a little distant, and his mother was definitely grand – mired in the straitjacket of old-fashioned etiquette. And what would Guy himself feel about her parents? The father who was not her father, the mother who had cheated on her husband and who had not been honest enough to tell her only child, even in death. Should she keep the whole horrible affair a secret, and allow her mother's deceit to seep down into the next generation?

"My God, how did I deserve this? What did I do wrong? And why did I ever write to her in the first place?" In the bath the warm, scented water swirled around her, bringing no comfort. Solange rubbed angrily at her skin, making a series of red, ugly blotches on her arms. "I've brought most of this on myself. She didn't need to know anything about my family, any more than I need to know about the Kirwans and their problems. It would have been better to acknowledge the letter and leave it at that. I should have let their lawyers in Paris handle it all."

Solange was certain now that she had said far too much in that initial letter. Her aim had been to give an impression of worldliness and independence, to show that her family was comfortably off, that she was well educated, secure, did not need the Kirwan money.

Stepping out of the bath, she reached for a towel. Her body was slender and well shaped, with a small waist and hips, and full breasts. She had always been pleased that her olive skin tanned so easily, and she was grateful for its firm, silken texture. Her hair was a deep golden colour, heavy and thick, and not at all like her mother's pale, shimmering tresses; she had assumed that she had inherited Henri de Valnay's grey eyes and aquiline nose. Now she made a wry grimace, mocking her previously straightforward acceptance of hereditary features. Tears welled. Her throat hurt and she felt heavy, dull, angry with herself. She wiped her eyes and applied a little make-up, mainly to boost her morale.

In the bedroom, Guy's letter caught her eye, lying still unopened on her tray. There was, at least, something in the bright morning that could make her smile. She wrapped herself in a robe and sat down in her chair by the window. A family quarrel over shares in a vast sugar plantation had taken him to Guadeloupe, to assist one of his law firm's senior partners. Guy was an accomplished letter-writer. His words were filled with tenderness and desire; Solange could feel his need to be near her. She raised one hand to the hair at the nape of her neck, where he loved to touch her, and was grateful for the rush of affection she felt for him. When she had read the pages again she put them carefully away, with his other letters. Then she dressed with more optimism than she had felt for many days.

Over breakfast she read the newspaper aloud for Henri and discussed their plans for the day. He quickly memorised their agenda and the list of correspondence she had prepared for him. The vine-yards needed close attention at this time of the year, as insects and weeds appeared daily in endless proliferation. As Henri made his way to the library and his morning's telephone calls, Solange watched his sure steps and suddenly wondered how long each piece of furniture had been in exactly the same place, so that he could negotiate his home in complete confidence. She had been so unobservant, taken so many things for granted. From now on she determined not to succumb to over-emotional reactions. Her father must remain innocent of the mad moment of desire and conception shared by her mother and another man. That was the most important aspect of her recently acquired heritage.

She climbed the stairs to her bedroom where several favourite photographs stood on the glowing, waxy surface. One showed Celine de Valnay, serene and joyous, smiling up at her husband, her hand resting on her small daughter's shoulder. Solange drew up a chair and sat quietly for a moment to compose herself. Around her she felt the nurturing walls of her childhood home. She decided now that she would conceal her altered background from her fiancé, telling herself — and knowing it was untrue — that it was for the sake of her Papa. He was the father she loved and respected. She was the same person as before, even if she had been born of a different union. She would banish the unwanted ghosts of the distant past from her future.

They were dead, the beautiful doctor and her unknown lover, and they must not be allowed to shake the foundations of Solange's calm, secure world. It was only the immediate shock that had stabbed at her normal composure, like a needle that her mother might have administered. There was always a sharp jab first, shock and fear, some pain. But then it was over, the mark of its entry disappeared, and all was as before. Solange took up her pen and began her letter.

*

Domaine de Valnay,
St Joseph de Caune,
France

12th April 1970

Dear Eleanor,

Thank you for your letter of 30th March. It was kind of you to write again, and to describe your family to me. I know that you are trying to piece together how my mother and I became a part of Richard Kirwan's life. All this must be very difficult for you, and for your brother and sister. Your letter is moving, as is the portrait of your mother. Evidently you, too, are an artist, but with words rather than colours and brushes.

As for myself, I have come to believe that there is no true advantage for any of us in pursuing the truth of the relationship between your father and my mother. Whatever took place between them, and what was probably the accidental result of their feelings, should be left alone. You are in Ireland surrounded by your family and you will one day recover. Eventually we may all come to realise that Richard Kirwan tried in some way to be a fair man, or perhaps to ease a burden of conscience carried for many years, although for the moment his methods seem cruel and unnecessarily dramatic. It is unlikely that we will ever see this in the same light.

I think we should now put the past aside, and live for the

present and the future. Our parents – all four of them, for Henri de Valnay has been a true father to me since my birth – must have numerous secrets, and this part of their past is surely best forgotten. Your mother has already suffered a great deal, and I cannot imagine exposing my father to something that could perhaps destroy him. Richard Kirwan's bequest to me remains both a dilemma and a mystery. I am sorry to have been the unwitting cause of additional upset in your time of loss, and I hope that you will all draw from one another the love you need to begin a new part of your lives. At least you have the comfort of close family circumstances.

There does not appear to be any reason for us to continue with our correspondence. I do not see what can be gained by digging into the roots of a drama long past, in which we are only small players in a scenario we cannot understand. Those who played the two main roles are dead. Let us leave them that way, and remember what we loved best about them.

Thank you once again for your attempts to be compassionate. I respect your desire to know more of your father's history, but I do not wish to take a part in such discoveries. Our best opportunities must, I believe, lie in being the people we were before this unhappy revelation. I hope that your life will be fulfilling and happy, and that you will find great reward in your writing. I learned early from my mother, and from all those whom I truly love, that the beauty of human thought on the printed page, often expressed with difficulty and after years of effort, is perhaps the greatest gift we have to guide us in our lives and loves.

Yours sincerely,
Solange de Valnay

Solange signed her letter with finality. It would explain her feelings clearly, without unnecessary sentiment. Eleanor Kirwan might be her half-sister, but she was a stranger. She took up her mother's photograph and looked again at the beautiful, laughing face. With sudden force she slammed the silver frame down on to her desk, cracking the glass. Then she went downstairs to join Henri de Valnay in his study, grateful for the familiar routine of their day.

Chapter 5

St Joseph de Caune, 1970

"Solange dear, I shall need aperitifs and something to eat, in the library around six." Henri de Valnay stood facing the terrace, hands clasped behind his back, shoulders stiff and tense. "There's a young man dropping in to talk to me – apparently he has some radical ideas about the development of wines in the area."

"Oh? That's a subject close to your heart. Who's your guest? Most young men in this area just want to sell their harvests to the co-operative for the best price they can get."

Henri had tried on many occasions to interest neighbouring wine-makers and the local co-operative in modernisation and the production of better quality wines, but eventually he had become disheartened at their inability to recognise the need for fresh thinking in the industry. "This is Edouard Ollivier from Roucas Blancs," Henri was frowning. "He's just returned here, having completed several years away in Bordeaux. I think he's spent time overseas as well. You probably remember him from summer holidays years ago."

Paul Ollivier's lanky son came to mind instantly, making Solange smile. He had been the first boy to kiss her, just after she turned thirteen, and she had fled from him, both giggling and frightened. The Ollivier family had been one of the very few causes of disagreement between her parents. A land dispute between the Valnays and Paul

Ollivier had been resolved in Henri's favour after years of bitter argument in the courts, and relations had remained strained between them. Solange did not think the two men had spoken since the time of the settlement. But when Paul Ollivier had suffered a heart attack, Celine de Valnay had insisted on treating him, and it was the only occasion when Henri had vehemently opposed something that she wished to do.

"Yes, I remember when his parents were divorced and he went off to live with his mother in some grand château in Bordeaux," Solange said. "He's coming over here to talk to you about wine? That's extraordinary."

"I must admit my first reaction was to say no to his suggestion."

Henri was clearly uneasy at the prospect of this visit. He had no wish to become embroiled in further disputes with his neighbour, or to stir up old hostilities. Solange saw him raise one hand to massage his forehead and the bridge of his nose, in a gesture intended to keep one of his violent headaches at bay.

"I doubt that you'll get along well with Edouard," she said. "Any more than you did with his father. Last time I saw him he was making disparaging remarks about our vineyards. Well, not ours particularly, but the whole production of the Midi."

"You can't fault him for that, my dear. No one around here can produce a wine that could be considered as a decent *vin de pays*, let alone an Appellation Contrôllé or something that could be drunk in Paris. And he comes from an old Bordeaux family on his mother's side, where they know how to make wine."

"True. But it's really very odd, his coming here. I wonder if he's told his father. I can't imagine Paul approving of his son visiting the enemy camp."

"Well, I certainly don't want to become mixed up in another futile argument with Paul. I don't think I've come across this young man in ten years."

"He was aloof and superior, with floppy hair that fell over his eyes,

27

and a rather long nose — crooked from having broken it. Maybe someone punched him. That's very probable. Actually, he was long and skinny altogether, and far too opinionated and intense."

"Sounds as though he made quite an impression on you, my dear!" Henri was laughing.

"Oh, it wasn't just me. No one cared for him really, although he was good-looking, and obviously clever. We all felt sorry for him when his mother ran off and left poor old Paul. We thought her very wicked and glamorous at the time." Solange smiled again as she remembered the gangly young man who had kissed her. "Edouard could be very appealing when he allowed himself to lighten up a bit. But that wasn't often."

"You're making me feel sorry for the poor boy," he said, chuckling at her unflattering sketch. "Perhaps like his family's wine in Bordeaux, he's mellowed with age. After all he must be almost thirty now. He tells me he's come back to help his father with their vineyards."

"I'll be surprised if he stays here more than a week or two. Like his mother, he's probably too high and mighty to cope with our rustic lifestyle."

"If he's really interested, he'll be running that vineyard before too long, because Paul Ollivier certainly isn't capable of doing so. He'd probably be glad to retire completely, or at least take a back seat."

"That seems rather unlikely. Anyway, it doesn't explain what Edouard might want to discuss with you. I think it's highly presumptuous of him to invite himself here. May I sit in on the conversation? I was going to spend part of the evening with Chloe and Aunt Jeanette, but this sounds much more interesting."

"An open-minded attitude might help, if you're going to join us." Henri was still laughing at her. "You mustn't write people off like this, my darling. Try for the British assumption of innocent until proven guilty. I worry sometimes that you'll have dismissed the whole flawed world of humanity, before anyone has a chance to display their most fascinating traits to you. But come and join us, by all means. Given my relationship with that pig-headed old father of his, I may need an ally."

"I'm sure this can't be anything to do with your old disagreement. It's all so long ago."

"Well, whatever Edouard Ollivier has to say about future conditions here, it can't be much worse than the true state of things." Henri sat down abruptly, his expression strained. "Perhaps when he's gone we can have a simple supper together, beside the fire. Or you could still go over and see Chloe and her mother?"

"I was planning to be back here for dinner," Solange lied. "And maybe our guest will want to stay on too." She rose to her feet and kissed Henri on the top of his head. "I'm going to telephone Chloe and postpone our evening."

"Oh, Solange, how could you?" Her cousin was full of woe. "I was so looking forward to this. Mama had stopped concentrating on my affairs, in order to focus fully on yours for a few hours. And you said you'd stay for dinner. I can't face another evening alone with the parents, and there's nothing else to do round here during the week."

"Well, this seems like an important meeting for my father."

"Why can't you leave your father and what's-his-name to rattle on by themselves? You spend too much time with Henri. You should go out more and let him get used to being on his own sometimes. Then it won't come as such a shock when you're married and living in Montpellier."

Solange sidestepped any discussion about Henri or her forthcoming marriage, escaping with the promise of an alternative day later in the week. She hung up and went down the stairs to the kitchen, where Madame Prunier presided over the most vital affairs of the house. Several large windows overlooked the river, flooding the room with light. Heavy beams were hung with pots and pans, bunches of dried herbs, and woven strands of fat garlic bulbs.

"Ah, Solange. You look so pale, and your young man will think you're much too thin." The cook's ample form embodied her idea of the perfect female form. Solange winced, but Madame Prunier was in full spate and warming to her theme. "There's freshly baked bread over there, and some cheese. Try a slice of the Cantal. Go on child, eat! Eat for heaven's sake!"

"Prunie, can you make a little alteration to this evening's plans? Edouard Ollivier from Roucas Blancs is coming to visit my father. Could we have something to accompany aperitifs at about six? And there may be three of us for dinner."

"My God! Young Ollivier's coming here? Well, maybe the father is sending him to make peace at last. He's getting on and his health isn't good." Madame Prunier sniffed. "But your father shouldn't be too trusting. Paul Ollivier's a crafty old man."

She lifted the whisk and began to beat a golden mixture into a creamy ribbon. Solange scooped out a spoonful.

"I'd heard the boy was home – just in time, in my opinion. I saw Paul Ollivier last weekend, and he won't be taking care of the Domaine for much longer. He's always been a grumpy old fellow. But he never was all puffed up, like his high-born wife. Always creating strife, she was, and trying to live in such a fancy way."

"It must have been hard for her, though, coming down here to Roucas Blancs from a big château in Bordeaux."

"Huh! She should have thought about that before she married him and then ran off and left him. It's a pity he didn't re-marry. That might have made him less bitter."

"Who would he have married, after that mistake?"

"He was young enough, then. And he has plenty of land, so he was a good catch. It would have been better for the boy too. It's good that he has come home, so young and strong. Everyone knows Paul Ollivier would be too proud even to ask him to visit."

Solange hid a smile. She should have known that the young

30

Ollivier's return had already been discussed in the village. "Well, I'm going back to work. We'll just have a salad about one o'clock. There's a lot of paperwork in the office today, and my father says he'll fall asleep this afternoon if he eats a big lunch."

Madame Prunier clucked her tongue in disapproval of such a frivolous midday meal. Solange picked up a freshly baked bread roll, spread it with a thick curl of butter and cheese and left the kitchen.

Edouard Ollivier arrived at exactly six o'clock. Solange studied him covertly. He was as tall as she remembered, but no longer skinny. His nose still looked as though it had been broken, and his hair and eyes seemed even darker. He was dressed in faded jeans and a deep-blue shirt, with a worn, but well-tailored jacket that gave him an air of careless style. He was sunburnt and sinewy, reflecting time spent working out of doors. His reserve gave way to a smile as he greeted Solange, taking her hand and bowing elaborately over it. She knew at once that he was deliberately trying to charm her. When he greeted Henri de Valnay he stood straight and stiff, his fists clenched at his side.

"I appreciate your making time to meet with me, Monsieur de Valnay. I understand you've been involved in discussions about trying to improve the winemaking in this area. And you have a keen aware-ness of progressive ideas here in France, and more particularly in America and Australia." Edouard was speaking very fast and Solange realised he was nervous. He must have thoroughly rehearsed his words. She bent her head to hide her amusement as he ploughed on.

"You're probably aware that my father is no longer in good health. I've come home to take care of Roucas Blancs for him."

"I'm sorry about your father's health," said Henri. "But you doubt-less know that we have not seen much of one another for some time. And I wonder if he would be surprised to know that you're here?"

Edouard hesitated at the blunt question. He looked around the room as though he had forgotten his lines, then made an impatient gesture with one hand. "We must move on past old quarrels, sir. There are more important issues at stake when it comes to discussing our land."

Henri was taken aback at the reply and its lack of respect. But the area was in need of change, and former grievances had to be laid to rest sometime.

"You have a point," he answered calmly. "And God knows the region could do with a few progressive winemakers. But how do you think I can help you?"

Lorette appeared with a selection of tiny pastries hot from the oven. Henri poured his guest a drink and waved him to a chair. Solange sat beside her father, but remained silent. Edouard took in her distinctive beauty, deeper and more earthy than the pale, delicate incandescence of her mother, whom he well remembered. The firelight flickered across her hair, making it shine like antique gold. Her clothes were simple. A pale blue sweater emphasised her breasts and small waist, and a short, suede skirt made her legs look very long. She wore a pair of heavy silver earrings and several silver bangles, and held her wine glass in small, capable hands that were tanned from being in the vineyards.

Edouard brought his attention back to his host and rose to his feet. "Monsieur de Valnay, I want to make some radical changes on our land," he said. "Our vineyards border on yours, sir, and between us we have enough land to experiment, to make wines that will be taken seriously. We can't continue to produce this undrinkable stuff for which there is no respect, and for which there will soon be no market. In a few years we will all be bankrupt. There can be no future here in the Midi without change."

"Any effort to improve the wines around here would require sweeping changes, and a great deal of capital. I've discussed various options with the co-operative, but I've never made any headway."

32

Henri's smile was unconvinced. "And quite apart from the strained relationship I've had with your father, I'm limited to some extent by my own particular disability. Solange here, with Jeanette my sister and Joel my manager, can barely take care of the daily requirements in the vineyards. In addition, I don't have large capital sums for investment at my disposal. And no bank in this area is likely to make a substantial loan in a wine region that is failing. Tell me, what specific plan do you have in mind for your land?"

Edouard paced the floor for a few moments before coming to a standstill in front of Henri. His voice was low, his words very clear. "My plan, sir, is to grub up every hectare of vineyard belonging to Roucas Blancs and to begin again!"

"Dig up all those hectares? Good God! And replace them with what?"

"I want to replant the whole property with new grapes. Not all at once, but within a relatively short period of time. I've been experimenting with a few hectares already. I want to return to the traditional Carignan, and to grow Cabernet Sauvignon, Syrah, Merlot, Grenache, Mourvèdre."

"You intend to plant all these varietals at once?"

"Yes sir, and I'm already experimenting with some white too. I'm going to produce wines that are delicate and fine, rounded and supple. I have a small amount of Chardonnay, and I'm going to add Sauvignon Blanc and Alicante." Edouard turned to include Solange, who was leaning forward, caught up by the scale of his grand vision. "I'm going to make wines with noses of myrtille and rose petals, and the scent of the *garrigue*. Wines that are floral and complex. Varietal wines that are consistent and fruity. There's no reason why we can't do this and more."

"At the risk of sounding prosaic, I assume you've had your soil checked and analysed, and you know what will grow?" Henri was now openly sceptical.

"There's no reason why the huge variety of terrain in this area could not produce a fine Chardonnay, or a good Sauvignon Blanc – even a superb, full red, as good as anything in France. And yes, I've had our soil analysed by experts and I have studied new winemaking techniques, not only in France but in California and in Australia too." Edouard swallowed a large draught of whiskey. Perhaps because he knew Henri de Valnay could not see him, he focused on Solange as he made his reply. She found herself holding the edge of her chair, exhilarated by the boldness of his plan and feeling the sharp, sweet edge of danger and challenge.

"We need only imagination, courage, dedication." Edouard continued to pace. "Together we could become the catalysts, the example, for this whole area. We could revolutionise the thinking of other growers in the region. Within a few years we could astonish the entire wine world."

"I'm a simple wine-grower, Edouard – not a Messiah for the region."

"Sir, if we can produce one or two harvests of superior wine, the government would be only too keen to come in and offer subsidies. To us, and to other wine-growers too!"

"How could local growers invest in vines that would take years to bring in a return?" Henri made a gesture of dismissal. "And what about the machinery and storage facilities required to improve the quality of the wine? We all talk about our beloved *terroir*, but we need modern equipment as well as the right soil."

"I've written a report for you, sir, containing all this information and detailed costs too."

"Well, I'm familiar with new techniques, yes," Henri shrugged. "Our region is one of the oldest producers of wine in France, and I'd love to see it become one of the most innovative as well. But I'm equally familiar with the cost of such an enterprise."

"I don't expect you to give me an answer now, sir. I've been working for over a year on plans and statistics, on projected returns based on conservative harvests over a six-year period. I'd be happy to send them over to you." Henri stood up, his back to the fire, and faced Edouard, his expression quizzical. "Apart from the question of finance, there are other aspects of this venture you haven't touched on. Who will manage and supervise this enterprise? And where are the buyers for these wonderful new wines you hope to produce?"

"I've spent more than eight years away from here working in the best vineyards of France. I have developed a passion for the art of winemaking, sir. My father says it could be better described as an obsession. And I've lived in California and Australia and studied their new techniques."

"You still haven't told me who is going to buy these magnificent vintages."

"I've been in London for the past two years, working for a leading wine buyer and distributor," said Edouard. "You probably know the best of the buyers, from your own experience in wine distribution. I believe England will be the prime market for our new wines at first. But I have contacts in Germany too. And there are other markets opening up – even as far away as Japan. If we can mix New World wine technology with our uniquely French, age-old understanding of blend and taste, we can reach for the brightest of futures."

Solange saw that he was intoxicated by his dream. But a nagging apprehension accompanied her assessment of his plan. "And who will put up the bulk of the money required for all this new machinery and equipment, and for the storage facilities?" she asked him. "For the bottling and distribution costs?"

He looked at her directly, pausing to select his words with care. "Some further research would have to be carried out on the actual plant. But not much. I brought a design expert to Roucas Blancs last year, and he prepared the drawings for a modern vinification centre. It would almost all have to be new and yes, it's very costly."

"We're talking about millions of francs here." Henri was grave.

"Yes sir — and that is why I can't undertake such a project on my own. I could never raise the finance on our land alone. The government and the banks would laugh at me. But I know it can be done and I know I can repay a partner and sponsor with a financial return, and a sense of pride and satisfaction."

"So what you're really looking for is money." Solange's words were deliberately direct. "Valnay money to invest in your land."

"Not just my land. I hope that you, too, will . . ."

Henri raised his eyebrows and turned to take up the decanter of malt whiskey from the sideboard.

"Well, before we discuss this any further, I'd like to see the written proposal. I must admit that your scheme could come to fruition with time and dedication."

"I'm glad you agree."

"But you know my position, my limitations, young man. I'll think over what you have put forward this evening, and then we will talk again. Now tell me, what role will your father play in all this? And how will he react to any input from me, do you think?"

"My father is old-fashioned and stubborn. He thinks my ideas are crazy. But he has already given me a number of hectares with which to experiment, and he is willing to let me take over the vineyards simply because he can't handle things himself any longer."

"That's somewhat different from having an old enemy involved in your land. What does he have to say about that?"

"I didn't tell him I was coming here." Edouard hesitated. "He would be angry, it's true. But I have said to him that it's time to let go of old disputes and concentrate on the future. I think you agree with me, and eventually he will too."

"Well, you're straightforward, at any rate. And when I've studied your projections and figures, I might be able to suggest someone who could help financially. In the meantime if we are to work together, I should like you to address me less formally. A simple 'Henri' will do.

Now, let us talk of other things. Perhaps you will join us for dinner?"

"You're very generous." Edouard smiled at Henri, his face no longer tense, his eyes lighting up with pleasure. "But my father is expecting me for dinner. Perhaps I may take advantage of your hospitality on another occasion?"

Solange led him through the hall to the door, and he bowed again over her proffered hand. Then he straightened quickly and grinned at her. "I always thought you beautiful and intelligent, back when I was an awkward, graceless schoolboy," he said, the smile spreading to his eyes. "You had great presence, even then. A little stern, though, with no tolerance for hypocrisy. I see that has not changed."

Solange was embarrassed. She began to murmur something in reply but he leaned towards her suddenly, and placed his hands on her shoulders. "My father and I were deeply saddened by Celine's death. And I know what you've done here since then, taking on so much responsibility."

"Oh, I don't look on my work here as a burden," she replied, flustered by his tone and his proximity. "It's been a long and difficult period and I've had a great deal to learn. But now I know enough to help my father with the wine."

"You're really involved in the vineyards, then?"

"Very much so. I'm out there every day. And in the *cave* and the office." She looked up at him, smiling. "I'd like to see your father and mine forget, or at least bury, their differences. It would be good for both of them."

"True. I've heard about your engagement. Your father is going to miss you when you get married, Solange. That must worry you. Your fiancé is a lawyer from Montpellier, I believe? He's very lucky." He paused, raising his dark brows, and she wondered if he was laughing at her. "Before you abandon real life and agriculture for the attractions of legal and political ambition in the city, I hope you'll be able to come and see what is happening at Roucas Blancs."

37

He was standing very close to her, his hands still resting lightly on the soft sleeves of her sweater. Solange was becoming increasingly uncomfortable under the intensity of his gaze when he suddenly bent and kissed her, slowly and deliberately, on the mouth.

"Just a reminder of more carefree times," he said, touching her cheek gently. Then the smile appeared again, this time full of something that she thought might be mockery. "Goodnight Solange."

She was still trying to collect herself as he turned and strode away into the darkness. Indignation swept over her as she heard him start his car and registered the spit of gravel on the driveway and the red tail-lights winking between the parallel lines of the plane trees. If he had been trying to win her support, his effort had been clumsy and foolish by any reckoning. She closed the door and glanced at her reflection in the hall mirror. Her face was flushed and her eyes were far too bright. She thought of their first embrace, so long ago, and her fingers strayed to her mouth. His bold, slightly wolfish grin flashed through her mind and she began to smile, and then to laugh out loud. So much for Edouard Ollivier, she thought. He's more impertinent than he was years ago, but now he has a first-class degree in arrogance.

Still smiling, she returned to the library. Lorette had lit the candles on the small table beside the window, and she began to serve the supper. Henri poured a glass of white Bordeaux for each of them.

"So what did you make of all that?" Solange asked. "Is there merit in his grand plan?"

"I think in principle he's right." Henri leaned back in his chair, thoughtful. "He has a vision of the future which could transform this area. We desperately need young people like this. But it would be a huge undertaking."

"Would you be tempted?"

"If I were in a position to join him, yes. It would be a lifetime's work and endlessly fascinating. I'd revel in the thrill of it all."

"You'd have to ensure that your advice would be taken into account, that you had control. He's so sure of himself, and what he's primarily after is your money."

Solange recognised that this venture might lead to an entirely new life for her father, one that would be challenging and absorbing. She could be here to help some of the time. Montpellier was less than an hour away. Joel, too, would love this project and the bright future it would offer for him and for his sons. She reached across and took Henri's hand, feeling a seductive prickle of excitement.

"Why don't you consider it, then? We could take on a full-time secretary and accountant to work in the office with Aunt Jeanette. Joel's eldest son would certainly join you in the vineyards, and I can be here some of the time."

"Now just a moment, young lady, before you –"

"With Edouard involved, and maybe some input from old Paul when he gets used to the idea, we'd have an adequate team to begin with."

Henri withdrew his hand. He did not look towards her as he spoke. "Solange, I must be brutally honest. I'm in no position to consider such a move. I'm deeply concerned about running costs here. Our wines have been more of a drain than an income these past few years." He could sense her agitation at what he was saying, but he had brought the subject up and he saw no way back. "Actually, I've been thinking of closing down part of the vineyard after your marriage. Or maybe leasing it out."

"What do you mean? This is our home, our whole life, our heritage! This is where we belong!"

"Of course we do, darling, but –"

"And what about Joel and all your workers? They're more like your children – your dependants. Papa, you can't be serious – say you are not serious!"

"Let's discuss this another time." Henri was folding his linen napkin. "It's much too late for us to begin on a complex subject like this, and I'm a little tired. In any case it's not a decision I've made or even discussed with anyone."

He looked completely calm, reassuring. He was even smiling. Everything was the same, yet nothing was the same. Solange was silent, frozen in the face of another revelation. Small beads of perspiration appeared on her lip and her hands trembled so that she had to fold them in her lap. She could not absorb any more shocks, any more betrayals.

"Papa, we can't give our vineyards over to someone else. The vines are our tradition, our existence."

"Come, my dear child, let's go on up to bed. I need to get an early start in the morning with Joel. I'd like to see what progress has been made with the pruning and weeding. This is only a vague notion, nothing more. Don't worry darling, your Papa and your home will always be here for you."

Upstairs Solange looked around her bedroom, half-expecting it to have altered in some way, but it was blessedly unchanged. She undressed slowly, stopping for a few moments to look at herself in the mirror. Her eyes appeared sunken, her mouth was tight, the jaw tense. She had always thought of herself as loved and wanted. Her childhood had been one of privilege and comfort and she had been secure in her identity, confident of her future. Now she saw a young woman whose mother had suffered an agonising illness and died, a child whose father was not her father, and whose beloved family home and heritage could soon disappear. She was looking at a stranger whose beginnings had been a mistake, a product of a passionate but fleeting wartime liaison.

The night was inky and unwelcoming as she leaned out to fasten back the shutters. Beneath her bedroom window the river suddenly appeared out of the blackness, with the emergence of the cold moon. An owl called and then called again, unanswered in the lonely darkness.

Chapter 6

St Joseph de Caune, 1970

Solange lay with her eyes closed, refusing to acknowledge the morning sunlight. Sleep had eluded her until after three, and when she had finally drifted off, her dreams had been filled with anxiety. For the first time in her life she felt a genuine understanding for insomniacs. She dressed warmly and pinned up her hair, her reflection showing eyes that seemed to have receded into her skull. Her entire body ached in tune with her troubled mind. Above all she was tormented by the idea that she was another of those children born every day to parents who had not truly wanted them. Now it seemed that her home and the family vineyards were also under threat. A curse of some kind had fallen on her.

She decided on a walk before facing her father across the breakfast table. It would help to restore some strength and balance. But he heard her footsteps on the stairs, and called out from the dining room. She embraced him briefly and sat down in silence, trying to draw energy and calm from the steaming coffee and the sweetness of the brioche. Henri carefully selected a cheerful subject of conversation.

"Well, my dear, Guy will be back soon. In the next two weeks I imagine?" He tested the plum jam from last summer's harvest. "Then we'll have to put the business of vines on a back burner, while we discuss wedding dates and dresses and guests."

"You must have been talking to Lorette."

"Wait until your grandmother gets to work on this in earnest! And we have the St Jorre family to consider, with that impeccable ancestry and love of pomp. We're going to need a huge amount of tact and diplomacy with all these players as the day draws nearer," Henri continued with relish, oblivious to her stricken expression. "Do you have a date in mind, darling?"

Solange flinched as the image of her future mother-in-law came to her. But she did not need to reveal her newly discovered lineage to the St Jorres, or to anyone. There really was nothing to fear. She had already decided that.

"Papa, I haven't planned anything as yet. And I don't know why we must focus on this one event, when there is so much else to be done around here that is truly pressing." Her voice was sharp, raised in abrupt retort, beyond her control.

"Solange, my dear . . ."

"Oh for heaven's sake Papa! Once Guy arrives all this fuss will, as you say, envelop us. In the meantime you and Lorette seem to be so well ahead with your ideas on the matter, that I don't really need to comment at all."

Henri looked towards her, surprised and angered by her tone, hurt that she was not sharing his enthusiasm. He said nothing more, and the unusual silence seemed to Solange to have created a small crack in the foundation of their relationship. She held her coffee cup in trembling hands and tried to find some inner peace. After a while she put her hand over his.

"I'm sorry Papa. I must be more nervous about the whole thing than I had realised. Of course it will be wonderful when Guy gets home. I'm so sorry."

She tried to smile, but she was unable to suppress the distress in her voice. He reached out and drew her towards him. She leaned against his corded jacket, willing herself to regain composure, increasingly

42

frustrated by her inability to quell her self-pity. She needed help. There was no one to help her.

Henri was dismayed. For several weeks he had been aware that his daughter's even disposition was off-balance. At first he had put it down to Guy's absence but as time went on he felt an increasing unease. Solange was distant, touchy, preoccupied with something she did not wish to share. As his loneliness grew he craved the presence of his wife with an intensity that made him clench the muscles in his body, as if to squeeze out the despair. Sometimes, at night, he would sit up in his dark, solitary world, a band of pain like a vice around his chest and arms. Celine would have been able to read Solange's eyes, her facial expression, the signals he could not see. He wanted to lie beside his wife, to inhale the scent of her hair and skin, and feel her hands massaging his temples, smoothing away the hovering demon of depression. They would be able to talk about their daughter and try to resolve her troubles together. He wanted to hear Celine's murmured words of love and comfort. He longed for her physical presence with an anguish he could barely contain. It was still so difficult to talk about her with Solange. Slowly they had learned to live with the pain, to bury it, and to turn their thoughts away from the gaping emptiness of the unoccupied breakfast chair, the car unused in the garage, the rain jacket hanging limp in the hall cupboard. When they mentioned Celine now, it was mainly in the company of others who could help them stumble over the sentences, and guide them gently back to normal conversation.

"Solange, don't worry. It's just pre-wedding nerves, darling. I remember feeling the same way, all those years ago. But I have a suggestion for you. Your grandmother has been asking to see you for months. Why don't you go to Paris and spend a few days with her?"

"No. Oh no, Papa."

"It would be a change of scene. Charlotte loves you very much, darling, and Guy has somehow managed to gain your grandmother's approval – a feat that takes most ordinary mortals years to accomplish." He placed his fingers beneath her chin and lifted up her face, touching the corner of her mouth lightly to see if she was smiling. "You've been working so hard outside in the vines – it would be fun to be all dressed up and to live the high life for a few days."

Solange moved her head to interrupt but Henri continued to speak, his finger pressed to her lips.

"Take some time for yourself. Go to your favourite museums and shops, see a play and a film or two, lie in bed in the mornings."

"I don't think . . ."

"You won't get much chance after this, you know, what with the vineyards and the preparations for the wedding and the harvest." He put his hands on her shoulders. "What do you say, darling? No, don't answer, because I know you'll make some silly excuse about what's going on here."

She was silent now, not resisting him, and he pressed his advantage.

"Come on, let's find out about trains. There's bound to be one around midday. Think of this as one of the last orders from your father, before he relinquishes you to another man."

"Papa," she said, her response sounding strange and unconnected, even to her own ears. "I am on edge, you're right. A few days away might be good. There's nothing urgent planned until the middle of next week. I can't believe I'm agreeing with you, but yes – I'd like to take a few days off."

She looked at him, grateful for the love and concern in his face. "I don't think I want to go to Paris though. I'd prefer to be very quiet, somewhere on my own. Maybe a small hotel on the coast in Spain, like the one we stayed in last year. It's not far."

"Spain? You want to go to Spain?" Henri was incredulous. "There'll be hardly anyone there at this time of year. It will be completely dead."

"That's exactly what I need. Time to myself so that I can think

44

and plan dates, guest lists, and all those things I haven't even considered yet."

"Well, it isn't quite what I had in mind, but if that's what you want, then go ahead and arrange it." Something she was saying did not sound right, but having initiated the idea he felt that he could not now dissuade her from her plan. Instead he smiled at her and buried a foolish stab of regret that she had not thought of asking him to join her. "You should leave today, before you change that mercurial little mind. How will you get there?"

"I'll drive down. And I'll take my camera and some books, write some long-overdue letters. Learn to be better behaved so that you won't feel you're sentencing Guy to marriage with a shrew!"

They stood up, relieved to be laughing together. It did not take her long to pack a few clothes and necessities. When she was finished she opened the locked drawer in her desk to take out her passport. Eleanor's letters stared up at her with bold insistence. She slammed the drawer shut and ran down the stairs.

The morning was clear and fine, and the forecast good. Solange looked up at the old house. Early roses covered the weathered trellis with tightly curled buds, but she noticed that the supporting wall badly needed repairs. There were loose stones, and parts of the edifice were crumbling. It would mean expensive scaffolding and at least two workmen. Had her father known about this and postponed it for financial reasons? A plague of doubts flooded her mind. Beyond the garden the vines stood in their orderly lines, marking the wild countryside with the signature of man's endeavours. She turned away, refusing to accept that all this might not be here for ever. Joel put her luggage in the back of the car and Lorette appeared with a flask of coffee and a basket of bread, cheese and fruit.

"I'll telephone you when I get there." She embraced Henri, lightly stroking the grey in his hair. "But don't worry if it's late, because I'm going to take the coast road as soon as it's practical."

Her home disappeared in the rear-view mirror as she drove away down the avenue of plane trees and out into the lane. She glanced at the letterbox and remembered her letter to Eleanor Kirwan, still in her handbag. Eleanor Kirwan. The faceless, unknown girl who had changed everything familiar and valuable in her life. She hated Eleanor Kirwan. At the main road she stopped, but instead of taking the right-hand fork to drive south for Spain and the Costa Brava, she turned north-east and headed towards Montpellier.

In the vineyards Joel straightened up from tending his vines and waved, noting with surprise that the car had turned away from the road that led to Narbonne and the Spanish border. He waited to see if Solange would return to the house. Maybe she had forgotten something. But the car continued in the same direction and was soon lost from sight. Joel shook his head, puzzled, and then returned to his pruning. A change of plan, perhaps. Lorette would surely know and he would ask her at lunchtime.

It was an easy drive and traffic was light. At Montpellier airport she parked the car and took her suitcase into the terminal building. Close to the newsstand, Solange saw a post box. She opened her handbag and drew out her letter to Eleanor Kirwan, watching as it disappeared into the yellow box. An hour later she was in the air, flying over the vineyards, out across the oyster beds and the glassy salt ponds to the sea.

It was almost dark when Solange swung into a gravel driveway between a pair of imposing stone gateposts. She stopped the hire car and got out, tired now, aware that she had come a long way. The main house stood on a rise, its stone terraces looking out over formal gardens and distant paddocks of grazing livestock. Leaded windows caught the last of the evening light. To one side there was a smaller building, the walls covered by a japonica in full flower. Smoke rose from the chimney. Her footsteps sounded loud on the gravel and she could barely contain her nervousness. But it was too late for a change of mind.

She rang the bell, and without waiting for an answer turned the heavy doorknob and stepped into the hall. She heard the scrape of a chair in the next room, and then footsteps. Her heart was thumping much too fast. She could feel it hammering against her breast, and there was a loud, rushing sound in her ears. Pressure mounted behind her eyes. An unbearable tension made her want to cry out.

Cedric Swann opened his study door. For a moment her life stopped completely, caught somewhere between her hidden fears and a surging relief. She stepped towards him, into his safe, welcoming embrace. She began to weep, not quietly but with loud, uncontrollable sobs, unable to say anything or try to explain what she was doing there. He led her into his study, and made her sit down by the fire. When he had dried her tears, he poured a pony of sherry and handed it to her. Then he opened his desk and unlocked a drawer and when he turned to face her there was a leather box in his hands and an envelope containing a key.

"Solange," he said. "My dear, dear beautiful little girl. I think you have come for these."

Chapter 7

Dublin 1970

Elizabeth flung her coat over the chair in the hall, and called out.

"Hi there! I'm home!"

Silence greeted her. The evening light streamed through the stained-glass door, hazing the oak panelling and the vase of tulips into soft focus. Grandfather Kirwan gazed down at her from his portrait by the stairs. Elizabeth looked into the hall mirror, and made a moue with full, red lips. Her face, framed by the mass of bright russet hair, stared back at her with a sultry pout. She made a rude gesture at her reflection, and grinned.

"Hey! Where is everybody?" she called out again. Then she caught the murmur of voices from the study. She opened the door with a jerk. "Well. Don't all answer at once! James? You're home early. Is something wrong?"

James was by the desk, the phone in his hand. "About twenty minutes then? Thanks Dr Mackay." He put down the phone. "He's on his way."

Elizabeth's glance swept the room. Helena lay propped against the cushions, a rug wrapped around her. She was shivering. Eleanor was on her knees by the sofa, talking to her softly.

"For God's sake, tell me what's going on! Mama?" Elizabeth ran forward. "What's happened to her?"

She gazed at her mother, taking in the tremor, the vacant expression, the fingers picking compulsively at the rug.

"It's all my fault." Eleanor's voice was choked. "I should have looked in on her at lunchtime. But I'd read the letter and I went out into the garden to think about it all. And then I just went up to my room." She paused, pushing a strand of hair back. Her shoulders began to shake.

Elizabeth took charge. "James, don't stand there like a dodo! Get El into a chair before she collapses as well. And for heaven's sake give her a handkerchief." She knelt by her mother and tried to still Helena's fingers, taking her hands and massaging them gently. "Maybe we should give her a shot of brandy?"

"I don't suppose that can harm her." James was opening the drinks cabinet, searching for a glass. "And Dr Mackay's coming any minute now."

"I called out to her this morning." Eleanor had control of her voice again. "She said she was painting and didn't want to be disturbed. I worked for a while on a manuscript I brought home from the office yesterday and then I found the post in the hall. There was a letter for me. From Solange . . ." She trailed off and blew her nose. "It put everything else out of my mind. I remembered Mother about three. I made a salad, and coffee, and brought it out to the studio. She was all huddled up on the floor in the corner, shivering and making a sort of wailing sound. Her paints and brushes were scattered everywhere, and she'd overturned a canvas and daubed everything with red."

She gave a stifled sob, twisting the handkerchief in long, thin fingers. "I half-carried her in here, but she wouldn't speak – she was making this weird, keening noise."

Elizabeth bent over Helena, looking into the vacant stare. James handed her the brandy glass.

"Come on Mama – look at me! It's Lizzie! I'm going to pour some brandy down you. And Dr Mackay's on his way." But Helena pressed

49

her lips tightly together and began picking at the rug again. Elizabeth turned to James. "Even if Dr Mackay comes, she may need to be in hospital."

Helena's teeth were chattering but her gaze focused suddenly on Elizabeth. The words, when they came, were clear. "No hospital. I don't want to go anywhere." She was shivering again. "I want Seamus. I just want Seamus. Seamus will know everything." Tears coursed down her face in glistening tracks as she repeated the words over and over again. "Please, please, find Seamus."

The doorbell rang. Eleanor went to answer it, and returned with Dr Mackay. He took Helena's pulse, checked her eyes and her breathing, and settled her back against the cushions. "Helena, listen to me. This is delayed shock and grief, my dear, and you badly need rest. I'm going to give you an injection now, to help you sleep. You've not been sleeping, have you?"

She stared past him, her lips moving silently, knots of wool gathering in her fingers on the edge of the rug. Dr Mackay turned to the others.

"Has she said anything at all?"

"She's been asking for Seamus," said James. "He's on his way back from a walking trip in Nepal. We tried to get in touch with him when Father died, but he's been in a very remote area. Finally we got a message to him through the British Embassy. He cabled yesterday to say he would be back as soon as he could."

Dr Mackay nodded, preparing the syringe. "Well, if you have any way of contacting him again, you should emphasise the urgency of the situation." He bent to give Helena the injection. "Your mother's physically and emotionally exhausted and Seamus is probably the best one to pull her through. He's a good doctor into the bargain. Meantime, I think we should get her into a nursing home for a day or two."

"Will she need to be there for long, Dr Mackay?"

"I can't really tell you, James. Your mother has taken Richard's death very hard, and she's locked herself away. She hasn't allowed herself to grieve or to rest. You can't do that for ever. Sooner or later, your body and your mind will say 'enough'."

The doorbell rang again, loud and urgent.

"Who on earth could that be?" Eleanor jumped up in agitation. "You're not expecting anyone are you James? Lizzie?"

"No." They both shook their heads.

Elizabeth went out to the hall. A large silhouette filled the glass of the front door and she flung it open. "Oh Uncle Seamus! Oh God, are we glad to see you!"

The man standing there was big and bear-like. Ice-blue eyes gazed from a craggy, weathered face, topped by tow-coloured hair that was streaked with grey. He dropped his rucksack on the step and opened his arms, enveloping his niece.

"Lizzie, my love." His voice was deep and gravelly. "I started back as soon as I could. I'm so sorry I wasn't here to help you all. Where's your mother?"

"Oh Uncle Seamus . . . " Elizabeth's voice began to quaver. "She's had some kind of breakdown. They're taking her to hospital."

She led him into the study, clasping his large hand. He smiled at Dr Mackay, took James's hand, touched Eleanor gently on the cheek as he embraced her. Then he strode over to the couch. "Helena, I'm home. Look at me."

Her eyes flickered open; then she reached out and took his big hand. Her eyes closed again. At once her breathing seemed easier. Seamus sat beside her in silence as James recounted the day's events.

"Is it all right if we keep her here, Peter?" Seamus asked Dr Mackay. "I'll stay with her. I'm sure she'll sleep now. Then, when she's ready, I'll take her down with me to the west."

Dr Mackay nodded agreement. Seamus looked over at Eleanor, taking in her strained face.

"Maybe you could take a few days off too, and come with us, Eleanor? Help me out?"

"She could do with it," James said.

Seamus looked at Eleanor, questioning, but she shook her head. "We'll talk later, Seamus. Let's get Mother to bed. Dr Mackay, thank you so much. Is there anything we should be doing?"

"No, she's much quieter already. I don't think we need worry too much, now Seamus is here. I can call back in the morning, on my way to the surgery if you need me." He picked up his bag and put on his coat, smiling reassurance, shaking hands with Seamus. "In any case, Seamus knows what should be done. Over to you Dr O'Riordan. I'll see myself out."

When he had gone, Seamus lifted Helena and carried her upstairs, while Eleanor went to the kitchen to prepare a meal for him. James and Elizabeth stood together in the study, looking out over the bay, silent for a while.

"What's going on?" Elizabeth was puzzled. "I know Eleanor's upset about Mama and about the will, but I've never seen her go to pieces like this. Not since that awful Matthew. She's not going to have a nervous breakdown, is she? She's not going to, well, to get into a state like Mama?"

James shook his head. He went into the drawing room and came back with a letter. "This came today," he said. "Solange has decided she wants nothing more to do with us. You know El. She gets so sensitive and she thinks it must be her fault. I've no idea what she wrote to Solange initially."

"I don't know why she bothered to write at all," said Lizzie. "I wouldn't have put pen to paper on her account."

"Oh Lizzie. You know Eleanor. She always worshipped Father. I suppose she wanted to – oh, clear his name, or at least be able to explain all this to us. To herself. Perhaps even to Solange."

"Can I read the letter?" Elizabeth held out her hand, frowning as he hesitated. "Oh don't be ridiculous, James. I'm part of all this too. Let me read it."

James handed her the letter and she read, swiftly. As she finished, she threw it towards the desk, furious. It fell on the floor.

"Selfish little French cow! Who the hell is she to decide that Father's secrets should die with him? Buzz off and don't bother me now I've got the money, is more likely! Poor Eleanor, no wonder she's hurt. I bet she poured her heart and soul out to Mademoiselle Solange and now she feels snubbed."

"Lizzie, try to see this in a more balanced way. How would you like to be told, just as you're about to marry, that your father isn't your father, and your mother never told you. And Solange can't ask the man she always thought was her father, because maybe he never knew either. Then there's the fiancé. Should she tell him or not? Anyway I don't think she needs money."

Elizabeth looked at him, her expression filled with scorn. "If the fiancé is any good and she really loves him, what's the problem?"

"Oh for Christ's sake! This girl must feel as though she was some unwanted mistake. Grow up. Try to see the whole picture, can't you?"

His sister glared at him, her small form stiff with hurt and resentment. He tried a kinder tone. "It may be more important in France, Lizzie, in these old, landed families. Even in middle-class Ireland, parents aren't exactly thrilled when their offspring choose someone with a less than respectable pedigree."

"She might be living in a shed for all you know. Maybe her mother tried to blackmail Father. Maybe she made him do this to us. She must have known he was wealthy. Maybe she's not his daughter at all."

James sighed, realising it was pointless to try and make his sister consider the situation from a more rational viewpoint.

"Come on, it's not likely that Solange has invented a background for herself, just to impress us. And her mother is dead. Maybe Father just felt guilty at the end, and money seemed to be the easiest way to make some final gesture of acknowledgement."

"Well if she survived without his support all those years, I can't see why he should have sprung her on us now. And what about Mama? What did he think this would do to her?"

Her expression changed as she looked at him shaking his head, and she chose her next words more carefully.

"I think you and I should find out what really happened. I think we have to, James, in order to try and understand. You know, when I first heard it, I felt as though he'd reached out from his grave and – stabbed us. As if he'd never loved us at all, and just waited to drop this bombshell on us when he was safely away. I was so angry, James, that night. I went down to the beach in the freezing cold, on my own, and walked right to the end where it's deserted. And I screamed at the top of my voice. I thought of all the swearwords I knew, and I yelled them all out at him. I wanted to shock him, beat him with them." She stopped, unable to keep her voice steady. "But I couldn't reach him, James. He was gone, away somewhere in a secret place. And I wanted him back, so badly."

James put his arms around her and hugged her tight. She whispered into his jacket. "I was so afraid, while he was dying, fading away before my eyes. Oh God, James, it was so selfish of me because I wanted him well for me. I didn't think of his pain. And suddenly, it seemed like a punishment. He'd been taken from me, and sort of given to a total stranger." She straightened, moving away from him and wiping her eyes. "God, what a lot of rubbish I talk. I hope I haven't smeared my mascara, have I?"

She gazed at her brother defiantly. He ran his fingertip under each eye gently.

"I think it looks fine now, Lizzie."

"So why don't you go to France and see what you can discover? About Father's life."

"You mean Solange or no Solange, we have to know what

54

happened?" James looked at her, mulling over the idea.

"Yes, James!" She grabbed him by the lapels. "You could arrange to handle a case in Paris, and I'll come with you. We can find out about Father's time there, all those years ago."

"That's crazy!" James was laughing, half in despair. "I can't just 'arrange a case in Paris' as you put it."

"But you do get involved in international cases, James. It happened last year!"

"Yes, but that was unusual. And I don't choose my cases. Solicitors send them to me. Although there's the Arlenne settlement that I glanced at a couple of weeks ago. And the law conference in Paris next week. I hadn't thought of going away and leaving everyone so soon . . ."

"You see? I knew we'd work out something."

"But what about Eleanor?"

"We'll tell Uncle Seamus everything. Then he can make sure Eleanor takes a break with him in Connemara. She shouldn't know anything about this, for the time being."

James nodded, bemused by the simplicity of Lizzie's plan, but troubled by its deeper implications. "I'll be working most of the time."

"Yes, of course. But I can do some research on my own. My French is just as good as yours or Eleanor's."

"Where would we start?"

"At the Sorbonne, where Father was before the war. We're bound to find people he knew. After all he did go back sometimes, didn't he? And what about the grandmother? Solange's grandmother is still in Paris. The first letter said so. I'm sure she must have known Father. Anyway, you can make the arrangements in the morning. Meantime, I've got an essay to write for tomorrow. 'Night, brother dear . . ."

Elizabeth left, blowing him a kiss. James sat for a while, grateful to be alone in the quiet room, wondering if he was going mad. He should not be considering such a wild scheme. But perhaps he owed it to them all, himself included, to try and find the truth. He would ring his colleague in Paris about the Arlenne case. First thing in the morning.

Eleanor sat in her room staring at the bright expanse of moonlit water, thinking over the letter. Why had she been so upset over Solange's reaction? Why hadn't she understood, much earlier, that Seamus would be the ideal person to help her mother. She should have reassured Helena that he was on his way.

"Will I ever be essential to anyone?" she asked herself, fighting stupid tears. "Father never really needed me – even though I loved him so much. Matthew didn't need me either, and I didn't even know it."

She stood up and drew the curtain with such violence that one end detached from the rail. Leaving it to hang jagged across the window, she got into bed and turned her head away from the light.

"Damn you, Father!" she whispered into the darkness. "I knew you didn't love me the way I wanted to be loved. But I always thought I could look up to you. Trust you. What legacy have you left us, with your noble bequest? 'To my daughter in France, Solange de Valnay, – the ashes of my family in Ireland!'"

Helena tossed uneasily in her sleep. Images floated behind her closed eyes in a menacing melange of nightmare and memory. There were voices in a muffled distance, and Richard's shadow drifted in some unattainable dimension. She needed to speak to him urgently. There was something she had to explain. She could sense reproach emanating from his dim figure. Helena gave a small cry of despair, which set up an echoing all around her, engulfing her in discordant noise. She tried to put her hands to her ears, but they would not obey. She felt panic building up inside her head.

Then her brother's voice came through the maelstrom, overriding all other sounds, and she felt his hand enclosing hers. It was as though all the years had been rolled away in the soothing cadence of his speech. The pain of the present was wiped from her memory by the vision of the wide skies of her Connemara childhood, when Seamus was the centre of her world. With a long, shuddering sigh she lay still and let the past enclose her.

Chapter 8

Connemara, 1927

Seamus and Helena stood by the seashore. A smell of fresh seaweed rose from the tide and the surf was heavy. The sun shone fitfully between gusts of rain. Helena's hair was tied firmly into a plait down her back, but unruly wisps had already worked their way free in the wind. At thirteen, Seamus was in that stretch of youth that left bony knees and elbows projecting from his shrinking clothes. His face was round and freckled, filled with fierce concentration. The summer – their last childhood summer – had left a wet trail across their memories.

In the final two weeks they had visited all their special haunts to say goodbye, hovering around the quayside amongst the fishing nets and boxes, breathing in the life that was going to be taken from them. In the small chandlery shop Helena inhaled the rich smells of rope, tackle, brass and varnish, grain sacks and bolts of canvas. She sat on a stool behind the polished counter and listened to the tread of the fishermen's boots on the swept, wooden floor. Dada became more silent than ever. He stared off into the distance, turned his porter glass around and around between his hands, and chewed on his pipe. Angela sorted and packed school uniforms and bedding, issuing advice and encouraging promises. Helena didn't believe any of it. She was being sent away. Away from everything and everybody that she loved, off to some prison of a convent boarding school to have "manners" put on her.

If it hadn't been for big Connor Sweeney, the perfect pattern of their days might never have been torn asunder. Connor Sweeney and his gang had long been the bane of their lives with their taunting and bullying. He was so big, he thought he could get away with anything. Until that one afternoon.

"Well! If it isn't little carrot head and her sissy twin brother!" Connor had sneered. "Have ye written any more 'verses' sissy boy? Come on, now, let's see them!"

Seamus had pushed past him, clearing the way for his sister, but Connor caught her by the hair. Helena had squealed and struggled, landing a sharp kick on his leg. Her twin, twice her size, had leapt to her defence and in the ensuing struggle Seamus's precious copybook of poems had been stamped into a puddle. It was the first time she had seen her brother cry. After the lads were gone, wheeling their bikes back up to the college, laughing and jeering, Seamus had tried to gather the sodden pages together. But the ink had all run and the lines were illegible. Quivering, she put her small hand into his.

"Won't you be able to remember them all, Seamus?"

He had shaken his head, unable to speak. Then he had squeezed her hand and they had left the ruins of his soul floating in the rain-soaked path. As they trudged up the hill the sun had come out, glinting on Connor Sweeney's new bike. That was when she had the idea. Moments later they were in the college bicycle shed. When they couldn't identify Connor's bike Helena had prodded Seamus, laughing.

"Come on – we'll let the whole lot down. They're all as bad as each other, these fellows and I hate the way they look down on us. If we do them all, no one will guess it was us after Connor Sweeney!"

Reaching down, she had unscrewed the valve on the front tyre of the nearest bike, then the back. Seamus watched, horrified, as she moved methodically down the line. She caught his eye and grinned. "I dare you, Seamus O'Riordan, or you're a scaredy-cat!"

He set to work and the noise from the shed began to sound like a steam engine. When they were all done he grabbed her hand and they fled across the road to hide behind a crop of boulders.

"Helena O'Riordan – you're the wickedest girl I ever met!" Seamus gasped. "If we're found out, they'll chop us up into little pieces."

"Get away! No one will know. No one saw us. If we go off home now, who's to say we were ever near the college?"

But they had stayed on to watch the fun as the boys came out of their afternoon lessons. The roar of fury had rocked them both in their hiding place and then they had run for their lives, with a posse of big lads fanning out from the school in pursuit. When Helena fell, twisting her ankle and losing her boot, Seamus had lifted her up on to his back and staggered on across the fields. At the house Dada had been standing by the kitchen range, Angela was making tea, and the Head Brother from the college was sitting at the table. Their elder brothers were outside mending the nets, but close to the back door where they could hear everything. Brother Fergus was a big man with a lumpy face and hair sprouting from his ears. It was clear from his breathing that he was barely in control of his fury.

"Is this yours, Miss?"

The boot, lace broken, sole caked in mud, was put on the table. Seamus, wide-eyed, had let go of his sister and as she slipped to the floor a searing pain shot through her injured leg. The room began to reel. Helena could faintly see the Brother, his fat finger wagging, his mouth opening and closing like a codfish, but the sound was drowned by the roaring in her ears. Then everything went blank. After that, Dada and Angela had come up with the plan to send them away.

Peadar O'Riordan had been widowed soon after the twins were born. On the night of the funeral he had sat beside the kitchen range, holding the infants in his lap. Seamus was a big, bonny baby, round-faced with a mop of sandy hair like his Da. But Helena was a fairy child entirely, with deep brown eyes and her tiny face framed in a crown of red-gold light. Angela Doyle had come to the house that night and offered to help him. She was a disgraced woman who had run off with the nephew from the "Big House", and he a Protestant. She had even married him in the Protestant Church. A year later she was back, in her black dress, with her husband dead from a riding accident. His family would have nothing to do with her, and her own had been less than welcoming. That night she appeared small, thin and dark-haired, with too strong a nose and chin. But her eyes were calm and she looked at Peadar straight as she made her offer to take care of the children and the housekeeping.

For four years Angela had looked after them all while the people of Roundstone cast disapproving glances. Then Peadar had married her and from that day on Angela slept in Dada's bed with him. Otherwise all was as it had been. But the slim, dark woman glowed and smiled, and often sang in a soft contralto in the kitchen, when she thought there was no one around. In the village the O'Riordans were considered unconventional and therefore suspect, and the twins were regarded as completely wild.

Now even Angela had agreed that they should leave home, that they should be separated. Her sister was a nun, the headmistress of a boarding school in Athlone, and a place was arranged for Helena. Seamus was to be sent to Galway to stay with his uncle and go to the College with his cousins. Helena wanted to plead – to rant and rave, cry and beg. But at the thought of departure a lump got in the way of her words and she could not speak. As Angela worked, brisk and busy, the vice around Helena's heart tightened.

"I'll not be able to breathe soon," she muttered to herself in panic, "And no one will notice. They're so busy with their useless discussions about school clothes and books. I'll be dead in the corner, and they won't even know. I hate them – I hate them all!"

She sought refuge outside in the wind and rocks and heather, — soaking into her memory the colour of her home, and the smell of it. Down at Seal Bay she lay on the flat rocks, studying their grain and their criss-cross lines and cracks. But even here, the future kept intruding. She went in search of her brother and the look of him was edged with pain, because soon he would be gone from her, and she feared he would change, grow away from her, and all they had shared together would be finished.

Now it was the last day. They stood at the sea's edge offering each other comfort without words. Helena, aware of fears that Seamus could not express, was ashamed of her selfish absorption in her own troubles. He had a piece of paper in his hand, rolled into a tight scroll. She knew he had sat out here last night at dusk, writing and writing. He raised his arm now, and cast the paper out into the deep water, standing with his eyes closed and his lips moving silently. Helena edged closer and watched the paper as it opened slowly on the tide. It was densely written. The ink began to spread and soften, leaving eddies of deeper blue on the surface of the water.

"What is it, Seamus?"

"I'm writing on the water," he said softly, taking her hand. "I'm signing our names on the bay, so that it will always know us, whenever we come back, whatever we look like. I've told our story to the tide, and the beach, and the seaweed. I've bound this place to us with the words. We belong to the bay, and the bay belongs to us. It's like writing a will, you know?"

He squeezed her hand, turned and walked away, back towards the village. She stood staring at the pulpy pages drifting away from her. Then she ran past him, racing up the stony road to the crag and the heather, where she could look down at it all – the house, the shop, the village, the boats bobbing on a shining sea. She could hear Angela calling and she saw Seamus reach the back door where Dada stood waiting. Dada said something to him, then turned to look up at her, squinting into the light. He signalled. Then she was running again, down, down to give him a last hug before grief closed over her, and set her adrift.

Her school was in the Midlands, a grey building with high windows, set in a flat, featureless landscape. She missed the boats, the smell of salt in the air. Here everything was so tight, so bound in. There were high hedges and iron gates, but no tumbling stone walls and dipping seagulls. The sheep and cattle seemed arranged in the landscape – not free to ramble the hills, or spring over ditches as they did at home. Even the water tasted different.

The nights were worst, imprisoned in the cubicle that contained her narrow bed. There was a small skylight above her, and in her imagination she rose through it into the starry sky, and out across the fields to Connemara. She wondered if Seamus had to sleep in a tight little space like this, without the wind whipping its wild song around the windows, or the sound of rigging slapping against boat masts on night water. That was when the loneliness became suffocating.

Helena grew thin and pale. At last she found a form of escape in drawing. It gave her comfort to sketch from memory the familiar scenes of home. One afternoon she was struggling with the cut of a sail on her father's boat.

"It is the mast, *ma petite*. When she moves into the wind it is like this."

A hand gestured at the page, and Helena saw that the speaker understood how the boat rode the water. She altered the angle of the mast and looked up. She had often noticed the elderly French nun who was retired and walked with a silver-handled cane. Her face was lined, her eyes sunken, perhaps with pain or just with age.

"Thank you, Sister."

"I am Sister Véronique. May I look at your work?"

Helena handed over her sketchbook. The long fingers turned the pages slowly.

"You have talent, I see. But you are often alone, are you not? I think you need to eat more and sleep better." The nun's voice was kind. "I know what it is to long for home, for someone who is far away."

Sister Véronique was a fine teacher, inspiring and cultured. Helena's French grammar improved, and gradually the old nun guided her pupil into finding a focus for herself in art and music.

Helena wrote long, rambling letters to Seamus, and more restrained ones to her father and Angela, assuring them that she was well. She did not say that she lived for the time when she could be home again and free. Seamus sent her poems, and funny stories about his life in Galway and his new friends. Helena began to fear that he was not missing her at all.

But at last summer came and they were home. The best times were the evenings when everyone gathered in the kitchen, or down on the quayside if it was fine, and Helena could lose herself in the wild playing of fiddles and flutes and spoons, in the whirl of skirts and the tapping of feet. Even her old enemy Connor Sweeney watched her with admiration but he did not approach her. Seamus was never far away and no one would take him on lightly now. When the evenings began to shorten and the school trunks came out again, Helena resolved that this time she would not be torn by partings. This time there would be a quiet casting off, so that her anguish at leaving her home and her family could be contained.

In the middle of her final year at school, when the cold March winds whistled down the corridors and the trees outside were bent flat against flurries of sleet and hail, Dada died. For a time Helena withdrew into herself, rarely speaking, unable to communicate in a world where Dada was no longer there to shelter her with his towering love. She could not even talk to Seamus about it. One grey evening, when grief had almost consumed her, she sat down with charcoal and pastels to create her own image of him. And it was then that she knew her future direction. She would paint, put all that she felt on paper and canvas. Say it in a sweep of colour, in the droop of a figure, the sharp line etched along the softer contour of a hillside. She learned that year to speak in magenta and green and cobalt blue – with oil or water and a brush and palette. Her adult years had begun.

Chapter 9

Dublin, 1970

A watery light filtered through the half-opened curtains, and Eleanor turned away and put her face into the pillow. Her head ached, her eyes felt gritty, and she wanted only to forget everything and to sleep. It was weeks since she had slept through the night without waking. She longed to be out of Dublin and away from the house, the city, everything. It would be good to walk on the beach at Seal Bay, to breathe in the heady western air and soak up the remote peace of Connemara. James had been right, she did need a break. He was almost always right, even though she didn't tell him so very often.

Showering quickly, she dressed in warm trousers, boots and a sweater and took up her hairbrush, studying her reflection in the mirror. A thin, pale face, a mass of wild, black hair, somewhat heavy eyebrows over startlingly blue eyes underlined by shadows, a straight nose and firm mouth. Her father's features stared back at her and Eleanor realised, with a shock, how like him she was. Tall and spare, with his slightly brooding expression. Her height had always made her feel awkward. Not much of Helena here, she thought ruefully, except for the unruly hair. The firefly look had been given in its entirety to Elizabeth.

She wrestled with her hair, then made her way along the landing to her parents' bedroom and looked in. Helena lay slumped on her pillows, but her breathing was easy and she was sleeping soundly. Seamus was nowhere to be seen. Eleanor closed the door gently and made her way downstairs. She set the breakfast table and left a note to say that she would be in the office for an hour or so. There were manuscripts that she wanted to collect and work on in Connemara, and things she must discuss with Gareth Duggan. He always arrived at the office very early in the morning.

Kirwan Publishing had an international reputation for literary excellence. The founder, Eleanor's great-grandfather, had passed on its mantle to his eldest son. In turn Jonathan and Dorothea Kirwan had hoped that their own son would follow them into the business. But Richard's great love had always been scholarship and his parents had had to be content to see the young man's star shining in the academic firmament. Since the death of Richard's parents the firm had been run by the senior partner, Gareth Duggan.

When Eleanor graduated, she went to work as Gareth's assistant and she was proud that she had risen on her own merits, to become his second in command. He had been a familiar figure since her childhood when he had joined Kirwan Publishing as a young graduate. Over time he had also become a close family friend. Eleanor had found him a demanding but inspirational colleague with whom she could have a fierce argument or a deep discussion with equal satisfaction. In addition he was a good editor, intelligent and incisive.

Gareth was a tall, rangy man, with broad, muscular shoulders and long arms, rather ungainly in his height, as if he didn't quite know what to do with the stretch of his legs and his large hands. He gazed down on the world from wide-set, penetrating eyes, and his big, square face featured a slightly off-centre nose and a generous, sympathetic mouth. His hair was worn a little too long, and stood up wildly when he ran his hands through it. Eleanor teased him about the pepperings of grey that had begun to appear at his temples.

It was still early when she knocked on Gareth's door. He greeted her with freshly brewed coffee that she drank gratefully, perched on the edge of his desk. The office looked out on to Fitzwilliam Square through long Georgian windows draped with mulberry silk. There was no other suggestion of formality in the room. Books and manuscripts were stacked in towering piles on the shelves, on Gareth's desk and all over the carpet, each volume tagged with a coloured marker on which he had scrawled copious notes. Eleanor looked at him with a rush of affection.

"You're looking a little peaky, Eleanor," he said, patting his pockets as he searched for his cigarettes and lighter. "It's just as well you're going off to the west. How is Helena this morning?"

"She's holding together, but only just. I'm so relieved that Seamus has appeared. But I'm not sure if I should be going down to Connemara."

"After all that's happened you could do with the break."

"But I was going to organise a meeting with Eammon Kennedy this week. His writings on the situation in the North are really good, Gareth, and we should get him signed up before someone else does. He's produced a brilliantly balanced series of essays, right up to this latest split of the IRA into officials and provisionals." She twisted her hands together and paused. "You know, Father was writing something on the development of the different Unionist and republican paramilitary groups when he got so ill, so I have his papers to help me too."

The mention of Richard brought the dilemma of his will into sharp focus again. In the days following the funeral and the reading of the will Eleanor had wanted her mother to tell Gareth everything, but Helena had refused to talk to him or to anyone. Eleanor had been obliged to wait in desperation for the arrival of her uncle, unable to discuss the subject outside the family, afraid that she would be betraying her mother's private grief. She had longed to turn to Gareth for advice, but she never seemed to find the right opportunity, and now was not the time to start on the whole story. She wished she did not have to go to Connemara. She was too tired to face her mother's silent struggles and she felt that it would have been better to hurl herself into the backlog of manuscripts.

"Won't you need me here?" She looked at Gareth wistfully.

He studied her for a moment, aware of the pull between family duty and her longing to bury herself in her work and shut out everything else. He knew there was something more she wanted to say, but he was at a loss as to how he could help her to break the barrier of silence that had surrounded the whole family since Richard's death.

"Your mother needs you more," he said at last. "She's had a pretty bad year of it – you all have. And maybe you'll get a little time to yourself, to take stock of things."

"You'd think by now I'd have remembered to bring a handkerchief everywhere with me." Eleanor bit her lip hard and smiled at him, watery eyed. "Are there any tissues?"

Gareth produced what looked like a small sheet from his voluminous pockets.

"It's creased, but it is clean – I promise. Now, dry the eyes and stiffen the back. We'll be in touch by phone every day, and I'll keep you up to date."

"Thanks for the pep talk. I appreciate it." She reached up and kissed his cheek. "When I come back there's something I want to talk to you about. Not business – it's about Mother and Father. You've been such a close friend to us all for so many years, and now I don't know if I ever understood my parents at all. Oh hell! I'm sorry." She turned away and began to gather up her papers.

"Eleanor – your family has always been special to me." His voice was serious. "It's impossible to imagine how the children and I could have got through Moira's death without the support you gave us. Your mother's alone now. She needs strong, kind people around her, and you're one of the strongest. That's what matters at this moment. That's all that matters."

"But I don't feel strong! I'm tired of picking up the pieces of everyone else's lives. I've never really picked up my own pieces. And their lives are proving too difficult for me."

"You're grieving. That's natural."

"It's more than grief. Much more."

"Look at me." He held her face in his big hands. "Something has happened at home since your father's death, is that it? Something to do with Helena and Richard?"

She nodded. He let go of her, walked over to the window and stood looking out at the square.

"I realised there was something terribly wrong. Apart from your father's death, I mean. Only I didn't want to pry. And yes. Richard weathered some pretty fierce storms along the way. The war and its aftermath destroyed a good many people. But it didn't destroy what Richard and Helena had together. You and James, Elizabeth, your home, all this." He gestured round the room. "If your parents had difficulties, then they got through them together, and they loved the three of you. I'm sure of that."

"I don't know, Gareth. I just don't know any more."

"I know that you're needed in Connemara. Helena told me once that when things are bad you've always been her one, steady light. You're going to have to go down there, just for her sake."

His expression registered something unfathomable and for a wild moment Eleanor wanted to reach out and touch him, feel his strength and support.

"It's too long a story to discuss now. But when you get back I'll tell you everything I know, I promise you. In the meantime you'd better get going. I'll ring you in Connemara tomorrow."

She drove back to Killiney wondering exactly what Gareth was going to tell her on her return, and why he had specifically mentioned the war.

*

In Eleanor's absence James had telephoned Monsieur Serge Bouvier of Descartes, Bouvier & Fils in Paris. After a lengthy conversation he turned to Elizabeth, smiling.

"We're all set, Lizzie. Serge Bouvier is handling the Arlenne case in Paris. He'll organise our hotel and meet us at Orly next Monday. I'll have to go down to his office during the afternoon, but you can amuse yourself for a while, I'm sure."

"Oh I'm not short of ideas for an hour or two alone in Paris!"

"I told him you were coming with me, to do some research on your thesis, maybe at the Sorbonne." James had begun to feel like a student on an escapade that would definitely earn disapproval. "And the Convention is starting on Monday too. We're invited to the opening reception. What do you say?"

"I shall floor the international lawyers with my style," Elizabeth practised what she believed to be a sultry look. "What about our flight?"

"I'll book now, and then ring Serge Bouvier with our time of arrival."

"Your time of arrival where exactly? And who's Serge Bouvier?" Seamus was standing in the doorway.

Elizabeth glanced at her brother and James shrugged.

"Well, we were going to tell you about this anyway, Seamus," he said. "So it's probably best to do it before Eleanor comes back."

"I don't know what you're planning, but as conspirators you both look guilty as hell." Seamus sat down in the big armchair, and regarded his nephew and niece, unsmiling. "Eleanor is no fool and neither is your mother. Luckily for you, they have their minds on other things. Do I take it you're going off somewhere as soon as we're safely on the road?"

"James and I are going to Paris next week to try and find out more about this Solange. How it all happened." Elizabeth attempted a winning smile. "This is something we have to do, Uncle Seamus.

Because of the letters. We thought we'd start at the Sorbonne, where Father was before the war."

"And we don't want to involve Eleanor. She's already upset," James said. "So we thought we would —"

"Whoa there you two! You're going much too fast for me. Let's go back to the beginning please." Seamus put up his hands in dismay.

"Honestly Seamus, there's no point in Mother or Eleanor hearing about this right now," said James. "We may not come up with anything. I'm sure Mother has told you about the will, and the letters from Solange de Valnay who's supposed to be our half-sister in France. I'm assuming you know about this, Seamus. And we want to learn more ourselves. We have to."

"So you're going off to try and find this Solange de Valnay, and to confront her?" Seamus was frowning.

"No, of course not!" Elizabeth cut in. "We don't expect to see her at all. She lives in the South of France somewhere. But James has business in Paris, and I'm going with him, to see if we can discover anything about Father's life before — well, before. This is a whole other life, Seamus. And if he'd wanted it to remain secret, he wouldn't have mentioned her in his will, would he?"

"I'm not at all happy with the idea of this precipitous journey." Seamus regarded them seriously. "I can't prevent you from going, but I don't think it's a sound plan. And I hope you fully understand that this is not a game or an adventure."

"Of course we realise that." James tried a conciliatory tone.

But Seamus had risen to his feet and turned away from them, still talking. "You may be digging into an extremely painful or even tragic area of people's lives. Looking at a period that's best forgotten. Just remember that war leaves an appalling trail of destruction. Things are not simple matters of black and white, right and wrong, in days of crisis. You must be able to interpret what you discover with compassion. In my view, you should postpone your research for a while."

James's eyebrows snapped together furiously, and Seamus realised how like his father he was in that moment of anger. "All right James. I'll say nothing. But I warn you – if Eleanor finds out you're doing this behind her back, she's going to be desperately hurt. I haven't seen her this shaky since the break-up with Matthew."

"Don't worry!" Elizabeth hugged him quickly. "We'll be back before she ever knows we're gone."

"Well, think it over." Seamus walked to the door and turned to face them. "And don't forget what I said earlier. You don't know, either of you, how living close to death can alter your perspective. Be kind to your father, – and anyone else involved. In the meantime I came to tell you that your mother's up and about, and she wants to leave for Connemara as soon as Eleanor's ready. I'm going to have breakfast with her now, and I think you should join me."

He went out, leaving Elizabeth and James surprised by his vehemence.

"What does he mean by all that, do you think?" Elizabeth was shaken.

"I don't know, Lizzie, and we're not likely to find out for the time being. Go and find Mother and see what you can do for her. I'll make coffee and toast."

Eleanor returned from her office to find James in the driveway, a rug and pillows in his arms.

"Aren't you rather jumping the gun?" she asked. "Mother might not be able to travel until tomorrow, or even the next day."

"She's just had breakfast with us. She's a little shaky but she's packed and ready to leave for Connemara."

"I can't believe it. You're sure she's up to it?"

"Seamus says it's all right. That she'll be better off down there and she can rest on the way. Tell me when you're nearly ready to go." James came to stand beside his sister. She was leaning against

73

the door frame, her eyes closed wearily. "Look El," he said kindly. "If you feel too tired or too stretched you could leave it till tomorrow to travel. Or I could drive you all and come back on the train."

She looked so vulnerable. James reached out and tucked her hair behind her ear, raising his black brows. She shrugged, straightened her drooping shoulders, and turned away briskly. "I hope you and Lizzie have everything you need. I'll write a list of shopping for Mrs Kenny, and she'll be here to do the cooking."

"I don't think we'll be in much. I have a lot of work to deal with, and Lizzie may stay with one of her friends." He glanced at her briefly, not quite meeting her eyes.

Eleanor looked at him sharply. There was something odd about the way he spoke and she felt she was missing some aspect of his statement, but she was too tired to follow it up. "Well, take care of yourself, and watch out for Lizzie. James?" She paused. She could read him so well and she always knew when he was keeping something from her.

He turned at the kitchen door. She was gazing at him in silent query. He felt guilty, but determined not to involve her. "We'll be grand. We're perfectly well able to look after ourselves you know."

He saw hurt cloud her eyes and was irked by her acute sensitivity. She'd been like this since the split with Matthew. It was like walking on eggshells.

Moments later Seamus and Helena appeared in the hall and Eleanor felt a wave of relief as she saw her mother's easel and other paraphernalia. Somehow things could not be so bad if Helena wanted to paint.

"We'll ring when we get down there," Eleanor said as she turned on the ignition.

James and Elizabeth waved nonchalantly, and Seamus was disturbed by their air of easy innocence. As soon as the car disappeared from view they went back to the study. James picked up the phone and dialled. "Hello – Aer Lingus – could I book two seats to Paris, Orly?"

Chapter 10

Gloucestershire, 1970

Solange drew back the linen curtains and looked down at the lawn. Only the English, she thought, could produce that flawlessly smooth expanse of green without a single blade out of place. Her watch said ten-thirty. She could not remember ever having slept so deeply for so long. The leather box lay still unopened on the tallboy. She had not been brave enough to delve into it alone when she had come upstairs the night before.

Cedric was reading the newspaper when she appeared for breakfast. Solange was suddenly ravenous. She ate a bowl of porridge with a thick yoke of cream and a sprinkling of brown sugar, said yes to coffee, eggs and bacon, and hot toast spread thickly with butter and home-made marmalade.

"Good heavens – I've never seen a self-respecting French woman dispose of an English breakfast so efficiently. Come outside with me now, my dear. It's a suntrap out in the garden. You decide how you want the day to pan out, and I'll go along with you."

They seated themselves in wicker chairs, faces raised to the warm sunshine. Celine's box lay on a small table between them. Solange had believed herself to be ready for the truth, but she could not look directly at Cedric as she asked her first question, opening the doors to long-hidden lives.

"Was he my father?"

"Yes, my dear. Richard Kirwan was your father."

Now that she had heard it spoken aloud, she knew it was the truth.

"I felt in my heart that it couldn't be a mistake. But it was so sudden. I couldn't speak to anyone, and I was terrified that I'd somehow make Papa aware of what had happened, that I would say something to alert him. I was so angry, so disgusted. I am still. But I knew it must be true." In spite of herself her eyes filled with tears. She brushed them away roughly and looked at Cedric. "Why weren't you surprised to see me last night?"

"I saw Richard Kirwan's obituary in the newspapers a while ago," Cedric replied. "Your mother had talked to me about him. And she gave me that little package about a year before she died. I assumed, then, that she had decided to talk to you too. She wanted me to keep the box for you, in case you ever asked about him. I've been half-expecting you to find your way here."

"Asked about him? They both made sure I'd ask about him," Solange said bitterly. "But she never warned me. I didn't know who he was until I received a letter from his daughter in Ireland saying he'd left me rather a large amount of money. To salve his conscience I suppose. Here are the letters. You can see for yourself exactly what has happened."

Cedric read the pages slowly and shook his head. "I think Richard Kirwan did care a great deal about you, about both of you. Your mother always seemed sure of that. But it does seem strange, this last gesture."

"It wasn't just strange. It was cruel. What kind of man would do that to his family? And why leave me money now, having ignored me all these years?"

"One can't know what thoughts and desires approach as death's companions, Solange."

"He must have been a selfish man. And cowardly. I don't know how Eleanor can still respect him, after such a barbaric gesture." She put her next questions with some hesitation. "How much do you know about all this, Cedric? Did they continue to see each? Were they . . . ?"

Cedric leaned forward and took her hands. "Solange, there's no easy way through this. I realise how you must have felt, how you feel now. Your mother was regarded as a shining light for everyone, almost a saint. Now you are forced to consider her in an altogether different way, as someone flawed like the rest of us."

"She cheated on us," retorted Solange savagely. "Even after my father married her, even though he loved us so much, even though he was blind, she cheated on him. How could she have dreamed of deceiving my father, when he loved her and needed her so much?"

Cedric looked at her, and she saw that his face was stern rather than sympathetic. "Everyone involved in an affair finds their own justification for it. And this one was complicated by war and separation. Don't judge too hastily, my dear."

"Richard Kirwan must have known Mama was dead," Solange rushed on, her face flushed with anger. "But he thought nothing of blowing our lives apart when he no longer had to answer for himself."

"Well, on the face of it, the bequest is a crude gesture. Why couldn't he have left you in happy ignorance? I can't answer that. I admit it was an extraordinary thing for him to have done." Cedric paused. "My dear, you've got to stop looking at this from your own narrow point of view. You must learn to understand. Now I want to ask you something. Have you discussed these events with your grandmother in Paris?"

Solange was stung by the rebuke, shocked by the mention of Charlotte de Savoie.

"Was Grandmama involved in this passionate little tryst too? Oh yes, I can see it all happening. The typical Parisian love affair. She probably had several of them herself in her day, so she didn't worry about Papa, either. None of them were concerned about deceiving him."

"That's enough, Solange. You're right, there was deception and unhappiness. One cannot conduct clandestine relationships without paying that price, no matter what the effort or the intentions of those involved."

Solange was shaking her head, her mouth set, hands clenched.

"You know, you've been exceptionally fortunate. You've always had a secure, comfortable home, no physical or emotional threats to face. You got through your school days, your university years, without any real challenges. In a pleasant haze, really."

"But I haven't spent my whole life in the vineyards, Cedric. I've lived in Paris, in Montpellier, while I was at the university. I've travelled, met all kinds of people. I even got arrested and put in jail during the student demonstrations. I don't think I have a narrow outlook."

"This is not about being narrow, it's about tolerance and experience. You've known terrible sorrow and your mother's death was the greatest tragedy. But I'm talking about things that force you to make difficult choices for complex reasons. Security can leave you unprepared, extremely vulnerable in the face of sudden changes of fortune. Now tell me, what does Guy have to say about all this?"

"Oh Cedric, Guy doesn't even know! I can't imagine trying to explain it to him. And you should see his parents. They're very grand, very conservative. They would never accept a bride in the family who is, well, illegitimate." Her throat closed as she said the word.

"Good God!" To her dismay Cedric began to laugh. "Half the French aristocracy has emerged from the wrong side of the blankets. You cannot keep this a secret from Guy. It's too important to you."

Solange turned away. She took up her mother's package and broke the seal. Inside was a square box made of black leather, with a monogrammed top, bearing the initials RDK in gold lettering and she opened the lid. A man's portrait gazed out at her in the form of an old photograph. He was handsome if a little severe, brooding almost, but his features were fine. Light and shadow emphasised the smooth plane of the cheeks, the high forehead, the dark shining hair and heavy eyebrows. His eyes stared at her, cool and direct, intelligent. The mouth was wide and the lips well defined. Small lines at the corners suggested that he could laugh.

Solange lifted the picture out of the box. On the back of the photograph was a note in her mother's handwriting. "Richard in Ireland in 1941." Underneath were more photos. One showed Richard Kirwan in a country setting which Solange could not identify. He was tall, graceful, and confident in the way he held himself. She studied two further pictures, one taken on the banks of the Seine, the second in the garden of Avenue Mozart, her grandmother's house in Paris. He looked thin and had one arm in a sling. She lifted this image and turned it over, but there was no note on the back. Looking back down into the leather box, she saw a photograph of her mother, radiant with beauty. Her hair was shining in the sunlight, flying loose around her laughing face. She was looking up at Richard Kirwan, her joy not merely visible but demanding to be recognised. He gazed back at her, his expression full of tenderness, his arm around her slim shoulders. Solange handed Cedric the photographs, tears blurring her vision.

There were several more pictures of Richard Kirwan and Celine de Valnay. But the man had changed. His face was gaunt, and his eyes seemed to have disappeared deep into shaded sockets. There was something wrong with his jaw – it seemed crooked and made his mouth appear lopsided. In one of the pictures his thick, dark hair looked like stubble growing back from a shaven head. The clothes he wore did not have the same costly look or cut, and they hung loose on him. It was a shocking contrast to the images of the carelessly good-looking man she had studied moments before.

"Why does he look so different, Cedric?"

"He was very ill at the end of the war. He had suffered terrible injuries. I'm sure your grandmother knows the details."

Solange came to the last of the photographs. Celine de Valnay was dressed in a summer frock of sprigged material. Her small waist was encircled by a thin belt from which the skirt flared out, as if she had just whirled around. In her arms she held out a small child wearing an organdie dress with elaborate smocking. Richard Kirwan was leaning forward, touching the little girl's cheek.

"She always kept that dress." Solange stared down at the picture. "I saw it in the drawer of an old trunk she kept in the attic. I suppose it's still there." Her hands were shaking. "My God, Cedric, she even brought me to see him. Where would it have been? And where did she leave poor Papa?"

There were no more pictures. A note was attached to one of the photographs, in handwriting Solange had never seen before.

My Darling,
    She is divine, a true beauty. You never leave my heart or my thoughts. I love you. I will always love you and think of you, and look after you both. R.

Tissue paper rustled in Solange's shaking fingers, her tears making blots on the fragile surface. Beneath the thin layers she found a medal in its velvet case. The green and red striped ribbon had not faded, and the metal still had a dull sheen. Underneath was the citation of Richard Kirwan's outstanding bravery, earning him the Croix de Guerre for services to France. It was signed by the President and bore his seal. There was one more photograph. In the centre of a decorated platform, surrounded by a number of solemn officials, Richard Kirwan stood to attention as the medal was pinned on to his jacket. The attached note was brief.

Paris, 1947.

Darling Celine,

This is for you and for you alone. You gave me my life. You are my life. You will always be my life, and my inspiration, and my love.

I never forget. I am forever near you.

Richard.

Solange sat unmoving. After a few moments she dried her eyes and came to stand close to Cedric Swann, bending down to look into his face.

"Cedric, my mother and Richard Kirwan are dead. Whatever they did, nothing can hurt them now."

She stopped, her courage faltering in the face of the knowledge she sought. Then she straightened and her question was spoken with a clear determination.

"But Papa, who has been my father all my life, who has loved me and encouraged me, who adored and trusted my mother – does Papa know that I am not his daughter? Tell me Cedric, has he always known?"

Her body was crooked and straining, her face close to his. She grasped the arms of his chair, shaking it slightly. Cedric Swann shook his head. "I regret, Solange, that I do not know the answer to that question. I just do not know."

Chapter 11

St Joseph de Caune, 1970

Henri de Valnay walked through his vineyards, bending to touch the young shoots emerging from the long sleep of winter. Joel moved alongside him, guiding his steps over the rough, stony earth and Henri put his hand on Joel's broad shoulder in a gesture of companionship and gratitude. The dogs raced back and forth in the spring sunshine, hoping for the trail of some irresistible quarry. Joel was proud of his winter's work – a misjudged snip of his secateurs could have damaged or even destroyed the shape of the vines for the coming year, and reduced the number of grapes that the plant could produce.

"Let's just hope that we don't get a really strong *tramontane* in the next few weeks, blowing all the flowers off those promising vines," said Henri. "We could certainly use more of this glorious sunshine too – and not just for the vines. I need the warmth and the light of it to seep into my bones – into my soul."

Joel smiled, but he wondered what kind of omnipotent power would make such a good man suffer so much. It seemed excessive, his blindness, the loss of the wife whose courageous support had made his world a habitable place. Soon Solange would leave him to marry young St Jorre, as indeed she should. The girl couldn't carry on living just for her father and his needs, no matter how close they were. What would become of his friend, Joel wondered, left alone on his estates, eating his solitary dinner at night, with only a handful of friends to keep him company occasionally.

"When is Solange coming back from Montpellier?" he asked. "You'll have to forget all about the vines after that. Such a to-do there'll be then, setting up the wedding."

Joel waited for a humorous reply, but Henri was frowning. "Solange went to Spain, Joel. She's not in Montpellier."

"Oh. I thought I saw her take the Montpellier turn the other morning. Maybe she wanted to do some shopping on the way."

"Yes, I imagine that's what she decided to do," said Henri, puzzled by the route his daughter had taken. "Anyhow, she'll be back by the end of the week. As for Guy, we're not sure when he'll arrive, but it should be soon."

They strolled towards the house, discussing the possibilities of the year's production. The smell of a serious luncheon drifted in the air – probably a cassoulet that would send everyone to sleep for hours. Henri sighed. Only in the heart of winter could he really appreciate the heavy mix of pork, lamb, duck, onions and garlic, tomatoes and white beans. But it was Joel's favourite from Madame Prunier's vast repertoire, and it would certainly have to be accompanied by several glasses of full-bodied red Corbières. This monthly ritual with Joel had been a pleasurable event for many years, but of late Madame Prunier's gargantuan lunches had become something of a trial for Henri. Sometimes in the afternoon or at night he would find himself in the grip of a sharp, stabbing pain that made him grimace and stiffen, hunching his shoulders to minimise his distress. He thought ruefully of the heavy lunches he used to eat as a young man, and wondered at the strength of his constitution. He must be growing old. He wondered whether he would even recognise himself if his sight were restored now. But he turned quickly from the consideration of his disability, for in that direction there lay only the seeds of depression and self-pity.

"Good God – there's no one in the kitchen, and it's so close to lunchtime!"

Joel's anxious observation brought him back to the moment and made Henri smile. He could hear loud exclamations from the hall, and a faint response from a male voice, punctuated by laughter and conversation. He climbed the stairs, trying to guess at the cause.

"Monsieur! Monsieur! Such a surprise!" Lorette was breathless and beaming. "Monsieur Guy is back earlier than expected! Someone to keep you company – isn't that good? Now Joel, you take up Monsieur Guy's bags. Madame Prunier will see to the lunch, and I'll set another place at the table."

"My dear Guy – we weren't expecting you for another few days." Henri walked with a glad heart across the hall, holding out his arms to greet the younger man with deep affection. "This is very good. Solange will be delighted!"

"I'm told you bundled her off to Spain for a break, before her hungry admirer returned to claim her."

Henri smiled with pleasure. He could feel the energy and excitement emanating from Guy, and his body felt strong and fit in Henri's welcoming embrace. Joel reappeared at their side.

"So, tell me Joel, how does our young friend look to you?" asked Henri.

Joel surveyed his subject, accustomed to making his descriptions come alive for Henri. "Well, he's certainly not one of those pale, stooped lawyers. What a suntan! I don't think he could have spent much time in the courtroom. No, he was lounging on the beach from the looks of him. He doesn't show any obvious signs of drinking too much rum, or eating too many strange, spicy things. There's no evidence of anyone having put a voodoo spell on him. Eyes and ears are still in place. He hasn't grown any extra hair though!"

They all roared with laughter. Guy's smooth forehead rose to a definitely receding hairline, a feature about which he was extremely self-conscious. His eyes, however, were remarkable – almond-shaped and more gold than hazel in colour, with a hint of green that seemed to come and go with the changing of his expression. Long lashes gave extra definition, but an underlying impression of shrewdness saved him from too soft an image. He had a generous mouth, whose turned-up corners suggested a man of even temper. Henri put his arm around the young man and led him into the study. Guy walked over to the telephone.

"May I call Solange?" he asked. "Perhaps she will come home tomorrow, or even tonight if it's not too far. What's the number in Spain?"

An unexplained uneasiness stirred in Henri, and he was ashamed of his evasive answer. "She's unlikely to be in the hotel in the middle of the day. Let's telephone around five this evening and see what plans she will make. In the meantime lunch is ready, and we must do it full justice. We'd like to hear about Guadeloupe and your court case."

They settled in to the pleasures of reunion, companionship and a fine table. When the coffee pot had been emptied they parted in the hallway. Joel returned to the vineyards and Guy retired for a siesta after the long hours of travel. Henri made his way to his study and shut the door. Then he lifted the telephone and dialled directory enquiries. With the Spanish number lodged in his memory he dialled again. The hotel receptionist came on the line.

"No sir, there's no Mademoiselle de Valnay here. No, she hasn't been here, sir."

Henri replaced the receiver. Where could Solange be? She had seemed definite about not going to Paris. Perhaps she had gone to Montpellier as Joel had imagined. But why would she have gone there? Certainly not to shop. At a complete loss, Henri dialled his mother-in-law in Paris. Solange was not expected. The girl had been far too elusive over the past few months although Charlotte de Savoie would love to see her granddaughter. There was so much to discuss, and of course plans for the wedding could not be left in the hands of provincials. Henri hung up and put his head in his hands, pressing his forehead with his fingers, resisting the beginning of a headache from the lunchtime wines, from his worry, from his blindness. He looked up wearily, straining his head towards a window or a lamp, waiting for a miracle in the form of a hint of light. Then he turned abruptly, took a deep breath and rang the bell for Lorette. Within moments, Guy appeared at the study door.

"Lorette said you wanted to see me?"

Henri braced himself, grimacing at Guy's question. He could feel the tight muscles in his neck, in his whole body. "The truth is that I don't know where Solange has gone. I've tried the hotel she was to stay at in Spain. I assumed that she was phoning me from there two nights ago, but she never arrived."

"Perhaps she went to Paris after all?"

"No. She's not with her grandmother, and I can't think of any friends she might have gone to stay with. I spoke to her late on the night she left. She said she'd arrived safely and was looking forward to a few days of relaxation. I assumed she was calling from Spain."

"She didn't leave a number where you could reach her?"

"No. She said she would be out every day, and that she would telephone me before the end of the week. I just can't understand this – it's so out of character."

The two men sat in silence for several minutes, Henri with his head back, eyes closed. Guy rose and walked around the room.

"Look, Henri, she must have decided to get away from telephones and family and everything," he said at last, at a loss for any other logical explanation.

"She's been subdued in the last few weeks, unsettled." Henri's voice was anguished. "But I pushed aside the idea that she might be seriously unhappy. I should have tried harder to draw her out. It's difficult, really, because it was always Celine who did those things. It's hard

86

for me to be both parents to Solange. I thought we'd found a balance, though, and I never expected anything like this."

Guy sat down opposite Henri. Solange's behaviour was more than strange, it was inconsiderate. He could see Henri's bewilderment and hurt. The man was always so stoical, too much so. He never complained about his blindness. He had barely left Celine's bedside during her illness and finally he had buried his wife in an almost unendurable state of grief, and had immediately turned his love and compassion, his undivided attention, to his daughter.

"Well, I'm sure Solange can't have had an accident or come to any harm, otherwise someone would have contacted you. Maybe she's changed her mind about me and run off with some respectable vigneron."

"How do we set about locating her, then?" Henri could not be sidetracked by an attempt to lighten the atmosphere. "Where in the world could she have gone? And why the deception?"

"I don't think she wants to be located. We'll just have to trust her to contact you again when she's ready. She said she'd be in touch within a few days."

The telephone rang. The noise was shrill and the instrument seemed sinister, the numbers jumping boldly out of their silver circles. Henri picked up the receiver.

"How are you darling Papa? Is everything all right at home? I miss you so much, but I'm fine. Tell me your news."

"Solange! Where are you? I telephoned the hotel in Spain and you weren't there. What happened to you? Why didn't you let me know that you'd changed your plans?" Henri could not suppress the rebuke and panic in his voice.

There was a short silence. Her response was hesitant and filled with regret. "Papa I'm so sorry. I didn't mean to worry you. I'm truly sorry. I went to a different place, somewhere to think things out from a distance. I just wanted to step right away from everything."

Henri's hands were shaking and his throat was dry. She sounded so casual. And he still didn't know where she was. "Solange, Guy arrived back this afternoon. His case in Guadeloupe finished early and he's home. Could you come back tomorrow?"

"Oh dear. I haven't really planned things very well. Yes, of course I'll come home. I'll try and return a day early, but it might be complicated. Papa, I'll be there as soon as I can. 'Bye, Papa, I love you."

"Wait a moment! I'm sure you want to speak to Guy before you hang up on me – he's right here."

"Oh – yes, of course I must talk to him!"

Henri handed over the receiver with a mixture of relief and annoyance.

"Solange? We've had quite an afternoon here, worrying about your secret whereabouts." Guy was curt. "Where are you?"

"Hello Guy. It's wonderful that you're there with Papa. He's probably been a little lonely, and he's very bad about going out regularly. I'll try and be back late tomorrow evening, but don't plan anything until you hear from me."

"Well, I hope we'll hear from you soon."

"Yes. Yes, I'll try."

"Where can we . . . ?"

"I'll talk to you again as soon as I can."

The connection went dead. Henri sat frozen in his chair. Solange had deceived him because he could not see her, because he could not help her by reading the visible signs she expressed.

"So what is really going on here, Henri?" Guy asked. "What has happened to Solange? We still don't even know where she is!"

But there was no reply from Henri de Valnay, and in the soft, early evening light Guy saw that he was quietly weeping.

Chapter 12

St Joseph de Caune, 1970

In the spring sunshine, Edouard stood looking over his experimental hectares. The healthy, new shoots were surrounded by his father's long-established rows of vines. He had waited with ill-concealed impatience for the first flowering to appear on the delicate tendrils. It was the wind that he now feared most. If the arrival of a strong *tramontane* coincided with this brief, crucial period, much of the potential yield might be blown away by powerful gusts, before the minuscule flowers began the transformation that would turn them into grapes. At least he could be grateful that this year no severe frost had damaged the crop.

More than three years ago he had planted these first vines. Paul Ollivier had looked on with scepticism as his son fastened the fan-shaped vines to costly stakes and wires. The tall plants looked bare and strange beside the low, rounded bushes of the older grapes, but Edouard was determined to do away with the back-breaking harvesting of the traditional goblet shape. His father shrugged at the idea.

"You have to remember that your tall 'eventails' will be more vulnerable to the winds – a big *tramontane* will tear through these high, thin plants of yours and leave them barren. Poof! Half your yield can disappear! My low-growing vines are better protected from the weather. Tradition doesn't come into being by accident, you know — it's here because it works and has worked for centuries. Well, we'll see how your skinny young plants come along." But in spite of his misgivings, Paul had helped his son to fasten the shoots to their supports, and later to prune them.

From the beginning Edouard had been certain that his plan would one day be recognised as an inspirational example. Although doubtful, his stepfather, Julien Montfort, had lent his expertise and offered valuable advice concerning the project in the south. It had been more difficult for Edouard to persuade Paul Ollivier that he should give up several hectares to experiment with new rootstock. The older man had no confidence in the costly, unproven methods advocated by his son. He was tired and dispirited, his health was poor, and innovation seemed to him dangerous and unnecessary. But he was secretly glad to see his son so passionately interested in the vineyards. At least the boy was not planning to run off to Montpellier like his younger brother who preferred the easier life and conveniences of the city. Eventually Paul had set aside a few hectares for his son to plant, if only to humour him.

"He'll see, in the end, that the easiest way to make a living is to produce a passable *vin de table*," Paul said to himself. "In the meantime the thing is to foster his enthusiasm – keep him involved in the land. It's the only way he's going to learn."

In the three years that had followed, Edouard felt only increasing confidence in his *terroir*, in the mix of minerals and the quality of the soil, and in the sturdiness of his rootstock. The verdant shoots that appeared each spring filled him with a deep satisfaction, and even a feeling of tenderness. Each year he had returned regularly from Bordeaux to Roucas Blancs, and he had even come from London to inspect his vines. Paul Ollivier waited for the time when his handsome, ambitious son would be captivated by some suitable young woman. But there was no sign of romance in Edouard's life.

"Where would I find the time to devote to a girlfriend?" he asked his father. "I'm too involved in the wines – in the planting, and all the travelling between here and the north. I'm in love with my vines. For the moment that's enough."

His intensity and seriousness worried Paul. What a crushing disappointment it would be if the quality of his experiment proved to be less than he expected. But the mistakes of youth were always hard, and there were no short cuts to wisdom and experience.

Now, in the spring of the fourth year Edouard knew that success was within his grasp. His grapes would be of good enough quality to make his own fine wines. But he needed capital to buy equipment, and he needed it now. His father's old *cave* and oak barrels could not deal with the kind of winemaking Edouard had in mind. New fermentation and storage tanks were needed and the existing *chai* and the *cave* needed to be reorganised and insulated for proper temperature control. His first thought had been to approach his stepfather for help. But asking Julien Montfort to finance a scheme on land belonging to his wife's former husband would be a bizarre request by any standards, and Paul Ollivier would never countenance such an arrangement. Edouard had discussed his ideas with the local co-operative, but they were unwilling to spend time or money on blending anything new or unusual. He had still not decided how he was going to explain Henri de Valnay's possible involvement to his father. But the time to organise financing was overdue. This year the harvest of new grapes would be picked by hand, and rather than being pressed with his father's undistinguished table wine, or sold to the local co-operative, the grapes would go into his first attempt at making a *vin de pays*. Next year's grapes were of even greater concern, and he knew that he must finalise a plan for the autumn that would allow him his own full harvest in the following year. There was so little time in which to put it all in place. He started back towards the stone house on the hill, its grey, bleached shutters closed against the invasion of the midday sunshine.

"Edouard! Come up – there's a telephone call for you! It's Henri de Valnay."

His father was leaning over the iron balcony outside the salon. Edouard waved and began to stride swiftly uphill, trying to stem the excitement that gripped him.

"Why is Valnay telephoning here? What the devil does he want with you?" Paul's tone was hostile. "You'd better explain what's happening here young man."

"Hello Henri?" He was aware of his father's proximity, the glare of unsuppressed anger.

"Edouard, hello. Thanks for your note. I've been going over your plan with the help of Solange, and Joel my manager. I'd like to talk to you, but I don't want to raise your hopes as to my assisting you with investment."

"I understand, sir."

"There's merit there, however, and your scheme looks to be feasible for the most part. Maybe I can help you to tighten it up, and get it looked at seriously where influence and money are available."

"Thank you. I'd be glad to –"

"Let's see. How about Saturday evening around seven? Perhaps you'd like to stay on for dinner? My future son-in-law, Guy St Jorre, is here, and perhaps Solange will be back."

"Thank you sir. I'd be delighted to accept your invitation."

"What about your father? Would Paul like to join us, I wonder?"

Edouard, taken by surprise at the invitation, glanced at his father. Paul's body was stiff with hostility, and he continued to glare at his son with undisguised rage.

"I'm not sure about my father – it's hard to winkle him out of the house at night. I'll pass on your message and I'm sure he will telephone you later in the afternoon."

He hung up, struggling with a mixture of elation and apprehension.

He had hoped Henri de Valnay would come up with an offer of finance himself, or perhaps a bank guarantee. Edouard was sure they could work well together. But at least his neighbour seemed willing to help in some way. He joined his father at the kitchen table and poured a glass of red wine for each of them, wondering how to get around the old man.

"Would you like to join Henri de Valnay for dinner on Saturday evening, Father? He wants to discuss my ideas for improving the quality of our wines. Will you come along with me? Solange and the future son-in-law will be there too. You always had a soft spot for Solange. She's rather like her mother, and I know you admired Celine."

"Don't try to fill me with that bullshit!" Paul's anger exploded into the room. He banged his glass down on the table, spilling the wine on his shirt. "What the hell have you been cooking up with Valnay behind my back? I don't have anything to say to him, and I don't expect you to be up there visiting, thick as thieves with him, without my knowledge!"

"Oh for God's sake!" Edouard could not contain himself. "You two had an argument nearly fifteen years ago. It was resolved in court and you've lived with that ruling ever since and it hasn't killed you. It's time to forget."

"Don't lecture me, or tell me what to do about my land and my business!"

"Father, we have to move on, take advantage of today's climate, concentrate on getting together with our neighbours to make better wines for better returns. That's more important than a few hectares of land and an old quarrel that only the two of you can remember."

"What bloody land would you have to plant and inherit, if I hadn't fought for it all my life? I don't need you running up there, discussing plans for my property with de Valnay, without even consulting me. You always were an arrogant piece of work, but this is beyond what

I will tolerate. I won't bloody allow it – do you hear me?"

The argument raged for two hours before Paul Ollivier finally looked at his son with some measure of calm. The young man sat on the opposite side of the table, his head bent, his mouth thin and angry, shoulders hunched. Neither one spoke for a while until Paul cleared his throat.

"Well, I don't like to go out at night you know. And eating late gives me indigestion these days and stops me sleeping." Paul's words were gruff but there was indecision in his tone. He looked at the simple platter of charcuterie and cheese in front of him and then glanced up at Edouard. "No – I'll stay here. But you'd better go and finish this discussion you've started."

"I'm sorry, Father. I should have spoken to you. It was stupid and arrogant, as you say."

Paul interrupted his son, waving aside the apology with an impatient hand. "We've been over all that. We don't need to begin again." He hesitated for a moment and drained his coffee cup. "Well, I don't know. That woman Prunier runs a formidable kitchen. And I'd like to see Solange. Yes, I would like to see her. She's a brave little thing, coming back from Montpellier to take on the vineyards, bearing up like that after Celine died."

"I think you'd be impressed by –"

"That's the kind of woman you should be looking for, you know." Paul pointed a finger at his son. "One with her feet firmly on the ground, and a real love and knowledge of the country. You should lighten up – you always look so serious. Play a little. Go out, laugh out loud, get drunk once in a while. It's not natural the way you carry on. A young man like you shouldn't be afraid to use his charm. All this talk of wine – even the best vintages won't do much to warm your bed."

"Father, let's stop this trivial nonsense, once and for all. You found out yourself that wives and winemaking don't go well together, and you've managed all right." The words were out before Edouard could control his angry reaction.

"How dare you tell me what was or wasn't right!" Paul stood up, his stick pointed at his son. His face was flushed and he was shouting. "You've been away, trotting round the world, living in big cities and grand châteaux. But that doesn't teach you anything about human nature! What in hell do you know about my marriage and my relationship with my wife?"

Edouard was shocked by his father's vehemence. Paul thumped his walking stick on the hard ground and continued to rail at his son.

"I was a fool, a bloody, stupid fool! Your mother came here from Bordeaux and tried to create a home and a vineyard that would have quality and grace. She saw it all, a whole generation before you ever thought of it. You're doing what she wanted to do thirty years ago! But I didn't have the imagination or the courage to listen, and after years of trying she left me. It was my fault. And don't you ever presume to open your mouth on the subject of my marriage to your mother, about which you know nothing! Not a goddamn thing!"

Paul sat down again heavily and stared at the cracks in the old slate floor. His son regarded him in silence, too amazed to speak.

"She never mentioned any of that, Father – no one ever put it like that," he said, after a long silence. "I always thought Mother had met Julien in Bordeaux, that they fell in love and she left you. We've never discussed it. Father, I apologise. I had no idea. I didn't know you felt like this."

Paul went to the buffet and took out two glasses, splashing cognac into the balloons and handing one to his son.

"Well, I've had enough of these family disclosures for one day. It's all long ago, and your mother is happy, and I'm still the old fool I always was. But don't you make the same mistakes. And don't make assumptions based on pure ignorance. Now, what were we discussing?"

"Whether you might go out to dinner with a neighbour, instead of sitting here lecturing me about my solitary life?" Edouard attempted to back away from the painful wound he had inadvertently prised open. "Otherwise I may turn into an old curmudgeon like you. Maybe it's hereditary."

Paul began to smile. He was embarrassed by his outburst, and it never took long for his son to coax him out of ill humour. He tried to sound grudging but Edouard was delighted by his response.

"All right, I'll join that old bastard Henri de Valnay. Might protect him from getting caught up in some mad, grandiose scheme for the young and reckless. You can telephone him and accept on my behalf. I hope he can produce a decent brandy after dinner."

Edouard smiled. Gruff as his father might be, he was always keen to be in the thick of any goings on in the vineyards. They drank their cognac and coffee in companionable silence. Then Paul disappeared into the cool recesses of the house for his siesta.

Edouard rose and brought out the file of facts and figures he had presented to Henri de Valnay. A few revisions could still be made, and he wanted to read through it all again. But he was unable to banish the memory of his father's astonishing outburst. He smiled as he considered the old man's concern about his future. But a wife was the last thing he needed just now. He could deal with only one dream at a time, and his present plan did not contain any place for a woman.

He thought about Solange, sitting by the fire, her hair gleaming in the shifting light, her eyes shining with intelligent interest, her lips curving in a half-smile as she looked at Henri de Valnay. What a pity her father couldn't see her like that. Edouard wondered if the man had ever seen his daughter. She had become a real beauty – not ethereal, or fragile and pale like her mother, but smooth and glowing. He liked her clear, steady gaze, the slightly imperious look tempered by the generosity of her soft mouth. The mouth he had kissed. Her eyes seemed to take in everything, consuming every detail in a glance.

Perhaps it was because she was seeing for two souls rather than one.

He could not remember how long Henri de Valnay had been blind, or even what had caused his blindness. Strange how the lives of neighbours could be veiled by constant proximity. But sometimes one could look at a longtime friend or acquaintance, and all at once there would be something new and wonderful about them, something entirely unseen before that could feel like a blinding revelation. He opened his folder for the hundredth time and picked up his pen but he found it impossible to concentrate. The numbers on the pages danced and wavered in front of him. He rubbed his eyes and tried to return to his report. But in his mind there was a persistent image of Solange looking up at him after their brief embrace, and he could not quell the surge of excitement he felt rising inexplicably inside him.

Chapter 13

St Joseph de Caune, 1970

Solange turned her car off the *autoroute* and headed towards St Joseph de Caune. She licked her lips again, her mouth dry with apprehension. As the long sweep of her valley came into view, she pulled over and stepped out of the car. Below her lay the symmetry of the vineyards, the gnarled trunks reaching out with delicate, curling fingers for new life. The river ran silver in the evening light, and the disappearing sun touched the walls of her home. She stood looking down at the scene for a long time, wondering if she had stopped out of love for its beauty, or in order to delay the moment of homecoming. How would she explain why she had lied, excluded her father from her plan?

"I know I've hurt him, Cedric," Solange had said to her old friend. "It's the first time I've lied to him about anything important. That's what I resent most – the feeling of being cut off from my father by this horrible secret."

"Solange, my dear," Cedric was firm. "You're not cut off from anyone, except in your own mind. Just explain to Henri how nervous you had become about your marriage. With Guy away, you had time to reflect, and suddenly it all began to seem rather frightening. Your father will understand that."

"But how will I be able to go on concealing all of this?"

"Now look, you're not the only young woman in the world to

have concealed something potentially hurtful from someone you love. You'll find that you can do whatever is needed, for Henri's sake. You know that you must. And I know that you will."

But away from Cedric's guidance her doubts returned, eroding her courage. She decided to tell her father that she had been to see Cedric, that she had talked to him about her marriage and the move to Montpellier, about her changed role, her dread of leaving him, of leaving the vineyards. That much was true at least. She had misgivings, too, about the letter she had written to Eleanor Kirwan. It had been too brusque, too final. She still thought that the Irish girl was overly keen to throw herself into her parents' past. But Cedric had made her see Eleanor's obvious turmoil.

"There's no need for you to try to become close sisters," he had said, looking at Solange over the top of his glasses. "But you can afford to be kind. This has been very difficult for Eleanor Kirwan too. And perhaps there is something that you can do for one another in the future, after the shock has subsided. Don't ever be too hasty in closing doors."

"You're right, as usual." She smiled ruefully at him. "I should have made the letter softer, less abrupt. Maybe in years to come we will somehow bring our paths together – when it's not all so new and raw."

She knew she had not handled any part of this crisis well. And now, in addition to the reconciliation with Henri, she would have to contend with the return of her fiancé. Solange wished that he had been delayed for another few days. She could not imagine crossing the barrier of unspoken deception that would lie between them. She was not ready for Guy to touch her, to embrace her. Her heart felt as though it was made of lead, dull and heavy. It was the first time that her spirits had not risen as she drove down into the valley.

Within seconds of hearing the car Henri emerged from the front door. She flung her arms around him and held him tight, wondering if she was imagining a slight reserve. He kissed her forehead, touched her cheek, and enquired whether she was tired after her journey. He did not ask where she had come from, and his deliberate omission lay like a barrier between them. Suddenly Guy's arms were around her, holding her firmly against him. He framed her upturned face with his hands, and his eyes held a question she knew she could not answer. Then he took her hand and the three of them entered the house.

As the evening progressed it became more and more difficult for Solange to raise the subject of her impetuous flight to England, her visit to Cedric Swann. The pall of her unaccustomed behaviour hung over them and immediately after dinner Henri retired to his bedroom, pleading fatigue and gently refusing Solange's offer to read to him or listen to some music. Alone in the library with her, Guy kissed her for the first time, whispering in her ear, but she broke away with a murmured apology.

"I'm sorry, Guy, but I need to spend a few moments with my father. I'm going up to say goodnight to him."

Henri was preparing for bed and she put her arms around him, laying her cheek against his shirt.

"I'm so sorry, Papa, to have rushed off without explaining. I had a case of nerves – it's something that has never happened to me before and I handled it badly. I'm truly sorry, to have alarmed you."

"It's all right now darling," Henri said quietly. "I know you're all right. You can tell me all about your travels in your own time. Let's just go on towards that."

Solange returned to the library. There was no sign of Guy. After a moment she bent down and picked up the telephone. Her hands were trembling and her heart felt as though it would leap into her throat. What would she say to Eleanor Kirwan once she got through? It took a few minutes before the international operator connected her with the Dublin number. Solange heard the telephone ring in Killiney, across the water that divided them. The trilling sound repeated itself seven, eight, nine times. She hung up abruptly, despising herself for failing to carry through the sudden impulse. Then relief coursed through her. It had been a crazy idea anyway. Eleanor would not have welcomed it, would probably have hung up on her. Or she might have got the brother or younger sister on the line. Worse still, even the mother. Good God! She should have thought the idea through more thoroughly. It was just as well no one had answered.

In her bedroom Solange took out the leather box that Cedric had given her. It seemed like a century ago, another lifetime, but she was certain the knowledge would never leave her. She placed the box in the top drawer of her desk, with her diary and Guy's letters, and turned the key. His knock on the door made her heart race. She was not ready for this. She did not want him in her bed now, could not love him as before. Guy entered the room and stood looking at her in the lamplight, her heavy hair already down on her shoulders. Her feet felt as though they were bolted to the floor.

"I love you, Solange."

He did not say anything else, or wait for her response, but reached out for her and began to kiss her, first on her forehead, then on her eyelids, on the corners of her lips. He touched her ears, turned her around and lifted her hair to kiss the nape of her neck. With a surging relief, she felt an enormous longing for him, for the sweet recollection of his lovemaking. Her body began to respond and she gripped him tightly and offered up her mouth for his kisses. Gratitude poured through her mind. He was the only one not affected by her hidden origins, the only one who was as he had always been. She felt comforted, exhilarated, knowing that there was something that had not changed. She lay back on the soft quilt and guided his hands, her action bringing with it the liquid sensation that was desire. She held him, felt his warm breath, delighted in the urgency of him, welcomed his body, and shared with him the first purely spontaneous happiness she had known for many weeks. Through the night they held one another, sometimes sleeping, sometimes waking each other for reassurance, for the long-missed union of their bodies. She slept at last with her head on his shoulder, her legs wound around him, her arm across his chest.

During the next few days they walked through the vineyards with Henri and Joel, wandered along the river bank, dined with Aunt Jeanette and Chloe, shopped at the market stalls in the village. Each time she looked at Guy, Solange felt a fresh surge of happy relief, of normality, of elemental joy. Life could be simple again after all. He would take care of her, love her, protect her. What did it matter really, this secret that she had feared?

From her bedroom window she watched her father walking with Guy each morning, his gestures animated, his face smiling. She sat down at her desk and wrote to Cedric, wanting him to know how much he had helped her.

> *There is peace here again. The worst part of this experience has passed, and I am sure now that it need never go any further. You have given me the confidence to accept what happened and to go on with my life, knowing I am the same person that I was before that first, shocking letter. Thank you a thousand times, dearest Cedric. Thank you.*

At the dinner table that evening, Henri made a small exclamation. "Oh good heavens Solange -- I'd forgotten that while you were away, I invited Paul Ollivier and young Edouard to dinner on Saturday. I did tell Madame Prunier, but you'd better liaise with her. We haven't had a dinner party here for a while."

"Paul Ollivier's coming here for dinner? I don't believe it! He's such an old grump, and your sworn enemy. I presume Edouard has a hand in this. But I can't imagine how he persuaded either one of you to have dinner together. Have you had any more discussions with him about tearing up all his vineyards?"

"Tearing up vineyards? What would that achieve?" asked Guy. "What would he do with the land instead? Surely the soil isn't suitable for anything but vines? And isn't Paul Ollivier the one . . . ?"

"Yes, that's him," replied Henri. "But his son Edouard is convinced that he can change the calibre and reputation of the wine in the whole area, and he's asked me to join him as a partner. He sent me a rather well written plan of the entire scheme."

"Good Lord. And is this something you're considering? I'd love to read the plan."

Henri lifted a good, red Bordeaux and poured, listening to the sound of the wine, judging accurately the right amount in the glasses. "Well, I've explained to him that I don't have that kind of money available. I must admit, though, the scheme is not as fanciful as it sounds."

"Revolution in the vineyards of the Languedoc! Sounds amazing." Guy looked at his future father-in-law and immediately realised what a new, challenging project could do for Henri, once he and Solange were married and living in Montpellier.

"I've gone over the figures several times, but I couldn't afford the investment required." Henri shrugged, regret plainly written on his face. "It would take up everything I own. If I had a large sum at my disposal, though, I wouldn't hesitate to back this young man."

"Perhaps you should consider this further before making any final decision, Henri."

Guy glanced at Solange for her reaction and was surprised to see her sitting stiffly upright in her chair. Her face was closed, her expression strained. He was about to ask for her opinion, but something made him stop. There was an atmosphere in the room that he could not understand, but he knew it would be wise to change the subject. He turned to Solange and smiled at her, concerned at her frozen expression, but she sat wordless, her face betraying inner turmoil. In her mind the secret had returned to taunt her.

"You have money!" a voice screamed in her head, and she looked around, almost believing that someone must have heard. The voice would not stop. "You have all that money sitting in a bank in Paris. You have the money to help your father begin again, but you can't give it to him. You can't use it!"

She rose abruptly. "I think I'll go up early if you don't mind. My head is aching and my throat is a little scratchy."

She kissed Henri on the top of the head and touched her fiancé's cheek. "Guy, why don't you read to my father for a while in the library. I think I'll just take a couple of aspirin and get straight into bed."

Late into the night he held her, disturbed by the renewed tension in her, wondering why her face was tight and closed. "Darling, I have an idea," he said. "I have to go to Paris towards the end of next week. There's a conference on international property law and old Thommeret wants to take me along. Why don't you come up with me? I'll take some time off and we can spend a few days getting there, stay at a couple of good châteaux on the way. I don't want us to be apart again so soon."

She made no reply, and he continued quickly, hoping to convince her. "You could visit your grandmother. Or maybe you'd like Henri to come too? What do you think? Solange, why the tears? You must talk to me about what is eating away at you."

But she could not tell him she was weeping because even his love could not dissolve the tentacles of the past, and she knew she must visit her grandmother with or without him. She turned and nestled close to him with her head on his shoulder, her fingers tracing lines on his chest.

"I'm just foolish and over-emotional. I'm fine really, and yes I'll come with you to Paris. But just the two of us. I'll see Grandmama, and I'll try to put everything together once and for all. Find my way through." She wiped her tears away with the back of her hand and closed her eyes.

For a long time he lay awake in the black night, puzzled by her words, disturbed by her sudden change of mood and her choice of words, realising that he was, for some reason, truly in the dark.

Chapter 14

St Joseph de Caune, 1970

Solange stood on the terrace sipping her champagne. A stirring of soft air touched her bare arms and she took a deep breath, absorbing the scent of the evening. Guy watched her from the French windows, excited by her beauty but distanced from her by a feeling of resentment. He had tried without success to coax her into telling him what was troubling her, and now he had begun to feel irritated by her closed attitude.

She had not looked forward to this evening with any great enthusiasm. Each time she thought about Henri and his interest in some joint venture with Edouard Ollivier, the existence of her inheritance pricked her conscience. The sudden reconciliation between her father and Paul Ollivier also puzzled her, and she could not fathom how Edouard had engineered such a transformation in his father's attitude. He must be manipulative, willing to steamroll over anything that lay in his path, driven by his own ambitions. She tried to focus on Guy's return, listening to his stories about life in the more exotic outposts of France. He was hinting at the French West Indies as a possible honeymoon destination, but she was not ready to be drawn into a discussion on this subject.

Lorette appeared from inside the house with a tray of hors d'oeuvres and Henri found his way to the stone table that was serving as a bar, to open another bottle of champagne. Solange moved towards him and found Edouard suddenly at her side, touching her elbow lightly.

"You're fortunate with the weather. And this must be one of the most magnificent views in France." He indicated with a long, surprisingly delicate hand the shaded terrace with its marble and scrolled iron furniture. "Your mother restored all this with such care. But of course there's no terrace anywhere graced by beauty such as yours, Mademoiselle de Valnay. I raise my glass to you." His eyes were alive with laughter, although his face was perfectly composed. His nose wrinkled as he drained the last of the champagne. "I always have to try not to sneeze at this point – you can imagine how a sneeze is received at a champagne tasting in Rheims."

She smiled at him, and refilled his glass. He was leaning on the balustrade, apparently relaxed, but there was an underlying wariness in him. He needs to have faith in himself as an individual, she thought. Or maybe he needs someone to demonstrate faith in him.

"I'm happy to see your father enjoying himself," she said, glancing across the terrace at Paul Ollivier. "I must admit I was concerned about his coming here this evening. I can't imagine how you brought about this thaw in their relationship, but maybe the two of them will get together from now on. I wouldn't mind collecting Paul sometimes, and taking him home, if he doesn't want to drive himself at night."

"That's very thoughtful Solange. But you won't be here, will you? You'll be settling down as a little housewife in Montpellier, with all your absorbing domestic duties. That will be a change from the vineyards. What in the world do you think you're going to do there?"

"I certainly won't have any trouble finding things to do," she retorted. "It's a city full of energy and culture, and I'll be able to enjoy it and share it with my husband. Isn't that enough?"

But he only smiled at her, raising his eyebrows and shaking his head slightly. Solange felt a current of anger. She was determined not to be provoked, and irritated by the fact that she sounded defensive. "I spent the best part of four years in Montpellier before going to Paris and coming back here," she said. "I would have spent longer there if I hadn't returned to help my father during my mother's illness. The city is forward looking, open to new ideas, new music and art and there's no shortage of things to do. It's a great time to be there."

"Ah yes, so it is. You'll probably be able to do something worthwhile like a nice course in musical appreciation or watercolours. And you'll be giving chic little dinners for your husband's colleagues and partners, advancing his career like a model wife. It will be challenging, I can see that."

Infuriated by his mockery she moved away to stand closer to Guy, acutely aware of Edouard's sardonic gaze boring into her back as she left him. What was the matter with him, she wondered. Why should he feel entitled to comment on her life?

Aunt Jeanette arrived, creating a welcome diversion. She was obviously delighted by an excuse to dress in her finest, most matronly silks. Solange often wondered how her father had always displayed such a casual, sophisticated sense of Parisian style, while his sister had remained stubbornly mired in the frumpish fashions of the provinces. Chloe followed her mother on to the terrace. Beneath a low-cut evening blouse, her breasts were clearly visible. A startlingly brief skirt, cut from some shiny fabric, emphasised her pert little derrière as she moved, and she was wearing thigh-length boots. Solange saw the look that passed between mother and daughter. Another skirmish on appropriate evening dress had evidently broken out.

Uncle Georges appeared several minutes later. He wore an expression of infinite resignation, and walked with the plodding gait of the survivor. He had probably fortified himself with a large whiskey from his host's decanter. Chloe was already smiling and pouting at something that Guy had said to her. Edouard stood nearby, his expression amused but guarded.

Solange had placed tall candles in the stone flower pots and urns along the terrace. Below lay the swimming pool that Celine had built so that Henri could exercise easily and safely. Now the surface of the water stirred, and in its trembling reflection the small group seemed to move closer together. As darkness fell, the cypress trees lining the path to the garden were silhouetted against the last of the indigo light, silent sentries guarding their fragile paradise. Henri took Solange's hand in his and called Guy to his side. His guests fell silent.

"It's time for a toast. I'm glad to be able to do this in the company of friends and family who have known Solange since she was a small child. I have been blessed with a daughter who is a young woman of considerable beauty. More than that, she is a steadfast friend who has shown me unfailing love and kindness, a person of remarkable strength and bravery." Henri's voice broke and he drew the couple closer to him. "Guy, you are indeed lucky. But I have seen in you all the qualities I could ask for in a son-in-law. I wish for you all that I was so fortunately given, in the years of my own marriage to a wife who fulfilled my every dream. I wish you joy. May God bless you both."

The small group stood together, joined in old memories and new hopes. They touched lips to cheeks, glass to glass. Tears and smiles were mixed with glad embraces and murmurs of comfort and support. Lorette appeared on the terrace. "Ladies and Gentlemen – dinner is served."

Dinner was a triumph. Paul Ollivier threatened to weep when the roast veal was presented with delicate mushrooms and truffles. Jeanette was certain that she could not eat both cheese and dessert, but she graciously overcame her qualms, and sighed with happy surfeit as the last morsels of lemon pastry vanished. Uncle Georges, who rarely ate more than a token of any offering, left nothing on his plate. Chloe smiled and pouted, leaned forward to voluptuous advantage, and made every attempt to ensure that Edouard should feel included in the intimacy of the family celebration.

"I think we should take coffee in the drawing room." Solange rose from the dinner table.

The men drifted into the salon, Henri heading easily and unaided towards the buffet which held the digestifs and cigars. In the smaller sitting room, the three women retouched unruffled hair, and applied fresh lipstick.

"My God, Solange, he's fabulous!" Chloe was full of optimistic desire. "Guy too of course, but that's different. What about those black eyes and the little twitch at the corner of his mouth. And that mouth! It could have been carved on some classic statue. Imagine putting out your tongue and . . ."

"That is enough Chloe! I don't know how or when young women became so vulgar," said Aunt Jeanette. "And I warned you to dress properly for this occasion. Young Edouard may look up to date, but men like that prefer women to have some delicacy and restraint. Don't you agree, Solange?"

Solange found herself irritated by Chloe's litany of praise for her guest, and she had no intention of becoming involved in the discussion. Returning to the drawing room she was aware of Guy's admiring gaze as she crossed the room to reach the coffee tray. Edouard stood beside him, an Armagnac in his hand. She allowed her eyes to flicker over him before turning away to lift the coffee pot and she was surprised by an unguarded sadness in his expression.

"Congratulations, Guy. You're a fortunate man." Edouard raised his glass.

"Thank you. Yes, I am." Guy smiled, lifting his brandy. "I understand you're about to embark on a lifetime's venture in the vineyards. Henri has explained your ideas to me. They sound like the shot of adrenalin this area needs to bring winemaking into the . . ." He did not have time to complete his sentence.

"You must feel guilty, though, every time you're here."

"Guilty?"

"Well, there she is — the original, timeless goddess of the vine-yards," Edouard was watching Solange as she bent to fill another coffee cup, her movements naturally sensuous. "Look at her, so full of that unique passion for the land that transfers itself down into the earth, and make the wines full and sweet."

"I had no idea that a few glasses of Henri's finest vintage would turn you into a poet of such lurid fancy," Guy snapped.

"I'm quite sure neither one of us requires any wine to recognise Solange's particular quality, and her place here. Henri will find it very difficult without her."

Guy's anger mounted and he struggled to remain detached and polite. Solange had been right — the man was arrogant and insufferable.

"I'm glad you admire my choice. And it's very decent of you to be so concerned with Henri's future," he replied coldly, realising that he had failed to sound ironic. It was a pity they had not met in a bar where he could take Edouard outside and use his fists. Why was he so offensive?

"Oh I am, indeed I am. And we all hope that you will not remove Solange too far from the vineyards where she belongs. It would be such a waste. She must be very aware of that herself, though?" Edouard shrugged and smiled.

Guy was seconds from an explosion of rage when Solange arrived to stand beside him. She was immediately aware of something between them, a black current that felt like hostility. She looked enquiringly at them both.

"Excuse me for a moment." Edouard moved away towards Chloe and Uncle Georges. Guy was about to speak, unable to contain his fury, when Henri rose to his feet.

"My friends, I am not one for speeches or announcements, as you well know. But now, in order to make up for the last twenty-five years of reticence, I ask you, for a second time in a single evening, to celebrate with me another beginning. What I am going to say will come as a surprise, even to Solange. But I know that she will support me in this, as in all else that we have achieved together."

Her body froze into an icy stream of fear. No. He could not announce that he planned to close down part of the vineyards. Not now. Not in the middle of this wonderful evening. She could not breathe and she glanced around wildly, placing her hand up at her throat. Across the room, Edouard watched intent and puzzled as her calm evaporated. Henri continued, unaware of her involuntary signals of alarm.

"I made a decision last week to embark on a new, independent and, I believe, fruitful phase of my life. Everyone here knows that Edouard has come back to us with radical, but in my view modern and logical, ideas about the operation of Roucas Blancs and the development of our vineyards. I want to tell you all that I have decided to support these plans with sufficient financial support to get this very ambitious scheme operational."

There was a stunned silence in the room. Henri continued, apparently oblivious to the stillness around him, but perhaps he was simply enjoying the element of surprise. "Please join me in a toast to our joint enterprise, and to its long-term success for ourselves and for the vineyards of our region."

His family and friends raised their glasses, trying to mask amazement, curiosity, excitement, alarm. Edouard stood completely motionless, utterly astonished, unable to ask a question even within his own mind. Then he raised his glass.

"To our enterprise and friendship, sir, with my deepest gratitude and respect."

Solange swallowed her cognac in one breathless gulp. She looked at her father's new partner as he raised his glass. All around him there seemed to be whirling currents of danger. She felt Guy's arm around her waist and was grateful. Without his steadying support she might have lost her direction and given in to the powerful sensation of drowning in a wave of excitement.

Chapter 15

Connemara, 1970

Eleanor pulled the brake and got out of the car. This was what she had been waiting for as she drove out of Oughterard and Maam Cross – this first glimpse of Connemara, stretching out to the Twelve Bens in a shimmer of rain-laden sky, and away to the unseen sea in a tapestry of sage-green bog, white rocks and gleaming water. The wildness of it! The silence, except for an occasional bird call or the rasp of a cricket, and that peculiar misty light loved by painters, a promise of another world hidden behind lowering clouds and the hum of the wind across the bog grass. It was a blessing, this tumbled land, scattering into the western sea. It felt so good to be here.

"Wonderful, isn't it?"

She hadn't heard Seamus getting out of the car. He was standing beside her, squinting into the horizon from under his dreadful old hat. Eleanor smiled. "I'd forgotten how peaceful it all is – like a photo you keep treasured, a picture in your mind of something special. Only it never fades and it never, ever looks the same from minute to minute. No wonder you're a poet and Mother is a painter."

The wind gusted, whisking her uncle's battered hat off his head and ruffling his hair. He grabbed at the hat and grinned. "Treacherous – that's what I'd call it! Peaceful? Only sometimes. Satisfying? Yes – always."

"Is Mother still asleep?" Eleanor glanced back at the rear of the car.

"Yes. Dropped off just before Galway and hasn't stirred since. I must have been dozing for a while myself."

"I couldn't believe it when she appeared this morning. Yesterday she was on the verge of complete collapse, and today she's on her way to Connemara. It's remarkable what your presence has done for her."

"Well, she's still pretty ropey and it's been a long day. Let's get her home, Eleanor."

As they drove off, Eleanor's thoughts turned to a night, shortly before her father's death, when he had been so restless. He had wanted to tell her something. She was sure of that now. But he had been unable to start and she had not known how to help him. When finally the morphine had quieted him, she had run from the room and sat on the steps of the porch where Gareth had found her. He sat down beside her, saying nothing for a while, just laying his hand lightly on her shoulder. She had broken the silence.

"Why can't I talk to him Gareth? I can't stop this hideous disease eating him up and there are so many things I want to tell him. Today I thought he was trying to say something important to me. And I wanted to say, 'It's all right, I love you. You've done your best and it's enough.' But I ran away from him, because I can't bear it."

She had sat, sobbing, while Gareth stroked her hair until she was quiet.

"You can speak without words, you know, Eleanor. And I'm sure he feels that love radiating out of you." He was silent for a few moments, considering. "But maybe he does want to talk to you about something and he doesn't know how to begin."

He turned her face up to him and looked at her seriously. "Why don't you write to him? Tell him all these things you've just said to me. Put it all down on paper, and let him read it, quietly, so he can soak it all in. And it may well open the doors for him. Think about it."

He had smiled at her then, smoothed her dishevelled hair, and brought her indoors. Now she wondered if Gareth had known all along what her father had wanted to say. This morning he had mentioned the war and the years that followed. Surely that could not have been a random remark. And Seamus, what did he know of her parents' past? Did everyone around her know their story?

At Roundstone they turned away from the village to the headland where Seamus's stone cottage stood, ringed with gnarled trees and crouched close to the huge rocks. Eleanor and Seamus brought Helena inside and went to get the luggage. There were fresh eggs, butter, and home-made bread in the kitchen and Eleanor set about making them supper. Sitting beside the fire afterwards, Helena began to droop.

"Mother, I think bed, right away. Don't you agree Seamus?"

Seamus nodded, and Eleanor led her mother down the corridor, aware that she looked very frail, almost old. She shivered involuntarily. Helena's hand was shaking a little as she lifted the latch and went in. The room had a high, old-fashioned double bed made of oak, with a patchwork cover. The window looked out to sea, framed by heavy wool curtains. There was a dark oak table, and a high-backed chair with a tapestry cushion, bedside tables, a small wardrobe and a brass-handled chest of drawers. Helena's face was alight as she moved around the room, touching familiar things, leaning on the deep sill to open the window. A light breeze and the soft shuffle of the tide flowed in. She turned to her daughter, smiling.

"I'll be all right now Eleanor. Just leave the bag on the armchair over there. Now that I'm here, I know I'll sleep well. Tell Seamus to put my easel and paints in the hall and I'll sort them out in the morning. Goodnight dear." She kissed her daughter lightly. "Get a good sleep yourself. And thank you for bringing me down – for everything."

Eleanor slipped out and shut the door. In the kitchen Seamus was feeding his dog, Chaucer, and banking up the fire in the range. He looked up at his niece. "Everything all right?"

"Yes, fine. She's gone to bed."

"Nightcap?" Seamus was opening a cupboard.

She chose brandy and he poured generous measures for them both.

"Do you think it's too cold to go outside?" Eleanor asked. "Could we go down to the beach? We could do with a walk, after being cooped up in the car all day."

"Good idea."

Seamus handed her an oversized jacket and opened the back door. They made their way along the path to the cove. Eleanor glanced back at the house and saw that her mother's light was already turned off. They found a large rock and sat down. The moon was lighting the bay. Eleanor looked up, then took a sip of her drink.

"Seamus . . ." She paused, marshalling her thoughts. "I know this may sound pretty mad, after all this time, but could I ask you – what did you do during the war?"

"I was just qualified then, looking for work." Seamus was gazing out across the bay.

"But did you go away at all? To fight, I mean. Or did you stay here all the time?" She watched him swirl his glass, and saw the moonlight dance in the liquid.

"I was here. Well, not all the time. I started work in a practice in Galway, but I was doing this place up. It was derelict when I found it. I used the money Dada left for me, to repair the house, and to work on a boat I'd bought with Ronan and Ciaran. It meant I had hardly anything left to live on. But I was clear about my goal. I wanted to set up a practice in the village. There was a lot of poverty around here then. Times were very hard and people were really suffering. I wanted to give them something back."

Eleanor nodded and took a deep draught from her glass. She began to splutter.

"Whoa there girl! What's the hurry?"

"Making courage I think," she laughed shakily. "You see, I've begun to understand that this whole business of Father's will is somehow linked with the war. I remember when I was little and he was so sick. We spent a lot of time down here then. So you must know some of the story. They must have told you, Seamus. You helped to look after him, didn't you?" She knew she should wait for a signal from him, for a comment perhaps or a word of encouragement, but she could not hold back any longer. "What happened to him, Seamus? And where did this Celine woman come from? Did Mother know her? God, do you realise I'd never even asked, till this happened, where my mother and father met. I never knew it was in France."

"I don't know where my father met my mother to this day." Seamus smiled over the rim of his glass. "At some country dance, or a cousin's wedding or something, I suppose."

"But Seamus, what about you? Why did you never get married? Didn't you ever fall in love with anyone?" Eleanor stopped, realising that she had never really considered her uncle's life before. He had always been the one who was there to comfort and advise them all. Seamus was gazing at her in astonishment.

"Well!" he said. "That's a lot of questions all in one breath, never having asked any before. I don't know if I can supply all the answers. But I can tell you about the first time I encountered your father. Helena had met him in France during the previous year. I came to get them out you see, Richard and Helena, just before war was declared." He took her empty glass from her. "And that also answers your second question in a way. Because I met a girl there, and I fell in love with her. But when I saw her again it was too late for us both. She was already married."

Chapter 16

Paris, 1939

Helena emerged from the doors of the Ecole de Louvre, Stefan and Daniel on either side of her, jostling to carry her gear. The golden light of an April evening poured through the trees along the square. It seemed to Helena that all of Paris was arm in arm and the air was full of laughter, of people enjoying spring and life and love. She felt the thrill of expectation as she glanced across to the bus stop, then a pang of disappointment when she did not see him. But it was early, surely? He might have been delayed by his students.

Stefan towered above her, more than six feet of blond Swede with pale eyes and fair skin. Daniel was small and slight, his face intense and fine-boned with a prominent nose and a swatch of black hair. He was squinting at her through the haze of his evil-smelling cigarette and smiling, his face sardonic.

"You are looking for someone perhaps? Are two willing escorts not enough for you, Mademoiselle?" Daniel scanned the square with exaggerated care, clowning as always. Stefan was frowning. He hadn't understood. Then Daniel gestured with a dramatic sweep of his arm.

"This one now? He looks promising. See how he hurries, how he scans the crowd? Ah! What is he searching for? A bright halo of copper, the sweep of a long skirt!" Daniel stepped in front of Helena, teasing her, pulling Stefan forward to help block her view.

But not before she had seen him. Richard! Striding down the far side of the square, searching the queue at the bus stop. She laughed and pushed Daniel aside for another look. Stefan was still puzzled and she turned to smile up at him. It wouldn't do to be looking too keen when Richard eventually spotted her. Richard Kirwan from Dublin. He was so cultured. A university professor for God's sake! What could he want with her, a fisherman's daughter from the wilds of Connemara, a penniless artist? But he had kissed her hand, held it in both of his and kissed it, with the fierce blue eyes piercing her. And he was so neat, so ironed. Even his shoes were shiny. She didn't know anyone who polished their shoes. But she'd be willing to polish his shoes, to put her hands inside them and feel the softness of leather moulded to the walk of him. She saw Richard smile as he spotted her in the crowd of students. All night she had wondered if their hours together had just been some interlude that he was already on his way to forgetting. But he was here.

"Stefan, will you bring my things over for me, please?"

He nodded and gathered up the materials cluttering her feet. He was so dear, Stefan, so solid and dependable. She sighed inwardly, knowing he would want to escort her home this evening, and take her out to dinner. Poor Stefan, he followed her like a great dog everywhere, waiting and hoping for some signal from her. He was a genuine friend and good company, a perfect foil for Daniel's wicked wit and fiery temperament.

Daniel flicked away his cigarette butt and watched as Helena crossed the street. She had been like a suppressed volcano all day. He had noted her restlessness and the shining eyes as soon as he had seen her that morning. His Irish princess was in love, glowing like a lighthouse with the amazement of it. He felt a twinge of regret, but he knew she was not for him. And poor Stefan was crushed with devotion, but she did not want him either.

She sang like an angel, and played melodies on her violin that brought grey seas and gulls, and tumbling hills and rocks floating out of the air around her bow. And she was a fine painter, committed to her art, with an affinity for light that transformed even the quietest work into something luminous. She would be known, Daniel thought, she would make a name for herself. He knew that soon he would lose the Irish firefly that had fizzed into his world and taken it by storm. How had she done it? His family, so reserved behind their customary politeness, had dropped their defences immediately. She had romped on the floor with his two younger brothers, shared the making of matzos and music with his mother, charmed his father. When his younger sister Leah had come home from the Conservatoire that first day, she and Helena had become instant friends. How strange that a Christian girl could walk unhindered through these barriers, as though they did not exist, and yet display respect and understanding for his family's Jewish traditions.

He told himself again that what he had with her was purely friendship, and in a way it was. They talked about everything, their dreams and their fears, their problems and triumphs. He knew her so well. Today when they had sat down together for coffee, she could hardly contain herself. With sadness he tried to listen, as a friend. What was his name, this Irishman who had swept her off her feet? Richard Kirwan! Older, she had said. A professor. He was her countryman, and of her faith. Seeing him now, Daniel shrugged in resignation and walked quickly after Helena and Stefan, catching up with them as they reached the other side of the square. The tall man had seen her, hesitated when he realised she had company, then smiled as she waved.

A lean face, heavy eyebrows, remarkably blue eyes that brightened and warmed as he smiled. Good-looking and powerful, older than any of them – perhaps ten years older. This man knew success. He was assured. His body was firm and he moved with surety and vitality in his step. He was well dressed, in a dark suit with a fine silk tie and good leather shoes. He swung his briefcase easily. Helena had reached him now and he was bending over her hand with an easy grace, bringing it to his lips. Daniel could almost touch the energy pouring from her as she looked up at him. She was like a bowstring, stretched to high tension, awaiting the magic of a song. She looked so lovely, so vulnerable, as she introduced them.

"Richard, these are my friends Daniel Nazarre and Stefan Svenssen. Daniel is from Paris, and Stefan is from Sweden. We are all studying together."

Richard's voice was deep and resonant. He shook hands and chatted easily in his perfect French, sizing up the two young men as he spoke. When the next bus came they boarded it together. At the boulangerie on the corner of Helena's street she bought baguettes, and they sat on her balcony sipping wine and eating the fresh, crusty bread with cheese and olives. Richard was good company, interested in their work, their lives, their backgrounds. The evening lengthened and the four of them went off in search of dinner and a jazz club with dancing. Helena watched Richard from behind her fall of copper hair, memorising every plane of his face, every crease around his eyes, every cadence of his voice.

When he danced with her, they were fluid together. She seemed to float against him, his hands holding her lightly, his bright blue eyes gazing down into hers. Sometimes he would reach out and smooth her hair back from her forehead, or brush it behind her ear, or touch her cheek or her lips with the backs of his fingers. She was oblivious to everything else in the smoky, crowded cellar.

Daniel chain-smoked and watched in silence. Stefan turned his glass round and round, and yearned. He caught Daniel's eye and smiled a resigned, lopsided smile. For both of them knew that for Helena, Richard was the one, and that there would never, never be another.

Chapter 17

Paris, 1940

"Professor Nazarre, things are going to get very difficult when the Germans overrun France and take Paris."

Simon Nazarre shook his head, but Richard continued to press home the urgency of his argument. "Believe me, the Nazis are evil. Look what has happened to Jewish families in Germany, in Czechoslovakia and Austria."

Richard Kirwan was at the Nazarre family home with Helena, Seamus and Stefan. It was time to leave France. He was anxious to take Helena to safety before the situation became any more dangerous. Tonight would be their last night in Paris. Seamus had landed in France just over two months earlier, embarking on his first holiday after sitting his final medical exams. During the past weeks Richard and Helena had delighted in showing him the city, introducing him to their friends and their favourite haunts. Daniel had laughed with astonished delight when he met Seamus, commenting that he might be Helena's twin but they were as unalike as it was possible to be.

Now Helena sat close to Seamus in the Nazarres' drawing room, her delicate form emphasised by his big, craggy physique. Yesterday their brothers, Ronan and Ciaran, had arrived in Brittany with Seamus's boat, ready to take him back to Ireland with Helena and Richard. The small group sat close together, listening to the news on the wireless. The atmosphere was edgy as the BBC announcer in London spoke of the German advances, his reports making a deadly contrast to those of the optimistic French broadcasts. Richard turned again to Daniel's father. "There's too much confidence here in France. Too much faith in the Maginot line. Belgium and Holland will not be able to resist a German invasion, even with the French and the British alongside them."

"The French army will make a stand around Paris. I'm sure of it." Simon Nazarre was emphatic. "And even if the Germans do come, what of it? I am a Professor of Music at the Conservatoire. And Hannah —" he gestured to his wife, "Hannah plays in a chamber orchestra. Our children study the arts. None of us is political, we pose no threat to the Germans. Why should they bother us?"

"Father, you are so blind!" Daniel broke in impatiently. "Why won't you listen to Richard? He studies these things. Hitler's Nazis have a record of terrible violence and aggression against Jewish people, against intellectuals, against gypsies. I know, I've been told."

"We are French, Daniel." Simon Nazarre was firm. "French citizens, all of us. Our religious heritage is immaterial. Besides there are international conventions."

"The Germans will drive their tanks over your conventions, as they are doing all across Europe," Daniel retorted. "Hitler is a madman. His henchmen are persecuting Jews in Germany and in Eastern Europe. Why would it be any different here? I have reliable information."

"Information from whom, Daniel?" Simon glared at his son. "From these Zionists and Communists that you consort with? This is a house of peace. You are allowing your head to be filled with unconfirmed horror stories. I don't know what has come over you."

"He won't listen, Richard. I have tried to warn him, to tell him what we know. But he doesn't want to hear it."

Daniel shrugged in weary resignation.

"Daniel isn't repeating radical nonsense, Professor Nazarre, truly."

Richard leaned forward earnestly. "I'm a historian, and this is my field of research. I have studied Hitler and the rise of his party. He is evil, and he has gathered a willing and dangerous following to his cause. You are a respected citizen of France, of course you are. But this will count for nothing when the Germans arrive. France will fall to Hitler, because your politicians have underestimated him, and the country is not prepared for a German invasion. It's like the Franco-Prussian War all over again, but this time it is not Bismarck against whom you will fight. You should listen to your son, sir, no matter what the source of his information."

Helena reached out and touched Simon's arm. "Come with us to Ireland. I'm sure Richard could find you a teaching post, Professor Nazarre." She turned to Hannah. "Madame Nazarre, we could get all of you on to Seamus's boat, I'm sure. It's large enough, isn't it, Seamus?" Her brother nodded assent. "It would be a new life, a new beginning, and we'll be there to help you."

"If I had to leave my country, it would be a comfort to go where you are, my dear. But France is our home and here we will stay." Simon Nazarre looked around the room, at the fringed lamps, the jumble of books, instruments and music, the rich carpets and heavy crimson drapes. Outside the long windows his two younger sons, Zachary and David, were playing on the lawn. He smiled fondly at Helena and squared his shoulders. "I will not be driven out of my country. My children were born here. We have our friends around us. I have my work, my students. Hannah has her colleagues in the orchestra. The boys are eight and ten and they are doing well in school. Perhaps in Germany people are more easily swayed towards barbarity. But not in France! We are civilised here."

Hannah Nazarre sighed as she stood up. "Simon, my dear, you do not always discern evil. There are those in this city who resent us because we are Jews. Prejudice will find a target in any society. They are no worse or better here than in any other country." She shrugged and walked to the door, beckoning them as she went. "But for now, dinner is ready. Tomorrow Daniel and Leah will travel with you to Brittany. Have you managed to get fuel for your journey, Richard?"

"After a lot of wheeling and dealing, yes. Stefan will be coming with us too. He has managed to obtain travel papers from the Swedish consulate. That should ensure that there are no delays going west, and that they get safely back to Paris afterwards."

A feast had been prepared. The long table gleamed with silver, crystal and starched napkins, laid out on a white damask cloth. Leah was lighting the candles as they entered the dining room. Zachary and David rushed in, and they all sat down.

Seamus would never forget that meal. The wine, the laughter, but most of all Leah – sitting opposite him, glancing at him over the candle flames, smiling and tossing her mane of black hair and teasing Daniel and his friends. She was nineteen and unlike any girl he had ever seen or encountered. He had never been so acutely aware of anyone in his life. He knew that he was in love with her, that he had fallen in love with her the day he arrived in Paris, when Helena had introduced them in the smoky intimacy of a small café.

Leah was tall, thin as a whippet, with high cheekbones and large, deep-set eyes. Her fingers were long, tapering to neat, unvarnished nails, and she wore no make-up on her pale skin. Her black hair was tied back in a twist of green chiffon. It was exactly sixty-four and a half days since they had met, and each day he had fallen more helplessly in love. Leah and Daniel had spent every day with their Irish friends. Between them all lay the need to fill each hour with shared memories, before Seamus spirited his sister and Richard away to Ireland. Now, on this last night in Paris, the chandelier above the table caught the evening sun from the window, and broke into a thousand rainbows that danced on the table, and on Leah's hair whenever she leaned forward. Seamus was mesmerised.

"And do you have any kind of specialty, Dr O'Riordan?" Simon

Nazarre's voice broke the spell, and Seamus tore his attention away from Leah while he gathered his words in French. This was the first time he had met Simon and Hannah Nazarre. He wanted to make a good impression.

"I'm only just qualified, and I'll be working in the city of Galway when I return to Ireland. It's a good place to gain the experience I need for a general practice of my own later on."

"But you do not come from Galway?"

"No. I'm from an area called Connemara, fifty miles from the city. It's where I hope to work eventually and the place I love most. I hope you will see it some day. And my sister is right, I would be happy to take your family to Ireland aboard my boat. Now or at any time."

After dinner they gathered around the piano in the drawing room, and the instruments were taken out. Only Stefan could not play anything, but he sang two Swedish folk songs and, under the influence of another cognac, he performed a wild dance around the room to great applause. Then Daniel took out his flute, and Hannah her cello. Leah and Helena played a duet that Simon had arranged for them. Richard took his turn at the piano and played some fine jazz. No longer shy, Seamus borrowed Helena's fiddle, and filled the room with the haunting melody of the Coulin, a traditional Irish air that brought tears to Leah's eyes.

Then Daniel said, "Leah, play the Wieniawski for Seamus?"

Helena and Richard urged her on. Leah stood up, directing a radiant smile at Seamus. "Yes, I'll play it," she said, looking only at him. "Papa? Mama?"

Simon went to the piano, and Hannah took up her cello.

"This is really a violin concerto," Leah explained to Seamus. "What I will play is the Romance from the second movement, which Papa has arranged for me. Do you know the piece?"

Seamus shook his head. "I've never even heard of the composer," he said.

"He was Polish, a very fine violinist himself. Not so well known yet. He has not been dead long enough," Simon said with a wry smile. "This piece is made for Leah. One day she will make it famous." He nodded at Leah and Hannah, and began to play the opening bars, softly. It was a beautiful arrangement, sensitive to the mood and structure of the music.

The first violin notes, when they came, were like a lover's tentative touch. Seamus was instantly caught up in the music, in the beauty of Leah's playing, her passion speaking out so clearly to him across the swelling chords and harmonies. He was shaken, overwhelmed by the music itself, and by Leah's eyes holding him riveted as the last, long sweet note faded into breathless silence. No one spoke for a full minute when it was over. Seamus and Leah were wrapped in the spell of it, oblivious to everyone else in the room. At last, Stefan let out a gusty sigh. Everyone laughed, and the world began to turn again. It was nearly dawn when the party ended. Zachary and David had fallen asleep on the sofa, and the first pale light was sliding over the rooftops.

They stood in the street, saying their last goodbyes. Silence fell. Helena gazed up at Simon and Hannah standing on the steps of their home, and felt suddenly afraid for them. She ran back up to them, tears in her eyes. "Come with us, please. Don't stay here!"

Simon put his arm around his wife and shook his head. Hannah was smiling at him as Richard spoke from the street below. "You know if you want help you have only to get word to us. And Madame Nazarre, if you need to send the children . . ."

Hannah nodded without speaking, then embraced Helena once more. She whispered as she held her. "He is a good man, my dear. Marry him. Do not let him walk away from you. And perhaps when this is over, we will come to Ireland and visit you."

"Dawn is here," Daniel called out to them. "We must prepare to negotiate the roads to Brittany. We need a few hours of sleep, or we shall be in bad shape. Stefan, we will meet you at Richard's apartment around ten. Ah, Seamus, my friend, it has been good to have you here with us." He turned to his sister with a wicked smile. "Say goodnight to the doctor, Leah, or he won't be able to tear himself away."

Leah ran down the steps. She kissed Seamus lightly on both cheeks, and then suddenly on his mouth, her lips caressing his for an ecstatic moment. Daniel caught Helena and whirled her around and around, then kissed her hand gravely. "Ah, my little Irish jewel, put this man out of his misery." He nodded towards Richard. "Even if it means you will consign Stefan and me to eternal despair. Are you going to take him?"

Helena laughed, then turned to Richard with an imperious gesture. "Well, Professor Kirwan, man of history, ask me again, one last time!"

And Richard went down on his knees, there in the Paris dawn, the rumble of a distant military convoy vying with the first birdsong of the day. "Helena O'Riordan, marry me when we get back to Ireland, or I shall have to throw myself off your brother's boat on the way."

Stefan gave a crooked smile as he explained the scene to an astonished Seamus. "They had a quarrel one day. She said he was a conceited upstart, and she would not marry him, even if he got down on his knees in the middle of the street and asked her. He said he would do it again and again until she said yes. This is his sixth time, I think."

Helena leaned towards Richard, her hands on his shoulders, and stared deep into his eyes. "I will marry you, Richard Kirwan. I'll marry you, and I'll love you, and I'll give myself to you for ever. Say you'll do the same for me."

He caught her and held her, kneeling in the street with his face buried against the folds of her dress. She wound her fingers into his hair, pressing him close. And the onlookers could hear them murmuring to one another, over and over. "I will my love, I will."

Then everyone was laughing and embracing, and Seamus found

himself with his arms around Leah, and for a second he felt the shape of her leaning into him, her fingers on the back of his neck. Then she was gone, to hug Richard and Helena.

Once more, farewells were said, and they walked along the boulevards to the morning's chorus of birdsong with the sun slanting through the trees, planning their journey to the coast, while Paris awaited the vanguard of her conquerors.

Chapter 18

Brittany, 1940

The May morning was warm and bright, and they travelled with the soft top of Richard's car down. Stefan, Leah and Seamus were in the back, with Daniel squeezed into the front between Richard and Helena. The roads out of Paris were dense with traffic, and progress was slow. Stefan had fastened a Corps Diplomatique badge from the Swedish consulate to the car and he carried a letter signed by his friend Anders Petersen, stating that they were travelling on consulate business and had a right to purchase extra fuel. For once he was glad of his powerful connections. During his student days he had been careful to eschew his family's title and influential network of friends, not wishing to be set apart from his peers. Now he was glad to be able to use them. They sang to begin with, and discussed the route they should take.

"We should keep off the main roads," said Richard. "There'll be more convoys on those and it will slow us up. Maybe we should go out by Versailles, across to Alençon, and down along the coast."

Helena was looking at the map. "Oh, Richard, if we're going that way, could we take in Mont St Michel? I've always wanted to see it, and it would be a wonderful place to break the journey."

Daniel nodded agreement. "I'm sure Seamus would like to see it too. After all, who knows what may become of it."

"It won't matter if we take another day to get there, will it?" Helena asked. "We could snatch just a few more hours together. Will it make any real difference to Ronan and Ciaran on the boat, Seamus?"

"No, of course not," Seamus thought of one more day with Leah and answered without hesitation. "I just need to get a message to them. I'd love to see Mont St Michel. Leah? Stefan? What do you say?"

Leah was radiant. Stefan looked at Helena's shining head in front of him, and felt that a few hours more before she left with Richard was worth the pain. He nodded and smiled.

"Great!" Helena flung her arms around Richard and the car swerved wildly. "Mont St Michel — we're on our way."

"Not if you do that too often." Richard kept one hand on the wheel and used the other to disentangle himself. "Sit still. You're like a small octopus!"

As they travelled west, the grim realities of impending conflict became more evident. The French army was on the move. Troop transports streamed east on their way to strengthen the tragic fantasy of the Maginot line. In towns and villages, people came out to watch them. Banners hung from the balconies, and cheers and offerings of flowers greeted the fighting men of France. On two occasions Stefan had to remonstrate with the gendarmerie, warning Richard that the army had started requisitioning cars, and that he should not leave the driver's seat under any circumstances. Despite the delays and difficulties of the journey, Seamus sat close to Leah in a suffused haze of joy. It was seven o'clock when they arrived at the coast. The stark silhouette of Mont St Michel rose out of the sea before them, the spire of the abbey reaching into a golden sky. They stood looking at it, entranced.

"Let's find somewhere to stay," Richard said at last.

"And something to eat!" Daniel added. "Then we can enquire when we should go out to the island."

They found a *pension* and were lured into the Restaurant Parisienne by the sight of huge dishes of langoustine. Champagne seemed the only thing to drink and there was an unspoken resolution to say nothing about parting. They would live for tonight and tomorrow, banishing fear and sadness.

Daniel watched his sister, wondering if this was just some transient romance blossoming on the edge of separation, inspired by the onset of war. He glanced across to see Helena whispering something to Richard as he held her glass of champagne to his lips. His heart twisted a little and he turned away towards Stefan. His friend was also watching Helena, but with a look of such unguarded pain and hunger on his face that Daniel was shocked. He had not fully understood how deeply Stefan had fallen in love.

"Damn!" he thought. "How we all spin and turn, full of hope and longing, with grief waiting at the close of our dreams! And my little Leah – will your Irish love sail away tomorrow and forget you? God how I fear for what this war may do to us all."

He crushed out a cigarette and stood up abruptly. "Now, what about this casino? Shall we go and lose our lives to the game of chance?"

Stefan gave a half-sigh of relief. They rose and went out into the kindly night. Outside, the casino lights blazed, and music came from the dance floor.

"Helena," Leah called to her softly. "Seamus and I thought we might just go for a walk on the beach. Is that all right, Daniel?"

"As the official chaperon I know she'll be safe with you, my friend." Daniel was smiling at Seamus.

"We'll be back to see you make your first million." Seamus caught Leah's hand and they were gone.

The night air held the tang of the sea as they walked along the harbour wall and down to the beach. A full moon shone, silvering the masts of the boats at anchor, and the ripples of sand and tide. Seamus gazed at Leah. She heard his sharp intake of breath and moved willingly into his arms. In the sweetness of her kisses they were fused together, melting, sharing breath and heartbeat.

"Leah – my love, my beautiful Leah!"

His hands trembled as he touched her face. He was afraid to hold her again, afraid of the desire rushing through his body, beyond control. She clasped his hands, kissing the inside of his wrists, each of his fingers, pressing her cheek into his palm. Then she moved closer against him, eyes closed, head back. He found himself kissing her neck. He wanted so much to take her. He heard her make a little moan, felt her go almost limp in his arms.

"Leah we can't." He pulled away. "This isn't the time. Not when I have to leave you so soon. Oh my darling – I love you. I want you. Ah, don't cry, Leah, please don't cry."

"I'm not crying because I'm unhappy!" she whispered. "I love you, Seamus. Just now, I felt as though we were one person. Did you not feel the same? You can't go away now. It's unbearable."

"Yes, it's unbearable, but I know already that this is for ever."

"It's the same for me. The same. I love you. But there are things we must consider, and for now I have to return to Paris."

She pressed against him and he stood rocking her in his arms. Before him rose all the obstacles they would have to face in their different backgrounds and different faiths, and through separation and war. "Come with me, Leah. I'm in love with you and I want you to come with me now, back to Ireland. I want to keep you safe. Come with me before any harm can reach you. Please."

Her face was buried against his chest but he felt her shake her head. "You know I cannot leave my family. I have to stay here for the present." She stopped, suppressing the terrible fear that he might never come back for her. "But in time, when this war is finished, then we'll be together. It can't be so long. And then you'll come back for me, Seamus, won't you?"

He kissed her over and over, cupping her face in his hands. "Whatever happens, I promise I'll come back for you. I'll take you away to a place at the edge of the world where we will always be together and I'll always be there for you. I will wait for you."

In silence they embraced again. Then he brushed the sand from her feet and smoothed her hair, and they left the intimacy of the night and made their way together towards the bright lights of the casino.

At the tables, Daniel and Stefan had done well but Richard had lost his stake. Helena was on a roll. On her final bet, they all followed her numbers with wagers of their own. Watching the silver ball clatter around after the spin, they willed it to fall into the right slot. As it came to rest and the wheel slowed, a cheer rose from the table. Number 33! The little redhead had won! Helena stood up, gave the croupier a brilliant smile, and tipped him generously. They made their way to the desk and cashed in their chips. Then they ran laughing down the street like truant schoolchildren. They crept into the little *pension* and went to their rooms with whispers and good-night embraces. There were only three hours of the night remaining before the proprietor woke them for their crossing to Mont St Michel.

It would be their last day together.

Chapter 19

Brittany, 1940

Early morning swept the tide away and in the pale light the fortress of Mont St Michel rose like a mirage, soaring proud and mysterious out of the dawn mist. It was cool, and a slight breeze blew around them as they made their way towards the stone gates at the base of the rock and the looming ramparts. They decided to climb up to the abbey first, and then work downwards. In the narrow alleys their voices echoed off the crumbling stone. From the windows above them they heard the first stirrings of the inhabitants, preparing food, hanging out bed linen to air from their balconies. It seemed extraordinary that routine, everyday happenings were part of this mystical place.

At the abbey, Richard was soon deep in conversation with their elderly guide Monsieur Le Brun, tracing the political history, the architecture and the social changes each age had wrought. Stefan watched Helena hanging on to every word from the Irish professor whom he both liked and hated. He knew, with cold certainty, that Richard was the right man for her and that he could never hope to rival him. The last of his hopes fell away, floating downwards into the sea. As they began their descent to the second level of the abbey the guide pointed to an area at the top of the long, stone staircase. "This is Gautier's Leap," he said. "A tragic place."

"Who was Gautier?" Helena stared at the steps, winding along the inside of the rampart to the level below.

"He was a political prisoner who knew there was no hope for him in those dungeons. As they led him to his cell, he broke away from the guards, sprang up on to that wall over there, and plunged to his death on the rocks below."

"What a terrible price to pay for freedom!" Helena shuddered and turned away from the wall.

Stefan stood alone and very still, gazing over the rampart. He leaned out, staring down. Down to the bare white rocks, the scrubby bushes, and the brooding mass of the outer fortifications. In a kind of dream he stretched his body out further and further, at one with the prisoner's despair, with the sensation of the man launching himself out of all his suffering, spiralling down for a few mad seconds into final oblivion.

"Stefan!" Seamus was running towards him.

Helena spun around, her heart almost stopping. She threw herself towards the wall and caught at his legs with a force she did not know she possessed, pulling him back into her arms. He stumbled, and slid on to the steps bringing her down with him. Helena cradled him, staring at his blank expression, at the beads of sweat on his ashen face.

"Stefan – are you all right?"

His vision cleared momentarily, and he shook his head, trying to banish the nightmare force that had seized him. She touched his face gently.

"I'm so sorry. I don't know what came over me. I think I just got a bit faint. I'm all right. I'm all right now."

"Don't get up yet. Seamus, is he all right?"

Her brother bent over the stricken man and took his pulse. "I think he needs air, Helena, and a little space to collect himself." He gave her a reassuring smile and she moved away to stand beside Richard and the others. Seamus sat down, shading Stefan from the hot sun. Stefan's eyes were closed, his breathing shallow and uneven.

"Slow, steady breaths now." Seamus's voice reached into the fog around Stefan's brain, calming his chaotic thoughts.

"I don't know what it was." His voice was raw and he clutched convulsively at Seamus. "I felt that man in my head. I wanted to jump."

"I understand." Seamus pressed his hand. "It was a bad place to be at such a moment, but it has passed."

Stefan turned his head away, dreadfully ashamed of his weakness. They sat for a few moments in silence, until he felt the strength returning to his limbs. He was grateful to the quiet Irishman, for his prescience and his tact. "You're a good doctor and a good friend. Thank you. I can get up now." He looked at Seamus directly, the unvoiced plea in his eyes.

Seamus nodded and helped him up, smiling at them all, their silence a contrast to poor Monsieur Le Brun's twittering distress. Never had his grand tour produced such an unpleasant effect on a visitor.

"He's over it now," Seamus said. "A bad attack of vertigo. It comes like that sometimes. And after a night of champagne, a long climb and the heat of the sun when we came out on to the battlements, it's not surprising. Let's link you down, Stefan, and you'll soon get your full vigour back."

"I do apologise. I've never felt like that before." Stefan smiled sheepishly. "I haven't ruined the tour I hope."

"What matters is that you're all right. But we don't have to go through the rest of the abbey you know." Helena reached up on tiptoe to hug him briefly.

"No, please," Stefan was standing stiffly, his heart hammering at her closeness. "I'd like to see the rest. I really am quite recovered."

They descended the long staircase and looked at the cloisters, Monsieur Le Brun pointing out the beauty and symmetry of the marble columns, the magnificent windows of the long refectory. Finally they approached the dungeons. A dank smell rose up from the gloomy darkness. The tragedies of broken and abandoned lives seemed to emanate from the walls, the rusted chains and musty cells.

"Seamus, I don't think I can go down there." Leah's voice contained a hint of panic. "I know it's foolish but I'm afraid of this place. I don't know what it is. Will you come upstairs with me and we'll wait for everyone up there? Please?"

"Let's give this a miss, shall we?" Richard's concern was immediate. He was watching Stefan closely too. "I think that's enough tales of suffering for one day."

They left quickly but the shadow of sadness and their impending separation accompanied them down the steep hill into the town. Helena glanced at Stefan and recognised anguish in his broad face. She took his hand and curled his fingers over her own, acutely aware of his silence.

"Now, since I am in possession of a large bankroll from the casino, I suggest we go somewhere for the most delicious lunch we've ever had in all our lives." She strove to raise their spirits once again. "No, Richard! This treat is mine."

Their last meal together was perfection. Richard, casting caution to the winds, ordered a white Haut Brion for its complexity of flavour, and then a purple, fruity St Julien, rounded and elegant. Oysters, succulent lamb and local cheeses were followed by a tart of Normandy apples with thick cream. They lingered in the afternoon sunshine, until at last the sound of the sea reminded them of the encroaching tide. They rose, mellow and filled with gratitude for their friendship, and made their way across the sands to the mainland.

At the turn for St Malo Stefan said, "I think we should swim. There are bathing huts and a magnificent beach. It will refresh us all." He seemed to have regained his good spirits.

On the beach they rented two blue-striped canvas huts, and rummaged in the car for swimwear. Richard took his togs from his suitcase, and provided shorts for the men. Stefan and Seamus emerged suitably clad from the tent, but Daniel was too slight for a good fit. His shorts sagged at the waist and drooped over his knees. His sister, laughing, gathered them up at the waist and deftly tied them with her silk headscarf. Helena had found a swimsuit, and came up with a muslin shirt and flowered shorts for Leah. A waiter arrived to ask if they would like drinks. On the beach, or served in the water?

"In the water?" Richard was intrigued.

"Voilà, Monsieur!" The waiter produced a light, round tabletop. "It floats. You bring it into the sea, and I give you your aperitif. It is good?"

"That is better than good. It's quite wonderful!"

They ordered a bottle of chilled Sauternes and ran into the sea, gasping with the shock of the cold, laughing and splashing. As evening drew on they floated in the calm water, the table sailing between them. Time faded and the future seemed far away. There was only the now, the sea, salty lips and sweet wine, friendship and the sound of surf breaking far out on the point. It was Stefan who finally broke the spell. "How long to St Brieuc?" he asked quietly.

Richard stood up, shaking the drops from his firm body. Stefan rose too, and they gathered their table and the empty glasses and walked up on to the sand. Helena watched the two men, one fair and broadly muscular, the other lean and dark. Daniel ran after them, his body slight but wiry and strong. She sighed and emerged reluctantly from the water.

Seamus held out his hand to Leah. Water cascaded off her gleaming skin as she rose from the sea. She raised her arms over her head to squeeze her dark hair. The thin muslin clung to her and he felt a jolt of desire as he saw her breasts outlined clearly against the wet cloth. He drew in his breath and felt fire in his throat so that he was obliged to turn away, reluctant for her to see his hunger.

"Are you coming, Seamus?" Daniel's voice broke through his jumbled thoughts.

He turned towards the shore. Leah was disappearing into the beach tent. He was both disappointed and relieved.

They drove on towards St Brieuc. Seamus held Leah's hand and tried to think of any words that might convince her to come with him to Ireland. He could not sail away and leave her encircled by the dangers of war. Her head was resting on his shoulder and he slid his arm gently around her and gathered her close as she slept. Helena, looking back in the driving mirror, caught his eye and smiled. She leaned across to Richard and kissed his ear. Daniel watched both couples and wondered what would become of them all. He knew this was his opportunity to persuade Leah to leave. His parents would be devastated, but surely it would be better to have at least one of his family safe from harm. How could he make his father accept the danger they were facing? The Germans would trample them all. But Daniel was determined that they would not be able to claim an easy victory. He would fight. His friends would fight. But if he sent his sister away, what about Mama, and Zachary and David? In the times ahead, they might need Leah. She was strong, would be resourceful in a sudden escape, and more importantly she might be able to shake some sense of danger into their father. Simon Nazarre was convinced that rumours of German atrocities originated with the Communists whom he abhorred, or with the Zionist movement in which he placed no confidence. Daniel shifted restlessly, and lit another cigarette. Helena turned to him.

"Poor Daniel, have you enough room there?"

"I'm fine. Just anxious about the situation here. If France capitulates . . ." They passed another group of soldiers and he made a gesture of disgust. "Poor fools led by officers living a grandiose dream. Our generals have spent too long filling their bellies and sleeping with women to get out and train an army for modern warfare. In the end the Germans will crush us like matchwood."

"I'm afraid you're right." Richard was sombre. "The French may find their only salvation in small, underground groups of fighters. People like your friends that we met last week. I was impressed by them."

"Yes, but what you were saying that night was right. We need to organise our communications, get information to the people. I don't know how much time we have to put that kind of thing together."

"You'll need radios and transmitters that are light and easily transportable, and some means of identifying each other. Printing presses will be important too. When I get to Dublin I can look into the question of equipment. My family has a publishing business. I'll see what we can do to help."

"Thank you, my friend. We'll have to organise a way of contacting you, if things become desperate." He glanced back and smiled suddenly. "Maybe Stefan can go to work in the Swedish consulate, and send you messages through the diplomatic bag. Eh, Stefan?"

"You mean give up my painting and become one of those little office clerks? I'd have to mix with the jackbooted oafs that my father seems to admire so much." Stefan put a hand on his friend's shoulder. "Seriously though, you know I will do whatever I can to help. My father would have a seizure if he thought I was using his contacts in the consulate, or our neutrality, for anything 'irregular'."

Seamus was surprised at the bitterness of his tone.

"Stefan's father is Count Carl Svenssen," Helena explained. "He has business interests in France and Germany, and considerable standing in the Swedish consulate in Paris. I'm sure you've gathered that father and son don't get on too well. Stefan says Daddy is a Hitler-lover, and Daddy thinks Stefan is a wastrel, because real men don't study art."

When they reached St Brieuc there was chaos all around them. People were crowded on the quayside, arguing and bargaining for passage on any available vessel. Foreign nationals and French refugees stood among trunks and boxes piled along the wharf. Seamus shouldered his way through the confusion and stood on the pier looking down. When he saw his boat tied up alongside at the far end, he gave a piercing whistle. She was a Galway hooker, fifty feet long, freshly painted and fully decked. Helena gazed at her with delight. "She's lovely! What have you called her?"

"*Famaire*. It means Sea Wanderer." He was looking at the boat proudly. "She'll sail through any sea. Come on – I'll show you."

Two men appeared from below at Seamus's call – tall, sturdy men, in jerseys, caps and sea boots, their eyes wind-weathered in their ruddy faces. They spoke in Gaelic, and Helena gave a whoop of joy and rushed to embrace them.

"This is Ronan, my eldest brother, and this is Ciaran."

The men shook hands all round, smiling shyly, their soft Irish voices offering greetings and welcome. They moved away on the deck to allow the party to board and Helena clattered down the companion-way. Seamus took Leah's hand. "Come and I'll show you over her." He caught her around the waist and took her on a tour of his great treasure. It was important to him that she should see it all and love it.

Later they sat on deck in the darkness, sharing a last bottle of wine together as they waited to sail on the midnight tide. They kept the conversation light, avoiding the pain of their impending separation. The cloud began to build up, and a fresh wind rose.

"It will be a rough crossing, I think," Ronan said, looking up at the sky.

"How long will it take?" Richard asked, suddenly aware that he was no sailor.

"I'd say four or five days to Galway, if we have the wind," Ronan answered.

"Oh, there'll be plenty of that I'm afraid. But you'll get your sea legs in no time, and *Famaire* sails like a dream." Seamus looked at Richard with some sympathy. Then he turned to Daniel and Leah, his tone desperate. "There's room on board for the two of you. You could still come with us. You, at least, Leah, could leave with us now while you have the chance to be safe."

But in his heart he already knew the answer. They had discussed it earlier, Daniel unable to persuade his sister and adamant that he himself must return to Paris. There was a sudden commotion on the quayside. People had gathered around a wireless set to hear the news. Now a man was running down the pier, shouting. "The Germans have invaded France! The Germans have invaded! They're coming!"

Murmurs of anxiety rose from all the boats and there were wails from people gathered on the quay. On the deck of the *Famaire* Ronan stood up.

"The tide has turned, Seamus," he said quietly. "It's time to put out to sea."

He went forward to the bow. Seamus stood, paralysed. Daniel rose and touched him on the shoulder. "We must get back to Paris as soon as we can. It is no use delaying now."

Seamus stared at Leah, and Stefan's mouth tightened in sympathy. He wanted to say something, anything, to help his friend through this terrible moment as Seamus had helped him earlier in the day. "I will take them both safely back to Paris, Seamus," he said. "And if there is any hint of trouble I promise I will contact you, and bring them down here. Then you can sail in and take them away."

They gathered, all together on the deck, holding one another, making promises, saying comforting things to hide the fear. Helena wept as she clung to Stefan and Daniel, and kissed Leah. At last, Richard had to tear her away to let them disembark. She stood in his arms, her face streaked with tears.

Seamus took Leah's hands. Then she was crushed against him and he was kissing her again and again. He could hear her whispering against his mouth. "Don't forget me, my Irish sea wanderer. Listen for me when the wind sings in your sails, and the sea sighs against the side of your ship. Soon you'll come back for me, Seamus, won't you? Don't forget to come for me."

She broke away from him, weeping. Daniel took her hand and she jumped down on to the pier. Ronan and Ciaran cast off and the boat pulled away from the quay. Eyes blurred, his soul torn asunder, Seamus stood at the wheel. He saw Stefan give Leah his handkerchief, and Daniel put his arm around his sister's shoulders.

The great sail shook itself out into the wind and drew *Famaire* towards the harbour mouth. Looking back across the moonlit wake of churning water, Seamus could still make out three figures on the end of the pier, caught for ever in a still, silent image, separated from him by the slap of the rigging and the whoosh of the bow wave as the *Famaire* carried him away, with the rest of the small armada. Away from the coast of France.

Chapter 20

Connemara, 1970

Eleanor rubbed her eyes and closed her file. She had been working for three hours and it was time for a break. The sun was already high, the tide full in on the beach. Through the window she could see Helena standing at her easel by the water's edge, shaded by her floppy, brown painting hat. In the kitchen she made coffee, mulling over the story of her uncle's lost love. Last night she had been touched by his trust, his willingness to share the feelings he had locked away for so many years. Slowly her family's complex story was beginning to unfold. And Mother was painting again. That was a good sign. Perhaps just being here would release Helena from the cocoon she had spun around herself, the distancing that had begun before her father's death. Some months before the end, Eleanor had noticed her mother moving away from everyone, drawing deep into herself. She had thought it was Helena's way of confronting death but now she wondered if this change had been brought about by something else. Perhaps Helena had realised, or had begun to suspect, that Father had someone else. But had this liaison, this affair with Solange's mother, continued after the war, or had it stopped so that he discovered his daughter in France only just before his death? The questions seemed to lead to more questions. She sighed with frustration and was considering a return to her manuscript when Seamus appeared at the door.

146

"You've been working like a beaver all morning. I didn't like to disturb you." He looked at her shyly. "I didn't destroy your first night here with my revelations, did I?"

"I felt privileged to be trusted with your precious memories, Seamus. I hope I didn't put you on the rack too much, cause you too much pain."

"Remember when you broke up with Matthew? You came down here and poured out your heart to me. So I knew last night that you'd understand about Leah."

"But there's so much more to tell. About Father, and what happened to Leah and Daniel and Stefan, after you left France." Eleanor paused. "Will you tell me the whole story?"

There was terrible sadness in his face as he gazed out of the window across the bay and she realised that the pain was as fresh for him now as it had been when he had said goodbye to Leah all those years ago. She poured the coffee and sat down with him in silence. He had met Leah again – he'd told her that at the start of the story – but she was married. So had Seamus gone looking for her when it was all over, only to find – what? The whole chain of events was so vital to her own understanding of her parents' tangled lives. Guilt jabbed at her. It was cruel to put her uncle through this. Perhaps Solange had been right when she said these memories were better left to die.

"I'm sorry," she said softly. "It still hurts – I can see that. If you'd rather leave it be . . ."

"There are some things, the darker aspects of our lives, that we are very loath to bring to light." He turned back to her and she shivered at his bleak expression. "We try to keep the shutters tightly closed over them, but maybe this is timely. I have a bit of a problem, however, when my story crosses someone else's."

"You mean things Father might have shared with you? Or Mother?"

"Yes. I have to respect their right to be silent if they do not wish to speak."

"But he's dead!" It came out far more forcefully than she had intended, driven out by a deep anger. "And he's left us a will that in effect says 'Go and discover all this for yourselves – I'm safely out of it!'" She looked away, ashamed at her outburst. "I'm sorry, but you must see that he couldn't expect us not to care about the daughter in France, or to want to discover who she is and how she came to be there."

"I do know what a shock it's all been. And I've no idea why he did what he did. Your mother hasn't said anything to me about that. But I just want you to go at it gently."

"Oh, Seamus. Have I been hectoring you?"

"I can't imagine you hectoring anyone, Eleanor." He laughed aloud suddenly, clearing the air. "Now, I think it's time you went for a walk out in that wonderful air. I'll be back in less than an hour with the post, news, gossip, and anything else that I think requires your attention. After that you can hector away, and I'll do my best to answer."

When he had gone she made her way down to the rocky headland where Helena was working, bringing with her a thermos of strong coffee and two mugs. She sat down quietly, at a little distance, so as not to disturb her mother's concentration.

"Goodness! Have you been here long?" At last Helena stepped back from the picture, and saw Eleanor. She wiped a brush on an oily cloth and considered her work.

"Not too long. I love watching you paint. Did I disturb you?"

"No – you never do. Even as a child you had a great capacity to sit very still, so one wasn't aware that you were there. Your grandmother used to find it quite unnerving."

"Granny Kirwan? Gosh, I wouldn't have thought she could be unnerved by anything!"

"She was a formidable lady all right." Helena laughed. "She unnerved me a lot in the early days."

"You mean before we were born?" Eleanor held her breath. Was her mother going to start talking about the past?

"Yes, before you were born." Helena turned back to her palette, selecting and mixing colour as she spoke. "She regarded me as an unsuitable match for her only son. A bohemian from the wilds of Connemara. I mean, what kind of breeding stock was that? We had our share of misunderstanding. In fact," she stopped working and stared out to sea, "it wasn't till your father recovered from his war experiences that she really began to accept me. Although I think she had a grudging respect for me after she saw me bringing you two into the world. That was hard going."

Eleanor clasped her knees and spoke carefully. "But Father wasn't with you? When we were born, I mean?" There was a silence. Damn, Eleanor thought. She's gone on me, back into her shell. Then Helena answered.

"No, Eleanor. He left from here with Seamus to bring some friends of ours out of France. I, well we, had spent the night before he left up on the hill there." She nodded up at the rocky outcrop behind her, smiling to herself. "It looks rather grey and unwelcoming from here. But there's a wonderful dip behind the rocks halfway up, a natural basin of good, soft grass that makes a great trysting place in fine weather." Her hand was moving fast over the canvas now and she frowned in concentration. "I'm quite sure you and James were conceived in a night of great love and passion, on the side of a mountain in Connemara. Granny Kirwan wouldn't have approved of that at all. But Angela now. Angela would have been delighted. She certainly took Dada up there a few times. Seamus and I saw them."

"Mother! You didn't!" Eleanor gazed up at the hill, laughing. "Spying on your own father?"

"Well, not exactly." Helena's smile held mischief. "We followed them a couple of times, but Seamus got embarrassed when Dada started kissing Angela, and he dragged me away."

"I wish I'd known Angela," Eleanor said wistfully. "And Dada.

I would have liked grandparents to spend time with, and Granny Kirwan wasn't very comforting, was she?"

"No. She wasn't." She took up a brushful of paint, and began to stroke it on to the canvas.

"But Father. Did he know you were . . . ? Did he know that we'd – started? Up there."

"How could he know?" Helena winced and worked the canvas harder. "He disappeared. I didn't hear from him. Everything went wrong you see, when they got to France."

"Who is 'they'? Who went with him to France?"

"Your uncles, all three of them. Seamus and Ronan and Ciaran. In Seamus's boat. I wanted to go, but Richard and Seamus wouldn't hear of it. I fought with them for days and I was devastated when they left without me. Even then I couldn't tolerate the idea of these macho men going off on their deeds of daring, fighting their great battles, and assuming that the women would wait patiently at home."

Eleanor was surprised by the bitterness in Helena's voice.

"I waited and waited for news. A week passed, nearly two and still nothing. Finally Seamus and Ronan and Ciaran got back to Galway. Stefan and Leah were not with them. And neither was Richard."

Eleanor felt a small prickle of excitement. This was the first time that Helena had mentioned these names. She held her breath, waiting for her mother to continue.

"I was sick all day, every day. I thought it was the worry. Eventually I discovered I was pregnant. And then Seamus told me I was expecting twins. That was so hard, realising that my babies were growing in me, and their father might never see them, never know them."

Seamus hailed them from the house, calling them in for lunch, and the thread of the story snapped.

In the afternoon Helena took up her canvas and brushes once more and returned to the headland. Eleanor was wondering whether she should follow when the telephone rang. Gareth's voice came down the line, anxious. "Are you all right, Eleanor? Is Helena feeling any better at all? I keep thinking of you both and hoping you'll begin to revive down there, with Seamus taking care of you."

"Yes, it's good. And we're beginning to talk. It's all right, Gareth."

They spent over an hour discussing the business of the day. Afterwards Eleanor returned to her manuscript, and then walked with Seamus and Helena across Gurteen strand. Before dinner they spoke to James and Elizabeth whose lives in Dublin seemed reassuringly uneventful. Helena read for a while beside the fire, but the sea air had worked its healing magic on her and she retired early, her eyes reflecting the beginnings of a new peace. Eleanor glanced at Seamus without speaking, afraid of pressing him. To her delight he smiled at her, his expression conspiratorial, and reached into the cupboard for the brandy.

"So El, are we to reopen my book of revelations?"

Impatient for him to resume his narrative, she blurted out the question that had been with her throughout the day.

"How could she not have waited for you, Seamus? You're such a wonderful person. How could Leah not have remembered that and held on? Who could she possibly have found and married to make her forget you?" She paused, realising too late that she was rushing ahead of his story.

"Stefan." Seamus's voice was cracking in pain. "She married Stefan Svenssen, in the Swedish consulate in Paris, so that he could get her out of France."

Chapter 21

Paris, 1942

The street echoed with the sound of breaking glass and the shouts of soldiers. In the rue des Anges, a knot of curious onlookers gathered to watch the families being herded from their homes into the backs of the trucks. There were men, women, children, frail grandmothers and tiny infants, each one wearing an armband marked with the yellow Star of David. The soldiers pushed them roughly with rifle butts, prodding and forcing them like beasts into the waiting transport. A German officer directed his men up the steps of Number 15. They rang the bell, but before anyone could answer they began to kick and hammer on the door, lifting their rifles to smash the glass. Simon Nazarre appeared on the threshold, and stood looking at the officer.

"There is no need for all this noise," he said, dignified and calm.

A soldier pushed him roughly aside. "How many in this house, Jew?"

Simon looked at him, taking in the cruelty of the young face. "Just my family. What is it you want?"

"You have to leave now, all of you. This house has been requisitioned by the German High Command. You will be transported away from here. Get your family! *Schnell! Schnell!* Now!"

"This is ridiculous," said Simon becoming angry. "This is our home and we are French citizens. You cannot come here in the middle of the night and –"

A truncheon smashed into the side of his head. He sank to his knees, blood streaming down his face. Outside, voices had begun chanting. "Jews out! Jews out! Jews out!"

"Scum!" The officer spat at Simon. "When a German officer makes an order, Jew, you will obey. Immediately. Or you will be shot. Now get your family out."

Hannah came running down the stairs. She helped her husband to his feet, drawing him away from the humiliation of the public gaze, speaking placatingly. "Excuse me officer, my husband did not understand. We will get ready at once." She guided Simon towards the stairs. "What can we bring with us?"

"One bag only allowed on the transports. How many in this family?"

Hannah pushed her elbow into Simon's side as he opened his mouth to answer. "Only ourselves, and our two little boys who are sleeping," she cut in. "I'll get them up now. We'll be down directly."

When they reached the top of the stairs Hannah pulled Simon into their bedroom.

"But Hannah," he protested. "What about Leah – she's out with Stefan. She'll be back any moment. And Daniel?"

"Daniel must not be mentioned. Or Leah." Her eyes shone with tears. "Oh my dear, she at least may get away. Pray God Stefan doesn't bring her back here till these monsters have gone. We must do the best we can for Zachary and David. It's too late now for Daniel to help us."

She cleaned his battered face with a damp towel and bandaged the wound on the side of his head. Then she hurried to the wardrobe and brought out a suitcase, already packed. If only they had been granted just a few more days, she thought dully. They had almost got away. Some weeks earlier, Simon Nazarre had at last faced his eldest son across the dining table late one night, his eyes filled with sadness and defeat. "You will have to help us, Daniel. Find a way for us to leave."

"I'll arrange for you to leave, Father. But you can't tell anyone. Not your friends, and least of all Zachary or David. There are informers everywhere. People you might have known all your life would sell you to the Gestapo without a qualm, and sleep peacefully in their beds afterwards." His voice was full of bitterness.

Simon had sat motionless in his chair, slumped in shame and regret. From that day, the small chores of daily living became a painful charade in their twilight world. Daniel had said his network would get word to Richard and Helena who were prepared to do anything to help. Leah had received continual letters from Seamus until all communication had been stopped. But they knew he would keep his promise to bring them out of France.

As the days dragged on, dark and ominous, their position grew more precarious. Ugly slogans were daubed on the walls of houses and in the park where they used to walk. Fear became a familiar, following shadow and hunger gnawed at them. Only yesterday Daniel had brought them hope, telling them that they could be leaving soon. Now it was too late. Hannah went to wake the children, helping them to dress, talking cheerfully about a surprise trip to a new place. "Put on this extra jumper, Zachary. It might be cold. And David, here are your socks. Now hurry, little ones. We are setting off with Papa on a great adventure."

"But Mama," Zachary was protesting. "We can't go without Leah and Daniel."

Hannah knelt in front of him and put her fingers on his lips.

"Children, Leah and Daniel will not be coming with us just now. It will be only Papa and Mama and you two. Now, downstairs there is a German officer who is very cross because he doesn't like to be kept waiting. Daniel and Leah will join us soon, but we don't want to get them in trouble because they are late. Do you understand? For now, we will say nothing about them so as not to hold anyone up."

"But Mama, how will they know where to find us if we go away without leaving a message?" David gazed at her, his brown eyes still heavy with sleep. Zachary began to whimper.

Hannah looked up in desperation. Simon stood in the doorway. He came into the room and put his arms around his small sons. "Your big brother is so clever that he will work it all out in seconds. Don't you remember how he could always find you when you played hide and seek?"

"Now stay close to me, my little love," Hannah whispered to Zachary as they walked across the hall, their steps crunching shards of glass on the carpet. Outside a bonfire had been lit. Three German soldiers pushed past them to enter the house. Cherished pieces of furniture, crystalware, china and books were hurled through the windows and thrown on to the flames. Further up the street stones and rifle butts were being used to enter another house. Groups of people huddled together, holding one another and stumbling towards the waiting trucks. Some were silent, others howled in terror. The two little boys shrank back and moved in closer to their parents as the chanting began again. The crowd of bystanders grew, their voices becoming more strident. Hannah and Simon recognised with anguish several former neighbours whom they had considered as friends.

"Jews out! Jews out! Jews out!"

Across the city in the crowded concert hall Leah pressed Stefan's hand, her eyes shining with delight. There were no seats for Jews in the concert halls, not even for those who, until recently, had formed an important part of the city's musical life. Leah had piled her dark hair under a felt cloche hat, and gone with Stefan for a few hours of stolen pleasure. The theatre was full of Nazi officers and their expensively dressed women, many of them French.

"How can they sit there without shame?" she whispered to Stefan during the interval. "How can they sell themselves like this, for a night of pleasure and a wardrobe of finery?"

"Just enjoy the music. They will not be here for much longer, you'll see."

"But in the meantime my little brothers are hungry because we are Jews with special ration cards, and there's never any food left when we reach the top of the queue. Someone even spat at my mother yesterday. And a young man threw a stone at Zachary and David."

"Just being here is one way of defying them," said Stefan. "And we will win in the end. People like Daniel will be recognised as heroes, and we will win."

Daniel had not lived at home for months. Only a few days ago he had warned her that the whole family was now in danger of being rounded up and sent away to a prison camp somewhere in Germany. He came home only at night and always left before dawn, and Leah knew that he had joined a resistance group. As the music swept over her, erasing the humiliation and indignity of her altered status, she fought the threat of tears. She desperately missed the Conservatoire where she was not permitted to pursue her studies. Jews could no longer occupy teaching positions or places in the arts. After thirty-five years in the Conservatoire, Simon Nazarre was not allowed to teach and Hannah had been told there was no place for her in the orchestra.

As the last notes of the symphony brought a rush of applause Stefan took Leah's hand and they slipped out and away from the theatre in case some member of the audience might recognise her. They set off for her home so deep in discussion, so focused on the joy of the evening's music that they almost walked into the jaws of the trap.

It was Stefan who realised what was happening. He pulled Leah into the shadow of a doorway at the end of the street. Flames lit the hellish scene that would haunt her always. She watched as her family was led down the steps, saw her father climb into the truck like an old man, looking back at his shattered home. Her mother comforted the two small boys and scanned the shadows looking, Leah knew, for some sign that her daughter had escaped the dragnet. She started to move towards them, wanting to go wherever they were being sent. But Stefan grasped her arms firmly.

"Stefan, let me go!" She strained to get away, tears streaming down her face. "Let me go to them, I have to be with them!" Her voice rose and she began to sob.

He clamped his hand firmly over her mouth and pulled her, still struggling, into an alley. Then he lifted her off the ground and carried her for four more blocks, away from the noise of the trucks as they began to move, away from the shouts of abuse, away from the sound of glass shattering and furniture being smashed and the crackle of the bonfire, away from the fearful sound of people wailing.

At last they stopped in a deserted side street. Leah leaned against the wall of a building and vomited, falling to her knees, retching and moaning softly to herself. Stefan rocked her and hushed her, took her hand and insisted that they must move on, faster now, through the dark streets. She stumbled along beside him in a fog of grief.

"Where are we going?" She gasped out the words.

"To the Swedish consulate."

"You can't, Stefan. You can't take me there. The consul will never accept it and neither will your father. And all the embassies have German guards now!" She slumped against the wall, in tears again.

"Oh, Stefan, we were almost free you know! Daniel was organising it."

"I know, Leah." Stefan's face was bleak.

She stared at him.

"Daniel didn't tell you. It's better for everyone involved that no one knows more than is absolutely necessary. Then, if things come apart . . ."

"You were helping Daniel to organise this?"

"Yes. I'll have to send word to his group." He wiped his face in a gesture of fatigue. "In the meantime, I must get you to safety. There'll be another patrol along here soon, and we need to make it to rue St Pierre."

"What's there?"

"My friend Anders Petersen. He's a secretary at the consulate, but he lives in rue St Pierre, and what's more he has a car."

"But where would he take us?"

"Trust me, please. Come on Leah."

It had begun to rain. An involuntary sob broke from her as she slipped and fell on the slick, cobbled street. Stefan grabbed her and pressed her hard against the damp wall. At the end of the narrow alleyway a patrol was moving purposefully in their direction, guns ready. Shouts came from behind the men, followed by the sound of running feet. Stefan and Leah froze, sure that they would be discovered. The soldiers turned abruptly and after a moment moved away in the other direction in pursuit of some other terrified quarry. When the sounds of marching boots had died away at last, they resumed their journey, slower now and even more wary. It took them almost two hours to reach rue St Pierre where Stefan went in search of his friend, leaving Leah in hiding among the garbage bins at the rear of the building. The minutes ticked by. Rain drummed steadily, soaking her light clothes. The smell of rotting waste and the black shapes of foraging rats plunged her into fear and despair. At last, Stefan was back with his friend. Anders Petersen was clearly tense and unhappy.

"We can't take her upstairs Stefan. The concierge might see her, and she's a nosy old bitch at the best of times. You'll have to wait here while I fetch the car. It's a pity we can't wait till daylight."

"There's nowhere I can hide her until then," Stefan answered. "Can't you tell the guards you've received urgent instructions from the consul that require your immediate attention? It's lucky he's away in Marseilles until tomorrow with my parents."

Anders looked down at the bedraggled girl, crouched and shivering beside the bins.

"All right, Stefan," he said softly. "I'll flick the lights twice when I pull up in the car. We'll have to put her into the boot."

"Just a few minutes more, Leah. We'll soon be in a safe place." Stefan squeezed her shoulder.

Exhaustion, grief and a kind of hysteria enveloped Leah as she huddled in the wet, afraid that she would begin to scream and not be able to stop. She clamped her teeth into her lip to prevent the sound and tasted blood. They heard the noise of a vehicle approaching and froze, unsure whether it was Anders or a German patrol. The car stopped, engine running. The headlights dipped twice.

"Now!" Stefan pulled the trembling girl to her feet.

They reached the car and he opened the boot. Inside was a tennis racket, some clothes and a rug. He helped her into the boot and began to cover her with Anders's belongings. Leah's limbs were stiff with cold. She lay curled up and shaking as Anders helped Stefan to pile the remainder of the load on top of her. Then they loosened the spare wheel and placed it at an angle over the haphazard heap. Anders opened the valve and let the air out.

"Just in case anyone should check," he explained. "They're very suspicious these days."

The lid closed and Leah was shut in the suffocating darkness, assailed by oily engine fumes and the smell of rubber and leather as the car accelerated away. The journey seemed interminable as she lay crushed beneath the weight of the wheel. Then they stopped suddenly. She heard a German voice, followed by Anders's explanation as to why they were out driving after curfew. She could not capture all that was said, but she thought they must have made some lewd remark because she heard the German laughing raucously. Then he banged on the car roof and let them go. They crawled away, Anders wary of appearing to be in any hurry.

At the entrance to the consulate they were halted again. An urgent message from the consul, Anders explained, showing his identity pass. The night officer had asked him to come in right away. It was a decoding task requiring urgent attention and only he had clearance at this level. This young man beside him was the son of Count Carl Svenssen, and a part-time member of the staff. The guard studied their papers. Moments passed. Then Leah heard him bark out an order.

"Open the boot if you please."

Anders got out of the car slowly. Leah heard his footsteps approaching and pressed herself into the floor. Lying still as death, hardly breathing, she heard the lid creak open. Anders was apologising for the mess. Leah began to shake uncontrollably.

"A puncture on the way. It always happens on a rainy night when one is in a hurry! See? The tyre is as flat as a pancake!" He thumped it. "It took us a while to loosen those nuts — they were jammed solid with rust. These French cars are not a patch on the German machines."

The sentry wrinkled his nose with distaste, frowning at the chaos before him. Then he nodded curtly, slammed down the lid and waved them on. Anders jumped into the car and gunned away through the gates, around the back of the building, out of sight of the guards. They lifted Leah out, rolled the rug around her and carried her into the consulate. Anders greeted the duty officer. "You know Stefan Svenssen? His fiancée's had an accident. The consul is away with Stefan's parents, but he suggested she should stay here overnight. He didn't want them rounded up in the curfew and involved in an embarrassing misunderstanding."

The duty officer nodded. Lucky young devil, Stefan Svenssen, with his rich father and the consulate to hide behind. His own parents would have left him to work out his problems himself.

Anders took the fugitives up to the official guest apartment and went in search of some food. Leah stood blinking in the brightness of the lights, filthy and dripping, unable to speak. The room began to spin and Stefan caught her as she fell. He carried her into the bathroom, stripped off her clothes and bathed her gently. Numb with shock, Leah was oblivious to her nakedness as Stefan dried her, slipped a towelling robe around her and lifted her into bed. Then he lay down beside her, holding her hand until at last she was quiet. When Anders arrived with a tray she had drifted into uneasy sleep. They sat quietly, eating and discussing Stefan's next move.

"Your father's going to be livid about this Stefan. You know that. And there's no guarantee the consul will let her stay here, even if you officially ask for sanctuary."

"Well, there's one thing I can do. She's my fiancée, you said so yourself. I'll marry her and take her out of France, as my wife. They can't touch her then. She'll have Swedish status and the support of the embassy of a neutral country. I'm going to marry her Anders."

"You'll be marrying a Jew. Your father will be insane with rage. He'll never consent." Anders looked at his friend in horror. "And it could compromise the position of the consul, and your father's status as a neutral businessman."

"I don't need anyone's consent," Stefan answered coldly. "I'm twenty-five years old. I can marry anyone I please. And Father is altogether too cosy with his Nazi friends. If my actions cause a rift, I'll be delighted. As for the consul, he's a man of principle whom I admire. I'll take my chances with him."

"Have you thought of your mother?"

"Ah yes, dear Mother who thinks of nothing but what she should wear to her next party, and where her next bottle of gin will come from. Too bad. But we won't be here long enough to upset anyone. We can take a train to Switzerland. Leah will be safe there and secure, away from all this, and no one will bother us." Stefan stood up with his cup of coffee in his hand. His normally benign expression was menacing. "Everyone will want to get us on that train, give us the necessary papers, just to get rid of the embarrassment of it all. You know that."

Anders shook his head in exasperation.

"Look, Anders," Stefan's voice was thick with anger, "you didn't see what I saw tonight. I watched this girl's family being loaded into a cattle truck like animals. They're going to be sent to a German prison. Their crime? They happen to be Jews. If she hadn't been with me she would have been taken too. I have to protect her, Anders. The whole family are old friends."

Anders stood up and put his hand on Stefan's shoulder. "You certainly know how to get yourself into a mess, my friend. God knows what the consul is going to say to me in the morning. I may be out of work and travelling on that train with you. Meantime, I've cleared you and your guest with the staff on duty. They all know your father so they aren't asking too many questions."

Stefan began to thank him but Anders silenced him. "I'll leave you to work out your plan, but whatever you decide you'd better do it before the consul gets back tomorrow night. There's a dinner planned with some general from the German High Command, so you'll want to be out of here fast. You're crazy, Stefan. But I have to admire your courage." Anders squeezed his shoulder and was gone.

For a while Stefan sat quietly, looking at Leah. Then he lay down on the bed beside her and put his arms gently around her. She gave a little sound, perhaps of fear, and he whispered to her gently. "It's all right. No one will hurt you now, Leah, I swear."

She turned her head into his shoulder. He closed his eyes and drew her nearer. In his mind he saw another face, floating in a halo of glowing, coppery hair, coming close to rest against him. How would it have been if he had rescued her, if he had saved her life, taken her out of danger to lie in his arms like this? But now at last he could do something worthwhile, something heroic, that would make her aware of his true worth. His eyes filled with tears as he gently smoothed the dark hair beside him and began to make his plans for the morning.

Chapter 22

It took three hours to talk Pastor Bruzelius round. He was a kindly man and deeply concerned about Stefan's proposition.

"Your family will have grave objections, Stefan. And she is of a different faith."

"That's why she's in mortal danger now. They've already taken her parents and her little brothers away. We both know that the consul general can't keep her here as an asylum seeker. And you know my father wouldn't countenance my marriage. But I'm twenty-five years old, Pastor Bruzelius. Old enough to choose my own wife." Stefan hesitated, frantically searching for a convincing argument. "I was planning to marry Leah anyway. We made the decision several months ago."

"But it will not be a proper marriage ceremony Stefan. To begin with she is not even baptised. She is not a Christian."

"She's willing to become one. We've discussed it often. You can baptise her first, and then marry us. Pastor, please. We are, after all, merciful Christians. We cannot condone persecution. This is wartime and it's her only chance — our only chance. Otherwise her blood will be on your hands. I'm telling you Pastor, I've seen incidents so horrible, so barbarous . . ."

"Please Stefan, the less you say about such things, the better for all of us. Now tell me honestly and truthfully, what are your feelings for this girl?"

"I will abide by the promises I make to her, Pastor Bruzelius." Stefan stood straight. "I will honour her and care for her. I will do everything possible to make up for what has been taken away from her. Now, will you marry us, Pastor?"

There was a long silence. "Very well Stefan. I will do it. But first I must speak to her alone, without you."

Stefan put his head into his hands, relieved. Then he led the clergyman upstairs to the guest suite where Leah was sitting on a chair, staring out of the window. She stood up as Stefan and the pastor entered.

"Leah, this is Pastor Bruzelius who will perform our marriage ceremony. He will be asking you to embrace the Christian faith as we have discussed, in order for our marriage to be valid."

He prayed that she would understand. This was the only chance of convincing the pastor that she had intended to become a Christian. He stumbled over the words, ashamed of what he was asking her to do. Then he kissed her cheek and left the room.

Leah regarded Pastor Bruzelius in silence. The pastor saw before him a young woman of considerable beauty, dressed in a crumpled blouse and skirt. He took in her strained face and haunted eyes. But there was a shining intelligence, a strength and dignity about her. He smiled encouragement and began to go through the basic tenets of the Christian faith. Each time he asked her did she believe, she nodded, her hands clasped tightly together, her eyes downcast. He baptised her at last, kneeling on the carpet, with the sounds of the Paris morning drifting in through the open window. Then he went to the door where Stefan waited.

"Now, we have welcomed into our midst a new and beautiful sister, in the eyes of God." He spoke warmly, wanting to bring some hint of joy to the day's strangely sad proceedings. "Stefan, let us find her something appropriate to wear. Every girl is entitled to that on her wedding day!" He strode off, calling out to Anders. "See if you can't find that wonderful assistant of yours, young man. If ever she was needed it's now." He turned back to Stefan. "At five o'clock I will perform your marriage ceremony. There's some paperwork to be prepared, in order to ensure that everything is in order. You'll need two witnesses and – ah, Marta! I have a little project for you my dear."

Marta was big and bosomy with a wide smile. She was fond of the priest and often helped him with his pastoral work.

"Inside there is a young woman about to be married. See what you can do, my dear, to help Stefan find her appropriate clothes. I know there's precious little in the shops. And Marta, I think she needs to do something with her appearance. Maybe her hair. You will understand." He did not wait for her answer, trusting her intuition. "Five o'clock then, Stefan. I believe the consul has a dinner here at seven, and your parents are among the guests. It would be better if this were all settled by then."

The light of the Paris evening had turned to gold when they assembled in the reception room downstairs. Armed with the Svenssen account number and signed letters from Stefan, Marta had visited several of Countess Svenssen's favourite boutiques and made her selections with care. Now she stood beside the bride, as her Matron of Honour.

Leah had been transformed into a perfect Aryan beauty. Soft coils of platinum hair were pinned up under a velvet hat with a small veil. Her cheeks had been brushed with colour and she wore a deep-red lipstick. A dove-grey belted suit, silk stockings, long gloves and high-heeled shoes completed the outfit, and a spray of white flowers was pinned to the lapel of her jacket. Stefan gazed at the stranger beside him, afraid that he had destroyed the Leah he knew, and that he would never find her again. He touched her hand tentatively and smiled encouragement.

Pastor Bruzelius began the service. Stefan recited the marriage vows. Leah stood beside him in a trance, Anders and Marta flanking them as witnesses. Silence fell. Leah realised all at once that everyone was looking at her, but she could not respond although she heard the words that sounded like a chant from far away.

"Do you, Leah, take Stefan as your lawful wedded husband . . ."

"I'm betraying them all," she thought. "My people, my family, my heritage. I am even betraying Stefan, just to save myself." She saw him through a blur of tears, heard him whispering urgently.

"Leah! Leah?" He was squeezing her hand, his expression frantic. She saw his concerned blue eyes. This man had shown so much bravery. He had risked everything for her, given so much. In trembling tones she spoke the words. "I do."

Stefan took his family signet ring and placed it on her finger. Then he brought her over to sign the register. Pastor Bruzelius handed him the marriage certificate, and pronounced them man and wife. It was just after six.

"May I ask what is going on here?" The cold voice came from the doorway like a whiplash. Count Carl Svenssen stood surveying the scene, taking in his son's jacket and tie, and the unknown young woman beside him in the fashionable silk suit, the veiled hat, the corsage. Stefan stared at his father with the sick realisation that the worst part of the day was yet to come. Nothing could ever be certain under that withering gaze.

"Good evening Pastor Bruzelius, what a pleasant surprise. What brings you here this evening?" The consul general of Sweden appeared, urbane and pleasant.

Stefan's mother, Aneka, drifted into the room, her blonde hair immaculately coiffed. Leah looked from her to Count Svenssen, and the cold rush of fear returned.

"It would seem that the pastor has been conducting some sort of ceremony here." Count Svenssen fixed his glare on the tall man in his shabby cassock, and waited for an explanation.

Stefan swallowed hard and stepped forward, holding Leah's hand.

"Your Excellency, Father, Mother, this will come as something of a surprise to you I'm sure, but I have just got married."

His father looked at him, then at Leah. He swivelled his gaze back to his son as his lip curled. "Indeed. Here on these premises. And you could not have postponed it for even a few hours, to enable your parents to join the celebration?" He turned to glance fleetingly at his wife, noting her shock as she stood rigidly behind him. "I see even your doting mother wasn't aware of this plan. You didn't see fit to mention this to us before we left for Marseilles, Stefan, or to consult with the consul."

" I . . . that is, we just decided suddenly. Yesterday evening." Stefan was gripping Leah's hand so hard that she winced. "Leah is, was, leaving France you see. Very soon. To work in Switzerland. She has been posted there. Tomorrow actually. So we decided to marry and go together. We didn't want to be separated. It would have been difficult to organise it any other way, because of the war."

He trailed off. His mother's glance was focused on Leah, taking in every detail of her clothes, her face and dark eyes, and last of all her hair. She put her hand on her husband's sleeve but he shook her off. Carl Svenssen's tone became more arctic. "Leah. I see. And may we know her other name?" The count addressed his question to Stefan, ignoring Leah completely. "Prior to her taking ours of course."

Leah felt a flush of anger suffuse her face. She looked directly at Carl Svenssen and her voice was firm and clear. "My name is Leah Nazarre, Count Svenssen."

The consul general looked at her sharply. Aneka Svenssen gasped and her husband set his mouth into a thin, narrow line. His gaze returned to his son. "Leah Nazarre. I see. I see it all very clearly. I take it that this travesty of a marriage is another of your hysterical political statements, Stefan. Another of your sentimental, ill-informed crusades?" The count turned on the pastor. "I think we all know what this young woman is, pastor. And I believe there are grounds for challenging what has been done here today."

"This young woman is my wife, Father. Our marriage is valid and legal, and has been duly witnessed." Stefan held out the certificate, defiant, standing with his arm protectively around Leah. "Pastor Bruzelius has done everything perfectly."

The pastor nodded emphatically, turning now to the consul. "He is right, Your Excellency. The marriage is valid."

The consul general was about to speak when Aneka Svenssen stepped forward. "Stefan, this is dreadful. Quite dreadful. How could you bring this – bring her here, tonight of all nights? General von Stroepper of the German High Command will be arriving soon for dinner." Her voice was shaking, and she moved towards the drinks tray.

"A brandy perhaps, Aneka?" The consul took her arm and guided her to a chair.

She nodded distractedly, and continued to address her son. "What possessed you to stage this charade, Stefan. And with a total stranger, and a ..."

"A Jew. She is a Jew, is she not?" The count's angry words interrupted his wife. "Is that what is really behind all this, Stefan? You have finally found the perfect way to bring the maximum shame and discomfort to me and to your mother."

The consul general took the furious count by the arm. "Carl, calm yourself, please. This is disturbing, and as a parent you have my sympathy. But I'm sure Stefan and his bride cannot have an agenda such as you suggest. Let us try to discuss this in a more restrained manner."

"This has nothing at all to do with your business interests, Father," Stefan cut in. "And Leah is not a stranger. She has been one of my closest friends and a fellow student for years. Her brother was in my class at the Ecole de Louvre and I know the Nazarre family well. They are fine, cultured and generous people. And would you like to know where they are now, Father? Mother? What your German friends have done with them?"

The Consul looked at Stefan and warned, "I think we should all be guarded in what we say on this matter, young man."

"Don't Stefan, please." Leah was tugging at Stefan's arm.

Stefan glared at his father, ignoring everyone else, his voice rising. "I have no intention, Father, of repudiating this marriage. And yes, I married her legally, here in the consulate, to keep her out of the clutches of your German cronies."

"You stupid young fool! Do you really think you can make a mockery of your country's diplomatic representative and of me?"

"Well, Father, if you don't want any unpleasantness, I suggest you make your car available to me and my wife, for our journey to the railway station tomorrow morning." Stefan ignored his father's wrath and continued. "Then we can be out of here and on our way to Switzerland at the earliest opportunity."

Count Svenssen's fury finally erupted and he moved over to take his son by the shoulders and shake him.

"How dare you speak to me like that, you useless layabout! I will do nothing for you and your Jewish bitch. She has curdled your brains to make use of our family name, and I'll have her handed over to the authorities as soon as possible."

The consul stepped between them, placing a restraining hand on Carl Svenssen's arm. Stefan spoke very quietly, but there was cold menace in his words. "If you do that, Father, I will go with her wherever she is sent. And I have arranged for a full account of this marriage, signed by myself, to go to the Swedish press and to newspapers in London and the United States, if you prevent me from leaving the country with my wife."

Aneka Svenssen had begun to weep. She poured herself a second brandy and sat down, her head bent. Stefan's face was grim. "Would you let him do that to me, Mother?" His voice softened. "Mother, help us please."

"Aneka!" Carl Svenssen spat the words at his wife. "Get out – go upstairs immediately. I will deal with this."

Aneka Svenssen drained her glass and left the room as the Count directed his wrath towards Marta and Anders. "You will hardly expect me to thank you for your role in all this. No doubt His Excellency here will be discussing this with you in the morning."

"Neither of them knew anything about Leah, Your Excellency, except that we were planning to elope together if necessary." Stefan turned back to address his father. "We want to leave for Switzerland tomorrow morning, Father. All we need is a car, and perhaps some help from His Excellency to obtain clearance for the train journey. I will never trouble you for anything else."

"I could drive them, sir," Anders said quickly. "That way they'll be gone from here first thing in the morning, and you can rely on Marta and myself to be discreet."

"See to the arrangements for one of the official cars, Anders, and have the clearance forms and travel permits prepared and stamped. I will sign them later this evening." The consul looked at Marta sternly. "Neither one of you is to discuss this marriage inside or outside of the consulate. I will hear details of your part in this affair tomorrow. Is that quite clear?"

When he turned his attention to Stefan and Leah his expression was sad but kindly. "You young people are embarking on a lifetime's journey, and I wish you all the courage that you will require. You are guests in your country's consulate tonight and I hope you will have a safe journey tomorrow. You, Pastor Bruzelius, must answer only to your conscience. And now I'll bid you all good evening."

The consul shook each one of them by the hand and left the room.

Moments passed before Count Svenssen could bring himself to speak. His voice came from between clenched teeth.

"I do not want to see this woman ever again." He looked at Leah with revulsion. "You have brought disaster with you, like all your kind, and you have made the Consul of Sweden and myself parties to a disgusting deception."

"Father . . ." Stefan stepped forward and extended his hand.

"Go upstairs, Stefan, and stay there until your departure tomorrow morning. You have put me in an impossible position. Take that woman and get out of my sight!" The Count opened his wallet and threw a large wad of notes on the table. "That is the last money you can expect from me. You are disinherited Stefan, and I assure you that she won't gain a penny from this liaison."

He turned on his heel leaving his son with his hand still out-stretched. Stefan picked up the notes and carefully folded them, putting them into his pocket. Leah took his hand. "Stefan, let's go upstairs."

Stefan ignored her, moving to the row of decanters on the side-board. He poured himself a full tumbler of whiskey and drank it.

"A safe journey to you both." Pastor Bruzelius put his hands on Leah's shoulders and then turned to Stefan who was refilling his glass. "God be with you Stefan. God be with you both."

"Come Leah, the bridal suite awaits." Stefan downed his second whiskey and held out his hand. "Marta, do you think you could organise a tray of food for us? It doesn't look as though we will be included in tonight's dinner party."

His smile was bitter as he led Leah towards the door. As they started across the hall the doorbell rang. A footman appeared and answered it. Leah's limbs turned to water as she looked at the man who entered. General Walter von Stroepper was impeccably attired, his uniform a statement in organised discipline. He was tall and very straight. His face would have been handsome but for the hardness of expression in the cold, pale eyes. Stefan froze where he stood, Leah a little behind him. The German officer was between them and their escape route to the staircase. The footman took General von Stroepper's coat, hat and cane as the consul appeared at his study door with Carl Svenssen. Formal greetings were exchanged. It was impossible to ignore the young couple on the edge of the circle. The consul general moved forward, graceful and unhurried. "Good evening Herr General. We are a little behind our schedule this evening. You know the Count, of course. We've been celebrating on his behalf."

"Count Svenssen." The general clicked his heels. "A celebration?"

There was an awkward silence, then Aneka Svenssen's voice floated from the landing above. She looked down at her son standing in the doorway, shielding his wife.

"My dear General, how good to see you again." She was smiling brilliantly as she descended the stairs. The general was captivated. She held out a bare arm. "May I present my son, Stefan, Herr General."

The general hardly seemed to notice the young man as he moved to the foot of the staircase and offered his hand to Aneka.

"Stefan is an artist," she continued. "He has been studying at the Ecole de Louvre where he met young Lise here. They have just been married."

"Indeed! My congratulations Herr Svenssen, Fräu." Walter von Stroepper turned as Stefan urged Leah forward. His cold gaze travelled over her slim figure and he smiled at her, his lips slightly open, perfect teeth on view for a second. But there was no hint of a smile in his eyes. "Shall we have the pleasure of your company at dinner?"

"Good gracious no." Aneka broke in with a purring laugh. "Lise's family is from the South, near Marseilles where we've just been. And our newlyweds are leaving tomorrow morning for their honeymoon in Switzerland."

"How very disappointing not to have such fine young people with us for the evening. My congratulations to you both," Walter von

Stroepper moved closer to Leah. "What is your family involved in, Fräu Svenssen? It's such a beautiful area. I know it well. Perhaps we have common acquaintances?"

Aneka rushed into the conversation once more. "Now, you know young love, Herr General. The Consul has kindly arranged for a champagne supper, upstairs. We have said our goodbyes, and they are going to . . ." she raised her eyebrows, deliberately flirting with him, "To retire, shall we say. And we mustn't stand in the way of wedded bliss."

Von Stroepper gazed down at her bosom and appeared agreeably preoccupied as Aneka drew a deep breath and looked for a long moment into his eyes. Then she turned again to the newlyweds. "Now my dears, off you go. You have an early start tomorrow." Her back was to her German dinner companion, her face bleak.

Leah felt the cold resentment directed at her like a stab to the heart, but she was grateful for Aneka's intervention. "Goodnight," she whispered. "And thank you."

Aneka turned abruptly and was gone in a swirl of chiffon. Stefan and Leah fled upstairs and stood trembling in the security of the guest suite. A tray had been placed on the table, laden with cold meats, a bottle of champagne and a vintage red wine. Marta had left a red rose on each plate. Leah tried a smile. Stefan walked over to the tray and poured himself a glass of wine. He stared at Leah, this strange blonde woman to whom he was now married. He drank his wine without pausing as his wife unpinned her hat and let the peroxide tresses fall around her face. Then he topped up his glass.

"Stefan, don't."

"Don't what, Leah?" Everything came apart inside his head. "Don't drink myself into a stupor? Because I know you don't want me as a husband. But at least you're safe now, whatever has happened, and tomorrow we can leave for Switzerland. So, you take the bed and I'll sleep on the chair."

"You didn't sleep on the chair last night," she said in a low voice.

He shook his head. Things were getting blurred, confused. "It wasn't the same. And you were frightened and cold. You needed someone to warm you."

"Stefan . . ." She was opening the buttons of her jacket. He could see her silk chemise. He poured another glass of wine and swallowed it in two long draughts.

"Listen to me, Stefan. I know that you married me to protect me. But I've always known about Helena. I understand all this and I realise you still love her. I cannot believe how courageous and generous you've been and I am overwhelmed by your bravery, by what you have done for me. And now we must go on, Stefan. We must attempt to love each other in our own ways, and take care of each other. I can try to do this, Stefan, if you will let me." She slid the skirt down over her hips and stood before him in her slip.

A jumble of emotions shook him – admiration at her honesty and beauty, rage at her persecutors, at his parents, and at everyone who had insulted her and robbed her of any choice in her life. Now, with her ash-blonde hair, she reminded him of his mother. He hated himself for his rising desire, for wanting Helena, for wanting everything to be different. He reached for her and carried her to the bed. His lovemaking was without tenderness, a heady combination of reaction to the fear and stress of the last two days, and triumph at having stood up to his father. The whiskey he had drunk, along with the wine, made him rough and insistent. When he had spent himself she lay under him, very still, afraid if she woke him it would bring him back to her in the same black mood of desperation. At last he rolled aside in a deep sleep, leaving her to lie wide-eyed in the darkness. She could not imagine that Stefan would ever truly love her, tortured as he was by guilt and regret. And Seamus. What of her love for Seamus? But this was too much for her to consider and she pushed the thought of him from her mind, because she knew that her nerve would fail if she

174

dwelt on her treasured memories of him. She knew that she would always love him. Wiping silent tears from her face, she turned on her side and closed her eyes.

Stefan woke her before dawn. He was kneeling by her side, his eyes bloodshot, his face puffy.

"Leah I'm sorry for last night." He touched her shoulder gently. "Please forgive me."

She placed her fingers on his stubbled jaw. "Nothing was normal yesterday, Stefan. We had all been through too much." She sat up, her body aching. "I'll get dressed, we'll be leaving soon."

"Yes. Anders just called. We must be ready in twenty minutes. Leah, it will be all right. It will."

"I know, Stefan." Her soul was filled with weariness. She was no longer able to evaluate or rationalise the events of the past two days. "Do you think you can get me some coffee? I'll go and wash."

Leah dressed quickly and drank the hot coffee that Marta brought. Then they slipped down the stairs to Anders and out to the car. As they drove away from the sanctuary of the consulate, the German sentries saluted smartly, and then they were speeding through the empty streets.

"Take a left here, Anders," Stefan said.

"It's not the best way to the station."

"Just a small detour, trust me."

Leah sat up straight, her heart thumping as Stefan directed them through a maze of small streets.

"We haven't much time, Stefan." Anders was worried.

"Stop here." At the corner of the street a scruffy old man was setting up a paper stall. The car drew to a halt, and Stefan jumped out. He muttered something to the paper seller and then called out in a louder tone. "Could you bring a paper to the lady please?"

The old man turned. Leah caught her breath and started to get out of the car. Daniel crossed to the door and put a restraining hand on hers. "No, Leah. We have only a minute." He handed her a folded newspaper.

"Oh Daniel! Papa, everyone . . ." Her tears were hot, her throat closing.

"Don't talk about them. There's no time. Just remember, the only way we can help them is to fight back. They were taken away to a work camp. If I get any news I'll contact you through Stefan."

"You know about the wedding? What Stefan has done?"

"It was the only way to get you out and he's a brave man. I know it's hard for you, but least you can get safely to Switzerland."

Anders glanced back. At the end of the street he could see a patrol car. "Time to get out."

Daniel raised his hand in a farewell salute. "All the news is in that paper."

"Daniel . . ." A desperate pain spread through Leah's body.

"You can help only if you leave, Leah. There are messages for Richard. Get them to him from Switzerland. Tell him what you've seen. Send back what we need. It will be over one day, Leah. We'll all be able to live our lives again, and we will have made it so. Now go. Go!"

Stefan slammed the door and the car sped away. In the rear-view mirror Leah could see the doddering old man, a Gauloise hanging from his mouth, sorting out the morning papers for his stand. The patrol car stopped beside him. She saw him shrug, gesture, spit in the gutter, wave his hands vaguely.

As the train pulled out, crawling through the Paris suburbs under a rain-soaked sky, Leah gazed out of the window, seeing her city sliding away into the grey morning. Stefan watched her, wondering how he could ever bring back the laughing girl he had known before their world had changed. He drew her towards him and at last she rested her head on his shoulder and fell asleep. The train rumbled on through the countryside, smoke from the engine drifting upwards into the sagging pewter sky.

There was a screech of brakes and a hiss as they came into a small station and shuddered to a halt. Stefan gently moved Leah's head and rose to his feet. He stretched and stepped out into the corridor to look out of the window. It was then that he saw the German patrol on the platform. They were questioning a guard, showing him what appeared to be a photograph. Two officers boarded the train as it pulled slowly away from the platform. Stefan stepped back into the compartment and shook Leah urgently, pulling her to her feet in panic. "There are Germans soldiers on the train, Leah. I don't know what they want, but they had photographs and they were questioning the guard."

"But what could they do to us, Stefan?"

"They're looking for somebody. We're not safe until we are out of France, Leah. I don't believe anyone could have tipped them off, but we can't take the risk. When the train pulls clear of the village and into the countryside, we're going to jump."

She looked at him, dumb with fear. Then she bent to gather her few possessions and prepared to follow her husband.

Chapter 23

St Joseph de Caune, 1970

Solange stood laughing in the midst of farewells, congratulations and embraces. Then everyone was gone, and the only sound in the night was the rush of the river.

They followed Henri inside and sat down in the library.

"Papa, your decision is wonderful. And I want to be a part of it." Solange clinked her glass against his. "It's obvious Edouard is dedicated to making this scheme a success. There'll be no stopping you both."

"You certainly astonished us all this evening, with your announcement. You really are a crafty old fox." Guy was shaking his head, taking the measure of Henri anew. "When did you make this momentous decision?"

"Well, the more I considered his plan, the more merit it seemed to have." Henri was plainly delighted by the news he had sprung on them all. "So I went to discuss it with my bank, and with Pierre Etienne my lawyer. To my surprise the bank was cautious but interested, and offered me some leeway with funds."

"But you have to be careful that you retain control Papa," Solange said. "Your new partner is enthusiastic, but he's also very ambitious for himself, and there has been bad feeling between our families in the past. You don't know yet whether he's the kind of person whose strength is in producing a good idea, but who perhaps doesn't have the staying power to see it through."

"Are you having doubts already?" Henri looked offended.

"No, of course I don't doubt you."

"Just my ability to run a successful, innovative vineyard?"

"Oh Papa, you're reading this all wrong. And I'm going to be here with you. I'm going to be part of all this."

"You may not feel quite so keen when I explain that this project will rob you of some financial security." Henri turned towards Guy. "You might ask me to take her back, Guy, since she won't have much of a dowry after tonight."

Solange laughed and went to sit on the arm of Henri's chair, her bare, golden arm around his shoulders. For a moment, Guy, looking at them, felt as though he would always be an outsider. He experienced a twinge of sadness, perhaps of jealousy, as Solange hugged her father.

"I didn't know you were giving away a dowry with me, Papa. Guy should be offering you huge herds of livestock and chests of gold coins for a treasure like me."

"Well, I could do with a few oxen to help plough up my old vines. But, my dears, this will affect some plans I had for you both. I was going to present you with a nest egg which you could use to set up your home in Montpellier." Henri rose, and helped himself to another large cognac.

Guy was silent as his future father-in-law crossed the room with a sure step, and poured a generous measure into the young man's glass.

"I'm sure Solange is mystified as to where I suddenly found the finance for this enterprise. But for many years, Celine and I built up a fund to take care of emergencies, including my disability. And we had money put aside for you, Solange, for the time when you married. I haven't needed the money up to now, and I'm going to gamble that I won't need it for myself."

"I'd much rather you . . ." Solange broke in but Henri shook his head to silence her.

"But I've also had to mortgage part of our property to be sure of having sufficient working capital for this huge venture. And the Olliviers will have to do the same."

"Well, I think I'll be able to take care of my bride all alone," Guy said smiling.

"I must also admit that I hope Solange will be involved in the project," Henri continued. "I'd like to think that she'll come home regularly to see what is happening to her enterprising father."

Solange put her arms around him, blinking away unexpected tears. She could not bear to think ahead to his loneliness, to solitary evenings when there might be no one to read to him, talk to him, love him. She could not imagine not being near to him and to their vineyards. "Papa, I'll never lose interest in our wine, just because I live an hour or so away. Guy and I will be here every weekend, I know. And I'm sure I can come to help on weekdays too, at the beginning."

Henri's smile registered relief. He put down his glass. "Well, I think it's time we went to bed. I said I'd meet Edouard tomorrow afternoon at Roucas Blancs, and I'd like it very much if you were there, Solange, along with Joel. Goodnight, both of you. It's been a memorable evening for us all."

Solange made her way upstairs, stopping briefly at Henri's door to wish him a last goodnight. She was smiling when she heard Guy open her bedroom door. He came to stand beside her, and she was surprised when he did not touch her.

"I don't think you were very realistic back there, Solange."

"Realistic about what?" She looked at him, frowning.

"Well, I think you should be careful about the signals you send to Henri. He needs your encouragement, but you're not going to be in a position to help him much with this new venture. He'll have to find his own method of dealing with Edouard Ollivier and the new vineyards. Personally, I came close to hitting that arrogant bastard tonight."

"Good heavens, Guy, this has been the happiest evening we've had here since before Mama died. Don't get all glum and spoil it. You're not jealous are you? Oh you are sweet." She began to laugh and to reach out for him, but he kept her at arm's length.

"I suppose it's flattering for you to be considered a goddess of the vineyards, Solange, but that man is downright unpleasant. And you are not going to be here to handle your father's business dealings with him."

"A goddess of the vineyards? Did Edouard say that?" She moved away from him, still laughing. "It certainly doesn't sound like you!"

"I don't think you heard me, Solange. We are not going to be able to spend every weekend here, and it isn't fair to give Henri that impression and then disappoint him. And you've obviously forgotten that we were going to go into Montpellier together, tomorrow afternoon."

"Well – not every weekend, perhaps. But Papa will need a great deal of help, especially at the beginning. You surely don't expect me to abandon him altogether? And we can go to Montpellier the day after tomorrow. You're being a little selfish, aren't you?"

"I hardly think you are in a position to describe anyone else as selfish."

"Oh? And how is that?" Her tone was cold.

"Hasn't it occurred to you that it was selfish to rush off last week, leaving your father to fret over your disappearance? And where were you anyway, Solange?"

"If you had any real understanding of me, Guy, you'd know that I would never have done such a thing unless I was deeply upset." Solange stopped brushing out her hair and threw down the brush.

"I've been hoping you would tell me. Come now Solange, don't be silly. We don't want to quarrel." He put his hands around her waist.

"This has been a perfect evening, and we should both be very happy with the outcome."

He bent to kiss her, but she turned away from him.

"I see you're very tired, darling. And it's no wonder when you had to organise such an elegant evening all by yourself. I think you should get some sleep now. Goodnight, Solange." He bent over and kissed the top of her head, then closed the door quietly.

Solange lay back, furious at having been put to bed like a recalcitrant child. She pushed at the pillows angrily. Guy should have pressed her for an explanation as to why she had gone away. And why could he not see how important it was for her to help her father now, at the start of this new venture? She switched out the light, and after a while her angry mood faded.

She stared out at the distant stars, and felt herself floating up into the velvet night. Somewhere across the valley she imagined Edouard Ollivier looking at the same sky, planning the new vineyards, dreaming of their first great vintage. He could provide her beloved father with a new direction, with excitement and challenge. She imagined Henri during their first *vendange*, tasting and blending the new wine until it was all they wanted it to be. They would share the triumph and recognition they deserved, and she would be their wine goddess, steeped in the nectar of their success. Beneath the sheets she ran her palms over her breasts and down her stomach, along the smooth skin of her thighs. And then she drifted away to sleep, smiling into the soft, receiving darkness.

On the following afternoon Solange and Henri drove up the twisting road out of the valley to reach the point where their property joined the Ollivier hectares. Between the dipping, sloping acres of the *garrigue* lay patches of vines, their roots clutching stubbornly at the shallow soil. When they came at last to the new vineyards, their neat rows and stakes evidence of meticulous planning and attention,

Solange stopped the car. "I'm looking at his experimental vines, Papa. They're strong and healthy, and you'll smile when you touch them. He must manicure them every hour on the hour. There isn't a single weed to be seen."

At the house Paul Ollivier and his son were waiting to greet them.

"Well, Edouard, my lawyer has given me a draft partnership agreement with some scepticism," said Henri. "But before we discuss it, let's go out and see the foundations of our folly."

They drove out into the vineyards, this time with Edouard, to view the beginnings of his enterprise. In the first area they visited, he had planted several hectares on a gently sloping section of land where the earth was red in colour and very fine, and the roots were buried in chunks of limestone. Edouard took Henri by the arm and talked him through the land, describing the nature of the soil, the drainage, the quality and potential yield of the vines. They walked on together, a bond already forming between them as they became engrossed in the details of their plans. Solange and Paul followed a few paces behind.

Edouard turned to Solange. "Where's Guy, by the way? I suppose too much time in the countryside might prove a little wearing for him? That's something you'll have to think about in your new life away from here."

Paul cleared his throat and stared hard at his son. "Well. Ah, let's see. Now that you've been over the new vineyards, perhaps we should return to the house for an aperitif. Why don't you come with me Henri? And the young people can drive that rattling old buggy of mine."

In the dusty truck, Edouard glanced at Solange. Her face was set and closed. "How dare you address me like that!" She made no attempt to conceal her fury. "I don't want to spoil this afternoon for my father with this kind of nonsense. You have no right to comment on my fiancé in those terms. He's a lawyer in Montpellier, and that's where he has to spend most of his time. It's no' worse and no better than your being out in your vineyards."

"You're right," he replied. His face, however, was sullen and showed no signs of remorse.

They rode in silence to the house. Solange began to relax. A silly storm in a teacup created by minor forces, a kneejerk reaction to his irksome comments, on both their parts. It really wasn't important. She smiled at Edouard as they entered the house and was relieved when he grinned back at her, raking his hand through his dark hair. His eyes were shining like black pools, and she saw them flash with some expression she could not quantify.

"All the same," he said, "I still wonder whether you'll be happy away from the vineyards. Whether you will really be satisfied in some suburban villa in Montpellier when you could be here, in the thick of this new project with your father and me."

Before she had time to form a sharp, clever response he was gone, striding ahead of her into the dim old house, where his new partner awaited him.

Chapter 24

Connemara, 1970

Several days had passed, days of quiet recuperation for Helena, filled with long walks and painting and sleeping. Seamus and Eleanor watched her haunted expression begin to soften, saw her face and body relax a little. For a time Eleanor, too, felt suspended in an altered existence, far from gnawing doubt and unanswered questions, content to let her uncle gradually reveal his past. Exercise and the bracing air brought a glow back to her face and she went to bed early and rose refreshed. Her work proved as absorbing as she had hoped. She made good progress with the Kennedy manuscript and kept in touch with Gareth through long phone calls each afternoon.

"Up Lazybones!" Seamus knocked on her door on the morning of their fifth day. "I've left the makings of breakfast for you. I'm going down to the surgery to give Jim a hand for the morning."

Eleanor smiled and stretched. Dear Seamus. She knew Jim Walsh, his retired partner, enjoyed being back at work and was staying on for three more weeks, but already her uncle was anxious to get back to his surgery and the work he loved.

"Where's Mother?"

"Breakfasted early and gone out to paint. The weather forecast isn't great for the afternoon, so she wanted to get as much time out of doors as possible. Maybe you could take her some coffee later."

After breakfast she went outside. The dog was already up on the hill, chasing rabbits. She could see her mother in the distance, out on the rocks, further down from where she had been working over the last few days. Eleanor set off along the beach. Looking up into the wide sky, and over to the haze of the mountains, she felt at last that the worst was over and that now they could begin anew.

"We've turned the corner," she thought, and a wave of gratitude washed over her. "We are mending. Whatever revelations come now will bring less pain and we will be able to accept them as part of our lives, our family history."

When she reached the point, she called out to her mother. Helena smiled and came to sit on a flat rock beside her daughter, sipping her coffee companionably. The wind had risen slightly, but there were still bright, sunny patches between the fast-moving banks of cloud.

"There'll be a storm this evening I'd say." She was gazing out to sea. "Maybe a Force 8!"

Eleanor knew Helena's uncanny knowledge of the wind and weather. It seemed instinctive in her, as it was in Seamus. These two possessed an affinity which enabled them to feel and understand things together that other people could not begin to comprehend. Eleanor felt a tug of envy. She wished she and James were that close. Perhaps it had to do with her own insecurity. If she could only break down this stupid wall she had built around herself, perhaps she would be able to share more with her own twin.

Helena was speaking, and Eleanor realised she was talking about another storm, about the past and about Richard. Without any prompting, she was telling the story of the voyage back from France in 1940. Eleanor listened spellbound.

"When we put out to sea that night from St Brieuc, there was a wind just like this, and a heavy swell outside the shelter of the harbour. I've never minded that, neither has Seamus. I suppose being brought up on boats you don't get seasick. I've always found storms exhilarating. There's something about wind and rain and a rushing sea that makes you feel a part of the elements. But that night was different. Seamus had fallen in love and he'd had to leave his girl behind. He was carrying his own storm inside. I ached with his pain, but then of course, I had Richard."

Helena stopped, her eyes shining into the dark tunnel of the past. "He was so sick. So dreadfully, appallingly sick. Soon after we got into the channel beyond the Ile de Bréhat, the boat began to yaw from side to side. We were standing on deck in the darkness. He was sheltering me inside his jacket and I could feel his heartbeat." She closed her eyes momentarily. "He always had a special smell that I loved. I would press my face against him and breathe it in, like taking his essence inside me."

She was silent again for a little while, her eyes fixed on some point out beyond the bay. Eleanor did not dare to move.

"Then I felt him begin to droop. He retched for hours, while I sponged his face, tried to ease his discomfort. I was anxious that he would become dehydrated. Seamus couldn't leave the deck. The wind was vicious and he'd had to pull in most of his sail and run some rope aft, to steady the boat. I'd never been in such a ferocious storm."

She laughed, a tender, gentle laugh, as she continued, talking to herself in a voice that was low and clear. "He was clammy, cold, shivering, and his lips were chapped. I climbed into the bunk with him, and in those desperate hours I knew we were for ever. It didn't matter any more if we never made it to Ireland. I would shelter him and hold him close, even if we went down. Sick as he was, I knew he felt it too. He said, over and over again with each crash of the ship, 'I love you Helena, I love you. Don't ever let me go. I want you with me always.'"

Tears gathered in Helena's eyes as she saw Richard in that capsule of time, some thirty years before. Eleanor wanted to reach out and comfort her, but she knew she must not stir or she would break the spell. Helena's voice was rough and hoarse with longing when she spoke again. "For almost three days we had to run before the wind, heading south into the Atlantic on a massive, following sea. The boat plunged down each watery slope, then rose at an impossible angle, as though she would rear right up and capsize. Seamus and Ronan and Ciaran took turns at the helm, lashed to the wheel to prevent themselves being washed overboard. The wind howled and the rain lashed incessantly."

Helena took off her old hat, pushed her hair back, and clutched at the brim with her fingers. Suddenly, Eleanor had a clear recollection of her father wearing the same hat when they went out walking. That was why Helena loved it so, put it on when she was painting out of doors. Oh God, how lonely her mother was without him, how totally lost.

"I woke to see Seamus gazing down at us, dripping and swaying." Helena had resumed her story. "The sea had gone down. The dreadful noise had stopped. 'I think it's over,' he said. 'Ronan and Ciaran are taking this watch.' He shut his eyes and toppled into the opposite bunk, still in his wet gear. As he collapsed into oblivion, I heard him say something, barely audible in his exhaustion, 'Thank God you're safe Helena, you and Richard. But Leah . . . Oh God, Leah, Leah.'

"Not long afterwards, Richard opened his eyes, those piercing eyes that could always read my soul. For the first time since we'd set sail he smiled. 'Helena O'Riordan,' he whispered to me. 'You have been sleeping with me, you're a fallen woman! An immediate wedding is the only solution. Do you think Seamus, as captain of this vessel, could marry us now?'

"'I don't think Seamus is capable of anything coherent right now. And just because I'm in your bed, it doesn't mean I've been taking advantage of you, Professor Kirwan. You haven't been exactly in your prime.' He touched me then, so gently, so tenderly, and gave me a funny little smile.

"'Just promise me, Helena, that we won't have to wait too long. Promise me.' We held each other in the rolling cabin, with the first signs of light filtering through the galley door, and Seamus snoring on the bunk opposite us. And we were married by old Father Connolly, here in Roundstone, a few weeks later."

She leaned back and sighed, stroking the brim of her hat, her gaze turning towards the village beyond the point. "Even Granny Kirwan, with her unyielding expression, could not blight my happiness that day. She came down from Dublin, and sat like a death's-head at the feast, so stern and joyless. But Seamus lent us his cottage and we spent our first night together in Dada and Angela's big bed. I wished that they could have known how happy we were." Even now she shivered with delight. Then her face darkened. "Poor Seamus, he tried hard to hide his grief. He was so generous, so unselfish. In the beginning she wrote to him nearly every day. Then the letters became different, no longer full of longing and love. He knew they were censored. We began to hear stories about what the Germans were doing to Jewish families in Paris, how they had been thrown out of their jobs, made to wear special stars on their clothes, forbidden to listen to the wireless or use the telephone. Then Leah's letters stopped altogether. Seamus became frantic. Richard went back to his post in the university, but he and Seamus were putting together things that they might be able to send over to France for the resistance movement that was starting. They got radio crystals, and equipment for the underground newspapers, and money too. They were in touch with Daniel Nazarre, Leah's brother, through the Swedish consulate at first. On two occasions they sailed out to the Bay of Biscay, to rendezvous with a Breton fishing boat. They handed over their cargo then headed back to Ireland. It all seemed such an adventure."

She paused remembering. "It was difficult back in Dublin. Dorothea, Richard's mother, expected us to live with her. It was a big house, too big for her by herself. I felt we needed to be on our own. But he was her only son, she said. He'd been away a long time and she was getting old. I gave in and we moved in there but during university holidays we drove down to Connemara. I wanted to be close to Seamus, to comfort him. And I was desperately afraid for my friends in Paris. Dorothea Kirwan didn't like me much. I think she wanted me under her eye, so I wouldn't lead her son into bad habits. She was deeply suspicious of my painting, even though I was beginning to sell quite well. And we had no children. I lost one at five months. Stillborn. After that, nothing. I think she suspected that I didn't want any more. If she could only have seen how I longed to carry his life in me, bear a child that he had planted in my body."

Helena ran her fingers through her hair, living again that loss and sense of failure, when darkness had enveloped her and she found she could not even paint. Her voice sank to a whisper, and Eleanor had to strain to hear what she was saying. "Everyone I loved seemed to be taken from me. Seamus and I, losing our mother at birth. Then I lost Seamus, who was my other self, when we were sent away to school. And afterwards Dada, my anchor in a harsh world. I feared that everyone I depended on or loved deeply would be lost to me. Only my painting was real."

Eleanor thought of her father's last days. The memory tore at her and she wanted to speak out, but she bit hard into her lip. There was a torrent pouring from Helena at last, a deluge of sorrow. Perhaps these were the words that would begin her mother's healing.

"It was Seamus who helped me through Dada's death. He brought me back to Seal Bay. Made me draw a picture of Dada, and put in it everything I could remember about him. Say in it all the things I wanted to tell him. Then we let it float out on to the water, just as he had done with his poems on the day we first left Roundstone to go away to school. Later, when Angela began to get frail, Seamus came back from Galway and began his practice here. She lived with him until she died, three years later."

Helena was silent for a long time. When she spoke again her voice was stronger. "It was Richard who gave me back hope, after the baby's death. So tiny he was, our little son. I wanted to see him and Richard insisted that I should be allowed. We laid him out, wrapped in a linen towel and we had a priest baptise him Richard Seamus. He was buried in the family plot. Then a mist came down on me and I couldn't hear or see anything clearly. It went on for weeks. I was frightened. I hated it, but I couldn't stop it. Everything was grey. I couldn't find colours any more.

"One day Richard came home early. He arrived in a horse and carriage full of flowers from the stalls in Grafton Street, bunches and bunches of them." Helena was smiling again, twisting the hat. "He drove up to the front door, and came upstairs to the bedroom. He took me down to the cab, lifted me in and told the cabbie to take us for a drive. He said our baby was in a garden surrounded by beautiful blooms like these, because he had been so much loved and wanted. And he begged me to paint the garden that I saw, and set the child free to run in it, to feel the sun on his spirit."

Eleanor knew the picture. It hung in her mother's bedroom. There was something about the light that gave it an ethereal quality. It was titled *His Garden*.

"He did things like that, a reserved man who could blaze out his love and not care who saw it. And I let him go to France without me." Helena's voice had become harsh. She stood up abruptly and returned to the canvas she had been working on. Eleanor followed, afraid to lose what might come next. She saw the painting for the first time, a ship, rising out of a storm with her father's face there, floating in the wind and the water.

"I should have gone with him. We were meant to be always together. Like that last night here on the mountainside, before they sailed for France. When the boat came back without Richard, and with Seamus so badly hurt, it was like the old curse striking out at me again. And yet I knew he wasn't dead. I knew in the whole of my being that if he had died, I would have felt it. I nearly died myself, giving birth. I think that was the beginning of Grandma's Kirwan's forgiveness for me. She had blamed me for letting Richard go. But at least I had done the right thing before he left. Seamus stayed with me for the delivery, and when I was strong enough, he took me back to Roundstone, and I nursed my new babies and longed for my husband."

"Oh Mother!" Eleanor could not remain silent any longer. At that moment she loved her mother with a fierceness she had not known she possessed. Helena did not even notice the interruption, continuing her trancelike narrative in a low, bitter voice that Eleanor had never heard before.

"More than three years he was gone. After the first communication saying he was alive, there was a second message several weeks later to say he was coming out. And then nothing. Not a single word. Seamus and I tried to trace him through the Red Cross, through the embassy networks. But there was nothing. When the war ended, Seamus went to look for him. He found him in Paris and brought him home. But he was like an empty shell. I couldn't find my resting place in him any more. He was imprisoned somewhere, though he tried." Her face crumpled and she lingered over a brush stroke, as if trying to summon him back from the abyss into which he had disappeared. "He had terrible dreams. Many nights he would wake up, sweating and screaming. I lay with him in my arms as we had lain in the bunk during the storm, and I tried to soothe his trembling, stroke him back to sleep. I had my husband back but I couldn't find a way to bring him out of the darkness. When Elizabeth was born, that's when it eventually happened." Helena's voice trailed away into silence and she seemed to become aware of Eleanor. Her faraway expression gave way to one of shock.

"Eleanor!" Her tone was sharp, almost resentful, as if she had caught her daughter eavesdropping.

Eleanor felt a flash of rejection, then resentment. Helena would not have used that tone with Elizabeth – Elizabeth, the love child of their reunion. "But all that time there was someone else. Solange's mother!" she burst out. "How could he do that to you after all the promises he made? How could he?"

"Don't dwell on that." Helena's voice was cold.

"But I don't understand it. Did you know about her? Did you ever feel her there in his thoughts? Did he tell you? Or was he giving you his all, and then speeding back to France to do the same for her?"

She wanted to stop, knew she should stop. The words were cruel and ugly but she could not help herself.

"I don't want to talk about this." Helena's face had that closed look that her daughter had come to hate.

"You never want to talk!" Eleanor shouted. "You're locked away with your passionate memories, while we're in limbo, James and I, and even your precious Elizabeth. We're still alive, we're still here and you can't even see us. We should be able to find out how we came to have a half-sister we never knew about."

"No. I don't want to discuss it."

"No one wants to say anything. Why? For fear of upsetting the dead? You're our mother, surely you can tell us. We're not trying to lay blame. We just want to know!"

Helena turned on her in an icy fury. "You want to poke about in the raw wounds of my marriage, so that you can make yourself feel better. How dare you! You have no right to ask me intimate questions about my relationship with my husband."

Eleanor had never seen such ferocity, such venom in Helena. The blast of it, directed at her, shrivelled her up.

"No! It wasn't meant like that at all. It wasn't." She began to stumble away, still apologising in distraught, disjointed phrases. "I just thought if I could understand that I could help. But I've done it so stupidly, so clumsily. I'm sorry."

She turned and ran, back along the beach.

Helena, trembling, called after her. "Wait Eleanor! Come back here, please! Oh damn! Damn!"

Helena kicked her easel and it toppled over. The painting landed face down on the sand. She screamed out at the top of her voice. "Blast you, Richard Kirwan! Is there no end to this agony you've left us?" She sat down and began to wipe her canvas, clearing off the sand and grit, saying softly, "Give me time, God. Please give me some time, give me some peace . . ."

Chapter 25

Connemara, 1970

Eleanor fled to the house and stood leaning against the kitchen door. She needed to talk to someone. She had never meant to cause such pain. She took several long breaths to calm herself. James. She ran into the hall and dialled.

"Law Library, Four Courts. Can I help you?"

"I'd like to speak to James Kirwan please. This is his sister. It's urgent."

Eleanor waited, trying to stop her hands from trembling, wondering how she would begin.

"I'm sorry, Miss Kirwan, James isn't here. He's in France until Friday."

"In France? Are you sure of that?"

"Yes, Miss Kirwan. There's a case he's gone to settle in Paris, and a conference. Can I take a message?"

"No, it's all right. I'll catch up with him at the end of the week. Thank you."

She put down the telephone. Now she was shaking in earnest. Gone to France? With a sickening realisation Eleanor remembered his odd expression, her suspicion that he was keeping something back from her. He must have known before she left for Connemara. A slow fury began to burn in her head. She rang home and the housekeeper answered.

"Mrs Kenny, it's Eleanor. Is everything all right there?"

"Fine, Miss Eleanor, thank you. You just caught me. I'm leaving now to spend two days with my sister. With no one at home, James said this would be an ideal time. How is your mother?"

"She's coming along well, thanks. The sea air is good for her and she's painting again. Mrs Kenny, could you just check in the diary and see when James is going to be back from France?"

"Sunday, I think, Miss Eleanor. Yes, he and Elizabeth will be back on Sunday evening."

"Elizabeth? She's gone as well?"

There was a pause. "Oh dear, perhaps I wasn't supposed to mention that. Isn't it some kind of surprise?"

"Not to worry Mrs Kenny." Eleanor fought to keep her voice normal, to stop herself from screaming with rage. "I knew there was a plan afoot, so there's no harm done. I'll call back at the weekend. If they telephone, no need to tell them you mentioned the secret and spoil things for them. Thank you, goodbye."

She dropped the phone, and rested her head against the wall. They had planned this, packed her off so that they could go to France without her. Solange's letter, her mother's accusation, and now this. How could they? How could they? The kitchen door opened and Seamus came into the house, laden with packages. At the sight of her his slow smile lit up his face.

"Oh El, I didn't see you there. Look, I've brought some freshly caught fish for lunch." A second look at her told him something was terribly wrong. "Eleanor? What's the matter, what's happened?"

"I made a mess of it." Her words streamed out, unstoppable. "Mother said I was poking and prying just to satisfy myself. That I had no right. I'm a monster, Seamus. That's what I am."

"For God's sake, that's ridiculous. You're hypersensitive. You're putting things into . . ."

"No, that's the way she feels about me. I'm no use to her, no use

196

at all!" Eleanor was sobbing. "She was so angry. And then I came in to ring James for his advice. Only he wasn't at the law library. He's in France. James has gone to France, and Lizzie too. They went together."

"Oh dear."

Something in the way Seamus spoke, his resignation and lack of surprise, caught her attention.

"You knew!" she shouted at him. The betrayal was complete. She straightened up and faced him, her eyes blazing. "My God, you knew, you of all people! Yes, they'd confide in you, of course they would. And you advised them not to tell me, damn you. Wasn't that it, Seamus? Wasn't it?"

"No, Eleanor. It wasn't like that at all."

She rushed on, ignoring his denial, her voice rising. "Good old Eleanor is needed to drive people around the countryside, act as nurse, make meals, say comforting things, walk the dogs. But she's not to be trusted with anything important. No one need bother to let her know what's really going on."

Seamus shook his head, distressed. "They were only trying to spare you. You were so upset by the letter from Solange."

"Spare me? Spare me from what? From living? Well damn the whole lot of you! You can keep your sordid secrets to yourselves. To hell with you all!" She snatched up her car keys from the hall table and opened the front door. The wind had picked up and a flurry of dust and leaves danced in the driveway.

"Eleanor, where are you going?" Seamus, paralysed for a moment by her outburst, found his voice. He ran outside as she got into the car. "Wait Eleanor. Calm down, please. Let's go inside and talk."

She slammed the car door and turned on the ignition. Seamus thought how like Richard she was in her fury – the same dark brows meeting in a black frown over angry eyes, the same stubborn set of the jaw.

"Eleanor, don't go like this."

She revved the engine, shouting at him through the window.

"You don't need me. Neither does Mother. You've got each other and you can drown in all your memories and your bloody angst, without any interference from me. James and Elizabeth can do as they please and you and Mother can go on brooding. But you can do it without me."

"Where are you going?" Seamus made a last attempt, shouting after her into the rising wind, but she was gone. Stupid, so stupid. He had known how affected she would be if she discovered what James and Elizabeth had planned. He should have done more to stop them. And what in God's name had happened between her and Helena? He had tried to warn his niece to go slowly. But Helena must have said something dreadful. She seemed to have forgotten that her children were grieving too. He sighed in frustration as he walked slowly back to the kitchen door. Helena was standing at the corner of the house and he wondered how long she had been there.

"Well Helena, I'm at a loss on this one, I'm afraid," he said. "And I'm partly to blame. What the hell are we going to do now?"

She walked past him without responding. He heard her in the sitting room, lighting the fire, adding a log and some turf, opening the drinks cabinet.

"I have to do a house call. If Eleanor phones, tell her we're expecting her back in time for supper. And be gentle. She's left her work and come down here to help you, Helena. I think you should keep that in mind."

When he returned two hours later there was no news of Eleanor. He picked up the telephone and started dialling, but after a dozen calls he had failed to trace her. Helena was curled up in an armchair, her head bowed, twirling her glass round and round in her hands. Seamus threw some turf on to the fire and a shower of sparks flew up from the blue and orange flame. He saw them reflected in his sister's eyes, in her hair, but she did not look up at him or speak.

"Well, I've tried everyone I can think of," he said. "I can only suppose she's gone some place where she can be on her own. But she left her handbag behind and her house keys."

He glanced at Helena again, his face creased with worry. She seemed to have slipped away into some distant world. He thought of Eleanor's look just before she drove away, and anxiety rose in him again. How much fuel did she have in the car? She hadn't stopped in Roundstone to fill up. He had checked with the garage. She had just vanished. Gareth Duggan had not heard from her, but Seamus asked him to keep checking the house, and any other places she might go.

"Of course it's possible she might not return to Dublin at all," he said to Gareth. "She may have decided to go somewhere she can be on her own entirely."

He stoked the fire unnecessarily, then shifted his big frame round to look at his sister. She was still staring into the flames, silent and remote. He felt suddenly angry. How could she retreat from them all like this. He had never realised how self-absorbed she had become.

"Damn it Helena, you've got to talk to me. This is your problem too." He reached down and took the glass from her hands, gripping her fingers, forcing her to meet his eyes. She looked at him for a second, then dropped her gaze to stare at the carpet. "What brought this on? Eleanor was so distraught." He passed a hand across his eyes. "And I didn't help. I should never have kept quiet about James and Lizzie going to France."

Her head snapped back. Seamus saw her staring at him in disbelief and groaned. Oh hell, of course she hadn't known either.

"If I'm going to work out where she might be, I need to understand what triggered this. Helena?" He wanted to shake her out of her muteness. "Helena, talk to me."

She wrenched her hands from his and covered her face. At last she whispered. "They left her behind like you left me. Why did you leave me behind? Why did you go to France and leave me here? If I'd gone with you none of this –" she stopped and took a long, shuddering breath. "It would never have happened. I let him go, Seamus, and I lost him."

"If you'd come with us you would probably have been dead, and your unborn children with you." Seamus's voice was harsh, desperation dragging long-buried guilt up to the surface. "He survived, Helena. You didn't lose him. He came back, to you and the children. He gave you the whole of the rest of his life."

"Did he?" She was staring up at him, desolation in her face. "Did he really give me the rest of his life? I don't know any more. I don't think so." She sounded bereft, like a child. "I thought we were one, that nothing could ever separate us. But he went that day without me. I thought I would die when you took him."

"For God's sake Helena, he came home, and you spent the rest of his life together."

She gave a bitter laugh. "He went away with you and I never really got him back. There was always that terrible shadow, the things he couldn't talk about. And there was her. If he could have said it then, if he could have told me, it would have been easier. I'm sure of it. It was knowing there was something hidden, and never finding out what it was, until all those years later. And then wondering had he been with her in his mind, all that time, down through the years, when his body was with me." She pounded her fist on the arm of the chair, her face taut.

"I never wanted or needed anyone else. But he had someone else who rescued him, and gave him solace, and protected him. It wasn't me. And he couldn't even share his memories. After all, how could I understand? That's what he said to me, how could I understand?" Her words were vehement. "He didn't realise that I needed to know every pain he ever knew, so I could carry it for him in my body, like

200

I carried his children. I loved him enough to carry anything for him. Why didn't he love me enough in return to know that?" Her head drooped in despair. "Maybe his love was always divided, maybe some part of him remained with her. Was that it, Seamus? Only the shell of him ever came back?"

But Seamus did not answer. In his mind's eye he was seeing Richard, all those years ago, standing at the stern of the boat, looking at the silhouette of Roundstone harbour slipping away from them as they headed for the open sea.

Chapter 26

Brittany, 1942

"We should have brought her, Seamus." Richard turned towards him. "We could still go back for her. Leah might be glad to have her on board, and I feel uneasy about leaving her behind."

"You know, and I know, that this journey is madness," Seamus shouted back over the rush of the wind in the sails. "We could be caught at any time, the boat seized. What we did was right."

"Right for us. But she's devastated, and very angry."

"We can't expose Helena to the risk of torture, even execution as a spy. Because that's how they would regard us if we were caught. And with all this equipment we're carrying for Daniel, they'd be right." He put his hand on Richard's shoulder. "If she was seen on board there'd be no way to explain her. We need to look and act like any other Breton fishing boat."

"You're right." Richard spoke with resignation. "And we'll be back in a few days with your lovely Leah, and Stefan." He smiled at Seamus, and the excitement of the voyage lit up his lean, dark face.

Daniel had made the initial contact with Richard through a source in London, and they had been told how to establish radio contact with someone called Gautier, whom they believed to be Daniel. Richard told his mother that he and Helena were going down to Connemara for a week or so. They left Dublin, armed with the equipment for setting up a radio connection. Helena had tried to reach Stefan through the Swedish consulate but had received a guarded reply, stating that Herr Svenssen was no longer in Paris. Seamus veered between frantic concern and delirious anticipation. They waited in Connemara with growing trepidation for Gautier to make further contact. Finally they received a second message. "The artist and the musician must leave immediately." Did the message refer to Stefan and Leah? And if so, what had happened to the rest of the Nazarre family?

Plans were made in haste. Seamus's two brothers offered to sail with him on the *Famaire*. Their instructions were to make for the Breton coast near Lorient, and rendezvous with two boats from the Ile de Groix fishing fleet. Once contact was made they should hand over their cargo, and take two passengers on board. It took four days to make the crossing, running in a heavy swell but with a good following wind. On the afternoon of the fourth day they made their rendezvous as planned. As the first boat drew alongside, her captain called out to them. "The fishing is slack today. Have you had trouble with your lines?"

Richard answered according to the pre-arranged code. "One was snagged, but we have released it now. We are ready."

There was no sign of Daniel and his sister, or of Stefan.

"Gautier will meet you in Port St Nicholas," said the French captain. "Keep between our boats so you will be less noticeable. We cannot sail into the main harbour today."

An hour later they slipped into the shelter of Port St Nicholas, a small cove with deep water hidden by a large, freestanding rock. One of the French fishermen beckoned and called out softly in French. "You must come with me now, but leave someone on your boat, ready to sail quickly if it becomes necessary."

Seamus translated for his brothers. Ronan and Ciaran would remain out of sight, but prepared for immediate departure. Seamus and Richard left the boat, Richard carrying the precious equipment in a fishing bag on his shoulder. Their companion introduced himself as Achilles and once on the quay he nodded to them to follow him up a steep, wooded track. At the top of the hill, they could see right across the island in both directions, but the cove where the boats were moored was hidden from view. To their right was a small hamlet, its houses dreaming in the afternoon haze. Achilles looked around carefully.

"There have been unusual movements of German troops today and Gautier is worried. He has had to move his party to another house. We had hoped to make the exchange in the harbour but it is too dangerous." He indicated the direction they should now take. "We will pass through the village where I must leave you for a while, to see what the Germans are doing. You should continue towards Le Trou de l'Enfer, to the cliffs." He pointed. "Go to the house that stands alone. An old man will be working in the field outside. He will ask if you have any shellfish. Tell him no, but say that you can offer him some fresh tuna. Then follow him."

On the approach to the village, the street divided, the houses wandering haphazardly in two directions, crowded together on a narrow crooked junction. Achilles nodded briefly and left them. Seamus and Richard took the right fork, and walked on until the road dwindled to a dirt track leading out on to the headland. A few trees bent away from the wind, stunted by years of salt and storms. The two men quickened their pace. Richard scanned the path and surroundings but there was nothing to be seen. The landscape lay empty and silent before them, with only the crickets singing their evening song in the tufts of grass. Soon they could make out a building near the sea's edge.

Seamus kept his eyes fixed on the house, his heart hammering. Any moment now he would see Leah. As they rounded a corner on the path their destination came into clearer view, a Breton farmhouse with a high roof and whitewashed walls. In front of the building stood the old man. Richard slowed his pace and called out a polite greeting. The man straightened and regarded them for a few moments without speaking. Then he spat, cleared his throat and asked if they had shellfish. Richard replied that they had none and offered him tuna. There was another long silence. The old man dug his hoe deeply into the soil, left it standing, and walked away towards the house, indicating that they should follow him.

Inside the house the waiting stretched, tense and seemingly endless. In the distance a truck ground its gears as it struggled up a steep hillside. Only Germans had trucks these days. Richard had begun to feel a deep unease. He glanced at Seamus, raised his eyebrows slightly, and saw the slight shrug that was Seamus's response. The man got up suddenly and left the room by a second door. They heard him go outside. Richard straightened on his chair. He could hear movement — more than one person, he was sure. He wished they had brought guns with them. Seamus was watching the half-open door intently. A shadow fell on the staircase. Richard and Seamus stood up. Then the door was flung wide, and Daniel stood before them, dressed in a Breton peasant's cap and blue drill trousers with a loose jacket. He opened his arms in greeting.

"Ah, how glad I am to see you!"

He embraced them several times before standing back to survey them, smiling the sardonic smile they remembered so well. He was thinner, more intense than ever. Dark shadows and lines of strain on his face betrayed the dangers of his chosen life.

"I am sorry you had to wait so long, but I had to be sure that you were not followed. I did not want to take any risk with this cargo. The Germans are particularly active in this area at present. There could be an informer in our group, or perhaps they are making random raids on these villages."

Seamus could not take his eyes from the door. "Where is she, Daniel? Is she all right?"

"I must prepare you for a shock, my friend." Daniel's voice was sombre, his expression distressed.

Seamus felt a rush of fear. "What is it? Has she been hurt?"

There was another sound and they turned to see Stefan enter the room. He was limping and his face was unshaven and haggard, but he was smiling broadly.

"Richard! Seamus! God, how good it is to see you!" He turned to the open door behind him. "Leah, it really is them. Thank God."

She came in quietly and stood by Stefan. Seamus stared at her, unable to move. Could this be Leah? His mind struggled to make sense of his vision. Her grey silk costume was creased and stained. Her face was gaunt, the beauty he remembered marred by anxiety and sadness. And her hair, her once gleaming river of black hair, was now twisted on top of her head in an ash-blonde chignon. It looked bizarre, a shocking travesty against the dark eyes and the pale, haunted face. Seamus, unable to speak, found himself searching for the care-free beauty and innocence of the girl he remembered. Leah stood like a statue, unsmiling. Then she took Stefan's hand.

"Tell them, Stefan," she said in a low voice.

Stefan put his arm around her shoulders. "We are married," he said. "For three weeks now."

Seamus saw the room blacken and spin. He groped for the back of the chair and felt Richard's hand under his elbow.

Daniel was talking quickly. "Our whole family was taken three weeks ago. From the house, at night. If Leah had not been at a concert with Stefan she would have been arrested too. He took her to the Swedish consulate, and married her there. They had hoped to get away to Switzerland, but a Gestapo patrol was waiting for them on the train, and they had to come back to me in Paris."

"Daniel, Leah, I'm so sorry. About your father and mother, and the boys. Have you been able to discover what . . ." Richard's face was filled with sorrow, and with the memory of his unheeded warnings to Professor Nazarre.

Daniel's voice was hard. "They were among many thousands of Jews shipped off to Germany. In cattle trucks. God knows what has happened to them."

Seamus moved forward and placed his arm around Daniel. It required a strength he had not been aware he possessed, but he found his voice and attempted to speak steadily. "Daniel, I'm grieving for you both. This has been a terrible time for you. But at least Leah and Stefan have something on which to build a future. I wish you both happiness. Now we must get you away from here, to some kind of safe future."

He could not look at her again, could not bring himself to embrace her. He had to keep control at all costs. Why should she have continued to love him, after all? She had been so young and the time had been so short. It was understandable that she would have turned to Stefan who had saved her life. She seemed to be speaking to him across the room in wordless communication, but Seamus could not take it in. Daniel, his expression agitated, muttered something and began to usher his party towards the door.

"We must get moving. From now on you know me only as Gautier. Richard, have you brought the supplies I asked for?"

Richard indicated the fisherman's bag.

"Thank you, my friend. We are a tiny force, but we have stealth on our side and determination, and we have already been able to do a great deal of damage. You will realise in years to come how much you have helped us with this! Are you ready to sail, Seamus?"

"We can cast off as soon as we have everyone on board."

They left by the back door. A narrow path snaked along the top of the headland and then plunged down towards the sea. They moved quickly and without a word, coming together from time to time as Daniel halted to listen. As they reached the cliffs, the first heavy drops of rain began to fall. Soon it turned into a steady downpour, and the ground was slippery as they moved through the camouflage of the trees on the edge of the path above the sea. Stefan's limp had become more pronounced and he began to lag behind. He lost his footing, calling out in alarm and reaching for a supporting branch. He was close to falling, when Seamus steadied him.

"I'll look at your injury when we get clear of here, Stefan. In the meantime, you'd better lean on me."

"It's my ankle. I hurt it jumping from a train." He winced, then clutched Seamus's arm. "I must explain . . ."

"It's not necessary," Seamus was terse.

Stefan limped on, leaning heavily on Seamus, his voice low and determined, the words coming fast. "She didn't love me. But it was the only thing I could do, to prevent her being taken away. With Swedish citizenship I thought she could be safe. I thought I could save her, that I could do something courageous that would make Helena see – that would be worthwhile. But that Gestapo pig, General von Stroepper knew from the beginning. And my dear father disowned me, maybe even told them who she was, where we were going."

His breath was coming in gasps and he stumbled on a rough section of rocky ground. Seamus trudged on, his teeth clenched in a different kind of pain.

"But she is a beautiful and courageous woman, Seamus, and she is mine now. I hope she will come to love me in time. Yes, I know she will." He stopped for a moment and swept his hand across his broad forehead, brushing away the sweat. Ahead of them, Leah's slight form moved through the darkening gloom.

"I think we should talk about this some other time." Seamus could feel rage rising in him.

God Almighty! Could Stefan not remember that he was talking to a man who loved Leah desperately, who would have died for her? He began to move faster along the precipitous path, urging Stefan on, pushing him to the edge of endurance, hoping to prevent him from saying any more. But Stefan rambled on, unable to stop, as if he were delirious.

As they rounded a sharp corner, Stefan slipped again and pitched forward with a cry. For an insane moment Seamus wanted to see him tumble away over the cliff. It would be so easy to push him. Instead he dragged the big, lumbering man away from the edge of the crumbling path, and pulled him to his feet. "Stop talking to me and concentrate, God damn you! Shut your bloody mouth! You'll have us all caught with the amount of noise you're making!"

Stefan stood still, looking into the blazing fury of Seamus's face and began to mumble again. "I'm sorry. I thought at last I had done something I could be proud of. I've lost everything for her you know."

"What is all this, Stefan?" Leah appeared beside them, smoothing his brow, talking quietly. "We are together now, wherever we go. Come along, hold my arm, and take slow steps."

She looked up at Seamus and he stared back at her. For a few seconds all the unsaid things passed between them. Then she blinked away the brimming tears, and moved on deep with purpose, support- ing her unsteady husband. The path led to the village through a narrow alleyway between two rows of cottages. They moved carefully now, walking close together. There was no sign of life, no movement as they stepped into the street. Only the sound of the rain broke the sodden silence. A curtain twitched at a window, and Daniel raised a hand in warning. They moved back into the shadows of a crumbling wall.

"*Halt!*"

The harsh order split the silence. There were shouts and then the sound of heavily booted feet. Daniel yelled out to the others.

"Scatter! All of you, go for shelter!"

They rushed for cover. Daniel and Richard ducked behind some barrels on the narrow pavement. Leah, Stefan and Seamus crouched down on the other side of the street, behind the flimsy protection of a small shed. The first hail of bullets whined past them. Daniel began to move forward, trying to get an idea where the firing was coming from. As he rose from his crouching position, a second volley of gunfire began. Swearing, he pushed Richard even lower towards the ground.

"Where is Achilles? He must be further down the street waiting to get you on board." He thought for a moment, then made a decision. "I will try and lead them away, Richard. There are more of our group somewhere down the street. They will come to our assistance soon. But above all, you must get Leah and Stefan to the boat."

Richard began to protest, but Daniel silenced him angrily. "She is the only one I have left. I must know that she, at least, is safe. I'm going to create a diversion while you get them down to the harbour. Achilles or some of his group will be waiting for you. They'll make sure you get on to the boat." He flashed his old smile. "You have been a true friend, Richard. I know what you and Seamus have risked in order to come here. Now I want you to take my sister and go, with my love and my gratitude."

Richard gripped his hand. "Daniel . . ." he said.

Daniel shook his head. "There is no Daniel any more. There is only Gautier on the edge of the precipice." He broke off as a new burst of firing began, this time further along the street. "Ah – Achilles is at work. Now, when I move, you must go like the wind."

He slung the fishing bag over his shoulder, pulled a gun from under his jacket and leapt up, zig-zagging crazily between the buildings, firing as he went. Richard was on his feet in an instant, racing across the street to where the others waited, shouting to Seamus to move along behind the houses and make for the sea. Shots rang out on all sides, endless volleys crackling around them as they ran, crouching and crawling, around the backs of the cottages. Achilles appeared with several heavily armed men, covering the small party from behind. Richard kept moving, leading them down towards the sea. He prayed that when they came to the end of the village Achilles would still be able to provide cover. There was one area of open ground to cross before the shelter of the rocks.

Daniel was still running from one side of the street to the other, sometimes taking shelter, sometimes disappearing into the shadows between the houses. The rain drummed heavily, making it hard to follow his lightning movements. Richard, glancing up, saw a German sniper on the roof taking aim. He shouted a warning and turned back towards his friend. The echo of the shot seemed to reverberate in his head, louder than anything before. He saw Daniel buckle and fall forwards, then stagger up again and begin to walk towards him, swaying like a drunk. Blood was seeping through his jacket from the wound in his chest. The sniper took aim again but Achilles had seen the marksman too. He fired and the German toppled from the roof. Daniel had sunk down on to the cobbles with blood coming from the side of his mouth in a dark trickle.

Richard, racing towards him, felt a thump in his shoulder and realised he had been hit. He pushed the knowledge aside and kept moving, desperate to reach the figure on the ground. Behind him someone was screaming and he realised it was Leah. She broke free from Seamus and Stefan, and ran towards her brother. Under cover of fire from Achilles's group, Richard inched forward. The German patrol had withdrawn a little under the ferocity of the counterattack. Daniel was holding out the bag.

"Take it Richard. Give it to Achilles. He will get it to the people who need it."

"Daniel – let me help you. Oh Jesus . . ." Richard tried to wipe the blood from Daniel's face, feeling a searing pain in his own body, as he attempted to lift his friend.

"No, my time is over. Now go with the radio, everything. You must get it to Achilles."

Then Leah was beside them, on her knees, cradling her brother's head, gathering him into her arms. His blood flowed, dark and glutinous, across the silk of her costume. Richard rose with difficulty, his head spinning, a terrible pressure behind his eyes. He took the bag from Daniel's hand. With one last attempt at a smile, his friend's eyes closed and he slumped against his sister. His voice rattled in his throat. "Please little one, please go with him. You cannot help me Leah. Go with him and be safe." His voice faded away.

Richard bent down and tried to pull Leah to her feet but he was light-headed now, and he fell to his knees. He felt an arm beneath him, pulling him upright.

"Just help Leah. Not me. Help her." He was aware of more gunfire as he was dragged away, into one of the houses. The bag he had taken from Daniel was still clutched in his arms.

"Achilles – the bag must go to Achilles." He wondered who had taken him. If they were not Daniel's men he should say nothing more about Achilles, not mention the bag. Loss of blood was making it hard to think. He felt himself being bundled into a cellar, heard a trapdoor close leaving him in musty darkness. Nausea and pain clawed at him as he struggled to crawl into the darkest corner of the room, every movement bringing him to the edge of consciousness. If the trapdoor opened again, he would try and make a run for it. He must get to Achilles. Try to find Leah. Get to the boat. Despair engulfed him as he realised that perhaps nobody had escaped. Maybe they were all lying out on the rain-soaked street like Daniel, their blood filling the gutters, trickling away down the drains. Oh God, the waste of it!

Above his head, he could hear shouts, heavy boots running and stamping, and the splintering of wood. There was more staccato firing and then the heavy crump of artillery. In his mind was the terrible vision of Daniel, falling towards him, his chest flowering in a grotesque crimson ball as he held out the bag. Richard moaned. His right side seemed to be on fire, and the bones in his shattered arm ground together each time he attempted to move. Silence fell for what seemed an eternity, and then the trapdoor opened. Hands reached out to him and the world exploded in a vortex of pain and whirling shards of light before he was catapulted into a blessed darkness.

Outside, two of Achilles's group had tried to pull Leah and Daniel to safety. A burst of fire took them down. Leah knelt beside her brother on the bloody cobblestones, cradling him like a baby, screaming out her rage and horror. A heavier gun fired now from the top of the street, and several houses were hit. Masonry began to fall. Seamus and Stefan had reached Leah and were trying to carry her away from the centre of the street but she clung to Daniel. His eyes were open, but he stared out at nothing. Only the bright red bubbles foaming on his lips indicated that he was still alive. Then Seamus heard the sound of artillery once more, and the wall of the building nearest to them began to crumble. He felt a blow on the back of his head. From a distance he could still hear Leah sobbing, her voice repeating the same words over and over.

"I won't leave you, Daniel. Speak to me, please. Speak to me!" Her screams carried in the damp, smoke-filled air.

Stefan rose to his feet, shouting in German.

"Hold your fire. We are Swedish citizens. Hold your fire and I will come out with my wife."

A heavy beam from the window of the stricken house fell where Seamus was kneeling and struck him a second blow. He reeled through blackness, fighting for breath, for consciousness. Buried beneath a pile of rubble he did not witness the terrible spectacle of Leah as she was dragged away from Daniel's body. He did not see Stefan fall, struck by the butt of a rifle, trying to defend his wife. He lay in the rubble, oblivious to the sound of the German trucks driving away. He did not hear Achilles return and dig through the ruined building to reach him, was not aware of the Frenchman carrying him through the back of the village and down to the boat. His brothers lifted him aboard and Achilles urged them to set sail with all speed, telling them that everyone else was taken, that all they could do was try to save themselves. Nor did Seamus know that Richard Kirwan still lay seriously wounded in the black gloom of a cellar.

In heavy rain and under a blanket of darkness, the *Famaire* left Port St Nicholas, on an oily sea. She carried only Seamus and his brothers. Seamus would not regain consciousness for several days.

Chapter 27

Paris, 1970

Charlotte de Savoie looked at her granddaughter and felt the familiar catch in her throat. It was not that Solange was a replica of her mother. Celine had been more delicate, her hair a paler blonde, her skin almost translucent. But Solange had the same grave beauty, an identical air of calm, an unmistakable presence. She possessed her mother's clear, direct gaze that seemed immediately to find the centre of any issue. This evening Solange sat close to Guy St Jorre, her hand clasped in his. But there was a new dimension to the girl that her grandmother could not quite fathom, a watchfulness, a tension in her body.

"Well, my darlings," Charlotte de Savoie raised her glass. "I'm grateful that Guy's legal conference has brought you up here at last. Solange, I'm planning to have you all to myself during the day, while this young man goes off to his meetings. There is so much to do, so many preparations for the wedding."

She turned her attention to Guy. "I know you have to be at the Hotel Crillon for the reception soon. So, I won't mind if you disappear upstairs and change into your evening clothes." She rose, smoothing the silk of her dress. "Would you consider going on ahead, Guy, and giving Solange a chance to bathe and change at a slightly more leisurely pace?"

"What a good idea, Charlotte. But no more than thirty minutes."

Guy smiled at Solange and touched her fingers. He kissed her lightly, embraced Charlotte de Savoie and was gone.

As she finished getting ready Solange felt a shiver run through her. The house was outwardly unaltered, yet it was no longer just her grandmother's Paris residence. It had become the setting for a series of deceptions. How could she approach her grandmother and what would she say? She tried to bury the dreaded subject in the recesses of her mind and returned her attention to the demands of the present as she pinned up her heavy hair, allowing a few tendrils to fall around her face and at the nape of her neck. Looking at her reflection she began to feel good. It would be fun to be a Parisian for a while. In the hall downstairs she kissed her grandmother.

"You look beautiful, darling. There is nothing like perfect tailoring and rich fabric." Charlotte was fond of Yves St Laurent and had bought the evening suit for Solange several months before. The velvet jacket was cut square and low across her breasts and tight at the waist, and the skirt flared above her knees, showing off her long legs. "I don't think I'll wait up for you, Solange."

"No, you mustn't. I'm sure we'll go on to dinner somewhere," Solange said. "Tomorrow though, we have a great deal to talk about. But it won't be only about the future, Grandmama. Tomorrow I think we should begin in the past."

She did not look back or give her grandmother an opportunity to respond and as the taxi pulled out into the evening traffic, Solange determined to keep her demons at bay for this one evening. Tonight she would enjoy the glittering reception at the Crillon. And afterwards Guy would find a small, romantic restaurant for dinner and then perhaps a jazz club. She sat back and began to relax.

In the magnificent surroundings of the Hotel Crillon, James Kirwan accepted two glasses of champagne from a passing waiter and handed one to his sister. Arriving in Paris at midday, James had found Serge Bouvier at the airport to greet them and drive them to their hotel. After lunch he had gone to the offices of Descartes, Bouvier & Fils, while Elizabeth explored the boutiques of St Germain des Prés. When she had joined her brother and Serge in the bar of their hotel, James had been astonished by her appearance. Only this afternoon she had been his little sister, but now she was a vision of sophistication with her hair caught up in a pearl clasp and her creamy skin offset by a short, black evening dress.

"James has told me about your bereavement. I'm so sorry." Serge took Elizabeth's arm, guiding her lightly through the throng. "I understand that you hope to find some of your father's old acquaintances while you are in Paris. We may come across a man called Jacques Lefranche this evening. His father was a Professor of Law at the Sorbonne before and during the war. Old Lefranche is not the most likeable of characters, but he might be able to put you in touch with someone who knew your father well. Was he in Paris for long?"

James frowned and shook his head. "We're not sure. More than a year at any rate, before war broke out. As for the period of the war itself, I'm afraid he was one of those who preferred not to remember. I know he became ill around that time. But he never discussed that period of his life."

"He met our mother here in Paris," said Elizabeth, hovering on the brink of tears. "But it's too soon, too painful, for her to talk about it yet."

"Well, let us dwell on happier things for the moment." Serge refilled her glass and smiled at her. "This is your first night in Paris, and after the reception we must have a fine dinner, and some dancing perhaps. In the meantime, here is someone agreeable whom I would like you both to meet. He's a clever lawyer who is just beginning to make a name for himself."

Elizabeth studied the young man coming towards them, admiring his physique and impressive suntan. She summoned a brilliant smile and held out her hand.

"Mademoiselle, it's a pleasure to meet such a beautiful and exotic visitor. I'm afraid I'm just another lawyer like so many here tonight. My name is Guy St Jorre."

At the entrance to the magnificent salon, Solange stood looking across the mass of moving heads, dazzled by the splendour of the room. There was no immediate sign of Guy in the crowd as she walked forward.

"Solange, what a vision you are! Is this the result of Guy's return to France, or simply the combination of the enviable southern climate and some Parisian elegance?"

Jean Papillaud, one of Guy's colleagues, was at her side signalling to a waiter, handing her a champagne flute. She greeted him with relief, glad not to be alone in the huge room.

"Jean, hello! I hope I'm not too late. Everything seems to be still in full swing here. I was looking for Guy."

"Oh, he's working the room, obscenely tanned and far too clever. Stay with me a while Solange, he doesn't need any more attributes with which to impress the legal profession this evening. He's talking to all the dry old sticks, in order to further his career. They won't be able to concentrate on his prospects if they see you."

Solange laughed at his flattery, and listened with enjoyment to his description of a scandalous case in which he was involved, a lurid tale of jealousy, revenge and a double murder. They moved though the glittering assembly, meeting friends and visitors from overseas. She was chatting in Spanish to a visiting lawyer and his wife from Madrid when she saw Guy. He was standing beside Serge Bouvier, whom she recognised from one of her grandmother's soirées. There was a couple with them. The man, unusually tall and dark, had his back to her. The girl was very young with an extraordinary mass of red hair, and perfect skin that had clearly never been exposed to the cruel rays of the sun. They did not look French, but there were hundreds of foreigners here for the conference. When she touched Guy's arm he turned around, his face lighting up at the sight of her.

"Solange, I've been looking for you. You know Serge Bouvier, I think? And darling, may I present two visitors from Ireland. This is Mr James Kirwan and his sister Elizabeth." He stood back to allow her into the small circle and smiled at the two Irish guests. "It's Elizabeth's first visit to Paris. I've been making some sightseeing suggestions that I'm sure you can improve upon. James, Elizabeth, this is my fiancée, Solange de Valnay."

A rush of heat made her throat close. She could not swallow or breathe, could not speak. The man and woman stood motionless, staring back at her, frozen. She saw Guy smiling and realised that he was waiting for her to acknowledge them. Rage swam up into her consciousness and broke the surface, spilling out through the pores of her clammy skin, demanding control of her speech. Her fingernails pressed into the palms of her hands as she tried not to give in to panic. A voice in her head screamed her outrage. How could Guy have done this to her? How could he have known? She turned away from him. James and Elizabeth still stood like statues. When she was able to speak her voice was low, brimming with fury.

"How dare you. How dare you come here like this, invading my life, tracking me down, turning my existence into some kind of witch-hunt." Solange struggled to keep her voice from rising as a torrent of fury obliterated all else around her. Her eyes glittered with tears.

"Solange, what on earth are you saying? Solange there's been some mistake." Guy put his hand on her arm but she shook him off, oblivious to everyone but the Kirwans.

"You have no shame, either of you. No pity, no human feeling." She knew she was talking a little too loud now. People nearby had begun to turn around and look at her curiously.

"Solange, I think you'd better come with me. We should discuss this elsewhere." Guy tried to take the situation in hand.

She turned to him at last. She had trusted him, treasured the refuge of his ignorance. But he had led her into a trap. He had betrayed her. "I can't believe you did this to me. My God, I've agonised for weeks over your feelings, what they might be." She did not notice that he was staring at her in amazement, dumb with horrified surprise. She forced herself to slow down, to ensure that they all would understand and remember everything she said. "I don't want to see you again, Guy. I do not wish to see or hear from any of you. Ever again."

James stepped towards her, his hand outstretched. "Solange," he said. "I – this is just . . . We never thought . . ."

"Mr Kirwan, you resemble your father in your total lack of compassion. If you are a respected member of the legal profession in your country, I pity the cause of justice and humanity." Solange was shaking now, as she fought to keep herself from screaming. She became aware of Serge Bouvier, standing close by, gaping at her. Suddenly she was very cold. Grief engulfed her as anger and courage fled. She had no recollection of leaving the crowded room, or stepping out into the damp Paris evening. She began to walk, rain wetting her face, washing the tears down her cheeks. Her hair fell from its combs and clips, her sodden clothes sagged on her shoulders. Occasionally she caught a glimpse of herself in a shop window, a face painted with shades of grief and bitterness. Black lines, clown-like, had appeared beneath her eyes and ran down her cheeks. Several passers-by stared, but in the anonymity of the city no one tried to speak to her.

When she came to a halt at last she realised, with surprise, that she had reached the entrance to her grandmother's residence in Avenue Mozart. She put her key into the lock, numb with shock, the tears and rain still running down her cheeks unchecked, mascara making muddy streams on her face.

Charlotte de Savoie was standing in the doorway of the drawing room. "Solange, darling, you're here. Guy has been telephoning every fifteen minutes, asking if you have come home. He's very upset. My dear, what has happened? He said he couldn't explain." She walked towards the shivering girl. "Darling, what is it? What has caused you such distress?" She reached out her arms towards her granddaughter, but Solange pushed her away violently.

"How did it happen? How did it really happen? And Guy knew, even he knew about it, and he tricked me. Did you tell him? Did you?" She could not catch her breath between the terrible rasps of her sobbing and she hurled her rage and fear at her grandmother. "Why must they reach up out of their graves, after all this time? How could you have let it all happen?"

Charlotte de Savoie stood still, her face grey, her eyes widening for a moment in dismayed comprehension. Then she reached out and took the girl by the hand. "You'd better come into the drawing room, Solange," she said. "You'd better come and sit down with me darling. This is going to take us a very long time."

Chapter 28

Paris, 1942

Celine de Savoie reached out to silence the telephone that drilled unremittingly into her consciousness, her eyes still closed, her response mumbled.

"Dr de Savoie? Celine my dear, it's Sister Dominique. I'm so sorry to wake you. I know you've only had a few hours' rest but we have a terrible situation." The nun sounded close to tears. "Dr Hartmann and Dr Rossi have been relieved of their duties. Forbidden to practise. They've been taken away from their homes."

Celine sat up, wide awake. Her clock said it was five in the morning. "What do you mean, taken? Taken where? By whom?"

"They have grandparents or relatives who are Jews. They're no longer allowed to treat anyone. The Germans took them away late last night."

"How do you know this?"

"A neighbour phoned a short while ago. It's abhorrent, completely inhuman. I can't believe this is happening to dedicated men."

"Ssshhh. The telephone lines . . ."

"Yes, of course. Could you come and help out, Celine? I'll try and get you some time off tomorrow."

Celine replaced the receiver. She put on some coffee from the last of her precious supply. It was weak because she was rationing herself, but at least it was hot and the real thing. She tried groggily to register the full implications of the telephone call.

In recent weeks the city had been pockmarked with ugly posters vilifying Jews, denying them entry to public places. Twice Celine had glanced around, and then pulled them off the walls they defaced. She had seen people forced to display yellow stars on their clothing and travel only in the last, filthy car of the metro. But it was hard to believe this was happening in the world of medicine. Even the Germans needed good doctors.

On the way to the hospital she passed the morning queues. Lines of women, some shivering in the cold air, stood outside food shops with empty windows and shelves. Often they waited for hours in rain and fog, only to find that there was no produce left when it came to their turn. In the hospital it seemed to Celine that every time she looked up, the queues had lengthened rather than shortened. Some came because they were ill, others simply to get out of the grey, empty streets. There were people looking for family or friends who were missing. By midday her head was pounding, and she squinted through a dry film that had formed over her tired eyes, but she forced herself on. In the late afternoon, the senior registrar ordered her to go home and take the telephone off the hook until the morning.

"You'll be no use to us over the next few months Dr de Savoie, if you don't pace yourself and conserve some energy," he said quietly. "This is the start, not the end of our crisis. They will not stop here. They will spare no one."

Celine wheeled her bicycle into the street outside the hospital, grateful that the day was over. The late summer evening was chilly, a hint of mist cloaking the silent city around her. The streets were deserted, window shutters were closed tight as if to block out the German presence. She avoided the broad avenues where German officers and their wives or mistresses strolled and shopped, revelling in their role as conquerors. It made her ill to look at the public buildings

223

where the flags with black swastikas hung, reminding Parisians of their humiliation. At last she was at her apartment door, fumbling with the keys, finally home, but unable to find the energy to prepare any food. She moved through to the bedroom and without taking off her clothes fell on to the bed, covered herself with a blanket and closed her eyes.

Deep in exhausted oblivion she was slow to respond to the shrill, insistent ringing that had begun her day. The sound seemed far away and she tried at first to ignore it. At last, without sitting up, she reached for the telephone and glanced at her watch. Eight o'clock. Had she slept through the night, or only for two hours?

"Darling, I think you were asleep." Celine registered her mother's tones, precise and languorous at the same time.

"Mother, I was practically dead. I've had hardly any sleep in the last two days. Can I telephone you tomorrow?"

"Darling, I want you to come over to Avenue Mozart. I want you to meet someone very special and he's here only briefly. Could you ride across here? I won't keep you all that long, unless you'd like to stay for dinner."

"Mother, I cannot get all dressed up and appear at one of your little soirées. I just can't do it." Celine was exasperated, too tired for tact or patience. "You've already introduced me to everyone you know, and you'll be glad to hear that I've seen your pick of the month, Henri de Valnay, on several occasions. I can't cope with social duties tonight. Now can I go back to sleep?"

"Darling, it's not a soirée. This is a little different."

Celine pulled the blanket up under her chin. Annoyance flooded through her. Her mother seemed able to continue her life as though the world outside revolved as normal.

"I don't have the time just now for polite conversation with strangers. I just need sleep. Please understand Mama. I really will telephone you in the morning."

"Celine, it is you who must understand." Charlotte de Savoie's voice took on a different tone. "I need you to come over here as quickly as you can. This isn't anything frivolous. Please Celine, just trust my judgement. And bring your doctor's bag."

"Are you all right, Mother?" Celine was wide awake now. "If you aren't well I could phone Dr Ducray. He might be more useful."

"No – don't telephone Dr Ducray. I want you to come. I know it sounds unreasonable, but I'd rather it was you. I do realise how tired you are, but this is important."

The bicycle ride was another endurance test for Celine's aching limbs. When she finally rang the bell at Avenue Mozart, Charlotte de Savoie opened the door immediately.

"Why are you answering the door?" Celine asked her mother. Inside, the house had an eerie feeling. "Where are the staff? Where's André? Isn't Louise making dinner for you?"

"I sent Louise off for the afternoon. She's visiting some cousins who send me vegetables and things from the country. I was planning to dine out, so I don't need André this evening. Come, darling."

Celine followed her mother's swift footsteps across the marbled hall and up the curved sweep of the stairs. Charlotte's bedroom did not present its usual orderly appearance. The blue silk curtains looked as though they had been hastily pulled across the French windows. Several pillows were stacked on one of the chairs, and two blankets had been tossed on to the large bed, wrinkling the quilted cover. Celine stopped dead, astonished by the sight of a large, antique chamber pot on the carpet beside the wardrobe, with a monogrammed towel draped over it. She tried to imagine her mother having to use such a thing, and stifled a laugh.

Charlotte walked over to the cupboard that ran the length of one wall and opened it. Rows of couture clothing filled the space. She pushed some hangers aside with each hand, and moved in behind the formal evening gowns. "Many old houses have these amusing little passages between the bedrooms, hidden away for discretion and secret trysts. Years ago, this one allowed your father and me to be alone together, after the supervised time in the salon was over."

Charlotte pushed on the wall panelling. A section swung open, and Celine moved forward to peer into a dark space measuring about two metres by three. A man lay on a mattress, wrapped in a blanket with several pillows supporting his lolling head. As her eyes became accustomed to the dim light, she saw that he was very still, but his breathing was irregular and laboured.

"Who is this?" she demanded. "What's he doing here? Bring me a light, Mother, please. And start telling me what this is all about."

She bent to look at the prone figure. His eyes were half open, and she recognised the glitter of high fever. His face was bruised and battered. He had a cut across the back of his head and his black hair was still matted with blood. One arm lay at a strange angle. A bandage had been strapped inexpertly around his right shoulder. He moved his head to look at her and attempted a smile. In normal circumstances, thought Celine, he must be very good-looking. The flashlight fell on his hands, cut and spattered with dried blood. A gold wedding band shone on one finger.

He tried to speak to her, his voice hoarse and very low. She leaned towards him to catch the words and at first could not understand him. Perhaps he was delirious. Then she realised he was speaking in English. "So sorry. Sorry to have made you come here. You've had . . . Must be so tired . . . Sorry . . ."

Celine lifted his right arm gently. The wrist was swollen, possibly broken. When she attempted gently to turn him over, he cried out in pain. She removed his jacket and unwrapped the bandage around his upper arm and shoulder to inspect the injury. Shock struck hard. She turned to her mother.

"He's been shot, Mother, this man has been shot! He has an infection and the bullet is still buried in his shoulder. Who is he and how did you get involved with him? Talk to me."

She bent to examine him further and he watched her in silence, making an effort to focus his eyes. The bruises on the face and head seemed to be superficial, but the cuts on the back of his head would need to be stitched.

Charlotte stood at the entrance to the hidden passage looking concerned but calm. "Celine, we are at war. You could not possibly imagine that I would sit back and allow those barbarous thugs to over-run this city, to destroy all that is magnificent and civilised in France."

"Mother, we all feel like that. But there are . . ."

"Celine, I have wept every single day since the meeting of that old fool Pétain with Hitler. That was tragedy. To ask us to collaborate is like asking a woman to allow a rape and never murmur about the violation. We cannot just settle into defeat."

"Mother, you can't start a private war against the occupying forces. No matter what you feel. This is so dangerous for you."

Celine began to probe gently at the bullet wound, which was open and seeping. Charlotte turned away but continued to speak, her voice dense with contempt.

"France is the only country in Europe that has been brought to its knees in this way. The only country to seek an armistice. It's shameful. It may take time, but we must fight to rid ourselves of the Germans, and I fully intend to play whatever role I can. There's a beginning now, a small nucleus of people who are banding together, organising cells of resistance, and I'm proud to have joined them."

"What people? I'd like to know all about this."

"Some other time, Celine. Now, what can you do for him?"

"I'll have to take him out of here. There isn't enough room for me to treat him."

"He can't come out. I can't risk traces of anything suspicious on the carpets or the furniture. I don't want André and Louise to know anything about this. I must not compromise them. You'll have to do the best you can in there, darling."

Celine looked at her mother, perfectly groomed and apparently unruffled, as though she were about to go out for a bridge game or cocktails. She shook her head in disbelief. "Help me lift him very gently into a sitting position," she said. "I'm going to have to cut off the rest of this torn shirt to get at his shoulder properly. I'll clean the wound, but I can't remove the bullet until I return with more medical supplies." She took out a pair of scissors and began to cut.

The man suppressed a scream as they raised him from the floor. Sweat poured down his face and his eyes filled with an agonised plea. Celine took out a syringe and administered a powerful painkiller. Then she constructed a splint, filled a bowl with water and sponged his head and face, cleaning the cuts, placing soft dressings on the deepest cuts. She would have to stitch some of these lacerations tomorrow. The last of her bandages went to strap his arm into place.

Charlotte moved between the bedroom and the bathroom supplying sponges, cotton wool, and items from her daughter's medical bag. She produced underclothes, a warm shirt and a thick cardigan that had belonged to her late husband. At last the man lay back, his body supported by a small mountain of pillows. His breath was short and rasping. Through half-closed eyes he watched Celine intently.

"Now, Mother, it's time you explained."

They heard the doorbell ring.

"Oh God, close the door, Mama. Quick. I'll stay in here with him. Put my bag in too."

The bell rang again, and someone pounded on the door knocker.

Shut away in the confines of the dark passage with her fugitive, Celine crouched down with her arms round her knees, leaning against the panelling. She clasped her hands together to prevent them from shaking, but her whole body was trembling. The man was making a wheezing, rattling sound as he tried to breathe. Celine put her finger to his dry lips. He made heroic efforts, sometimes grinding his teeth in pain, struggling not to make any sound. A kind of wild excitement began to overcome Celine. After an interminable wait she heard Charlotte de Savoie's footsteps, quick and light. A male voice was speaking, addressing her mother in good French with a slight German accent.

"I must apologise, Madame de Savoie, for this ridiculous intrusion. Of course I have looked forward for some time to the opportunity of visiting your residence. Ah, what a restful room, full of grace and style, like its occupant. So quiet and secluded, an ideal hideaway."

His boots trod the thick carpet and he pulled back the silk curtains to look down on the small garden below. "I did not want a group of clumsy soldiers wandering around in your exquisite home. That is why I came myself. We have picked up some fugitives this afternoon and we believe there is another still at large, hiding somewhere in this area. But there is no reason why you should be disturbed beyond a few moments."

He opened the bathroom door, lifted one of the heavy blinds and peered into the street. Then he returned to the bedroom. Celine heard the wardrobe door opening. She drew in a breath. It tasted of fear. Her throat was dry and burning. She wanted to cough. Her head ached. The man on the floor stretched out his hand and she felt his eyes searching for her in the darkness. She gave him one of her hands and they stayed there together, silent, immobile.

"A superb selection of gowns." The German was flicking through the hangers. "I hope it will not be too long before you feel able to accept one of my invitations. You must not lock yourself away for too much longer, Madame de Savoie. Your beauty and style are the essence of Paris."

Charlotte de Savoie made no response to the request. Celine could hear his footsteps as they circled the room. "It would be an honour if you would join me for dinner one evening. I will not tire of sending you invitations, Madame de Savoie. I'm a very persistent man."

The wardrobe door closed and his voice gradually faded. Celine continued to crouch in the hot, dark space, the injured man still clasping her hand. Finally she heard the front door close and there was silence in the house. They remained motionless until her mother's familiar footsteps approached the wardrobe. The panel opened. Charlotte de Savoie stood outside, her face composed but strained. Celine's limbs seemed glued into her cramped position, and she unwound herself slowly and painfully to emerge into the bedroom. Her mother's arms were around her instantly, and then they were hugging, touching one another's faces, wiping away tears.

"Darling, I never dreamt you would be involved in anything like this. No German has ever set foot in this house before. I never meant to put you at such risk. Celine, my beautiful, precious daughter. Never again, darling. I promise." Charlotte dried her eyes and released her daughter. "Well, that was the Boche in all their glory. A handsome, cultured example of brutality who goes by the name of Walter von Stroepper. He has been telephoning constantly, asking me to soirées with those dreary, treacherous French men and women who are making fortunes from the occupation. I've told him that it is less than two years since your father died, and I cannot bring myself to go out. But now, finally, he has found an excuse to enter my house."

"Mother, how did you ever become entangled in all this? Do you realise how dangerous it is? You could be imprisoned. Shot, even."

"Celine darling, I can see that you're exhausted." Charlotte chose to ignore her daughter's admonishments. "I think you should sleep in your room here for tonight and go back to the hospital in the morning properly refreshed."

Celine looked at her mother with exasperation. She tried to be angry, but she could feel only amazement and admiration. "Mother, I'm not staying the night here. If you feel it's safe, it would be better for your patient to have the door open just a little. And he does smell a bit you know. We'll have to do something about bathing him tomorrow, otherwise he'll give you away. We must bring him out of there, so that I can remove the bullet from his shoulder. It's already been left too long and it's infected."

"He was delivered here only this afternoon." Charlotte de Savoie gave a small smile and a shrug of her shoulders. "He came in with the laundry van. Luckily I'd already sent Louise away."

"This gets worse and worse. I'll be back tomorrow in the afternoon, unless there's a problem at the hospital."

"And if he takes a turn for the worse?"

"You'll have to telephone me. You can say the pharmacy has run out of your medicine. My God, now I'm playing cloak and dagger. This is insane."

She turned back towards the hidden passage for a last look at her patient. He was fighting to keep his eyes open, and in the light she saw that they were very blue. He was aware of her standing there in the doorway, a silhouette of long legs and delicate ankles, and a crown of pale, shimmering hair. Celine bent down and placed a cool hand on his forehead. He whispered something that she could not hear. She moved closer to listen, and this time he spoke in perfect French, his breath rasping between the words.

"Goodnight, Celine. So brave, very brave. Your hair, a halo . . . Like Helena. Please can someone tell Helena Kirwan that Richard is safe."

"What is he asking for? Is there something I should bring him, Celine?"

"No, Mother, he just wanted to thank me, and he's asking if someone can tell Helena. Who's Helena, do you know?"

"He's anxious to get a message to his wife in Ireland. He's Irish, Celine. We're trying to get something through to her." Charlotte bent down towards the man on the floor. "We're doing our best to let her know you're safe." She turned away from the wardrobe to face her daughter. "I couldn't ask anyone else to come, Celine. Do you understand?"

"Oh, I think I'm safe enough for the time being. But you'd better start considering what to do with him. He's not going to be able to move very far for a while. We'll talk about it tomorrow. Goodnight, Mama, I love you."

As she embraced her mother the man looked up at her again and then drifted into sleep, an attempt at a smile on his battered face. She saw him like that in her mind, all the way home.

Chapter 29

Paris, 1942

Celine folded her stethoscope and placed it in her doctor's bag. In the harsh light she looked drawn and tired. As she left the wards the sister on duty looked up briefly to say goodbye. At the end of the corridor Celine glanced quickly over her shoulder. There was no one in sight. She slipped into the store where the medical supplies were kept, cleared a place on the counter and started opening drawers and cupboards. Splints, dressings and bandages, catgut and antiseptics, needles and syringes, tablets and instruments quickly formed a neat pile on the table. She took her keys out and opened the safe where the restricted drugs were kept.

"Morphine. Poor devil needs that."

She looked through the selection of painkillers and made her choice. The register lay on the counter and she signed for each item before locking the cupboard. She had made a false base for her medical bag the night before. The Germans often stopped people on the street and demanded to look into their bags or baskets. An overzealous soldier could make a great deal out of this little cache of drugs, might even confiscate them. She placed the false panel on top of the medicines and piled in her usual paraphernalia. As she snapped the locks shut the door swung open. She jumped.

"Celine, I thought you'd gone home. You look as though you need some rest." Dr Duras, a senior consultant, was smiling at her. "What are you doing in here? Raiding the morphine supplies?"

"I've just signed for a few dressings and some painkillers." She wondered if he could hear the strain in her voice. "My mother had a fall this afternoon and needs patching up, maybe even a couple of stitches. Fortunately it's not too serious and I can take care of it at home."

"Well, I'm glad it isn't anything major. Give my regards to Charlotte. We haven't seen her for bridge lately. Tell her we miss her. And don't get caught in the curfew, we're short of doctors as it is."

"Goodnight, Dr Duras."

She cycled away from the hospital, enjoying the fresh air after the clinical smells of the wards. There was little in the way of traffic, even on the Avenue Paul Doumer. The Germans preferred to strut on the Champs Elysées and frequent the well-known shops and restaurants. When she rang the doorbell at Avenue Mozart, Louise appeared, taking the bicycle inside and offering her something to eat.

"No thank you Louise, I don't have all that much time, but I wanted to look in on Mama. Is she upstairs?"

"Yes, Madame is in her bedroom. I don't think she is feeling well. She cancelled her lunch appointment, and she hasn't been downstairs all day. It's good that you are here, that is the best medicine. Ah, Miss Celine, these are such terrible days. If only your father was still here to take care of her." Louise spoke her next words with slow deliberation. "Everything carries its dangers now Miss Celine. Your mother must be prudent and very, very careful."

Climbing the stairs Celine wondered if there was some particular significance in Louise's remark. Charlotte was sitting on the sofa in her bedroom, composed as ever. She seemed younger than her forty-eight years as she looked up from her book, proffered a delicate cheek and smiled at her daughter.

"He's asleep. He didn't have a good night so I gave him some of your painkillers and sat up with him, hoping it might help. He managed some soup and bread, but he couldn't cope with the warm milk or the egg. When he recovers he'll regret having refused those rare treasures. He's very weak, Celine."

"Since he's asleep, Mama, let's talk about your involvement in all this."

"Darling, the first rule in this undertaking is never to tell anyone anything, in case they are questioned at some time in the future. The less one knows, the safer one remains. You just have to bring the right medicines."

"Mother, I want to join in what you're doing." Celine sat down opposite her mother. "I'm a doctor, I can help people like this."

Charlotte de Savoie stood up and turned away, using her favourite way of terminating an undesired discussion. She opened a small cabinet and took out a bottle of cognac. "Celine, darling, you are caring every day for people who are ill, injured, hungry because of the occupation. Your role is to deal with this war as a doctor. That's enough."

"Oh God, Mama, we can't take a walk without looking over our shoulders in case we're stopped. We can't move around in our own towns and cities because there's no fuel for our cars. We're short of food in a country rich in agriculture. We're living in constant fear. And it's not enough for me just to dispense aspirins to a few people in the hospital. It's not."

Charlotte touched her daughter's hair in a soothing gesture, tucking in a few escaped strands. But Celine took her hand impatiently and pushed it aside. "Scores of people have vanished during the past few months. You know that." Celine was determined not to be rebuffed. "And look at what's happening to Jewish people, how the Germans have rounded up thousands of them and detained them in terrible conditions in the Vélodrome d'Hiver, without proper food or sanitation. Apparently they're going to be deported to prison camps in Germany. It isn't enough to take care of regular hospital patients and pander to ridiculous German phobias about epidemics. I have to fight like you, Mama, and you must tell me how."

"Well, let's deal with the case in hand first."

Charlotte heard a sound and moved over to the wardrobe. Celine took her bag and followed her mother. The man was covered with blankets, and Celine saw that he was wrapped in her father's wool dressing gown. He heard their steps and opened his eyes with difficulty. His face was swollen and livid with bruises. He lifted his left arm and grasped her hand and she placed her fingers on his wrist, feeling for his pulse, touching his forehead.

"I'm going to give you more medicine to take, and another injection," she said softly. "I need to remove the bullet from your shoulder and strap you up for support. There may be some shattered bone in there. It will be very painful for a time, but the morphine will help. Do you understand me?" He nodded slowly, his breathing uneven, his blotched, bruised face flushed with fever. She took some gauze and dipped it in cooling alcohol, wiping it across his head.

"Your head needs stitching too, this wound is infected. You won't be able to do much for several weeks, I'm afraid." She worked quickly, unpacking her supplies and putting them to use within minutes.

The man groaned occasionally, beads of sweat on his face and a clenched fist the only signal of his pain. At last it was over and she bandaged him gently, a thick dressing covering the bullet wound, his deep lacerations cleaned and stitched. His swollen wrist was held in place by firm strapping. The morphine had done its work and he seemed to be drifting between sleep and vague consciousness but after a few moments Celine heard a sound and returned to her patient, moving him a little on his mattress.

She floated hazily across his consciousness like a vision surrounded by light, her face concerned and tender, her hands efficient but gentle. She wiped the sweat from his face, then touched him lightly on the cheek, and on his dark eyebrows. He whispered to her in French, hesitating over the words, his mouth dry.

"Celine. Thank you a thousand times for your courage. You and your mother are true heroines of France."

She placed an extra blanket over him, touched by his effort to speak.

"He'll get cold quickly Mama, lying here like this. And very stiff, too. Tomorrow we must get him up and walk him around a little. Maybe when everyone has gone to bed, he could sit in your chair for a while, with a couple of blankets wrapped round him. If he feels strong enough to try it." She looked down at him. "Do you understand?"

He nodded slightly, his eyes closed. "The letters, the crystals . . ." His voice was a dry rasp and he tried to lick his lips. "Urgent. For the press."

The effort of trying to speak made him clutch her arm with a grip that hurt her. Celine turned towards her mother. "What does he mean? What letters?"

"He's carrying printing and radio equipment that need delivering. I'm trying to arrange it, but my contact has had to move to another location because of the German patrols. I received the new address just before you arrived this evening. I'm going to call for a courier. The man who came before is dead, Celine. He was killed at the same time that this one was wounded."

"Call a courier? Don't be ridiculous Mama, you can't do anything that would draw attention to this house. I'm your courier. Give these things to me, whatever they are and I'll deliver them, now, on my bicycle. I can hide everything in my medical bag. I put a false bottom into it last night. There's still room even with the dressings."

"No Celine. Within an hour I'll be able to find someone who's used to doing all this. I don't want you to get mixed up in it any further."

"Mother, give me whatever he brought. No one will stop me. I'm a doctor, which is a perfect cover for something like this."

"Celine, you cannot do this. You must not become involved."

"For God's sake just tell me where to go. Presumably someone has been waiting for all this equipment for days."

"Since he arrived. He came ashore to hand over the equipment, and to take out two other people. But the Germans were there, waiting. Two of the group were taken and at least one was killed. He's carrying typeface for a printing press, and spares for a radio operator. And there's money, a good deal of cash."

Celine had already opened her bag, quickly reorganising its contents. Her mother walked over to the patient and knelt down beside him.

"She will take everything, Richard. Celine will deliver it all to Achilles and his friends. May God help us all." Charlotte opened the drawers in her armoire and handed several packages to her daughter.

"Take this to rue de Grenelle. Here's the number. There's a young man there with the code name of Achilles. Just say 'I have come to collect the bitter oranges'. If it is Achilles, he will answer 'They are good only for jam.' Give him the packages, and then leave as soon as he tells you to. Don't come back here tonight, but telephone me when you get home."

Their embrace was quick, but Celine had never experienced such an intensity of feeling for her mother as in that moment. They were joined in fear, in pride, hope and determination, and in their love. Moments later she wheeled her bicycle out into the Paris evening and was gone.

Chapter 30

Celine took a last look at her reflection and was satisfied. Now she was almost ready for him. She outlined her mouth with a deep-red lipstick and took out a small hat of dark-blue velvet. Her dress was a paler shade of blue, and the soft crepe clung to her figure and flowed with her movements. The doorbell rang and she smiled. He was always on time, Henri de Valnay, seemingly able to triumph over all obstacles including weather and transportation. Henri kissed her lightly on both cheeks, handed her a bouquet of roses, and accepted her offer of an aperitif. He removed his hat and threw it on to the coffee table, settling himself easily on the sofa in front of the open windows.

As a respected wine merchant, Henri had supplied the Savoie family for many years with a selection of his finest wines, champagnes and cognacs. Celine was not the first ambitious young woman he had come across, but when he met her at one of Charlotte de Savoie's soirées he was impressed by her straightforward way of looking at things, and he liked the gentleness about her that spoke of both dedication and compassion. On their first evening together he had looked into her eyes and realised that he was lost. But he knew she was not short of suitors and he sensed that he must go slowly, exercise every ounce of patience and skill within him, if he was to obtain this magical prize.

"I've chosen a restaurant that's only a few streets away," he said, raising his glass in a silent toast to a deeper liaison.

"Perfect. If it's near here, it won't be full of loud Germans and their good-time girls. I wish I knew how to keep them out of the smaller restaurants altogether."

"You look beautiful Celine – as though you've had a month's holiday." Henri surveyed her carefully. "And there's something else about you this evening, an extra spark of excitement in you. As though you have a secret, or you've won a lottery and not told anyone about it. Better still, perhaps it's just the pleasure of my company?"

She smiled but his observation unnerved her. He could not know that she did indeed have a new, thrilling sense of focus, an edge to her vision that was intoxicating. The arrival of the fugitive at her mother's apartment, and her contribution to the fight against German occupation, had given her a feeling of purpose and reward she had never experienced before. At night she had dreamed about Richard Kirwan more than once.

Henri talked easily about events in the city, new films, Parisian gossip. They enjoyed the same tastes in literature and music, and most of all she loved his sense of humour. But for all their common interests, Celine was disturbed by his careful avoidance of the problems of war. He seemed carefree always, speaking about a delightful book he had recently discovered, or an encounter that had been intriguing or amusing, but never about the occupation of his country. It was as if he had not noticed that France had been overrun by a foreign power. He sold fine wines to high-ranking German officers, and to the restaurants who catered to them and there was something about his increasing wealth and success in these difficult times that made Celine uneasy. She had said as much to her mother, but to her surprise Charlotte de Savoie had raised her eyebrows a little and come out in Henri's defence.

"Well, there doesn't seem to be much point in his sitting in his apartment on the Ile St Louis and starving, darling. And he does supply a great many more French people than he does Germans, you know. He can't help being wealthy and successful, Celine."

The restaurant was full, and there were people sitting at small tables outside on the pavement, enjoying an aperitif or a coffee, or waiting at the long bar with its array of polished glass and bottles. There was no hint of war or misery in this oasis of pleasure. In spite of the chronic shortages, an aroma of good cooking assailed them, and waiters rushed to the tables with dishes whose appearance became more tantalising with each passing moment. Across the table, Celine shimmered in the candlelight, leaning forward to listen to him, above the clatter of plates and the hum of conversation.

"I can't believe we're eating like this," she said, her mouth moist, the stain of berries still on her lips. "It's been so long since I had decent meat, or a fresh egg, or butter. That was phenomenal, Henri. I'd be a hypocrite if I said righteous things about black-market profiteers tonight."

He put down his glass and looked at her, his heart hammering. "Celine, you know I'm in love with you." He reached for her hand. "I'm afraid if I don't touch you, you might suddenly vanish, and I'd never know whether I'd really seen you at all."

She looked at him, her head on one side, lips slightly parted. She liked his square face, the steady grey eyes and slightly diffident expression, the mouth that suggested humour and kindness, the thatch of thick brown hair above the wide forehead. He was not handsome, but he was pleasing to look at and he exuded an impression of warmth, and the promise of laughter.

"Let's not go too fast," she said. "I love being with you. But I've only been qualified a short while, and my time and my life are not my own. You may get tired of taking out a girl who is constantly on call, and often half-asleep from too many hours on duty."

"Oh, I could live through that if I thought it wouldn't go on for

241

ever. In the meantime you could rescue me from my agonised state, and tell me there isn't anyone else serious in your life."

"There's no one else serious in my life." She was smiling at him still, and she had not moved her hand from beneath his. But as she said the words, an unbidden picture flashed into her mind of another man holding her hand, a man with blue eyes and dark hair, staring at her from his makeshift bed, whispering to her, thanking her for the gift of his life.

"Let's finish our coffee and go on somewhere to dance, and have a cognac. Would you like that, Celine?"

But to his disappointment she began to shake her head.

"I can't do that tonight. I promised Mama I would go over to Avenue Mozart after dinner. She isn't feeling well. I've been there almost every day recently."

"I'll come with you then. I'd love to see Charlotte, and perhaps we can find her some flowers on the way."

"That's sweet. But she's quite fatigued for some reason, and I won't be there long. Besides, I want to get to my apartment well before curfew, otherwise I'll be rushing back there in the morning, before making my way to the hospital. You see? I did warn you."

They walked to the top of Avenue Mozart, and he reluctantly took his leave of her, holding her hands in his and gently kissing her wrists and her palms. Then he tilted her face up and kissed her mouth. She stood still, her eyes closed. He kissed her again and felt her lips parting, and her wine-sweet breath. His tongue tasted her, found the softness of her, and her arms slid up around his neck as she moved closer to him, pressing her beautiful, curved form against his body. She withdrew from him, flushed and laughing.

"Goodnight, Mr de Valnay. You'd better hope that Mother is not gazing out of the window or you might be grilled about your intentions."

"My intentions are to make you fall wildly, passionately in love with me, Celine. Not very subtle, perhaps, but very direct."

"Goodnight, Henri. Thank you for a wonderful dinner, for the roses, for everything."

She rang her mother's doorbell, still humming to herself, feeling a little tipsy. André, the elderly butler, answered the door, his face creasing into a smile of welcome.

"Madame is upstairs," he said. "I'll let her know you are here, Miss Celine. Can I bring you a coffee, a tisane, perhaps?"

"No André, thank you. I'll go straight up." Celine began to climb the stairs.

"Miss Celine, if I may have a word with you?" Celine halted and looked down. André stood at the foot of the staircase, his expression sombre. "I hope you will not think I am speaking out of turn, but Louise and I are concerned about Madame de Savoie. She spends her time upstairs in her suite, and she is very tired. I think you should tell Madame that she should not try to look after her —" he hesitated. "To look after her 'guest' all on her own. We are here to help her, Louise and I."

Celine stood still, shocked. She wanted to respond to him, but she had no idea what to say.

"These are terrible days for France. The country has been shamed by defeat. We cannot be crushed by these brutes, or we will have no future. Not for our children and grandchildren, or for the country. We would like to help Madame de Savoie. We would like to fight. She does not need to be concerned about our loyalty."

"André, Madame was never concerned about your loyalty." Celine returned to the hall and put her hand on his arm. "But she has been afraid for you and Louise. She doesn't want to put you at risk."

"We cannot stand silent, and see the destruction of France. Two million of our young men have been taken away already. They are

243

prisoners and slaves. God knows if they will ever return. We have to fight to retain our dignity."

Charlotte was deeply moved by André's message. She looked across at Richard Kirwan, sitting in an armchair, pale and silent but beginning to heal.

"I suppose I was foolish to think they wouldn't notice," she said. "It's a relief in a way. And at least Richard will be able to move about now, and talk in a normal voice."

"I think it's time I left you," he said. "I've been here over a month, and I'm strong enough to move on now. There must be somewhere else I can stay while Achilles is arranging to get me out."

"You still have some way to go before complete recovery, Richard." Celine's tone was firm but she was smiling at him. "It's certainly time you got out a little. You look dreadful. Frightening in fact. I can't let any patient out of my care looking like that. It would be bad for my growing reputation!"

He smiled back at her, the brief light in his eyes startling in the gaunt face. Two weeks earlier Charlotte had broken the news to him that Daniel Nazarre was dead, that his friends Stefan and Leah had been taken by the Gestapo and his brother-in-law had been put aboard his boat gravely wounded. Through a contact in London, Achilles had at least been able to send a message to Helena confirming that her husband was alive. Richard watched Celine now, as she checked his pulse, took his temperature, cleaned and re-dressed his wound and inspected his lacerated arm. Her hair shone in the lamplight, and she looked bright-eyed, as though she had been — what? With a lover perhaps? He hoped the man was deserving of such a courageous, beautiful woman. He thought of Helena, and his body filled with pain as he imagined her anguish. She would be distraught. She was so fragile.

"What is it? Are you hurting somewhere?" Celine asked him.

"If the boat has returned safely to Ireland, Helena — my wife — will be frantic to know what has become of me, and the people we were supposed to bring out. It gnaws away at me. I'd just like her to know that I'm safe."

"Well, I don't think 'safe' is a particularly good choice of adjective." Charlotte raised her eyebrows, her expression wry. "But Achilles did manage to get one message through via London. And we'll send another when we know the date you can leave."

"In the meantime, Mama, I think Richard should put on some normal clothes again, get dressed, wear a shirt and jacket. In fact, it's time we let our fugitive out for a little fresh air and sunshine. I was thinking I could take him somewhere tomorrow afternoon."

"You can't go wandering around the streets with a hunted foreigner, just to get him a suntan."

"Of course I can take Richard out. He speaks perfect French, and he can pass for a Frenchman easily."

"I don't know, Celine. It's risky. You need to be so careful."

"Besides, Richard, I have a surprise for you," Celine said, ignoring her mother. "One of our group has made an identity card for you, and a ration card. With these, you can go out and tear up the town."

She opened her bag and removed the papers. He examined the forged documents, smiling a little at the near likeness on the identity card.

"As of now, you are Monsieur Emile Vallon of Sète, visiting Paris from the South. Here are your family details. You should memorise them and get your story right, in case you're stopped." Celine turned to her mother, enjoying Charlotte's surprise. "We can dress him in some of Father's clothes, and take him out for a stroll."

"You absolutely must stay far away from any of your previous haunts," Charlotte warned. "From streets or cafés that you used to frequent. And at all costs you must avoid your former colleagues from the Sorbonne, Richard. Contact with them would be a dangerous complication. But Celine is right. You need a change of scene." She gave him a long, cool inspection, making him feel like a small boy being scrutinised before being allowed out. "Perhaps you should think about a change of appearance. How about getting rid of the black hair? We could lighten you up to brown. Or you could try a moustache for a while, or even a beard. Meantime I have a very good idea."

She pressed the bell that rang downstairs in the kitchen. There was a knock at the door and Louise entered. Charlotte de Savoie took her hand and led her over to Richard, her gaze serene and unwavering, her voice steady.

"Louise, this is Monsieur Emile Vallon, a cousin from Sète. He will be staying with us for a few days. I know you will help me look after him while he is here. Perhaps you can get the guest room prepared for him?"

"I'll see to it immediately, Madame. Welcome to Paris, Monsieur Vallon. I'm honoured to meet you. Please ring for me or André if there is anything at all we can do for you." Louise's plump face had lit up with pride and she was gone before he could reply.

Celine looked at her watch. "I must be leaving Mama. I want to be home well before the curfew."

"I'll come downstairs with you, darling. I think I might have a drink in the drawing room. Richard – perhaps you would like to join me? We can help you with the stairs. Celine, why don't you delay for a few moments? It's almost a celebration, isn't it?"

"The bird flies from his gilded cage," Celine smiled at the delight and anticipation in Richard's face. "Yes, I'll join you for a few moments."

She took her patient's arm, conscious of how much she enjoyed supporting him. As they started down the stairs, she felt a glow of satisfaction and relief at his progress.

"Now Richard, let's take this slowly. You haven't been moving around much and one flight of stairs will be exhausting. You'll be surprised by your wobbly legs."

"Your room is ready, Monsieur Vallon. I hope you will sleep well after your journey." Louise had emerged from the guest room. She was beaming at him when the doorbell rang. They stood without moving on the marble staircase as André appeared in the hall and made his way slowly towards the door. Celine tugged at Richard's arm and led him back to her mother's bedroom. As she closed the door, she heard André's announcement.

"Madame de Savoie, General von Stroepper is here to see you."

Chapter 31

Paris, 1942

Almost an hour later, Charlotte poured them each a large cognac, willing her hands to remain steady, determined to bring their collective emotions under control.

"The Aryan conqueror arrives armed with quotations from Rilke and bouquets of flowers, whilst the terrified quarry shivers in fear only metres away. It's all been too much for me." Celine was unable to suppress the laughter that surged through her, surprising them all as they recognised the note of hysteria in its pitch. She swallowed a draft of cognac. "So General von Stroepper is paying court to you, Mother?"

But Charlotte's expression remained glacial. Walter von Stroepper's last words had been cold, and she knew that he had intended her to find them threatening. Her smile was forced as she tried to define the real purpose behind his visit. He would be disappointed and offended, he said, if she was not present at a reception he planned to host shortly. An invitation was on its way. She hesitated, wanting to escape into the spirit of Celine's laughter but acutely aware of her predicament.

"Celine darling, you'd better resign yourself to staying here tonight. It's past curfew time, and I'm sure you can't cycle straight, after that huge cognac."

"I couldn't even have stood up straight without it, after that little visit. Anyway, I don't have my bicycle this evening. I walked here after dinner with Henri. So, Richard, we can all help to celebrate your first night in a decent bed by sending you upstairs a little drunk."

"I'll make up your room, Miss Celine." Louise was still pale but giggling with the unaccustomed sensation of the brandy. "Goodnight Madame de Savoie, goodnight Monsieur . . ." Her memory failed her.

"It's Monsieur Vallon," Charlotte said. "He is a cousin from Sète, here in Paris to attend to some business for his father. Goodnight Louise. André. And thank you. I do not imagine any of us will forget this night."

They sat in silence for a while, each one of them allowing their narrow escape to penetrate their consciousness. Richard was the first to speak.

"Well, this evening's little episode has proved to me that I cannot remain here and continue to put you in danger, Charlotte." He stood up unsteadily. "There must be another place I can stay until my passage out of France is arranged."

"Of course you will remain here, Richard. But you're not ready to be presented to German generals. You look as though you've just stepped out of the grave. That grey tinge is difficult to explain." Celine smiled as she spoke the unflattering words.

"Your doctor is right." Charlotte relaxed into the restored calm of her salon, amused at Richard's bruised expression. "Tomorrow I think you should spend a few hours reading in the garden, taking a walk."

"But I cannot allow you to take the risk."

"It would be an even greater risk to transfer you elsewhere at this point." Charlotte surveyed him over the rim of her glass.

"Let's go up to bed, Mama. I'm exhausted by the evening's events." Celine did not want to become involved in a discussion that would lead nowhere. "I must be at the hospital early tomorrow and I'll have to go via my flat. I'd look a little out of place floating around the wards in a blue crepe dress, don't you think?"

Celine was smiling as she opened her bedroom window and leaned out into the garden. She could imagine Richard's pleasure at being able to sleep in a comfortable bed, with space and light around him. Lying in her own bed she thought about her dinner with Henri de Valnay, the touch of his fingers, their kisses, his words of love. It seemed so long ago. She thought again of Richard, released from his dark, cramped hiding place, his bedroom window open to the scent and sound of the garden below. She slept then, and left early in the morning, refreshed and revitalised.

The hospital was busy. Celine was deeply worried about the increasing number of old people and children suffering from a lack of nutrition. She was severely hampered by a shortage of drugs and medical supplies. German sentries were now posted in many areas of the hospital. Doctors, nurses and nuns went about their work, guarding their words as carefully as their patients. It was close to five o'clock when she left the wards to return to Avenue Mozart. Charlotte was waiting for her in the drawing room.

"Richard spent the morning in the garden, and he's had a siesta this afternoon. He's ready to go out with you. Putting on a jacket was rather painful, I'm afraid. Do you think he's all right without a tie? It's a warm evening."

Celine smiled inwardly. Here was a man with a gunshot wound, a hunted fugitive, and her mother was still concerned that he should appear in proper attire.

"Don't worry, Mama, I don't think there are any unbreakable dress rules for a September afternoon stroll. Are you coming with us?"

"I don't think so, darling. I'm behind on social commitments, and it might be best if I try and get back to near normal. By the way,

Henri telephoned. He was worried that you hadn't got home last night. I told him you'd decided to stay here, and he was relieved. He'd like to see you later this evening if possible, even for a drink."

Richard chose the river for his first outing. The water slapped against the ancient stones of bridges and quaysides, and they sat for a while on a bench near the Viaduc de Passy, enjoying the steely fantasy of the Eiffel Tower and the irony of the Statue of Liberty. He told Celine about his tenure in Paris, and how he had met Helena and then Seamus who had come and taken them back to Ireland when war was declared. They strolled a little further, Richard reluctant to leave the joy of the late summer evening, Celine content to prolong the intimacy of their conversation. She liked the sound of his voice and his rare, vivid smiles. They found a café and over watery cups of coffee he told her about Seamus and Leah, described both Daniel and Stefan. He came at last to the tragic afternoon when he and Seamus had come ashore, full of hope, to carry Leah and Stefan away to a better, safer world. His voice echoed with grief and regret as he described that night.

"God knows whether they are still alive. And Seamus – did he make it safely back to Roundstone, to Helena? Oh God, Helena. She's so tiny, so defenceless. You have no idea." His eyes blurred with tears and he put his hand up to hide his face, ashamed of his weakness.

"Stefan is from a neutral nation," Celine said, taking his scarred hands into her own. "Perhaps they somehow got away, or were detained and then deported. You said Stefan's father is influential, and pro-Nazi. Maybe he managed to have them released and sent to Sweden. You must stay hopeful, Richard. You must. That's your doctor's advice."

"Well I have some advice for you, too, Dr de Savoie." He looked across the table at her and attempted a smile. "This running of dangerous errands and dropping off of messages and leaflets is not for you."

Celine's face changed, annoyance clouding her expression of tenderness, but Richard either did not notice or chose to ignore it.

"If anything happened to you, I don't know what your mother would do, Celine. We've had plenty of time to talk about this during the past few weeks, and she needs you, especially since your father's death."

"A worthy speech, Richard." Celine looked at him, her eyes narrowed. "Of course it's fine for Mother to shelter fugitives, and for you to smuggle money and equipment into France, and rescue fleeing Jews, and for people like Daniel Nazarre to get shot. But I should just put on my little white coat and listen to the dying heartbeat of France while administering an occasional aspirin. Is that it?"

He regarded her seriously for a moment before responding. "You're right. It's presumptuous of me to tell you what to do. This is your country, your city, ravaged and invaded. I respect what you are saying and I admire the morality behind it. But war makes strange, unrecognisable people of us all, even those who appear to be our friends. Every turn in the street may bring some fatal encounter, perhaps mortal danger, even death. Be careful, there are no safety nets beneath the wire on which you tread."

He gripped her hands, leaning across the table, his face dark and serious and very close to hers, his eyes piercing her with the gravity of his warning. Celine gazed back at him, lost in his words and the acute sensation of his touch.

"Celine? I just called in at Avenue Mozart. Your mother was out, but Louise told me you might be by the river." Henri de Valnay was looking down at her, taking in the clasped hands, the intensity of the contact between her and this unknown companion, the way she had jumped in fright when he addressed her. He shifted his gaze to the dark-haired man. "I don't think we've met?"

"Emile Vallon. I'm a cousin of Charlotte's late husband," Richard said, in his impeccable French. "I'm in Paris for a few days. We were just about to return to Avenue Mozart. Celine, why don't you stay here, and I'll make my own way back."

"No. That's not a good idea Emile. No. And at any rate I've left my medical bag there. We'll go together. Will you come back to the house with us, Henri?"

They started up the incline, Henri making polite small talk, Celine filling in, trying to cover up her initial confusion. She glanced at Richard and saw that his face was very pale, his forehead beaded with sweat.

"Are you all right, Emile?" Her heart was beating fast. The uphill walk was too much for him and he could not maintain their pace. She tried to figure out what she could do to help him, without drawing attention to his frail state.

Henri saw him trip on a rough paving stone and wince. "You look unwell, my friend," he said. "Let's just sit down, here in this café, for a moment or two. There's no hurry, is there? We'll get some mineral water and then you may feel strong enough to continue."

"I'm so sorry to be holding you back. I was unwell before I left home, a stomach upset last week. I thought I'd recovered, but sometimes these things hang on for a while. I'm fine now, we can continue."

They stood up, Richard still a little unsteady. Henri put his hand out and firmly grasped his arm to offer support. Celine heard her patient draw in his breath with a small gasp of pain, saw Henri frown for a second. Then they moved forward, walking slowly until they were back in the hall at Avenue Mozart.

"I hope you'll excuse me, I think I'll lie down for half an hour. Thank you for your support Mr de Valnay."

"Not at all. Perhaps we'll meet again during your stay?"

"I'm only here for a day or so more. But if you are ever in the area of Sète..."

"My family has vineyards down there, a little further west. So perhaps our paths will cross again. Goodbye Monsieur Vallon. I do hope you'll be fully recovered soon."

There was silence in the hall as Richard slowly climbed the staircase. Henri looked at Celine. "Are you planning to go home now?" he asked. "Perhaps I can escort you."

"Well, I think I'll stop on the way and see if I can get something light to eat, and then have an early night. Why don't you telephone me tomorrow?"

"I don't think so, Celine." His mouth was firm, his jaw tight. "I think it would be much more interesting to take you home this evening."

They walked in strained silence for a while until he broke the impasse.

"You didn't mention that your mother had a guest?"

"He arrived unexpectedly last night." She smiled at him and quickly changed the subject. "Thank you for a wonderful evening, for a superb dinner. I haven't seen that much food for weeks."

"Louise told me he arrived several days ago. I think you should all get your stories straight. And I've never seen anyone from the Mediterranean with a face as pale and grey as that, never mind the hollows under the eyes and the bruise on the side of his head. Is he a cave dweller of some kind? And what's wrong with his arm?"

Celine stopped in the street and turned towards him, her face coloured with anger.

"What difference does it make to you who Mother has as a house guest, or what his background might be? You're bullying me, Henri, and I don't care for it."

"I don't know who this man is. I only know that some hollow-eyed stranger suddenly turns up at Avenue Mozart, takes you out, sits in a café clasping your hands and looking into your eyes, can barely walk, and has some sort of injury to his arm. And no one in your household seems to know when he arrived in Paris."

"He's been sick. You heard him say so. And Louise must be confused about which day he arrived. You know how it is."

"No. I don't know how it is. But I do know that Charlotte lives to release this city and the whole of France from the grip of German occupation. And I know that there are many small, clandestine groups involved in the very dangerous game of resistance and defiance." He stopped and took her arm, gripping her tightly. "You and your mother could lose your lives like this. The Germans have no mercy on people who are involved in any form of resistance. They don't even question most of those who are caught, they just shoot them. And those are the lucky ones. The rest are beaten, tortured, deported to prison camps with unspeakable conditions. Do you hear me, Celine, do you?"

He had begun to shake her, his voice low and insistent, drawing the attention of several passers-by. She pulled away from him. "Don't talk to me about the war and the Germans, Henri! Don't tell me how I should feel about these murderers trampling all over my country, killing innocent people, rounding up gypsies and deporting Jews just for being Jewish, starving small children and old people." She was trembling with rage, and they walked on without speaking until she reached the entrance to her building. She took a deep breath and tried to speak calmly. "I think I'll just go up now, and try to have a quiet evening, if you don't mind. Thank you again for yesterday. Goodnight."

"You must listen to me." He caught her hand and made her turn to face him. "I don't know what Charlotte is involved in exactly, or what your part in it might be. But I want you safe, Celine, because I love you. Do you understand me? Let others defy the Germans underground. You can fight by being a good doctor. That's enough to be proud of, darling, it's enough."

"Oh for God's sake, why does everyone keep telling me it's enough to be a doctor? And it's not enough, Henri, to drive around selling fine wine to bloated Germans, to buy and sell on the black market, and to supply restaurant owners who are collaborators. It's not enough to sit back and make more and more money out of circumstances that have destroyed your country, and put millions of French people into prison camps and forced labour in Germany. It's not enough! It's immoral and cowardly!"

A stone slab of silence descended between them as she stood there bristling with anger. Then he turned on his heel and left her. Exhausted, she put her key in the lock and climbed the stairs. The telephone was ringing as she opened the door.

"Yes?"

"Darling, we've managed to book a trip for Emile Vallon. It will be two weeks from today. I'll tell you about it tomorrow. Did Henri find you? Louise said he called in here."

"Yes, he found me. But I don't think he'll be looking for me again in the near future, if ever."

"What happened?"

"Henri didn't much care for our visiting cousin. He said he looked more like a cave-dweller than someone from the sunny South. An argument about our present lifestyles ensued."

"Oh my dear, I am sorry. But misunderstandings like this blow over. I think he's very much in love with you. He's just protective."

"And I think we have some giant differences of principle which certainly won't blow over. I'm very tired, Mother, and I'm going to bed early. I'll see you tomorrow, but not until late in the evening. I'm on duty all day. Goodnight."

For a long time she sat in her armchair, thinking about Henri de Valnay. It was probably best out in the open, this basic difference in their attitudes to the German occupation. She could not become further involved with him as things stood. All the same, she had half-expected him to phone. She sighed and got into bed. Although she was still wide awake, the strident sound of the telephone made her jump.

"Celine, I hope I'm not disturbing you. I just wanted to thank you for listening, for your kindness, for all your care. I hope your admirer isn't upset? And thank you again, so much."

It was not the voice she had expected to hear, but it made her heart beat crazily. An alarm sounded in her mind as she answered him. She tried to keep her tone light and friendly and the swell of gladness in check. "Sleep well. Be well. Goodnight."

She was smiling in her sleep almost before she replaced the receiver on its cradle.

Chapter 32

Paris, 1970

Elizabeth and James stared after the departing figure of Solange in stunned silence. Conversation around them ceased, as heads turned to watch her departure. It seemed as if the world had stopped, caught in mid-gesture by the click of a camera shutter. Guy's mouth tightened in a grimace of embarrassment and distress. James caught his eye momentarily, and then looked down at the floor. Elizabeth reached out to put a hand on Guy's arm, but he stepped back sharply.

"You must excuse me, Mademoiselle. Monsieur Kirwan. It seems you have an advantage over me, if one can describe it as such. Serge, I'm sure you will understand that I must leave now." He strode from the room.

For a few seconds there was an air of acute discomfort in the small group surrounding James and Elizabeth. Then the hum of conversation filled the vacuum once more. Serge summoned a waiter and handed them each a glass of champagne. James took a gulp of the sparkling liquid and cleared his throat. "Look Serge, I'm most terribly sorry about this incident. I'd like to explain."

He stopped, aware that this was not something he could really discuss. It was patently obvious from the scene they had just witnessed that Solange de Valnay had not confided in her fiancé. James realised that their appearance in Paris had precipitated a real crisis for his half-sister, and he did not think he should reveal her situation to anyone. He was frustrated and saddened that their first encounter should have been like this, and ashamed that he had not fully understood the terrible quandary in which she found herself. Serge was still waiting, too polite to press for an explanation. James tried again. "Serge, this is extremely awkward. It's a delicate family business. A problem with a legacy involving Solange de Valnay. We've never met her before, and we certainly didn't expect to find her here. Now she obviously thinks we engineered this encounter deliberately, but we would never have planned such a thing."

"And it would seem that Guy is also somewhat confused." Serge broke into James's stumbling account. "Look James, I don't require any elucidation of your private affairs. There has, as you so discreetly put it, been some awkwardness. But now it is over and we should go and dine."

"Serge, would you by any chance know where we could contact Solange de Valnay?" James asked. "I know she doesn't live in Paris, but perhaps we could find out where she is staying. I'd like to apologise for this frightful misunderstanding, both to her and to Guy St Jorre."

"Well, I imagine someone owes poor Guy an apology. That much seems clear. Solange usually stays with her grandmother when she's here. A formidable lady, Charlotte de Savoie, one of the most influential hostesses in Paris. She lives on Avenue Mozart. I can find the address for you if you wish to call. I would have thought Guy might be staying there too, at least until this evening."

Each of them stared into the distance, alone with their private thoughts in the crowded room.

"I'm not sure about dinner, Serge. Perhaps we might just go back to the hotel." James shifted his balance.

Serge turned to Elizabeth who had been silent since Solange's departure. She gazed back at him, her face troubled. Then she put her glass down on a marble-topped console. "Well," she said with finality. "I'm not going to let Solange de Valnay cast any gloom over my first night in Paris. I definitely want to go to dinner!"

She gave Serge a radiant smile and turned her back on James who was looking at her with exasperated disapproval. Dinner plans now seemed to him inappropriate, in the wake of Solange's distress. But Elizabeth showed no sign of regret or remorse for the shock they had imposed on their half-sister.

"Ah, I see Jacques Lefranche over there," said Serge. "Let me introduce you."

Lefranche was in his early forties, handsome but fleshy. He inclined his head towards Elizabeth and his glance travelled slowly down her body so that she was acutely aware of his unspoken message. He took her hand as Serge made the introductions, holding her fingers a shade too long and standing too close.

"Jacques, my guests are hoping to find someone who knew their father, Professor Richard Kirwan, when he lived in Paris just before the war. I wondered if your father might have come across him?"

"Well, I'll certainly ask the old man, and let you know. Where are you staying?"

"At the Raphael," Elizabeth answered.

"We're unlikely to be back until very late," said James. "It might be better if you telephoned me at Serge's office tomorrow."

Serge interjected. "I'm afraid James will be engaged all day tomorrow, Jacques, but perhaps he could contact you in the evening?"

"And Elizabeth is also busy." James spoke in clipped tones.

"You may ring me in the morning, Monsieur Lefranche." She nodded to him and left the crowded assembly, furious at the two men for making decisions on her behalf.

Dinner was an uneasy mixture of brittle gaiety and sudden silences. Serge was initially uncomfortable, but he was gradually drawn into Elizabeth's undisguised enthusiasm. James tried to join in the festive atmosphere, but his mind was clearly elsewhere. The evening finished early and Serge drove them back to the hotel.

In the morning Elizabeth ordered breakfast, and dialled her brother's room but there was no reply, and she was looking for Serge's office number when the telephone rang. She picked it up, resolving to be especially pleasant and co-operative with James.

"Ah, Mademoiselle Kirwan. I was afraid you would have already gone out. It's Jacques Lefranche. I spoke to my father last night. It appears that he does remember Richard Kirwan."

"I was just on my way out. Where are you, exactly?"

"I'm right here in the lobby. Why don't we go to my father's apartment on the Quai d'Orsay, and then have a little lunch?"

Elizabeth thought fast. Her brother would be angry if she went out with Jacques Lefranche. On the other hand, what a coup it would be if she could present James with new information about their father, when he returned in the evening. And she could always make some excuse to get away, once she had met Professor Lefranche.

"All right. I'll just leave a note for James."

Elizabeth found herself trying to quell a vague feeling of unease. But Jacques was a reputable lawyer. What harm could he possibly do her? She shrugged and took the lift down to the lobby. She could smell alcohol on his breath as he held the door of his car open for her. At the Quai d'Orsay he turned away from the Seine into a narrow street and drove through the gates of a courtyard, enclosed by nine-teenth-century buildings with ornate balconies and long shutters. In the entrance hall they stepped into the lift that resembled an old brass birdcage and rattled up to the second floor. Jacques tapped on the apartment door, using a key at the same time.

"Father, here is the young lady from Ireland, Elizabeth Kirwan. I told you I wanted to introduce her to you."

He led her into a drawing room that overlooked the courtyard. An old man sat in an armchair near the window, his knees covered by a plaid rug. His skin was paper-thin and mottled with liver spots. The veins stood out on his hands and on his head, around his temples. Elizabeth felt Jacques's pressure on her elbow and stepped forward.

"Elizabeth, this is my father, Maurice Lefranche." The old man looked up at her with rheumy eyes and remained silent and unmoving, as Jacques repeated his introduction. "This is the daughter of Professor Richard Kirwan. You remember him, don't you? You told me you did last night."

"Professor Lefranche, it's a pleasure to meet you. I am so glad to meet a friend of my father's from that time."

The old man nodded to her and waved one hand, as if to dismiss his son. Jacques brought Elizabeth a low chair, and then began to prowl around the room restlessly, picking up objects here and there. Maurice looked at him with irritation. "Jacques!" His voice was reedy and trembling. "Sit down and stop meddling. It will all belong to you soon enough!"

He gazed at Elizabeth. "My son can't keep his hands to himself. But you probably already know that?" He gave a dry cackle. "They're getting younger by the week, my dear Jacques!"

"Jacques tells me you knew my father before the war?" Elizabeth began to wonder which was the more unpleasant, the father or the son. She wanted only to conclude the interview as quickly as possible.

"Clever man, your father." The old man's watery eyes examined her carefully. "Not at all like him, are you? He was a tall man, with a dark complexion and very dark hair as I recall."

"You knew him well, then?"

"I saw him at conferences and in the dining halls of the university. Brilliant historian, going up the ladder fast. So everyone said. Not my faculty, but in those days all the professors knew one another. And our subjects overlapped sometimes." A small trail of saliva appeared at the corner of his mouth. "We weren't exactly friends, you know. He made bad errors of judgement. Took up with some arty set. Jews and wastrels, and even communists. A pity!" His eyes narrowed suddenly. "That's it — one of the girls I saw him with a few times, she was just like you! Same hair!"

"That was my mother, Helena."

"Married her, did he? Well, better than that uppity doctor, or a Jew from the family he was always visiting. One of them was in the Music Department here, little monkey of a man with a big nose and a small beard. We got rid of his kind in the end."

His voice rose and he coughed in his excitement, the sound of phlegm rumbling in his throat. Elizabeth was beginning to feel ill. She wanted to get away.

"Did you know any of my father's friends? Can you tell me anything else about him?"

"He should never have associated himself with those vermin. Communists and Jews. I don't know which was worse." He reached out and took her hand in a claw-like grip. "They said he left in 1940, ahead of the German troops. But I saw him again much later than that. It must have been in 1942."

Elizabeth was surprised. Why would her father have returned to France after the declaration of war and the occupation of Paris by the Germans?

"I thought it odd at the time," the old man continued. "He certainly wasn't at the university any more. And he looked different. Thin, with a hat on, sitting in some low-class café. He'd grown a beard, but I recognized him. Arrogant man, he was, always defending the underclass and warning us about the Germans. But the Germans were all right if you co-operated with them. And they knew how to get rid of the vermin."

"But did you talk to my father when you saw him in 1942? Are you quite sure it was him?" Elizabeth was convinced that he had been mistaken.

"Oh yes, I'm sure. He was with that aristocratic bitch Charlotte de Savoie, and her daughter. A doctor she was, the daughter, but not the sort who mixed with the likes of us. Too grand, they were. And all the time hobnobbing with the dregs. Jew-lovers and allies of the communists, all of them." He cackled again. "Well the great Charlotte de Savoie got her comeuppance in the end. Sent to prison, and her property seized. He didn't pick his friends wisely, your father. I heard the Gestapo spent a bit of time on him. It won him a Croix de Guerre. Saw it in the newspapers, after the war."

Elizabeth gazed at him, unable to disguise her amazement. Could this really be true? The old man's grip tightened.

"Ha! Didn't tell you about that, did he? Ashamed in the end, of the company he kept. All those Jews and criminals. Probably having something on the side with the doctor, from what I saw. She disappeared out of Paris too. But he didn't manage to save that fellow Nazarre. Sent away and never returned, and I was glad of that. Better to avoid those people teaching your children. You don't know what kind of contamination and propaganda they might be spreading!" Spittle had formed in the corners of his mouth. He was beginning to dribble.

"Father!" Even Jacques realised that his father had gone too far.

Elizabeth was staring at him unable to release herself. Her skin was crawling. Jacques bent forward and prised his father's fingers from her hand.

"Take her away, son. Take her to the Bois de Boulogne or take her to one of her father's old haunts." He waved his son away, cackling in his high-pitched, cracked voice.

"I really have to be going, Professor Lefranche. Thank you for seeing me." Elizabeth was already at the door.

Her head had begun to ache. Had her father really been in France with Solange de Valnay's mother and grandmother during the war? But that must have been while James and Eleanor were being born in Ireland. How could Mother have taken him back? Maybe Maurice Lefranche was right about the shame Richard Kirwan had felt over his liaison with Solange's mother. Perhaps that was why he had never told his family he had received the highest award for bravery in France. But what had he received it for and where would he have kept it? Elizabeth decided that Professor Lefranche must be confused. He was just a repulsive old crackpot. Jacques brought her down to the car, talking to her as he went, but she was barely conscious of what he was saying.

"I'd like to go back to the hotel please, Jacques."

"We are going to lunch now." Jacques's expression was petulant. "And then I would like to show you my own apartment on the river. There is a fine view." He reached across and placed a hand on her thigh.

"No. Thank you. I need to get back to the Raphael."

His expression was livid and his lip twisted in ugly scorn. He was cursing as he turned on the ignition and sent the car roaring out on to the main road, racing and weaving recklessly through the traffic. At the hotel he made no attempt to open the car door for her. She fled gratefully into the security of the Hotel Raphael and went to collect her key.

"Mademoiselle Kirwan, there is a gentleman waiting to see you."

Elizabeth closed her eyes in despair. All she wanted to do was to go upstairs and sink into the bath, cleanse herself of the whole disgusting episode and try to make sense of what she had learned about her father. But the receptionist was signalling to her visitor.

"Mademoiselle Kirwan, you don't look well."

She felt a firm hand beneath her elbow and looked up into the tanned face and hazel-green eyes of Guy St Jorre.

"I've obviously called at a difficult time. Please excuse me. I'll come back at a more convenient moment."

"No," she said, striving to control her voice. Suddenly she did not

265

want to be alone. "Monsieur St Jorre, would you mind very much escorting me up to my suite?"

They rode up in silence. Delayed reaction to the ugly interview was making her feel sick. Her head still ached and she rested it against the wall of the lift. She wanted to hide like a small child, and cry. Guy led her into the suite and guided her to the sofa. Then he sat down on an ottoman beside her.

Elizabeth lifted her feet off the floor and drew her knees up under her chin. She tried unsuccessfully to smile at Guy. Then she took a deep breath and began to explain. The words tumbled out in tearful sentences. Her father's death, the will, the letters between Eleanor and Solange, the trip to France, the awful encounter at the Hotel Crillon, and finally the disastrous visit to Maurice Lefranche. Guy listened without interruption, except for a quiet question here and there. He did not seem to judge her, or lay blame on anyone.

"So Solange would have received Eleanor's first letter in February? Almost five months ago?" Guy asked, when she had finished. He shook his head, and buried his face in the palms of his hands. "I knew there was a problem. But this! And she never told me anything at all."

"So, what shall we do now?" Elizabeth looked at him, seeking guidance. "I do really want to know about my father, and Solange's mother too. It's important to get the whole story. Don't you agree, Guy?"

Her eyes began to fill with tears. He leaned forward and placed an arm around her shoulder, dabbing at her eyes with a handkerchief. "You must make that decision for yourself. But no one else should be hurt or embarrassed by this. Perhaps the first thing is to look up the records of all those who received the Croix de Guerre. There is always a detailed citation to accompany each award. I could arrange for you to do that, perhaps."

"Oh thank you Guy, thank you so very much." Elizabeth flung

her arms around his neck and embraced him. A key turned in the lock and the door swung open.

"I'm back, Lizzie!"

James Kirwan stepped into the room and stopped, stunned at the sight of his sister, sitting forward on the sofa, locked in an embrace with Solange de Valnay's fiancé.

Chapter 33

Paris, 1970

Solange had breakfast in her room, knowing better than to disturb Charlotte de Savoie before eleven. She had climbed the curving staircase in the early hours of the morning, following the same steps taken by her mother when she had come with her doctor's bag on that evening in 1942.

"Can I see where you hid him? When will I hear the rest of the story?"

"Solange, this isn't some thrilling bedtime serial. This is a part of my life, and your mother's life, which has not been spoken of for years. It's very painful, all this remembering." Charlotte's tone indicated her displeasure.

"Even at the end, she didn't trust me enough to tell me. She must have known what he was going to do. And why did he include me in his will?" Solange waited for a soothing response, but no kindly words of reassurance were forthcoming.

"My dear, you know perfectly well now that it wasn't that simple. She had to think of Henri."

"So she loved this other man, carried his child, and at the same time she married my father. Does he know I'm not his daughter?"

"You are his daughter," Charlotte's voice was angry. "He adored you from the moment you were born. He has protected you, guided you, shared everything in his life with you. He is your father, and that is all."

"Well, what happened to him during the war? I never heard that period mentioned in our house, or here for that matter. And yet you and Mama were members of the resistance. Shouldn't someone have told me before that our family fought bravely, made a difference in the history books? I just can't grasp it all."

"Solange, the Second World War is still a difficult subject in France. Many people are unable to speak of it, even now. The lines between those who were considered collaborators and those who just continued with their lives as best they could are blurred. There's still so much shame and confusion attached to it all." Charlotte de Savoie leaned back in her chair, her body drooping with tiredness. "It's three o'clock in the morning, Solange and I'm an old lady. I'm not going to give you a lesson on the resistance at this hour."

"Richard Kirwan couldn't have put me in his will without Mama's consent," Solange said stubbornly. "And how come you, of all people, didn't know?"

"I knew that Richard had died, and I was deeply saddened by it. But I did not know about his will. And I don't believe your mother did either."

"He must have been insane as well as cruel." Solange saw her grandmother wince. "What other explanation could there be for what he's done to us all? This is destroying my life, and now my relationship with Guy."

"Your encounter with the Kirwans this evening sounds too melodramatic to have been engineered by Guy. And totally out of character too. Perhaps you haven't heard the whole story." Charlotte de Savoie stood up. "I'm going to bed. We'll continue this tomorrow."

She took her granddaughter's arm and for the first time Solange noticed the lines in the chiselled face, recognised the sadness behind the clear authority of her grandmother's gaze. At the door of her bedroom they hugged, holding one another with tenderness. Solange fell into bed exhausted, but her mind remained full of vivid images that prevented sleep. Was this where her mother had slept with Richard Kirwan, in this very room? Was this where she had been conceived?

At nine there was a knock on her door and Louise appeared to tell her that Guy was downstairs. He looked tired and grave and made no effort to embrace her.

"I think we have some explanations to offer one another," Solange began nervously.

"You certainly have things to explain to me. But only one of them is important. I realise now that you discovered something of major importance in your life while I was away. Something painful and difficult."

She stepped nearer to him, trying to maintain her composure, pressing her lips together firmly. He backed away from her.

"No, let me finish please. You couldn't trust me enough to confide in me." He was speaking evenly, but she saw that he was angry. "We're engaged to be married, Solange. I love you and you're going to be my wife. This is no way to start a life-long partnership."

"You don't understand how shocked I was. How desperate."

"You don't understand that people who plan to be married have to be honest with the person they love and trust. And I realise now that you do not trust me."

She burst out again, defensive rage turning her words into further miscalculations. "No. It wasn't like that. You knew all along what had happened and you brought those people to meet me. I trusted you and you betrayed me."

"Trusted me!" Violent anger directed his volley of words. "What can you possibly have to say about trust? How dare you suggest that I deliberately confronted you with the Kirwans. My God, Solange, this is far beyond anything I could have imagined!"

He sat down, gripping the carved arms of his chair, his face full of fury. Doubt and fear made Solange hesitate for a moment. "You knew them before, didn't you? You knew they'd be there?" It was a question now, and not the accusation she had intended to make.

"I never dreamed you thought so little of me." He stood up and walked towards the door. "We should consider breaking off our engagement. I suggest you think it over for a day or two, and I will do the same. I'll be at home in Montpellier when you want to get in touch with me."

She could not move or respond as she began to realise the enormity of her mistake.

"I'll see myself out. Give my fond regards to your grandmother."

Solange was left alone, staring at the space he had occupied. A new fear was forming in her mind. If Guy had not brought the Kirwans to Paris, why were they there? Were they planning to appear at Avenue Mozart? There had been no sign of Eleanor last night. Why had she not been with them? Solange turned swiftly and ran up the stairs to arrive in her grandmother's bedroom breathless and distraught.

"What is it darling? Oh I know, it's Guy." Charlotte sighed. "Louise told me he was here. Well, whatever you both said, something will be sorted out when you've had time to think things over."

"No, it's worse than that Grandmama! It's not just Guy. You see, two of the Kirwans were at the Crillon last night. But there are three of them. I told you that. And Eleanor, the one who wrote to me, wasn't there. I think she's on her way to see my father!"

Charlotte sat quietly for a moment, her gaze focused on her granddaughter. Then she sighed. "Darling, sit down. Too many hasty decisions and assumptions have been made and acted upon over the last few weeks. Now, let's begin again and try to take it slowly and logically."

Solange attempted to speak more quietly, but the words were punctuated by sobs. "Guy has broken off our engagement. And I'm afraid that Eleanor Kirwan has gone to find me, and that she'll tell my father who she is."

"Solange, you have no idea whether Eleanor Kirwan is even in France." Charlotte looked at her watch. "But we'll telephone Lorette and make sure Henri is not disturbed by any unknown callers, either by telephone or in person. You'll stay here tonight and we will talk all this through. And you'd better make sure that there isn't anything else you haven't told me because, darling, I absolutely will not deal with any more shocks."

Chapter 34

Paris, 1942

There was a knock on the study door and Charlotte looked up to see Richard Kirwan standing in a beam of slanting light. He was still rake-thin although he had acquired a healthier appearance.

"Let me guess." He smiled at her as she finished writing on a card lying on her leather blotter. "An invitation to a small dinner party, to keep the spirits up, defy the ugly Boche?"

She looked at him with a flash of amusement, then continued her work, holding her gold fountain pen in perfectly manicured fingers. "Actually, these are false identity papers," she said, holding up the card to study her handiwork more closely. "I'm a marvellous forger. It's probably from having been taught to faithfully reproduce ancient manuscripts as a child. I don't think this is what the nuns had in mind, but I can copy signatures faultlessly."

Richard laughed with delight. "And who delivers all these documents for your expert work?"

"Celine collects them from mail drops, or from one of the presses. As a doctor she has a perfect excuse to be cycling all over Paris. She brings identity papers, ration cards, passes into the unoccupied zone. But we're held up at present. One of the presses has broken down."

"Well, I don't think I'm talented enough to be a good forger. But I

273

could help with the collections and drop-offs." Richard was leaning towards her, his eyes lit with enthusiasm.

"No, Richard. It won't be long before we receive a message that your passage home has been arranged. It would be madness to do anything that might jeopardise that."

"Charlotte, I can't continue to sit here week after week, reading in your garden, strolling along the river, sunning myself as though I were on holiday. I have an identity card, and I can pass as Emile Vallon in any circumstances."

"Celine will oppose this idea, Richard."

"It isn't necessary for Celine to know."

"It's out of the question Richard. There's too much risk involved." Charlotte was adamant.

But as the days of waiting followed one another, Richard became withdrawn and tense. He ate little and his spirits were low. One afternoon he was recognised by a former university colleague as he sat in a café with Charlotte and Celine. After that he was reluctant to let either one of them accompany him on his walks, and he went out less. Finally, Charlotte relented and gave him a small package of documents to deliver to a drop-off near the Place de la Concorde.

He returned from his first errand full of energy and purpose. From then on Achilles, who led their small group, came quickly to rely on Richard's courage and clear thinking, and Charlotte was humbled by his solitary acts of bravery. His new role remained a secret until the inevitable evening when Celine arrived at Avenue Mozart before his return.

"Where is Richard? André says he went out more than four hours ago. Isn't that a little long to be safe?" Celine's tone was sharp with concern.

"You may as well know, darling, that Richard has taken some papers to a drop at Etoile. Achilles thought he was being followed yesterday and Richard offered to take his place this afternoon."

"Why would he do such a thing?" Celine gazed at her mother in astonishment.

"He couldn't cope with feeling cooped up and useless any longer. So I agreed, some time ago, to let him do a few deliveries."

"How could you send him out to risk the life I've worked so hard to put back together? I can't believe you put him in such danger!"

Charlotte sat still, surprised by the ferocity of her daughter's anger, stung by it, measuring Celine's reaction through a new awareness of her own. "Don't you think you're overreacting to this, darling? It's been wonderful for his morale. He was getting very depressed with all the waiting."

"I can't believe you allowed this."

"Celine, be reasonable." Charlotte's voice was measured. "I'm sending my own daughter out on these errands all the time. I'm putting the person I love most in terrible danger, each and every day."

There was a sound and they turned to see Richard standing in the doorway, pale and drained.

"There was a trap. They were waiting." He sat down heavily. "When I arrived at the rendezvous there were two men sitting on the bench where I was supposed to meet my contact, so I walked past and went into a shop. From the window I saw two other men on the pavement opposite, just standing there."

"You didn't approach them Richard – they didn't notice you?" Charlotte was tapping the table, drumming hard on the polished surface.

"No. There was something about them, something wrong about the way they looked. Then I saw the car parked not far from the bench, with the back door open."

"What about your contact?" asked Charlotte.

Richard rose and walked to the open French windows. He stood with his back to them, his shoulders hunched. "I sat in a café and waited. At two-thirty, a young woman arrived and sat down on the bench. I knew she was the courier I was supposed to meet. She was very young, barely in her twenties, and obviously nervous." Richard turned abruptly away from the window. "She should never have gone to the bench when she saw the two men, but she did. One of them spoke to her and I saw her face flash alarm. Then they marched her to the car, and she was gone."

"Oh God! The poor girl." Celine was white-faced, close to tears.

"It could have been you, Celine, or your mother." Richard's voice was unsteady. "God forgive me, I felt like a monster, because I was so glad it was her and not one of you. I was just so glad."

"You shouldn't have been there, Richard." Celine spoke coldly.

"We've had this conversation, Celine, but in reverse. It was just a few weeks ago. I had to respect your courage, as you pointed out then. You don't have a monopoly on feeling you should be doing something to fight."

He saw that she was stung by his tone. Charlotte de Savoie saw it too. "The question is what were the Gestapo doing there? Could anyone have followed you back here?"

"I don't think so. I returned by a very circuitous route, which is why I'm so late."

"I'm due at the printing press. They had another breakdown earlier, but if they've managed to get things working again, I'll pick up some blank cards." Celine stood up and kissed her mother. "I'll telephone you later, Mother."

"I'm coming with you," Richard said firmly. "Don't even begin to argue with me. I know something about printing presses and I may be able to help."

They set out together in silence. Darkness began to cloak the city as they moved through streets subdued by the grim force of occupation.

"I'm sorry I spoke so sharply," he said. "Relief has strange ways of expressing itself. That was a terrible thing to see. She was so young, so frightened."

276

Celine looked up at him, still not giving any signal that he was forgiven. "You should have told me."

"Yes, I should. But I didn't want you to be upset. I realise that I owe you my life and perhaps more importantly, my sanity."

"You may not thank me for saving your life, if you end up in the hands of the Gestapo. And after today's episode, I'm not sure about your sanity."

She was smiling at last. But Richard remained serious. "It's hard to imagine feeling guilty at being alive and safe. But I think of that girl, and I'm reminded of Helena frantic with worry. And I wonder about Seamus, and what might have happened to Stefan and Leah." He felt the sympathetic pressure of her fingers on his arm. "You've helped me through those moments so many times, Celine. And no one will ever be able to understand the strength I've drawn from Charlotte." He stopped for a moment and took her hand. "She told me about your father's heart attack, about coming into the study and finding him on the floor, dying there in front of her. And the effort she's had to make to continue without him."

"He was a wonderful, special man." Celine smiled as she summoned her memories of her father. "He married her when she was eighteen years old, so they were together almost thirty years. It seems a long time to be married when you're not even fifty."

She stopped and pushed open a door set into a wall of crumbling masonry and peeling paint. Richard followed her across an overgrown courtyard towards a shed at the back. They went through a narrow door and down a flight of steps. Inside the small room the heat was stifling, and the pounding noise of machinery hammered in their ears.

At a trestle table a young man pored over some photographs of German soldiers, their guns pointed at several bodies lying dead on the ground. A girl stood close to him, wrestling with the clanking press as it roared into life, shuddered and then stopped. Celine touched the girl's arm and shouted into her ear. "Lisette, this is Emile. He knows something about printing equipment."

Richard tried to start the engine. It was difficult to concentrate, or even to breathe, in the heat of the cellar. When he straightened at last he was bathed in sweat and grinning as he pressed a button. The old machine sprang into life, rattling and snorting like an ancient beast and Celine wondered how the presses could remain undetected from the hostile world outside. In that moment she felt a prickling on the back of her neck, a sense that someone was watching her. She turned round. A fall of loose stones made her glance up at the ventilation holes in the wall above her and she saw the tip of a gun barrel appear.

"Get down!" She shouted above the noise of the presses. "Get down behind the machines! Run for the back door!"

She raced across the room towards Richard. Lisette turned from the press and caught her arm in the machinery. She screamed out in horror and pain as gunfire tore through the thick, stale air.

"Halt! You are surrounded! Move and you will be shot!"

They ran towards the back door, ducking down behind the machinery to give them cover. The young man fell, drops of blood spattering the photographs of the German soldiers and their victims. Lisette clasped her mangled arm as Richard guided her towards the doorway. Behind them they heard the sound of boots clattering down the staircase.

"Quick, Celine, there are only two of them. We have a chance."

They stumbled up the slope in the darkness, half-dragging half-carrying Lisette, and clambered over the broken wall to fall, gasping, into the adjoining courtyard. There was no one in sight. Richard forced his way into an abandoned warehouse and they stood for a moment in the gloom, Celine holding Lisette close to her, cradling the bleeding arm.

They crouched behind a pile of sacking, the stench and filth making

Celine gag. Lisette was pale, her breathing harsh. Celine placed a hand gently over her mouth to quiet her as a German soldier used his rifle to push open the door. He stood silhouetted in the dying light, his gun in front of him.

The soldier shone a torch around the walls. Rats and cockroaches scurried for cover as he raised his gun. There was an explosion of sound, and then the German turned on his heel and left, prodding the piles of vermin infested sacks with his bayonet, stepping over mounds of rubbish to get to the doorway. From the adjacent yard a plume of smoke spiralled into the sky. Within moments they heard the deafening noise of the dilapidated building collapsing on to the machinery hidden below.

"I'm going to take a look outside," said Richard. "Wait here until I make sure there are no more unpleasant surprises."

Celine held on to Lisette, counting the long minutes until Richard returned.

"I think we can leave. There's no sign of anyone out there and I've been all the way along the street to the corner."

"Lisette's in shock and she's lost far too much blood. I'll take her to a safe house near here. Then maybe to the hospital." Celine searched in her pockets and handed Richard a key. "You can go to my place and wait for me there."

An hour later Richard let himself into Celine's apartment. He sank gratefully into an armchair and telephoned Charlotte de Savoie.

"We're fine," he told her. "Celine's gone to check on a patient at the hospital and I'm waiting for her in her apartment. She'll phone when she gets here. Very soon I hope. Be careful, Charlotte, and wait for her call."

In the hours that followed, each movement of the hands on the clock signalled an eternity Richard could never have imagined. Then he heard the soft tap on the door and she was there, her face alight with triumph, her hair shining in the dim light as she stood in the doorway. She rushed into his arms, laughing and crying at once.

"Oh thank God you're here and you're safe. We stitched Lisette's arm at the hospital and they've hidden her until someone comes to take her to a safe house. I never guessed that Dr Ducray was working with us, and some of the nuns too. But that young man who was on the presses, he's dead before his life had even begun."

He held her as she wept. At last he tilted her face up and made her look at him as he wiped away her tears. Then he bent and kissed her gently. She put her arms up around his neck and he drew her closer and kissed her once more. She could feel his breath, hear his heart beating. She offered her mouth, tasting his lips with her tongue.

The telephone rang in shrill warning and Charlotte de Savoie's voice came clear and firm over the line.

"Emile is leaving tonight. A message has been sent to his wife and she will be expecting him. Achilles is waiting for you at his apartment. Take care darling. Take great care."

Celine turned and looked at Richard without speaking as she tried to quell the wrenching in her heart. Then she took his hand. "You're going home, Richard. Back to Ireland. Achilles is taking you tonight."

He stood silent, his heart beating too fast, his emotions burning out of control through the cool layers of accustomed logic. He could not smile because he saw her eyes, glittering with tears. The telephone rang again, shrill and insistent. Charlotte's voice was strained. "Celine, something is wrong. There are Germans downstairs at the door. Take Emile and leave the building."

In the background Celine heard shouting. Then the cord between mother and daughter was broken by a click and a long, long silence.

Chapter 35

Paris, 1942

Richard and Celine had been sitting tense and upright on two small, hard chairs for more than an hour when Achilles arrived at the safe house in the rue de Grenelle. The dingy apartment on the third floor had access to the surrounding rooftops as a possible escape route. It served as a cramped base for the decoders who spent their days and nights working on the radio messages that flew between London and France. Richard stood up and opened the door when he heard Achilles's triple knock and the whispered password.

"Celine, I'm so very sorry. Your mother has been arrested. We're doing everything we can to find out where she has been taken."

Achilles passed his hand over bloodshot eyes. His small group had moved, with equipment and transmitters, more than a dozen times in the past eight months, and his keen awareness of danger told him that it was time to seek yet another base of operations. "It seems I will be losing a valuable member of my team." He turned to Richard. "You'll be leaving by plane tomorrow night, my friend. I'm taking you now to a farmhouse where they will hide you near the landing field. But first, there are documents and messages to give you, all to be taken to London."

Celine listened quietly to the briefing. Her mind, trained to analyse and resolve the most grotesque of situations, now refused to grasp the full horror of what had happened. Where was her mother? Who, amongst their small, trusted cell, could have betrayed them? She recognised the added danger involved in Richard's departure. Nausea swept through her, making her hands icy cold and turning her face ashen. Achilles glanced at her with sympathy and opened a cupboard. He took out a bottle of cognac, poured a generous measure into a cup and placed it in her shaking hands. In a swirling current of despair Celine tried to think of some plan of action.

"Achilles, is the phone safe?"

"Make a call if you wish. But be wise, and be brief."

Celine picked up the telephone, a fervent prayer in her heart. Then she heard his voice, quiet and deep. Her own words were sharp with fear. "Henri, Mother has been arrested. Is there anyone you know, anything you can do to find her?"

She could not prevent the choking tears. Achilles moved to her side and took the telephone, speaking quietly to Henri. At last he replaced the receiver on its cradle and turned to her. "He will do everything that he can. I assume he is completely trustworthy?"

Celine stared at him for a long moment, then nodded. No matter what his beliefs, Henri would surely do everything to help her mother.

"He advises you not to go home, and certainly not to Avenue Mozart. Call in to the hospital sick, if you are expected on duty. I'm going to leave here with Richard in about an hour. Perhaps the best thing is for you to come with us. Your friend says there will not be much he can do until tomorrow at the earliest. We are at war, Celine my dear, and this is how it affects us all in the end."

"Yes, I'll come with you. I have to keep occupied, and perhaps I can be useful."

"You can help with the landing lights," replied Achilles. "The pilots need every bit of direction we can provide for them, and the forecast is for a cloudy night."

Celine sat down again beside Richard. He took her hand, pressing comfort into her palm and she rested her head on his shoulder. He placed his arm around her, cradling her, holding her close to him. When Achilles finally signalled that it was time to go, he had a selection of documents for Richard to carry. Additional messages, and information written in code on tiny scraps of paper and fabric, were hidden quickly in the lining of his jacket and the soles of his shoes.

They emerged into rue de Grenelle, making no sound, walking swiftly. A ghostly moon dimmed and then disappeared. In the maze of darkened streets, Achilles stopped suddenly as they heard a noise behind them. It was a harsh, croaking sound like an animal caught in a trap. They moved into the shadow provided by the door of a church and waited. A tall figure lumbered out of the gloom behind them, shuffling, dragging one leg awkwardly behind him. An arm, attached to something that looked like a large paw, was raised in what seemed to be supplication.

"Achilles! It's Stefan!" The whisper was hoarse with desperation. "They released me. They beat me, but I didn't speak Achilles. I have to talk to you. I've been following you for the last few days, trying to find a safe place to stop you, but it's been too dangerous."

"Stefan, you're crazy! You shouldn't have come here."

"My father's sending me to Sweden tomorrow, but I had to see you first."

Richard turned to look back at his friend. Stefan's face was twisted and broken, his left eye drooped downwards. A livid scar drew a line of indelible pain across his cheek to his ear. One arm dangled from a crooked shoulder, and his hands were bandaged as though he was wearing thick gloves. Occasionally he grasped his right leg and hauled it over the cobbles, grunting with pain and effort.

"Richard! Thank God you're alive! Have you any news of Leah? For God's sake, is there any news of her?" Stefan's voice rose to a wail.

Achilles reached ferociously out of the dark and put a hand roughly across Stefan's mouth. "Quiet, God damn you! Do you want to get us all killed? Be quiet, Stefan! You should never have come looking for me like this."

But Stefan could not stop babbling. Tears poured down his slack, beaten face and his ungainly, broken body heaved. The huge, bound paws gesticulated wildly in the moonlight. Then there was a flash of light. Achilles reached for his gun as Stefan turned in a grotesque pirouette. Achilles's body jerked upwards, jumping into the air like a puppet, before falling on to the street, his twitching limbs stilled by the hail of bullets. There was a gurgling sound from his throat. Stefan stood still, frozen in the terrifying realisation that he had unwittingly led the Germans to his friends. Celine began to run, grasping Richard by the hand. Their pursuers stopped to ensure that Achilles was dead, and to push the wailing, ranting figure of Stefan aside, kicking his misshapen frame into the gutter. Gaining vital seconds, Richard and Celine raced through the dark streets, hearing occasional shouts behind them. They came at last to the river and crouched in the shadows beneath the Pont de l'Alma, trying not to gasp for breath, straining to gauge the proximity of pounding feet.

"There aren't many of them, and I have a gun. Leave now, Celine. Run, while I create a diversion. Warn the rest of your group that Achilles is dead, and that Stefan has probably blown our cover."

"There's another safe house not too far. Try to get there. I'll wait for you." She whispered the address and the password and left him, creeping away from the dark protection of the bridge, from the shouting and the running feet. She stumbled and her ankle turned, causing her to cry out and to pause for a moment. The moon emerged to pour a detached, indifferent beauty on to the water and she glanced around. Richard stood, one arm around the neck of the German soldier, the other braced against the support of the bridge. Celine saw the grey helmet fall, clattering on to the pebbles, and stood transfixed as Richard increased his pressure on the German's thick, muscular neck and gave a violent twist. The man's eyes bulged silver in the moonlight and she heard a cracking sound as he struggled and collapsed on to the stones. Richard picked up the rifle and raised his arms in the moonlight, making a strange primitive noise as he thrust the bayonet deep into the padding of the grey uniform. Then he dragged the body towards the edge of the river. Celine could hear him panting with exertion, swearing in a low voice as he heaved. There was a soft, splashing sound and the bulky figure was gone.

She was about to turn back to him when several soldiers appeared on the bank above them, shouting for assistance and leaping on to the solitary figure below. The river's edge was alive with Germans and Celine heard the sound of a vehicle. She crouched, trembling, in the shadows as they hauled him away. Doors slammed, a motor roared into action. Then there was nothing but the timeless lap of the water and the echo of her own sobbing.

She set out again, through the ominous quiet of the night streets, fear walking swift and soft beside her as she sought to avoid being trapped out of doors after the curfew. At last she climbed a flight of steps and came to Henri de Valnay's apartment. She tapped lightly and when he opened the door she saw that his face was drawn and grey. He reached out to her and pulled her inside the room.

"Celine! I prayed it would be you. Thank God." He held her against him, and she clung to his solid stability as she wept for the terrifying fate of her mother and the man she loved.

Chapter 36

Paris, 1942

Charlotte de Savoie turned from the telephone to face the two men in her drawing room.

"May I ask who you are?"

"Gestapo. You are under arrest Madame de Savoie. Please pack a few personal belongings and come with me for questioning."

"What right do you have to enter my residence? And on what matter do you wish to question me?"

The man who had first addressed her spoke in German to his colleague who disappeared into the study. Within moments she could hear him pulling out the drawers of her desk, riffling through papers, moving furniture aside. There was a crash as a piece of porcelain fell to the floor. Upstairs she said a silent prayer of thanks that Celine had taken all the documents she had worked on earlier in the week. There was no evidence to incriminate her and now she would have to rely on instinct and courage.

She packed a few toiletries and night clothes into a small suitcase and descended the staircase, breathing calm and resolution into her soul. In the car she began to calculate how she should present herself, but her determination was shaken by a fissure of fear as she was led into the Gestapo headquarters in Avenue Matignon. The room she entered on the first floor was bare except for a table and several straight-backed chairs, one of which was occupied by a uniformed officer. He was a big man, his complexion slightly florid, but the broad planes of his face had an open expression. At his side was a slight, balding man with glasses, dressed in a civilian suit. His face was sallow, his eyes fixed on his papers, his mouth thin. Neither man looked up or acknowledged her. Charlotte stood erect, waiting for one of them to speak, recognising their intent to humiliate and intimidate her. Then the questions began.

"Madame de Savoie, you are involved, unwittingly or otherwise, with saboteurs determined to undermine the authority of Germany. If you will co-operate with our enquiries, I am sure you will not be detained here for long. I am Captain Reiner." The uniformed officer had a voice that was pleasant, educated. He glanced up at her with a suggestion of sympathy. "You will begin by telling us about the group of criminals led by the man Achilles. He was shot this evening and his companions have given us information which will result in further arrests tonight."

"I think you have made a mistake." Charlotte's words were quiet and steady, triumphing over her racing pulse and dry mouth.

"Madame de Savoie, I can assure you that your best interests will be served by truthfulness and a spirit of co-operation. We know this man Achilles visited your residence earlier this evening, so we can begin there." Reiner was still courteous, but he was watching her carefully for any sign of weakness. She held her head up and slightly back, levelling her eyes with his.

"I did not receive any visitors this evening, Captain Reiner. If you have been watching my home for some reason, you will know that. And I am not familiar with anyone by the name of Achilles."

She was sure that denial was her best, perhaps her only, opportunity. Achilles had not entered the house this evening, stopping briefly outside to pass a pre-arranged signal to Louise, confirming the address from which Richard would begin his journey home. The second man rose to his feet, flinging his spectacles onto the desk, and began to hurl abuse at her, ranting in a high-pitched voice as he bent towards her, hatred pumping through his mean, spare features. He knocked his chair to the ground and strode over to where she stood. Then he produced a small gun and held it beneath her chin. "We will not tolerate denial from so-called aristocrats that are sluts! Speak up, French bitch! We know you are engaged in criminal acts. We have many ways of getting information from people like you, and we have time. Plenty of time."

He was pressing the gun to her throat, screaming into her ear, pushing his body against her so that she arched sideways, fearful that she might fall. She turned her head, addressing the man at the table. "You are making a mistake, Captain Reiner. I am neither a political activist nor a hero."

She gasped as the butt of the pistol hit the side of her head. The sound resonated through her skull, as the small man hit her again, screaming invective.

"That's enough for the time being Dr Weissman." Reiner's voice seemed far away. "I'll have her taken somewhere she can think about more helpful answers."

A guard appeared and pushed Charlotte out into the corridor towards the street entrance of the building. The car ride was short. At the prison she was ordered to strip. The women guards shouted at her, throwing her clothes on to the filthy floor, searching her body with rough hands so that her spirit shrank back from the indignity of their probing.

"*Schnell, Schnell!*"

The words ricocheted off the bare walls, as she dressed again and was taken along the corridors to climb several flights of stairs. An overpowering stench hung in the passages through which they walked. Nausea rose up through her stomach and filled her throat and her mouth.

288

"Halt!"

The guard placed a key in the lock of a door with a peephole and pushed Charlotte forward. Inside the cell she was overcome by the odour that assaulted her, making her eyes smart. Tears streamed down her face as she choked and gagged. Behind her the door swung closed. She stood still, gathering the last shreds of her dignity, willing herself not to collapse. It seemed important not to fall down, even now in the confines of the stinking cell. As her vision cleared she took in the iron beds, three of which were occupied by other women. The dim light was yellow and ugly. In one corner was a bucket from which the sickening smell that permeated the whole floor seemed to emanate. She heard the sound of the peephole sliding back. Then the tiny eye closed again, there was a clicking sound, and the cell was plunged into darkness.

"Sit down on your bed and find your night clothes. There won't be any more light until morning. The bucket in the corner is for relieving yourself." The whisper came from the bed on her left where she had briefly seen a young woman with blonde hair.

Charlotte undressed in the rancid darkness, shivering in spite of the heat. The foul miasma had taken away any appetite, but her mouth was parched. "Is there any water?" she whispered into the darkness.

"Our meal time was at six. There's nothing now until tomorrow. But we all try and save a piece of bread from our evening ration. Take this and hold it in your mouth until it dissolves. It will help. I'm Claire – I've been here six months. They accused me of smuggling British soldiers into the unoccupied zone. On the other side of you are Sylvie and Adèle. They've been here longer. You'll tell us your story tomorrow."

Within moments Charlotte heard the regular breathing of sleep around her, even the sound of an occasional light snore. When she lay down, waves of pain pounded through her head and into her neck and shoulders. She could not sleep, her brain chasing an endless series of unresolved questions in fruitless enquiry. Who had betrayed her? Was Achilles really dead? Where were Richard and Celine? Finally she was forced to feel her way through the tiny space between the beds, in order to use the bucket. Then the tears came, hot and incessant as she made her way back to the narrow bed and lay down once more. She tried not to make any sound, inspired by pride and by gratitude for the stale ball of bread. Twice she opened her eyes in fear as a blinding light speared the blackness. She heard the peephole slide shut and realised that it was a guard, making an inspection. The other women slept on, the piercing beams no longer able to penetrate their dreams. At last her mind refused to entertain any further thought, her stiff, aching limbs found a position in which they could remain still, and she fell asleep. It was not long before the sound of banging invaded her uneasy, half-conscious state.

"Madame, you must get up right away, put on your clothes and make your bed. If you're not quick they punish you. Look, fold your bedclothes this way."

Charlotte stood at the edge of the bed, looking down in disbelief at the grimy sheet, the stained blanket, on which she had slept. Her skin felt raw and irritated. A guard appeared at eight, bearing tin mugs filled with a thin, black liquid, which her companions described as coffee. The three women questioned her endlessly for news of the war, for descriptions of the areas of Paris they knew best and in which they had lived. Her arrival was the highlight of the last few weeks, particularly since she had come from the outside world and not from another prison. After a few hours, hunger and fatigue began to manifest themselves and Charlotte unfolded the dirty blanket, but Sylvie tugged at her. "You can't lie down during the day, Madame. You have to remain sitting or standing until tonight. They'll punish you if they look through the spyhole and see you."

The door swung back shortly after eleven, and bowls were passed inside containing a grey, jelly-like substance covering a few vegetable scraps, and a plate bearing two slices of cold, greasy sausage. Charlotte could not bring herself to taste these offerings, and she sat in silence on the edge of her bed, watching the younger women consume the vile fare.

"You'll have to force yourself, Madame. It's the same each day and there's nothing else between you and starvation. In the evening they bring only tea and a small amount of bread. You must eat this, or they will win by starving you."

In the days that followed, Charlotte learned to hold her breath so that she could not smell the food she put into her mouth. She lived with pangs of hunger that she realised were part of a calculated scheme to dull her senses, to induce despair and exhaustion.

Her second interrogation lasted for two days. Captain Reiner questioned her repeatedly, using the same words again and again, never failing to indicate that he had time on his side. Dr Weissman sat silently at the table, writing endlessly. On the third day, Captain Reiner was alone. He offered her a chair and began to talk in a quiet, civil tone, trying to create an air of intimacy and reason.

"Madame de Savoie, it is not in our interests to detain someone as well respected as yourself in Paris. We are trying to integrate our two nations' cultural strengths, not destroy them." He leaned back in his chair, smiling at her as though he were waiting for her to make some sociable rejoinder. "All we require is for you to explain to us how you inadvertently became involved in some foolish scheme to damage the great partnership between Germany and France. Was it something that was begun by your house staff who are perhaps secret members of the Communist organisation?"

"I cannot help you with information I do not have." Charlotte's voice was tired but dogged in its insistence.

The German leaned forward, his tone suddenly aggressive. "We have captured several of this cell. We know that your house was used for the transfer of information between traitors and criminals. Your servants have been detained in Fresnes prison." He stood up, suddenly, and his next words froze the vein of courage that ran through her body. "You have been very foolish and very stubborn. I'm afraid we are going to have to remove you to Gestapo headquarters."

At rue de Saussaies the guards shouted orders as they forced her into another bare room. She could not suppress an exclamation of pain as the first blows caught her in the small of her back and she raised her hands to shield her head as she fell, curling her body into a foetal position on the floor. Her ribs felt the impact of heavy boots as she tried to roll away from the brunt of the attack. Through half-closed eyes she saw Captain Reiner, inexplicably bending over her, holding out his hand to help her to her feet. Dr Weissman appeared as she tried to steady herself. He raised his hand as though to hit her so that she backed away from him.

"Now you will tell us what we want to know! We have your friends, filthy traitors and Jew-lovers and Communists!" His eyes bulged in their sockets and his face was a mottled portrait of sadistic rage as he hit her. "Bring in the prisoner!"

He screamed an order and the door opened. Charlotte looked up. At first she could not clearly see the man who shuffled between his guards. His skin was scarred and savaged, the side of his face swollen beyond recognition. His hands hung limp at his sides, bloody and torn. Her stomach heaved as she saw his fingers, gnarled and black, the nails gone, the bones crooked and broken.

"You know one another I believe. And you will assist us now with our questions." Dr Weissman approached the distorted frame, turning the man around to face her.

The lips moved, cracking the dried blood, breaking open the cut on the corner of his mouth as he uttered the words that saved her life. "I do not know her," he whispered. "I don't know this woman. I have never seen her before." Dr Weissman delivered a blow to his prisoner's shoulder, and turned to Charlotte. "Save yourself now!" he roared at her. "This is the last chance you will be given to co-operate. And maybe you can save this man too."

In a blur of horror Charlotte looked at him, standing there in all his agony. He gave an imperceptible shake of his head. She was barely able to form the words. "I don't know him," she said.

They dragged him out, and as they took her to a solitary cell she heard a long scream, followed by the sickening thud of blows. Then there was silence, punctuated only by the sound of her own weeping as they locked her away with her vision of Richard Kirwan.

The cell was dark and so small that there was no room to sit down. Charlotte stood, her weight against the damp wall, trying to breathe away her pain. Hours faded into one another in a haze of semi-consciousness. She closed her fingers into fists, trying to prevent herself from tearing at her lice-ridden skin, waiting for her turn to be beaten and subjected to all Richard Kirwan's torture. When the door opened she had no way of knowing what time it was or how many hours or days she might have been there. Captain Reiner was waiting for her.

"It seems there has been a mistake Madame de Savoie." His voice was indifferent, toneless. He spoke briefly to a guard. "Take her outside. There's someone waiting for her."

In the street she stood alone, eyes cast down, trembling with shock and filled with shame at her filthy unwashed appearance, at the stench of sweat and urine, and the raised fleabites on her arms and legs. She felt a gentle hand on her elbow.

"Charlotte. Oh, my dear, it's all right now. Look, I have my car, and I'm taking you to somewhere you can rest. You're going to be all right now."

"I'd like to go home, I'd just like to go home now," she whispered. "And I must see Celine."

"Celine is safe and you'll see her very soon." Henri de Valnay's face was filled with shocked compassion and sorrow. "But you can't go home, my dear. The Germans have taken over your home. A General Walter von Stroepper has moved into your house in Avenue Mozart."

Chapter 37

Dublin, 1970

Eleanor drew up at the iron gates. For a few moments she sat resting her head on the steering wheel. Two passers-by glanced at her but moved on with a sympathetic nod. People were often distressed outside cemeteries. Best to leave the poor girl to her private grief. The sky was overcast, the wind cold, and the disasters of the past few weeks had accumulated in her head as she had driven away from Connemara. Now, almost without thinking, she found herself at the place where her father was buried. She made her way down through the memorial crosses. Richard's grave faced out over the wide sweep of the sea, the bough of an oak tree dipping like a blessing over him. She touched the cold granite of the newly erected cross.

"Why have I come here?" she asked herself. "This is only the shell of him. Why would he hear me better from this hole in the ground, than from anywhere else?" Kneeling on the wet grass that edged the plot, she began to tidy away the bouquets of dead flowers, murmuring aloud, oblivious to her surroundings. She wanted to understand, not to judge the man who had gone to his grave carrying his untold burden. Yet she knew how difficult it was to bare a flawed soul. In that, at least, she thought wryly, she was very like him. She herself had retreated into silence after her break-up with Matthew. Walled up, enduring the tactful concern of James and Lizzie and her parents, she had fled at last to Seamus in Connemara.

Matthew. He had never been unsure of anything. He was polished, urbane, aware of his own success and at home within it, charming in any social gathering. He was the darling of television chat shows, always certain to be entertaining and controversial. She had met him at a theatre festival, and she could not believe it when he had telephoned her a week later. During that first dinner she had lost herself in his piercing brightness, in his wit and laughter and the soft Donegal accent that crept sometimes into his carefully cultured voice. He brought her flowers, held doors open for her, and introduced her to Schoenberg and Strindberg, Le Broquet and Jackson Pollock, Ezra Pound and William Faulkner. Richard Kirwan watched the transformation in his daughter with deep contentment. One night, when Eleanor returned from an evening with Matthew, Richard was in the hall. He looked closely at her. "Happy?"

She turned and flung her arms around his neck. "I love you, Father, do you know that? I love you so much. You and Mother and everyone. And I'm in love, and I've never been so happy in all my life. I can't possibly deserve such joy!" She kissed him on both cheeks, looking into his lean, lined face and he stroked her hair and traced her smile with his finger. She touched the welts and puckers on his hands that were never talked about. He always wore a long-sleeved shirt, even in the hottest weather, but she had seen the marks of a skin graft on his arm.

On that evening she had, not for the first time, wanted to ask what had caused these terrible scars. But she was reluctant to break the spell as her father gazed down at her, and spoke in a tone that was soft with love. "Take it all, dearest girl, every ounce of joy that you can soak into your spirit, and hold on to it. It will be your salvation when times are hard, a reservoir to draw on, when it seems everything has been torn from you. Keep a sanctuary of good things."

Soon afterwards, Matthew had left her. He had married the heiress whose father financed his first play and their large house overlooking the sea. Then it was Seamus who had sat with her on the rocks at Seal Bay until the tears had finally been cried out, and she had begun to tell him some of what was in her heart.

Eleanor sat back on her heels beside her father's grave. The sweep of car lights in the evening gloom brought her back to the wet greyness of the cemetery and the silent headstones that surrounded her. She was overcome with anxiety that everything she valued would always be taken from her, so that she would spend her life in awkward transition and shifting affections that were not of her choice. She walked slowly towards the low wall bordering the edge of the cliffs and looked down into the suck and flow of a restless tide, churning against the rocks below her. There was a magnetism to the movement of the water that drew her, and she placed her hands on the edge of the wall and leaned out over the sea.

"Eleanor!"

She realised that someone was calling her name.

"I guessed you might come here, so I took a chance. Come away from the wall, Eleanor. You're far too close to the cliff."

"Gareth." She clung to him, shivering in the cold, wet evening. "I left my keys in Connemara, and my money too. But I had to come here, to try and talk to him." She turned back towards the grave, pulling her hand from his grasp.

"You're coming home with me. You're all in, and you're soaked." Gareth helped her into his car and fastened her seat belt. "Seamus has been very worried about you."

"I left my car near here. But I've no petrol, Gareth."

"I'll lock it now. We'll collect it in the morning."

At the house she drank the soup he gave her and sank gratefully into a hot bath and bed. When he was satisfied that she was sleeping,

Gareth went to the telephone. "I've found her, Seamus, at Richard's grave. She'll ring you herself tomorrow. Tell Helena not to worry, I'll take care of Eleanor for a few days. She'll be fine when she's had some rest."

In the morning she found him rummaging in the kitchen.

"Thanks for coming in search of me last night, Gareth." She did not know how to explain her actions of the previous day, and she could not look at him directly. "How did you know where to look for me?"

"I'm glad I got it right." He touched her cheek. "It wasn't a night to be out in the dark and the rain."

"I'm sorry. Everything sort of congealed in my brain in a big lump and I just stopped functioning coherently. It was pretty stupid of me."

"Well, I'd say you could do with some breakfast right now."

He had laid out two places, and she watched as he put bacon and eggs in the pan, picked up the teapot and brought it to the table.

"Where are the children?" she asked.

"They're away with their grandmother for the week," he replied. "And it's just as well, because there's something important I have to do."

After breakfast he led her into the study, and moved a pile of papers from an armchair. She smiled at his jumble of books and files, and at the enormous desk buried under his papers.

"I had a long talk with Seamus last night," he began. "I know some of the story, and I do understand how bad you feel."

"You don't know the half of it, Gareth." Her voice was angry. "I had a terrible row with Mother. Then I discovered that James and Lizzie had gone off to Paris, and that Seamus knew all about it. I still can't believe that part. It's bloody difficult to accept that I figure so little in the scheme of things. Poor, awkward Eleanor who only gets in the way. We'll let her know afterwards. Well damn them anyway. Damn them all!"

"Don't run yourself down. You're not one for self-pity. And if the real truth were known I'd say James and Elizabeth knew you wouldn't agree to such a mad escapade. Yes, Seamus should have told you. But he desperately needed you down in Connemara. And so did Helena."

"Helena doesn't need me for anything. She doesn't want me around."

"You know that's not true. Your mother is drifting, grieving, trying to deal with her bereavement and God knows what else. And as the one closest to her, you're getting the backlash. She's so vulnerable right now. She needs unconditional love and support. It's hard without you here, Eleanor, but she needs you more." He held her gaze for a long moment.

"I said I wanted to tell you something. It concerns some instructions your father left with me. Something he wanted you to do for him."

"Something he wanted me to do?" She stared at him, uncomprehending.

Gareth opened a drawer and took out a large manila envelope. Her heart turned over as she took it and saw her name written in Richard's familiar hand. She opened it slowly. The letter was short, a single page in his spiky handwriting. It was dated a week before his death. Her eyes blurred. She squeezed them tight and looked down at the page again.

My Darling Girl,

My time is nearly done and I am aware that I am leaving a legacy of confusion behind me. I look at you all as I slip away on this inexorable tide, and I know that in many ways I have failed you. I want you to understand that I love each one of you so much it pains me to be constricted so in my expression of it. But time and circumstance have made me as I am, and I ask for your acceptance of that, unfair as it may seem.

I see in your eyes your love for me, my dear child. I have seen it throughout my life, so steadfast and strong. It has always been a great comfort to me, particularly in the past year. Now I have to ask you to do one last thing for me. I ask you because it concerns a promise of silence that I gave many years ago, that I cannot break even now.

Enclosed are the papers for a trust fund I set up in Geneva, shortly after the war. I cannot name the beneficiary, but I want you to go to Geneva and take with you the papers I have left with Gareth. They are to be given to my beneficiary, after my death. I cannot explain further, darling.

Your mother is going to need you. She has been left with a painful legacy, and I cannot tell how she will cope with it. But I do know that you will care for her and help her.

Help me dearest Eleanor, child and beautiful young woman. Help me this last time.

Your loving father,
Richard.

Eleanor sat holding the letter, tears coursing unchecked down her face. In the distance she heard Gareth's voice drawing her back to the present, away from the vision of her father's lined and suffering face.

"Eleanor, I've booked two tickets to Geneva. I know your father has a commission for you there, and the sooner we go and take care of it, the better."

Chapter 38

Geneva, 1970

Eleanor unpacked and went out on to the balcony of her room at the Beau Rivage Hotel. Below her lay the city of Geneva, straddling the shores of Lac Léman and the waters of the Rhône. Gareth emerged from his adjacent room and came to stand beside her, looking out over the expanse of shining water, the yachts and steamers and the summer crowds. She longed to forget the circumstances that had brought her there, to become part of the laughter and music that drifted up from the lake shore. She had read and re-read her father's letter, but now she felt that she understood less than ever.

"Shall we go out somewhere special for dinner?" he asked. "We could put all this behind us, just for this evening."

"So that you can avoid telling me all the other secrets you've been keeping from me?"

"I haven't tried to keep anything hidden from you," Gareth said quietly. "There are just as many things I don't know in this whole mess."

"But you kept this from me." She held out Richard's letter. "Do you know the identity of his beneficiary? Is this another little item that everyone has heard about except me?"

"I don't know who it is," Gareth said angrily. "Richard didn't tell me."

"But he must have said something," she persisted.

Gareth frowned in exasperation. "Look, Eleanor, your father spoke to me the week before he died. He asked me to hand the letter over to you when I felt the time was right. I've been waiting until I thought Helena had turned the corner and you had less on your mind. Now I'll tell you what I can. But first can we just have a quiet dinner somewhere? Because I'm tired and hungry, and I could do with a couple of hours of relaxation."

"I'll get my things." Eleanor was ashamed of her ill humour, and felt determined to make amends.

They took a *mouette* up the lake to a restaurant recommended by the hotel, and lingered over dinner. Afterwards they wandered along the shore, reluctant to break the magic of the evening. But Richard's presence stalked them at a distance and they returned to the hotel sooner than Eleanor would have liked. Gareth ordered drinks to be sent upstairs, and they went out to sit on the balcony that linked their rooms. The moon was up, tracing a silver trail across the city. At last it was time to talk about her father, and Eleanor felt all her apprehension return.

"He was so dreadfully ill, in such pain." Gareth was trying to find words to make his story clear. "And towards the end he became extremely anxious. I wanted to let him know that he could confide in me, if it would help. Your parents were so good to me when Moira died and I owe them an enormous debt of gratitude. Helena was always there to comfort me, to keep me afloat. But it was more than that. You know that Moira worked in the theatre. After her death I discovered that she had put every penny we had into a production that failed hopelessly. And she had huge debts, on her credit card, in the shops she loved. She'd never told me, and I never checked. Moira always took care of our domestic finances. So I was left penniless, with two small children, an expensive nanny, and the mortgage on the house."

"Gareth, I'm so sorry. I never knew any of this."

"Richard helped me then, lent me money and never mentioned it until the day I was able to pay it all back. And when I asked him, at the end, if I could do anything for him, he gave me that letter and the instructions for the bank in Geneva."

"But he must have given you some kind of explanation?" Eleanor rose to her feet and went to look at the moon drifting out over the lake.

"He told me that he had set up a trust after the war, and that he had given his solemn word that he would never divulge the name of the beneficiary." Gareth went to stand beside her, his expression grave. "He said it was destroying him. That he had to put things right."

She could see that he was pleading with her to understand.

"Eleanor, in times of trauma people sometimes deal with things in a way that makes it near impossible to put them right later. Your father told me this was his last chance."

"But have you no idea at all who this beneficiary could be? Who he could have been protecting all these years?"

"I only know that he wanted you to deal with this. He said you had the kind of wisdom to do what was right for everyone."

"But I can't handle this, Gareth. I've no experience, no idea what is expected of me." She was drained. It had all become too painful, too complex.

He reached for her and now he was holding her tightly, his face close to hers, his fingers in her hair. "Eleanor, you are so splendid, so dazzling. God knows when it happened, when friendship and admiration turned into something else. I've seen you grow from a sweet, gentle child into the most fascinating and beautiful woman. Then I watched that bastard Matthew tear you into shreds and I wanted to kill him. I wanted to tell you then that there was someone else who would give you all the love you could ever need. I realise I'm a lot older than you. I'm forty-three now, but . . ." His arms were round her and he kissed her. "Oh God, this is the worst time to say this, but I love you, and I'd do anything to see you happy."

"You're in love with me?" She looked up at him, her heart racing, and put her hand out to steady herself. "Gareth stop. I need time to think."

He stepped back immediately and turned away from her, covering his eyes.

"Gareth, you've got to give me time."

"I'm sorry. I shouldn't have imposed on you." He searched his pockets for his cigarettes and lighter and she saw that his hands were trembling.

"No Gareth. It's not that. It's just that I've had so much to take on board recently."

"Please forget my outburst. It must have been the wine and the surroundings. Goodnight Eleanor." He couldn't meet her gaze as he wheeled away from her and went to his room.

Eleanor sat alone in the cool air, shaken but strangely elated. She thought of his fingers in her hair, his strength as he held her, his passion and tenderness, and she recognised an overwhelming longing to let him sweep her into real happiness. Back in her room she lay on her bed with the door to the balcony ajar so that she could look out at the moon riding high over the city. And she wondered if Gareth was lying awake too.

They met for breakfast in the dining room, avoiding direct eye contact and keeping to the business of the day. At Credit Suisse a Monsieur Doumier greeted them in his office. Eleanor hid a smile as he bowed. He was almost a caricature of himself, a small, dapper man in striped trousers, a pale grey waistcoat, silk tie and black jacket. He eyed them from behind rimless spectacles.

"Monsieur Duggan, I am glad to meet you. And Mademoiselle Kirwan, I am sorry for your bereavement. Your father was a true gentleman. I was happy to have been of service to him over the years."

He directed Eleanor and Gareth to gilt chairs in front of his desk. A third seat had been placed beside them. It appeared that he was expecting only one other person.

"I'm aware, Monsieur Doumier, that the identity of the beneficiary of this trust has been kept secret." Eleanor hoped that her nervousness was not too obvious. "But my father's instructions on his death were that I should deliver a package personally to this individual."

"We received a copy of this instruction from Mr Duggan. The lady will be here in a few moments."

"The lady?" Eleanor felt sick. Was this to turn into another unwelcome revelation? Another sister, another lover? I can't go through with this, she thought, panic rising. He shouldn't have asked me to do this.

"Have you met the beneficiary before, Monsieur Doumier?" Gareth's voice steadied her. "As Richard Kirwan's executor in this matter I am at a disadvantage, not knowing the person in question. I will be glad of any background information that you can provide."

Monsieur Doumier opened a heavy leather folder and removed a sheaf of papers. He passed them across to Gareth. "You will need time to study this Monsieur Duggan."

Gareth looked at the first page of the deed, dated 18th June 1947.

There was a knock at the door and Monsieur Doumier's secretary entered. "Madame Revere is here, sir. Shall I show her in?"

Monsieur Doumier nodded. Gareth turned and stood up. Eleanor held her breath.

The woman who walked towards them was tall and thin, dressed in a simple, tailored suit. Her hair was dark, shoulder-length and smooth, well cut. She moved gracefully but with a slight limp, and she gripped the shoulder strap of her bag tightly, with long fingers. Eleanor could not pinpoint her age, but it was clear that in spite of the lines that etched her face she could not be more than fifty. Monsieur Doumier came forward to greet her.

"Madame Revere, this is Monsieur Gareth Duggan, who is Monsieur Kirwan's executor. And this is —"

The woman held out her hand to Eleanor, looking at her with unmistakable affection and sympathy. "You must be Eleanor." She spoke in French, her voice low. "I see Richard in your every feature. The likeness is uncanny."

A tray with coffee and biscuits was placed before them. Monsieur Doumier cleared his throat discreetly.

"I think perhaps you will prefer to have some privacy for your discussions. I will be available whenever you require."

Eleanor barely noticed his departure. The woman was still holding her hand.

"Oh Eleanor," she said. "He should not have done this. It is hard enough that he is gone."

"Please," Eleanor whispered, "I need to know who you are."

"He did not tell you? No, of course not. He promised. I made him promise."

She was silent for a moment, staring through Eleanor, her mind somewhere far, far away. Then she smiled.

"Here in Geneva I am Madame Revere. But to your family, my name is Leah Nazarre. Or Leah Svenssen. That is who I am."

Chapter 39

Geneva, 1970

"Leah?"

Eleanor stood speechless and staring, absorbing every detail of the woman's face, the large, dark eyes and strong mouth. Seamus's lost love was alive, here in Geneva! And her father had known, all through the years.

"Leah." Eleanor said the name again, shaking her head in bewilderment.

There was a pause, then Gareth touched her arm gently. "Maybe we should sit down for a moment and catch our breath?" He guided them both to the chairs in front of Monsieur Doumier's desk.

"I'm sorry. You must think me very rude. It's just that I never expected . . ." Eleanor shook her head again, her eyes still fixed on the other woman's face.

"I realise this has been a shock. Richard was always a man of his word. A true friend and protector to the end." Leah looked away, her voice desolate. "I wish I could have seen him, done something for him. But it was impossible. Did he tell you about me, then, in the end? You knew who I was?"

"He never mentioned your name," said Eleanor. She knew that her next words would sound harsh. "It was from Seamus that I learned about you. But you never contacted Seamus. Or Mother, who was your

307

friend. How could you and Father not have said anything, let them know, at least, that you were alive?"

"Eleanor." Gareth squeezed her shoulder hard. "Before you ask any more questions we should try to understand the circumstances that have brought us here today."

"Monsieur Duggan," Leah interrupted him, her face tight. "She has a right to ask these questions. And I must try to answer them."

"Maybe I should leave you now." Gareth stood up.

"No." Eleanor took up Richard Kirwan's envelope from the desk, and held it out. "My father wanted me to give you this in person. Mr Duggan, Gareth, is his executor. He has been part of our family for many years and he's my dearest friend." She leaned back against Gareth, drawing reassurance from the feel of his hands on her shoulders.

Leah held the bulky envelope in her hands, turning it over and over, her fingers stroking it gently. Her face was unreadable as she stood up and went to the window that overlooked the cobbled street and the clanging trams below them. "I wrote to him three or four times a year," she said quietly. "And I asked him to destroy the letters, but I think perhaps he kept them. I don't know . . ."

She opened the envelope and drew out a bundle of correspondence in blue envelopes, and a separate white sheet of paper with some photographs attached to it. Then she raised her eyes to look at Eleanor and Gareth and spoke in her low voice.

"After that first time in 1947, when Richard found me, I couldn't let him come again. But I wrote several times each year, to tell him how we were. And he wrote to me. He understood me, and I knew what he was going through. We had been there together."

Her eyes blurred as she held the letters and photographs against her breast, keeping Richard's last letter separate in her other hand. She read it in silence and then looked up again, not at Gareth or Eleanor but past them as though there was someone else standing there in the room.

308

"Oh Richard, what are you trying to do? It's too late for all this!" She gave a ragged sigh and leaned her head against the window frame. "Eleanor, between your father and me there was a friendship of the deepest kind. A bond that could never be broken. We were both in the prison camps that became the most terrible, the ugliest heritage of that war. I was in Auschwitz and Bergen-Belsen. Your father was in Buchenwald. In the chaos at the end of the war I did not know he had survived. Until he came to find me."

She looked back at Eleanor who waited, dumb with astonishment.

"It may seem to you an extraordinary cruelty that I would insist upon his silence, but that is what I did. I made him promise he would never tell your mother." She hesitated. "Or your uncle. But you see, it had to be like that. For Stefan. For the sake of my husband."

"What are you saying?" Eleanor jumped to her feet, and Leah put out a hand, as though to fend her off. "That my father was in a concentration camp, and Stefan too?"

"Could we talk outside?" Leah asked. She was clutching the package close to her and she looked suddenly hunched and tired. "I find this room claustrophobic in spite of its size."

"I'll let Monsieur Doumier know that we'll be back later," Gareth said.

They left the imposing marble of the bank, and walked to the Jardin Anglais. Gareth found a bench near the floral clock, and they sat down in the sunshine, looking out across the lake. Leah's words came slowly, without reproach or self-pity, as she began to speak of that world of horror in which she had lived.

They had dragged her from Daniel's lifeless body on the street, kicking her, hitting her across the shoulders with their rifle butts. Stefan, Richard and Seamus had disappeared in the dust and smoke of the fighting. She thought she had heard Seamus shouting to her desperately above the roar of gunfire, and she was afraid to think what might have become of him. In the days of interrogation and beatings that followed, her own blood dried and crusted on her dress, mingling with Daniel's. Time seemed to collapse in on itself. She did not know where she had been taken. There were days in trucks, in cells, in the glare of interrogation rooms, in stinking holes with other filthy and battered women. Rats, cockroaches, lice, and the stench of despair were her constant companions.

Her captors were quick to tell her that her husband and companions had been executed as traitors. But as the days wore on, a stubborn core of resistance formed inside her. Her beloved Daniel was dead, but the questions she was asked made her suspect that some of the others had escaped. Stefan's father had strong diplomatic connections and she thought he might have been able to arrange for his son's release. And if Richard and Seamus had managed to avoid capture, her silence might be their only protection. So she held fast through every session of degradation, mockery and pain.

She did not know how long it was before she was put on a transport to the prison camp, or how many days it took to get there. There was an eternity of raging thirst, starvation and misery, and the horror of people dying around her. She knew with a terrible certainty that her family had gone this way before her. When the train drew into Auschwitz the living were herded from the filthy cars, stumbling over their dead companions on to the floodlit platform. Those who had managed to survive the hellish railcars were forced to stand half-naked in the night air, exhausted by fear, assailed on all sides by the shouts of the guards and the ferocious snarling of dogs. SS officers stood in impeccable uniforms, their polished boots reflecting nightmare images of violence under the glaring arc lights.

"This way. Move along. Hurry please. Mothers with young children are to step to this side."

A detail of prisoners passed them and began to pull the crushed, bloated corpses from the freight wagons, and to clear away the mounds of human excrement. Leah stood paralysed on the ramp, unable to force her trembling limbs into motion. A prisoner in filthy striped trousers and jacket shambled forward, pushing Leah in the ribs. "Move! Move now! Or they'll kill you. Stay to the left."

She was not sure if she had really heard him. She looked into his fever-bright eyes, took in the shaven head, the sunken eyes and hollow cheekbones. He was no more than a shuffling scarecrow. She moved to the left, in the direction he had indicated. For those surviving the initial selection, the quarantine barracks tore away the last vestiges of human dignity. They were ordered to strip off all their clothes. Naked and shivering, Leah watched her long, peroxide tresses fall to the floor as they shaved her head in retribution, perhaps, for her denial of her race. After the icy shower she was made to run into an open yard where she received a rough, blue and white striped prison uniform and a pair of ill-fitting wooden clogs. In a fog of shame and misery she huddled in the queue for registration. They still had no food or water.

The man at the rickety desk did not look at her. "Name?"

"Leah Svenssen. I'm married to a foreign national. I have Swedish nationality. You have no right to keep me here." Surely if Stefan were free he would come and take her from this place.

"You are a Jew." It was not a question. "Mixed-race marriage is not permitted. Occupation?"

Tears of furious despair rose in Leah's eyes but she said nothing more about Stefan. Their marriage could be used against him if he was still alive. She did not respond.

"Occupation?" The officer's voice had risen sharply. A guard on the edge of the line moved towards them, his dog straining at the leash.

"Musician. I play the violin."

For the first time he looked up at her. "Violin? Where did you play?"

"At the Paris Conservatoire."

"There is a women's orchestra in the camp. You could be useful. Stay in the quarantine section. If they want you they'll let you know."

She was prodded into a run once more, stumbling forward to be tattooed. Looking down at her left forearm she saw them scratch away at her identity and replace it with the marks they had selected. From now on she would have no name. They would know her only as a number.

In the Geneva sunshine Leah fell silent, gazing out at the beauty of the gardens. Mothers pushed babies in prams. Lovers and students lay on the grass, and an old woman fed the birds. Eleanor, humbled by what she had heard, was at a loss for the right words in the face of such suffering.

"How long, Leah? How long were you there?" Gareth asked her gently.

"Three years. All my life. Part of me is still there, can never escape." Leah's face was very pale.

"Would you come back with us to our hotel for some lunch?" Eleanor asked quietly.

Leah stood up. "Thank you, but I've been away too long. I really must go home. To Stefan."

"Stefan is with you? Oh Leah, there's so much to know. Can we meet him?"

Leah's face was as still as stone. "I'm afraid Stefan doesn't see anyone. He never recovered from the war." She brushed her hand over her eyes. "He needs constant nursing and he doesn't react well to strangers. He's subject to fits, convulsions. After we were captured he was taken to the Gestapo headquarters in Paris, and he received terrible injuries. Eventually his father managed to get him out. They put him in a clinic, here in Switzerland. It took me a long time to find him after the war."

Leah's voice faltered. "I was sick myself then. I had no money, no family left except Stefan. And I had nowhere to live, no means of supporting him or looking after him. My only chance was to finish my musical training, so that I would be able to work. I would have died then, if Richard hadn't found me. And Stefan would not have survived either. He was an embarrassment to his family, a useless shell who had married a Jew. They left him and went away. That was when your father came, Eleanor. Dear, brave, wonderful Richard."

Her voice had dropped to a whisper and now she began to sob. Gareth took her arm.

"It isn't fair of us to put you through all this," he said quietly. "Your bravery and your courage are beyond our understanding. You don't have to explain all at once. Let us see you home, and we can deal with the trust tomorrow, or whenever you feel ready."

"Gareth is right." Eleanor put her arms around Leah. "I'm just so utterly astonished, so terribly glad that you are alive, that Father found you and was able to help you. Could we meet again, tomorrow perhaps? We're staying at the Beau Rivage."

"Now that you have discovered me, I realise that I cannot vanish again." Leah disengaged herself, gently. "I'll take a taxi home, thank you. We'll meet again, perhaps tomorrow. Your father was a great man, my dear, and in a little while I will try to tell you more. But now Stefan needs my attention. Goodbye, Eleanor, Gareth." She embraced them both lightly, placing her palm against Eleanor's cheek. Then she turned and walked quickly away.

At the bank Eleanor found it hard to concentrate. Gareth and Monsieur Doumier didn't really need her and Leah was right, the office was oppressive.

"Gareth, I think I might go back to the hotel. Would that be all right?"

"Of course. We've only got about another half-hour here."

She walked back towards the Beau Rivage, gulping in the fresh air of the late afternoon, mulling over the extraordinary events of the day. At the hotel she went out on to her balcony and stood looking down at the lake. What should she do about Gareth? She flushed, remembering his embrace. When the telephone rang, she rushed inside and lifted the receiver.

"Eleanor?" Leah's voice sounded strained. "Could you come out here tonight? But on your own. I think I should talk to you, and it's best to begin sooner rather than later. Would Gareth mind if you came alone?"

"I'm sure he wouldn't," Eleanor said immediately, afraid that Leah might change her mind. "I can come straight away if you like?"

"Around eight o'clock would be better. Stefan is restless, but I should have him settled by then."

Eleanor was writing down the address when she heard Gareth's knock on the door. She said goodbye to Leah and put down the phone. "Come in Gareth. That was Leah. She wants me to go and see her this evening." She hesitated. "Do you mind if I go alone?"

"Of course I don't mind. I'm glad she wants to see you." He paused. She wouldn't need him now and neither would Leah. His next words came out in a rush. "I can't be away from the office for too long but I think you should remain in Geneva at least until the weekend. I'll go back to Dublin tomorrow." He sounded so casual, so matter of fact. She felt a sting of disappointment. But he was right, they needed the distance. Maybe he was regretting what he had said the night before.

"Whatever you think is best," she said. "I'll order a cab and get ready. I don't know what time I'll be back. Goodnight Gareth, and thank you. For everything. You're such a wonderful friend."

"You know I'm always here." Gareth heard her message and knew that friendship was all that existed between them. His reply was slow and deliberate. "As your friend. Whenever you need me."

He said goodnight abruptly and closed the door behind him. Eleanor sighed, turned to the telephone and rang for a taxi.

Chapter 40

Geneva, 1970

The taxi pulled up outside a house on the lake shore with a blue painted door and scarlet geraniums in the window boxes. Eleanor paid the fare and rang the bell. Leah opened the door and stood in the muted light of the hall, shadows hollowing the planes of her face.

"Please come in Eleanor."

The double doors of the sitting room opened on to a stone terrace and a sloping lawn that ran down to the lake. Bruch's violin concerto was playing softly on the stereo. Eleanor paused, absorbing the atmosphere of the room. There was a comfortable couch, deep armchairs and a coffee table that held a neat stack of books. Plain walls were hung with a few good paintings and tapestry cushions lent a splash of colour to the room. In one corner was a piano, Leah's violin and music stand, and a table piled high with sheet music. This was the only area that seemed to suggest Leah's presence. Otherwise the room contained no photographs or personal objects.

"I think it might be warm enough to sit outside," Leah said. "I've put a tray with wine and some cheese out on the terrace."

"It's beautiful here, Leah. So peaceful."

Eleanor accepted a glass of wine. Now that she was here, it was hard to know how to begin. Leah, too, seemed to be waiting, or listening for something. Was it Stefan, Eleanor wondered?

"Stefan is sleeping." Leah seemed to have read her thoughts. "He gets agitated if there's any change in his routine and he always senses stress. It upsets him. I was late home this afternoon, and I went out earlier than usual this morning."

"But he wasn't on his own, was he?"

"No. He can never be left alone. I have nurses who take care of him during the day when I'm teaching, or in the evenings if I am playing in a concert. Today, when the nurse came early, Stefan was aware that something unusual was going on."

"Leah," Eleanor hesitated. "Could you bear to tell me what happened to him? The last thing Seamus remembered was the ambush, on the Ile de Groix." She flushed, then ran her fingers through her hair, realising that she should not have mentioned Seamus. This was not the right time. "Father never spoke to us about this period of his life. We were told he'd been ill during the war, that he didn't want to talk about it. Now, with all these recent revelations, I feel I've lost the father I knew."

Leah walked over to the edge of the terrace and stood looking out at the lake, her face averted. "It was inevitable, I suppose, that some day I would have to emerge from my hiding place and face the past. Your father said so, and he was right. But you will have to be patient with me, Eleanor. After the war everyone was keen for us not to dwell on the horrors we had experienced. They wanted us to put it all behind us. It was embarrassing for those who had not experienced the devastation. Better to set about the business of living and forget the past, they said. But we can't forget, those of us who were there like your father, and like me. So we never speak of those years, but we live in two dimensions. In the world of the camps, and the world of the present where we try to function in what is considered real life."

Leah stopped for a few moments. Then, with a long sigh, she refilled their glasses. "We lived in a continuous nightmare of fear, violence, starvation and thirst. They tried to destroy every bit of humanity we possessed. They degraded us, beat us, killed us at random. Every shred of civilised normality became precious. A piece of soap, an item of underwear, a toothbrush, shoes. Bread was the camp currency. We paid in bread for those things, even though we were dying of hunger. I was one of the lucky ones," she said, with a bitter smile. "They put me in the camp orchestra. Otherwise I could not have survived."

"Your family?"

"I found out about them when I got to Auschwitz. All dead."

"So you were left alone. All your family taken. Oh God, how you must have felt."

"We hadn't much time for emotion." Leah's tone was hard. "Survival was everything. The ones who let anger find expression were beaten or shot, or sent to the bunkers to die of starvation. Sometimes that seemed better than continuing to live in such a hell. But we have such a tenacious will to live."

In her expression of icy determination, Eleanor caught a glimpse of the person who had managed to cheat the Nazi death machine.

"We helped each other, looked out for one another, tried to organise the weaker ones into work details with the less brutal guards. We supported the sick ones when we had to stand for hours on endless roll calls in the freezing cold or rain. We hid them during selections. Always there were the selections. We tried to share our bread, the few portions we had, to save a little for the very sick who were too tired to fight. But there were so many. So many, Eleanor. All dead."

She leaned back, her arms folded tight across her breast, her eyes closed. "When the Russians began to close in, they evacuated Auschwitz. We were forced to march to Bergen-Belsen. It was January and the snow was deep. We had no food. Some of the time even the guards didn't know where we were going. If anyone flagged they were shot where they fell. We walked over a trail of frozen corpses." She shuddered, her eyes still closed. "Belsen was worse, much worse. Overcrowding, brutality, starvation, disease. There were rats feeding

317

on the unburied victims of typhus and dysentery and tuberculosis. I do not know how anyone survived that place. I will never know."

"How did you get out?"

"As the Allies came closer they marched the ones who were still able to walk to a railway, to transport us further into Germany. I was deathly ill, but I knew they were executing anyone too sick to travel. There was no food left, no water. The guards shot prisoners on any whim that took them." Leah's eyes were still closed but her words came faster now. "We always marched together, holding one another up. But my legs were so painful I could hardly walk. I had pneumonia, and dysentery. I kept falling. The girl I was with, the one I was leaning on, she stuck with me for a while. Finally she let go of me, and walked on. She wept as she left me, said she was sorry, but she couldn't carry me any more. I crawled into a ditch and lay there waiting for the guards to shoot me.

"A Polish woman dragged me to my feet. She saw me moving as she passed and she forced me up, pushed me, even carried me some of the way. Her name was Hanka. I remember her dragging me up into the cattle car, lying down with me, trying to warm me. Trying to warm us both. At some point the train was bombed and the side was blown off our car. We lay there for days. The allied troops who found us took a long time to sort out the dead from the living. I spent weeks in a coma, in some hospital. When I regained consciousness I had no memory. No name, no possessions, no identity."

"And when you recovered how did you find Stefan?" Eleanor was awed by Leah's courage and perseverance.

"Eventually the Red Cross sent me to Paris because I spoke French. They thought if I got there, I might be able to remember something. I was given a job as a cleaner in a centre for displaced people."

She could not describe to Eleanor the terrifying emptiness of those days, living in a hostel, surrounded by the void of emptiness that was herself. She could not speak about hoarding the morsels of stale bread under her mattress, of stealing rotting cabbage leaves from the grocer's display to ward off the fear of hunger. At night there had been the aimless wandering from street to street after work, searching for anything familiar that might offer a clue as to her identity.

"The Red Cross gave me food and found me somewhere to stay," she said. "There was a woman in charge of the offices where I was working. A kind, aristocratic woman." Leah stood motionless for some moments. Eleanor wondered how she could stay on her feet for such a long period in the same position, back straight, head up, eyes closed tight, almost as though she was standing to attention. "She made time to talk to me each time we met. One day, when I was cleaning the floor, she saw my tattoo and asked me my name. I said Jeanne. That was what they had called me in the hospital. I didn't have any name, you see, only a number. She insisted on taking me to see her daughter who was a doctor, because I was still coughing and my legs were painful. The doctor had beautiful, pale gold hair. Not peroxide like mine was once. I thought I should tell her that I was a Jew, in case she wouldn't want to treat me. But then I wasn't even sure if I was a Jew!"

Leah broke off again and picked up the bottle of wine. "She was my lifeline, that doctor. A kind word here, a gesture there, medicine and supports for my knees, a better pair of shoes. In the meantime her mother was trying to trace where I might have come from. She was sure I was Parisian because of my accent."

"But wasn't there anyone from the camps who might have recognised you, or come looking for you? Anyone from your group?"

It was hard to explain the chaos of the liberation, the thousands of shifting, displaced, distraught beings who emerged from hell and walked into limbo, waiting for someone to place them back among the living. They wandered and searched, but for many everything had been swept away. Leah smiled as she recalled the final irony of her liberation. "The woman who abandoned me on the march told people

I had died in her arms on the roadside. I suppose she was ashamed that she had left me there. But in exonerating herself, she took away my last hope of someone finding me. Leah Svenssen was listed as dead."

A light wind had risen and the temperature had dropped. Leah shivered and turned to Eleanor. "Perhaps we should go in. I'll make us something to eat."

There was a noise inside the house, an odd, dragging sound. Leah moved swiftly across the sitting room as the door by the piano crashed open. "Stefan! What is it? Why are you up?"

She reached the swaying figure and tried to steady him. He was in the throes of a fit. The huge body was jerking. His eyes were glazed, spittle formed at his mouth and a gurgling sound came from his lips. He let go of the door, sinking to his knees, arms flailing. Leah knelt down and began to talk to him softly, almost crooning. "Hush Stefan, it's all right. I'm here. It will be over soon. Hush now, lie still."

She soothed the movements of his arms with capable hands. Eleanor crouched down beside her and gazed at Leah's husband. He was very tall with a solid frame. His hands were badly maimed, the arthritic fingers curled up. His face was scarred and deeply lined. One eye and the left side of his mouth drooped as though paralysed. The eyes staring blankly from the ruined features were Nordic blue, the hair white. Leah placed a cushion beneath his head and within a few moments the gasping, wheezing sounds died away.

"He'll sleep for a while now. Later I'll help him back into bed. He can walk by himself, using a stick, although he's very unsteady." Her expression was bleak. "You may want to go, Eleanor."

"I'd rather make you some coffee, and something to eat," Eleanor said, getting up. "I'm very good at poking about in other people's kitchens."

She busied herself searching out the coffee, milk and sugar. There was a loaf of bread and she cut several slices, placing them on a tray with cold chicken, lettuce, cheese and some fruit. Her mind was filled with the image of Leah, kneeling over her husband as he lay helpless on the floor. She wondered how often it happened, how Leah coped with it alone. When she carried the tray into the sitting room, Leah was still beside Stefan but his body seemed relaxed, and he was even snoring gently. Eleanor smiled.

"Come and sit down." She pointed to one of the chairs. "From here we can see that he's comfortable."

Leah's body was drooping with fatigue as she took her coffee with hands that trembled slightly. She made an attempt at a smile.

"I'm sorry," she said. "I'm not much of a hostess I'm afraid."

It was the first time Eleanor had heard despair in her voice. She looked at Leah from under her dark brows, frowning. "Until today I could never have imagined such bravery. You make me feel very humble, Leah. And you mustn't ever criticise yourself."

"You look so like Richard when you frown like that." Leah was laughing. "And you sound just like him too."

"It's good to hear you laugh," Eleanor said, smiling. "Now tell me, how did Father find you when everyone had given you up for dead?"

"Providence, Eleanor. Providence and Charlotte de Savoie."

Eleanor's heart stood still. Solange's first letter flashed across memory. "My mother was born Celine de Savoie. She studied medicine in Paris."

"Charlotte de Savoie?" Now it was all beginning to fit together. The camps, the displaced people returning after the war, the compassionate woman from the Red Cross and her daughter, the doctor, caring for them, helping to mend their shattered lives.

"I was trudging aimlessly around one day, as I often did. I hated to stay in my room. I passed a large building with a flag and stopped. A window on the second floor had caught my eye and suddenly I knew I'd been there. I knew what it would be like to look down from that window, and I saw myself in a car, driving away and looking back up at it. I went to the man on duty at the door, and asked what place it was. He said it was the Swedish consulate. I knew I had to go inside, and I was still arguing with the guard when one of the consulate staff arrived. Desperation made me bold. I wept and told him I had just returned from the camps in Germany and was trying to trace a Swedish relative. The only member of my family still living."

Leah smiled at the memory. The junior trade attaché didn't want a public scene. He brought her into his office, thinking it might be easier to deal with her in the consulate. Inside the building she remembered nothing. She was unable even to think of a name for her imaginary Swedish relative. The young diplomat became embarrassed and sent for his secretary.

"She was the first link," Leah said quietly. "The first person whose name I remembered. Marta. I looked at her face, and I knew her name."

"Is your name Marta?" she had whispered.

The woman had gripped Leah's thin shoulders. "Leah! You're alive!"

"Is this lady known to you?" The young man was astonished.

"Yes, sir. She's the wife of a friend who used to live in Paris before the war." Marta had nodded, dropping her voice. "Her husband is Swedish. Would you like me to take her into my office?"

Marta led Leah to a smaller office down the hall and embraced her, smoothing her hair, smiling as she tried to conceal her shock at Leah's appearance. "I can't believe you're here. We knew you had been arrested and we feared you were dead."

Leah stood very still. She knew only that this was Marta. Nothing else. She associated this place with danger and she felt herself begin to tremble. Marta helped her into a chair and brought her coffee.

"Anders was transferred soon after the wedding. Count Svenssen wanted him dismissed, but the Consul arranged to send him elsewhere. He was the wisest of men, the Consul. You and Stefan weren't the only ones he helped. But you needn't be worried about Anders. He didn't lose anything by his actions. But oh, my dear, it was so terrible about poor Stefan. I'm so very sorry. Have you been able to see him?"

Marta was looking at her with concern, trying to understand her dazed expression, her silence. Leah shook her head, desperate to understand some part of this story.

"I don't know what . . ."

"The count wanted everything done quietly. I doubt any of us would have known if it hadn't been for Countess Svenssen. Just before they took Stefan away, there was a terrible disagreement between them." Marta put her hands up to her face. "The consul told me to bring Stefan's travel papers. They were in one of the reception rooms and Countess Svenssen was shouting at the count. He'd abandoned his own son, put him into mortal danger, she said. He'd allowed the Germans to use Stefan, and then discarded him when he was destroyed. The count told her to go home immediately, but she followed me into my office."

Leah's nightmare of confusion deepened. Her life was connected to a Swedish countess. It was like a scene from a fantasy, but she could not visualise any of the players.

"The countess had been drinking heavily. You knew her problem, I'm sure. She asked me if I was the one who had witnessed your wedding. Then she opened her handbag, and gave me this envelope. She was weeping, Countess Svenssen. At least she cared about him."

"Yes. I'm sure she did." Leah nodded, trying to look as though she understood.

"'We're taking him away,' the countess said. 'Carl would like everyone to believe he's dead. But he's not dead, although it might be better if he was.'"

Marta reached into her desk, then handed Leah a thick envelope.

"She was crying as she said to me: 'This girl he married, he must have loved her very much to do such an insane thing. And maybe she feels the same love for him. He's finished now and she's probably dead. But if by any chance she survives, if she should ever come to look for him, I want you to give her this.'"

Leah could only stare at Marta, silent and frightened, unable to make any connection between herself and the events the young woman had described. But Marta did not seem to notice her confusion.

"She told me that no one was ever to know about our conversation, least of all her husband. Then she was gone. I never saw either of them again, but you probably know what happened to them. The count was a hard man, very unpopular here in the end. Too close to the Nazis."

Leah waited for some other piece of information that would make sense, help her to remember. Marta asked if she could do anything else for her. But there was nothing anyone could do for a woman with no memory, no identity, no past. Leah found herself standing on the pavement outside the embassy. She looked at the letter. It read "Madame Nazarre–Svenssen. To Be Collected". Nazarre–Svenssen. Neither name held any meaning for her. She found a small café a short distance away, and opened the envelope. Inside was a single sheet of paper, wrapped around a thick sheaf of bank notes and a certificate. The letter was short.

Paris
12th November 1942

Dear Madame Nazarre,
Should you receive this, my son will have paid a very high price for your survival. Stefan clings to the shreds of life remaining to him. His father is transferring him to a clinic in Switzerland where he will receive the best care available.

My husband and I will be leaving Europe and are unlikely to return. I pray that if you come to look for your husband, the enclosed sum of money will enable you to go and visit him. He deserves that, though he may not recognise you. In the aftermath of this frightful war you are the only person that he has.

He is in Switzerland, in the Clinique St Martin on the rue du Lac just outside Thonon les Bains.

Aneka, Countess Svenssen

The money was in Swiss francs. With it was a marriage certificate, signed and witnessed by Pastor Bruzelius, Anders and Marta. Leah sat for a long time staring at the money. It represented vast wealth to someone who owned nothing. Until now not even a name. Leah Nazarre, Leah Svenssen. She murmured the names, trying to make them fit. What should she do? The tone of the letter was frosty. But it seemed that she had a husband. How could she get to Switzerland? The prospect seemed impossible. She felt drained of energy, of imagination.

"What did you do?" Eleanor was on the edge of her chair.

"I went to see Charlotte de Savoie. I told her that I'd discovered a member of my family, still alive, in a clinic in Switzerland. I was afraid to tell her any more. I didn't know if this man really was connected to me, and there seemed to be such secrecy surrounding him. She was right at the centre of things, organising housing and transportation for war refugees, seeing to the return of French prisoners from the camps. She got me on to a train going to Switzerland and gave me papers in the name of Jeanne Revere."

Leah looked up at Eleanor, her face softening with a different kind of recollection. "It was then, Eleanor my dear, that the miracle happened. It was some months after I left for Switzerland that Richard came back to Paris. Back to Charlotte de Savoie and to Celine."

Chapter 41

Paris, 1942–1944

The new apartment was in modest surroundings close to Place St Augustin. Two large windows compensated for the size of the cramped salon, and there was a small balcony shaded by a leaning tree.

"It belongs to someone who went to live in the South when the Germans arrived. It isn't much, I know," Henri's expression was regretful. "But no one will come looking for you here, in this district."

On her release from Gestapo headquarters, Charlotte climbed the stairs with Henri, her face bruised and cut, her clothing torn, her skin covered in fleabites. She stood in the centre of the small sitting room gripping the table, her face blank. Celine tenderly dressed her wounds, gently washed and combed out her tangled hair, and took the soiled clothing away to be burnt, in case the lice and fleas would spread. Then she helped Charlotte into bed and administered a sedative. Henri reappeared, carrying a suitcase of personal clothing and some family photographs in silver frames.

"I managed to have these removed from Avenue Mozart," he said to Celine. "I thought she might need the photographs more than the clothes. They wouldn't allow me to take much."

"How did you arrange all this? Mother's release, getting into Avenue Mozart?"

Celine felt the current of tension flash between them and saw that he realised her question was framed by doubt. But in truth she did not want any revelations for the moment, preferring to live with gratitude.

"You don't need to know, Celine. For the moment you are both safe, and that's all that matters. But neither of you can continue as before. They have identified Charlotte, and they never forget. It is thought that she has gone south to Montpellier, so she must keep a low profile here in Paris."

Celine returned to work and waited for her mother to emerge slowly from the trauma of her imprisonment. A week later, she arrived at the little apartment to find no one at home. Three hours of anxiety passed before she heard a key turn in the lock. Charlotte was dressed in a pair of baggy slacks and a poorly tailored jacket, with a scarf wound around her hair. Her face was flushed with triumph.

"For God's sake Mother, I've been frantic with worry. Where have you been?" Celine's voice was a mix of anger and relief. "Why are you wearing those awful clothes? You've got plenty of decent things that Henri managed to rescue from Avenue Mozart."

"It's my new look. Much less conspicuous this way. And I've got a bicycle, Celine. I haven't ridden a bicycle since my childhood, and I love it."

Charlotte's eyes were bright, her face full of energy. All traces of her terrifying experience, her exhaustion, her sorrow at the loss of her home, seemed to have vanished. Celine looked at her in amazement, wondering if she could be in the grip of some post-traumatic hysteria.

"I've started work as a decoder, darling. There are so many messages and not enough people to work on them. I've spent all day learning the process, and after a few more sessions I'll be able to work on my own."

"But you know you're marked, Mama. This is madness."

"Don't you feel this malignant presence growing, spreading, choking us every day?" Charlotte's words were venomous, her eyes cold with hatred.

327

"Of course I can feel it. But you've been through so much, and it's too soon to start all over again. You could lose your life, Mother."

"We all have to die, Celine. Sooner or later we're all going to die. In the meantime it's how we live that counts. I'm not afraid of death any more."

It was as though Charlotte had become fearless, invincible in her contempt for her enemy, determined that there were no boundaries too dangerous for her to cross. Her ability to act against the occupation once more had transformed her, and given her new life and hope.

Throughout the long months of hunger and deprivation it seemed that France could never emerge from beneath the crushing strength of the German occupation. Henri appeared intermittently at the apartment, always laden with gifts of food obtainable only on the black market. On several occasions Celine tried to raise the subject of his feelings towards the occupation and the progress of the war in Europe, but his answers were vague and non-committal. The issue marred her gratitude, creating a gulf that she could not bridge. But his kindness and loyalty to the two of them were beyond dispute. He had rescued her mother from imprisonment and torture, even death. But gradually Henri's visits became less frequent. They did not know whether this was because he suspected their continuing involvement in the resistance movement. They missed his company, his ability to make them laugh, the shared luxuries of fresh bread and butter and cheese, and a bottle of fine wine.

It was several months before Charlotte learned that Richard had been deported to a prison camp in Germany.

"Darling, I know. I watched your feelings for Richard develop, and I wasn't surprised." Charlotte was unprepared for the grief in her daughter's answering gaze. "You saved his life and you shared a common danger. And there's hope that he is still alive, that he will come back one day."

"Do you really believe that?"

"I pray for it every night and day. But then he will have to return to Ireland. That is what will happen."

"I don't care what will happen. I just pray that I will see him again."

As the months wore on the messages from London became more urgent and more optimistic. Paris was alive with rumours, hopeful that liberation was only days away but fearful that the city would be destroyed by the Germans before they surrendered. On a soft August evening in 1944 Henri knocked at the door. His face was aged and tired, his clothes dishevelled. He spoke quickly, glancing down into the street below.

"I've got to leave Paris for a time. I'm afraid these are the last of your additional supplies for a while. These are tense and dangerous days and I beg of you to exercise caution."

He left a food parcel with them and moments later they saw him walk swiftly away, the brim of his hat pulled low over his face. They sat down together, disturbed by his agitated manner and sudden departure, his new role as a fugitive.

"I hope that he'll be safe, wherever he's going." Charlotte's eyes were troubled.

"Mama, you have to realise that he may be fleeing Paris because of his contact with the Germans. When the Allies reach the city he may be considered a collaborator. I don't know how we will feel then."

"Celine, I am certain that Henri is honourable. He wasn't accepted for the army because his sight wasn't good enough. He's spent the war doing what he's done all his working life, supplying wines to his customers."

"But what customers? He's made a fortune during the occupation and contributed nothing towards the defence of France. And now that German defeat seems within reach, he's going away."

In the groundswell of hope and optimism that followed the Allied landings, convoys of German soldiers flooded back from Normandy, exhausted and wounded. They did not remain in the city for long, and when they left Parisians stopped in the streets to jeer. But their relief was followed by an even greater shortage of food and supplies. The violence and uncertainty of the insurrection pervaded the city and Celine threw herself into helping the men and women who were wounded on the barricades, as they fought to free the city from the last remnants of the German army. Charlotte worked day and night, coding and decoding messages between Paris, London and Algiers, stopping only when her eyes could no longer remain open and she was forced to snatch an hour's sleep on the sofa.

When the news finally came through that there were French tanks in Paris, at the Hotel de Ville, Charlotte and Celine stood together on their small balcony. They held one another and wept, their embrace a celebration of freedom, of joy and hope, of life revived and restored. All around them there was shouting and cheering. They heard the first notes of the Marseillaise, initially a little uncertain, then swelling gradually into a wild crescendo of voices as all the bells of Paris began to peal and the entire city sprang into light.

In the aftermath of that exuberant August day euphoria was replaced by a dogged search for food. Anger and violence erupted, directed at those who had spent the past four years collaborating with the German occupiers and a savage cleansing began. On the last day of August, Celine climbed the stairs to the small apartment, worn out from a long shift and the afternoon heat. Inside she found a young man seated beside her mother on the sofa. He rose to introduce himself.

"Good afternoon, Dr de Savoie. I'm René Fabre. I work for Henri de Valnay. He asked me to come and see you."

"Darling, you'll never believe what has happened!" Charlotte interrupted, her eyes shining with tears. "Henri has sent this young man to help us. We are to return to Avenue Mozart, Celine. We can go home!"

An hour later they stood in the hall, surveying the ruins of their once beautiful house. The walls had been stripped of paintings and mirrors, the empty rooms were bare of carpets and echoed with their footsteps. The panelling was cracked, the windows broken. All Charlotte's most valuable furniture and family heirlooms had vanished with the Germans. André had died in the final, cruel months of the occupation, but Louise greeted them with tears of joy.

Ten days after their return, the front doorbell rang.

"Henri! We had no idea what could have happened to you. You've been hurt!" Celine reached up to touch him.

There was a cut over his right eye, and one side of his face was bruised and swollen. He looked tired out but his elation was obvious as he held her tightly, looking at her with joy. She returned his embrace, truly thankful that he was back.

"It's all over. Thank God it's all over and you are both safe." His voice was choked. "The rest we can deal with as time goes on."

"Oh, my dear, how will we ever be able to repay you for all these years of kindness!" Charlotte had appeared in the hall and hurried to embrace him. "Good God, what has happened to you?"

"I ran into a few problems but it's nothing serious. Not all of France is free yet. Paris was only the first celebration."

After that first reunion he visited them frequently, coming to the house as before, armed with treasures that included packets of butter, soap, some meat or a few eggs.

"I don't know how I feel about this, Mama," Celine said. "I'm afraid for him. There are so many people being denounced, even shot, for having been collaborators."

"In time we'll hear an explanation." Charlotte looked up at her daughter. "Has he told you that he's having agonising headaches, and blurred vision? What could cause that, do you think?"

"I don't know. He was injured when he first returned to Paris.

Maybe it's a result of that. I'll arrange for him to see a specialist about it."

But over the following weeks Celine put in so many extra hours at the hospital that she barely saw Henri, and his problem slipped out of her mind. Often when her shift was over she remained in the corridors outside the wards, comforting the women who were trying to come to terms with the sight of their sons or husbands returned to them with missing limbs and sometimes hideously disfigured.

Henri came one cold November evening to take Celine out for dinner. It was his birthday and he had chosen a restaurant that, despite the shortages and rationing, still produced a wholesome meal.

He greeted her, drawing her close to him, but her body stiffened involuntarily. He relaxed his hold on her immediately.

"Is this because of Emile Vallon, the cousin who was not a cousin? I think you should talk to me about him, Celine. Perhaps between your mother's contacts in the Red Cross and my own, we can discover what happened to him."

She told him the whole story then, from her first meeting with Richard Kirwan to the fateful night's events that had led to his arrest. She wept as she described those last moments beside the river when he had been taken from her, and the horror of Charlotte's encounter with him at Gestapo headquarters. But she did not tell him that Richard had a wife in Ireland, because she could not bring herself to say the words.

"Many of those who were arrested were either shot or sent to the terrible camps we are now hearing about," he said finally. "And many of them have not survived. But we'll try to trace him by whatever means we can. Now let me take you to dinner. You won't object to black market champagne tonight will you?"

In the restaurant Celine lifted her glass to wish him a year of fulfilment and happiness. He did not hesitate to toast her in reply. "To the most beautiful doctor, the most enchanting woman in Paris. And to our future!" Her hesitation was immediately evident. "Are you so reluctant to drink to a shared tomorrow, Celine?"

"We've shared a great deal already. I don't know where Mama and I would have been without you." She heard herself babbling on, trying to prevent him from expressing himself further. He reached out and placed his fingers gently on her lips.

"Something has come between us, and I can't seem to get beyond it. Is it Richard Kirwan? Or is there something else that we haven't discussed?"

"I do feel great affection for you, Henri. And so much gratitude." She searched for the right words, knowing she owed him honesty at least, not wanting to hurt him. "But the war has made me realise that we don't share the same basic views. And that disturbs me."

"What is it that upsets you exactly, Celine?"

"Each of us has had to make choices, desperate decisions, during the war. And now that it's all over, I wonder what you felt about the German occupation." She drew a deep breath. "You lived comfortably during those years. You did very well out of your wine business, supplying the restaurants and the Germans and the black market. But all around you there was so much violence, so much deprivation and suffering. And I always wondered why you didn't feel you should do something about that?"

"You're asking me why I didn't take up arms, join the resistance? Look after fugitives like your mother, carry messages, sabotage German trains?"

"Yes, I suppose I am asking that. But I'm also asking about being passive, about benefiting from the enemy occupation and not feeling soiled by it. I don't know who you are really, or what you believe in."

He did not flinch or look away from her, but he withdrew his hand. He lit a cigarette. His expression was tight. "You're wondering if I could be classed as a collaborator. That is what disturbs you, isn't it?"

333

She sat with her head bowed, knowing she had probably destroyed their friendship for all time.

"It's been difficult to know that you doubted me, and to live with that knowledge. But I couldn't speak about what I was doing, any more than you felt able to talk to me about your work. The Germans did more than occupy the country. They created a situation in which friends could no longer trust each other. But I had a small role to play during the last three years."

"You were working in some way against the Germans?" Relief and shame surged within her.

His face was so sad that she leaned forward and touched his hand as he continued. "I had access to high-ranking German officials. When a powerful member of the army or the SS placed an order for wines, I delivered them myself, taking a few bottles of a fine Bordeaux, or an exceptional Armagnac. Soon I was asked to stay on, smoke a cigar, sample a brandy. After a few measures of cognac I would hear of plans for movements of supplies in and out of Paris, where troops were being sent, special projects they were involved in. Men tend to try and impress one another when they've had a few drinks, and I often received useful information that I could pass on. At no danger to myself, I may add."

Celine wanted to break in, to ask his forgiveness for her lack of trust, to tell him about her mother's unwavering belief in him. But he was speaking again, glad to tell her his story at last. "After the terrible episode at Dunkirk, I helped to set up an escape line for British soldiers and airmen who were trapped here, and later for undercover people being sent into Vichy France."

"How did you do that?"

"I'm friendly with the Legrand family, whose vineyards straddle the border between the occupied area and Vichy France. I would go down there for wine tastings and to place orders." He smiled at her, and she saw that he was enjoying her surprise. "I collected people in Paris who had to get out, and took them down there. If they were French-speaking I passed them off as members of my staff. If they were British I hid them in the boot of the car, or said they were labourers. Then they could cross the line that ran through the vineyards. Most of them got away safely."

"I know how dangerous it was to get people out of Paris. It took such courage."

"It was my friends who were courageous. They were the ones who hid the men, organised guides, identity papers."

She looked at him, recognising the integrity that should have been evident to her all along. "I only wish I had known."

"And I often wished you had guessed. It would have made those years more bearable. But in the end it was best that you didn't know. Because there was always the possibility that I could be caught."

"And just before the liberation? Where did you go?"

"The rest of the country was still occupied. We had two agents who had to be hidden. But even at that late moment someone tipped off the *Milice*." He smiled and touched the scar on his forehead, just beneath his thatch of brown hair. "We were hiding in a barn when the Germans arrived and started shooting. One of the soldiers threw a grenade into the building. There was a terrific explosion and then stones and dust everywhere. I was unconscious for more than a day. But as you can see, I survived, unlike some of my friends."

"So much bravery, such heroism. And you were a hero for Mama and me."

"So many sacrifices, so many friends dead or vanished. Sometimes I cannot imagine how we will all recover from this." Henri stubbed out his cigarette and smiled, but there were tears in his eyes. "But we have to try and restore our lives. And those of us who fought have memories that will bind us together and help to heal many of our wounds."

She suddenly remembered that she had planned to make an

335

appointment for him with a specialist. How could she have forgotten, after all he had done for her?

"Do you still have the headaches, Henri? I'd like to arrange for you to see someone at the hospital."

"I don't think it's anything I should worry about. Just write his name down for me, and if I need him I'll make an appointment myself."

He raised his glass again, smiling but shy. "You know, I brought you here this evening to tell you that I want you to be with me always, to share my life. I'm very much in love with you."

"I don't know what to say to you Henri. We're ordinary people who were called on to do things we never imagined possible. I've watched people being killed in front of me, seen things that even a doctor never dreams of having to experience. I don't know how to find the way back to normal life. Maybe I'll never find it."

He interrupted her quickly. "Together we can put all this behind us. And I will always take care of you, Celine."

"I need time to get over the circumstances of the last three years. Can you give me a little time?"

From that evening their friendship deepened and as the weeks passed Celine acquired a sense of security that she thought had disappeared from her life. But something held her back from committing herself to this man who had already given so much of himself to protect her. She would return exhausted from the hospital, or elated after an evening with Henri and their circle of friends, only to meet the ghost of Richard Kirwan wandering through her haunted dreams.

Chapter 42

Paris, 1945

The city was awash with exiles. They poured into Paris, carrying their possessions in bundles clasped by bony fingers. Those who had fled at the beginning of the war hoped to return to their old jobs and small apartments, to pick up the lives they had known before the occupation. Parisians were stunned into speechless horror by the return of those who had been deported to the camps in Poland and Germany. Prisoners of war, sent away after the fall of France in 1940, arrived in Paris in the company of surviving members of the resistance who had been captured, tortured and deported, and with the few remaining members of the Jewish community. There could be no preparation for the vision of these skeletal figures that stumbled out of trains on to the station platforms to wander dazed in the streets, milling helplessly, with vacant expressions through relocation centres and hospitals, in the hopes of tracing relatives or finding help for their fractured bodies and souls.

Food shortages became more acute as the city tried to accommodate the swelling tide of refugees. In the hospital, Celine used every last ounce of energy to ease the sufferings of those who had returned. In each of their faces, in all their pain and anguish she saw Richard, and she grieved for him.

The Hotel Lutetia became the focal point for processing the deluge of deportees. Charlotte spent each day working to create some sense of order and comfort for people whose experiences were beyond comprehension.

"You and your mother are going to kill yourselves soon. Then what use will you be to anyone?" Henri looked at Celine one evening as she opened the door at Avenue Mozart. He took in the shadows beneath her eyes, the pale face, noting how thin she had become. She laughed at him and leaned across to kiss him lightly on the cheek.

"I promise I'll eat everything in front of me tonight, and I'll go to bed early and sleep for at least half of tomorrow."

"So, are we ready to go? Where's Charlotte?"

"She's upstairs and Louise is going to prepare dinner for her later. I need a few minutes to change, but I won't be long."

She poured him a drink and left him in the salon. As she crossed the hall the doorbell rang. There was a man on the doorstep in the pale dusk. His head had been shaved and his scalp was covered with a stubble of growth through which she could see numerous scars. His clothes hung loosely from stooped, bony shoulders. He raised his head so that she could see his waxen, yellowed complexion and she stared into eyes that were red-rimmed and sunken. He half-raised a hand with contorted fingers and attempted a smile, revealing broken, blackened teeth.

"Celine de Savoie. I'm looking for . . ."

She stood paralysed, unable to breathe. Horror coursed through her, followed by a terrible joy and compassion. He looked back at her and she saw tears beginning to run down his gaunt cheeks.

"I never wept in all the years I was away." His voice was thin and dry. "But I'm weeping now. I'm weeping with happiness at the sight of you, Celine."

She stepped down and gathered his shaking frame into her arms, holding him close to her, stroking him, touching the livid welts on his scalp and on his calloused hands, feeling the sharp prominence

338

of his bones beneath the thin fabric of his jacket, her tears falling unchecked and unheeded on to his wasted face. Then she led him slowly up the steps, calling for her mother and for Louise to help her.

Charlotte appeared on the landing at the top of the curved staircase and stared at the swaying figure in the hallway, partly supported by Celine and Louise. Her mind refused to acknowledge the possibility of his identity, of what was happening there below her. But when she could see that it was truly Richard who was standing there in the hall, she rushed to embrace him again and again, in all her joy and pity. From the door of the drawing room Henri watched them, unnoticed and forgotten, as they helped Richard upstairs.

"I didn't know where else to go."

Celine sat beside him, smiling through her tears at the wreckage of the man she loved. It was Charlotte who was able to make a first attempt at conversation, struggling to overcome her emotions.

"Oh Richard, God is so good! Our prayers for you have been answered and nothing else matters, nothing."

He looked around the bare room that had been his first refuge. "They took everything?"

Charlotte nodded. "But it was only my possessions. And the pictures and china and glass. They would have taken my life, had it not been for your courage."

She could not prevent herself from weeping once more when she thought of him as she had last seen him, beaten and tortured, firm in his determination not to betray her. Finally Celine rose to her feet, touching Richard's head, letting her fingers rest on his grey face.

"I think we have to put you to bed, Richard. I'm going to have Louise give you a light supper. After that a sedative, and a long, undisturbed sleep. We'll put you in my bedroom. There's no furniture left in the room where you were before."

Celine ran a bath, gently taking his clothes from him, helping his fragile body into the water, trying to conceal her shock at the sunken ribcage, the shrivelled frame. She persuaded him to eat a little and then she adjusted the pillows to support his head, and made him comfortable in the bed. He turned to her, tears running down his face, and she placed her hand on his forehead as he closed his eyes. He slept almost at once, but she was afraid to leave him. She sat on a chair in the half-dark of the evening, holding his hand, until she too fell asleep beside him.

The first morning passed slowly. Celine insisted on a complete physical examination. "I'm reverting to the role in which you first met me Richard." She was smiling at him, searching for a spark of light in the dull resignation in his eyes. "I'm going to go over you from head to toe, and then we'll know what sort of plan we should make to get you back on your feet."

He lay quietly on the bed, his eyes closed, allowing her to examine each damaged part of him. She emerged from the bedroom appalled, and wept in the privacy of Charlotte's bedroom, her mother's arms around her.

"You cannot imagine what they have done to him. I don't know yet what the long-term results will be. He's had a bad head wound and there are several other minor cuts on his scalp. His ribs have been broken and one of his legs is badly scarred. His feet have had frostbite from standing and marching in the snow without proper shoes. All his fingers seem to have been broken and were never re-set. He says he almost died of typhus, and he ought to be checked for tuberculosis, although mercifully I see no sign of it. And most of his teeth are destroyed."

"What kind of people would do this?" Charlotte's voice was barely audible. "Didn't we cast aside such acts of barbarism centuries ago? How could this have happened in our time?"

They sat in silence, numbed by the realisation of an experience so brutal, so alien, so dehumanising that it was beyond their ability to understand.

"We have to be so careful with him, Mother. He's very delicate, damaged psychologically. He won't be able to do very much for a long time. Everything will exhaust him. I'm sure he's anaemic and he's suffering from malnutrition. His digestive system has to get used to food very slowly. Anything rich will make him extremely ill."

"Well, that shouldn't be a problem at this particular moment." Charlotte was quick to enjoy the irony of the situation.

After a meagre lunch Celine wrapped a rug around Richard and sat down with him in the garden. The slightest exertion tired him out within a few minutes, and their conversation was slow and sporadic. He seemed content to sit quietly, saying nothing, his eyes half closed.

"I think we should try to contact your family in Ireland and tell them you're—"

He rose suddenly from his chair, shaking his head vehemently, staring out at her in panic, his hands trembling. His legs were unsteady, his face was bathed in sweat as great gulping sobs of grief and fear overcame him in his agitation.

"No! I can't see them — I can't let Helena see this. It would destroy her to see this horror!" He put his twisted hands up to his face. "I'm not ready for them. I can't see them, Celine. Oh please, God, no!" He fell back into the chair, his body rocking to and fro.

"It's all right, Richard, don't be alarmed, please. When you're ready we'll think about it."

"You have to promise me."

"I promise. And now I want you to rest. Come on upstairs with me and I'll put you into bed for a while." He began to shake again and she gently unwound his arms and began to stroke his hands. "You're going to be fine. We're going to take each day as it comes and I'll make you well again. I promise."

On the third night after his return she sat up in the dark, her skin prickling at the sound of screaming. In her old room, she found him sitting on the side of his bed, the sheets soaked with sweat, his body trembling. He was gasping for air, coughing and choking, his terror surrounding him like a thick, impenetrable mist.

"Ssshhh . . . It's all right Richard, it's just a dream. Your mind went back there, but your body is safe. You're safe here."

His shame at having awakened her, at the state of his bedclothes and pyjamas, at his fear, made him avoid her gaze. But she ignored his silence and humiliation, and went quietly to change the linen on his bed. Then she helped him to lie down and sat with him, watching him fight the need for sleep, lest it transport him back to the hell from which he had escaped.

During the daytime he made a determined effort to be cheerful, commenting with pleasure on the weather, the colour of the sky, the luxury of having a chair to sit on and clean sheets to sleep in. His appetite improved, and his joy at the simplest of food was heartbreaking to see. He seemed mesmerised by the simple action of cutting a slice of fresh bread, or pouring a glass of water. Charlotte made several trips to the library to find books for him and Richard sat in the drawing room or the garden with her, sometimes reading but more often in wordless contemplation.

One afternoon Celine decided that they should take a short walk. Richard appeared eager to accompany her, and it was with contentment and anticipation that she helped him on with his jacket and they began their slow descent of the stairs. Louise was smiling as she opened the front door for them. But Richard stood frozen on the steps, his face ashen, his hand moving up to his throat, clutching at his collar, struggling to breathe.

"Close the door, Louise." Celine tried to keep her voice calm. "Monsieur Kirwan isn't feeling very well. It's the chill air that suddenly came in from the street. We'll go walking another day."

She led him into the drawing room and removed his jacket and hat. She saw that his face was beaded with sweat and that his hands were trembling. He sat down on a chair, unable to control his limbs, and began to cry like a lost child.

"I can't go out. My heart is racing and I have terrible nausea and I think I'm going mad Celine! I can't even escape from myself, from the ruins of my own mind. My God, what am I going to do?"

She sat on the floor at his feet and began to stroke his knees, saying nothing until the shaking gradually stopped and he was calm.

"Richard, this is a well-known medical condition that causes palpitations and often attacks people who have experienced terrible trauma. These symptoms will fade. All these terrible feelings will fade in time. Even the nightmares will disappear. And you'll be able to go anywhere you choose if we are patient and work together every day. In the meantime, it may help you if you can talk to me about what happened to you."

But he shook his head firmly. "No one who did not see it should know about that place – no one should be exposed to what we saw there. It isn't right to pass on that burden. I can't talk about it. Not to anyone."

"It's not passing on a burden, Richard." Her voice was low and steady. "The human psyche needs to acknowledge these things in order to be free of them. I know Mother has begun to tell you her experiences over the last three years."

"No, it's not the same. You must never know how it's not the same." He was becoming agitated again and his hands had begun to flutter.

"Richard, you must let me share your pain, work on your hurt mind, just as you've let me work on your hurt feet and head and hands. I'm your doctor, and you have to be my partner if we are going to heal you. We have to heal all of you and we're going to do that. In time, we will do that together."

But he turned his face away from her and went to his room alone to rest. On the following day he was cheerful once more, talking to

Charlotte about the book he was reading, eating his lunch with evident relish. When he did not appear for dinner in the evening, Celine went in search of him. She found him upstairs in the corner of the bedroom, his hands covering his ears, his body rocking, his voice crooning on a strange high note to block out the nightmare sounds that had lodged themselves within his head. She took him in her arms and cradled him, smoothed his hair, held him against her breast until he ceased to move and was quiet.

There were days when Celine began to feel that she would never make any progress, and that he might perhaps be better in hospital. But she knew that any sign of defeat on her part could do him immeasurable damage, and she feared that putting him into hospital or any kind of institution would be unbearable for him. As the days multiplied into weeks she searched in vain for signs of real improvement, but she could not identify any major indication of change.

When the nightmares attacked him yet again, Celine sat on the edge of the wide bed and looked at her mother. She took a deep breath in the darkness and pressed Charlotte's hand. Then she gathered her dressing gown around her and left. In Richard's bedroom she found fresh sheets and laid them on the bed. Then she took him by the hand and helped him as he lay back against the pillows. When she had switched out the light, she lay down beside him, close against his bony frame, winding her arms gently around him, cradling him and whispering to him, until she heard the soft breathing that told her he was asleep. She closed her eyes and moved closer into the arc of his body and then she drifted away.

In the morning she found Charlotte up early and waiting to have breakfast with her.

"Why are you here so early Mama – I thought you weren't working until this afternoon."

"Celine, I want to talk to you. You loved him very much, even

344

before he went away. You want to cure him. But you must get help with Richard – you can't do this all by yourself. You can't carry his suffering, make up for his nightmares and all his agony, for the rest of your life."

But Celine shook her head, deliberately deaf to this oversimplified logic. She knew that she must find some point of entry into the closed world that held his grief, but she did not know what route she might take without destroying him. She kissed her mother and left for the hospital, refusing to be drawn into any discussion about Richard and his brittle, protective shell.

In the evening they all dined together. He was relaxed and smiling, his face showing real animation as they sat down to play a game of cards. He seemed to be completely submerged in the simple activities of the present, and some of the shadows left his face. Celine watched him, hopeful that this small signal would be the first step on the long road to healing, and she felt gratitude flow into her body, leaving her calm and content. It was Louise who answered the telephone.

"Miss Celine, Monsieur de Valnay is on the telephone for you."

Charlotte de Savoie caught her eye as she rose from the table and went to the telephone in the drawing room.

"Henri – yes, I know. Louise told me that you had left a message that night. I must apologise to you – I'm so sorry. It's been very, very difficult and tiring. He was in a place called Buchenwald – well, we've all begun to hear the stories of those camps." She listened to his voice, to his invitation to dinner on the following evening. "I don't know. I try to work with him each evening when I come home from the hospital. I haven't made much headway, no breakthrough yet. He's still a captive of that unspeakable place. But I've got to continue until I find a way. Perhaps I can telephone you in a week or so? And I'm sorry – so sorry about last time. We were just so carried away by the whole –"

345

"It's all right. It was an extraordinary moment and I knew I was superfluous. Let me know when you're free."

He hung up abruptly without saying goodbye and she was left holding the receiver, a sense of guilt making its insidious way into her mind. She returned to the dinner table.

"How is Henri?" Charlotte's voice was neutral but Celine felt her concern.

"He seems fine, busy as always. I told him I'd have dinner with him in the next week or two."

"Did he say whether he'd seen your eye specialist colleague again? Or whether there were any results from the first examination?"

"No, he didn't mention it at all." Celine felt the colour rising in her cheeks as she chided herself for not having enquired.

"Is this the man we met one day when I was first playing fugitive?" Richard looked up suddenly showing signs of genuine interest. "Wasn't it Henri who helped you so much, found you an apartment after Charlotte's release from prison? I'd like very much to meet him again. He's a very fine man indeed. Quite a hero, I'd say."

"Are you ready for a little socialising?" Celine was surprised.

"Yes, I think so." His answer was slow, but he was smiling. "I'm not sure I could handle a crowd of people, but I think I would enjoy the stimulation of some wider contact."

The small dinner party was modest and though they no longer dined off heirloom china, the atmosphere was one of contentment and spontaneity and Richard enjoyed the conversation and the sense of normality. On the following day Celine returned from the hospital to find him waiting for her in the drawing room, his coat and scarf lying over the back of the chair.

"I thought we might go out," he said. "I'd like to try again, Celine. Will you come with me?"

Her weariness evaporated as she helped him on with his coat and took his arm. He smiled down at her, uncertainty clear in his eyes. She had to stay close to him to hear his words. "They used to beat you when you went out of the door into the cold. You had to rush past them and try to dodge the blows. But I've spent a little while each day at the door here, opening it and looking into the street, getting myself ready to begin again."

Celine led him across the hall, sensing his fear as she opened the front door. He drew a deep breath and stepped out into the street with her, his heart racing, choking him, robbing him of breath. On the pavement they looked at one another and then she flung her arms around him.

"A victory! And now we will move on, slowly and at your pace, to the next one."

He stood with his arms about her, holding her to him in his relief. Their short stroll marked the beginning of his journey to recovery. Gradually he started to talk to her of his experiences. She could see him struggling to accept what had happened to him, to give it meaning. "Strangely I feel guilt more than anything," he told her one evening. "I feel guilty at the burden I'm placing on you and Charlotte. And I had friends there, in that terrible place, who are all dead. I ask myself what I can ever do to make their suffering worthwhile."

It was several weeks before he agreed to visit the dentist and begin the repairs that were necessary for his teeth. In the white, clinical space Celine saw the stalking giant of his dread return and watched him tremble in the chair. She was afraid to raise the subject of his family again, in case he retreated into the solitary shell in which he had lived for so long, in an effort to protect himself from insanity.

At the first sign of summer Celine suggested that they catch a train out to the countryside, taking a picnic with them. She brought a small camera and Richard took a photograph of her lying on the grass in the sunlight, with her hair spread out around her laughing face in a golden fan. He objected at first when she raised the camera to photograph him, but at last he agreed that it would mark their first real outing. Afterwards he opened the wine and they toasted one another and began to eat their chicken with uninhibited relish.

As they sat under the trees, Richard began to speak hesitantly of the wasteland he had inhabited, of his struggle to stay alive, and to retain his sanity. He described his initial horror at the walking skeletons that surrounded him, and the gradual realisation that he had become one of them. He told of the beatings, the starvation, the foul stench of dysentery, and the gnawing rats among the rotting bodies of the dead.

"They kept us alive only so that we could work in the factories. When anyone became weak, they were no use any more, and were killed."

Haltingly he described the dark hours spent freezing during the roll calls, of the dogs that leapt at the throats of weakened men and savaged them, of the irrational shootings and disappearances. At night he would lie on the piece of bread he had saved for the morning lest it be stolen from him while he slept.

"They took everything from us. We were starving and filthy and degraded. We had no names, only numbers. But we fought with the one remaining weapon we possessed. With our intellect. We were determined that they would not take away from us our power to think.

"I did not believe that I could ever speak about all this, Celine. I didn't think that there was another person alive with the courage to hear these things, and not turn away from me in pain. You've become my way back to life."

On the train they sat close together, their fingers touching, their faces soft with the knowledge of what was to come. They ate supper slowly, sipping their wine, looking at one another and smiling. Then they climbed the stairs together.

In the bedroom he kissed her again and again, whispering to her, touching her gently. Celine reached up to him and stroked his face, her body against his, helping him as his damaged fingers unfastened the small buttons at the back of her dress and she felt his touch on her bare shoulders for the first time. Downstairs the telephone rang unanswered, until Henri de Valnay abandoned his idea of asking her out on the following evening and replaced the receiver in his apartment.

From that day Richard began to feel the signs of healing that he had once despaired of ever recognising. He was unable to make any connection with his former existence. The idea of it filled him with an illogical and paralysing dread that he could not explain either to himself or to Celine. She had become his guide, his safe harbour, and he could not envisage a future without her sustaining love. Sometimes in dreams he saw his wife, weeping at the sight of his damaged body and faltering mind. On these occasions he would feel the tremors in his hands, the shaking in his legs and the sick anxiety seeping once more into his brain, and he would gather up every atom of strength to return to the world of Avenue Mozart. Celine counted each small step he made towards a full recovery, lying beside him each night in the darkness that could still terrify him, banishing his fear of sleep and nightmares.

Charlotte de Savoie watched with compassion and a sense of foreboding as her daughter was transformed into a radiant creature, overflowing with love and joy. There was no doubt that Richard's health was improving, and she feared for Celine, for what would happen to them both when he was ready to contact his family, and possibly return to Ireland.

One autumn morning, Charlotte was at her desk at the Hotel Lutetia. The building was no longer surrounded by crowds of people searching for missing family members and friends. But inside, a steady stream of enquiries continued, and each day brought its quota of tragedy in the faces of those whom she tried to help. She was writing a report when she heard the unusual voice. He was speaking in French but with a strong foreign accent, and she looked up to see if she could help the rugged, sandy-haired man who was trying to explain his problem to a secretary on the other side of the room.

"I realise he wasn't a French citizen," he was saying. "But at the Irish Embassy, they told me I should come here. Maybe in your records, someone mentioned seeing him or meeting him. Something . . ."

Charlotte rose to her feet and approached him. "Can I help you, Monsieur? I speak English and that might make it easier."

He followed her to her desk and sat down opposite her, holding his hat in his hands. She saw a faint glimmer of hope in his craggy face. "My name is Seamus O'Riordan, Madame," he said. "I've come to France to try and discover what happened to my brother-in-law who disappeared here in 1942. His name is Richard Kirwan."

Chapter 43

Solange arrived home to find the old house peaceful.

"Lorette! I'm so happy to be home. Is everything all right? Where's Papa? Have we had any visitors?"

"I don't know what you and Madame de Savoie have been hatching up, Solange, but in spite of your warnings from Paris I haven't received any strange telephone calls or surprise visitors. If it's some fancy wedding caterer your grandmother is sending down, they haven't arrived yet. Your father is in the library. We don't see much of him these days. He's always out in the vineyards, or talking to barrel makers and soil testers and God knows who. But it's good for him, all this activity. You'll see."

Solange entered the library and Edouard stood up, his dark eyes questioning. She embraced her father, hugging him fiercely, her arms tight around his neck. He looked tanned and fit.

"It's lovely that you're home, darling. But I thought you'd be staying in Paris for another day or two." His smile showed surprise. "You surely can't have arranged everything already?"

"Well, I decided to postpone all that until there were fewer distractions." She was acutely aware of Edouard's gaze. She moved towards him and he kissed her on both cheeks.

"I'm delighted the vineyards have drawn you back so soon," he said, his tone neutral. "I think it's wonderful that the glories of the capital haven't completely seduced you."

She was unreasonably irritated by his comment, certain that he was laughing at her.

"There's so much to tell you, Solange." Henri reached for her hand. "We've been out in the vineyards for most of the morning. The new storage tanks and the barrels for the *cave* will be delivered next week, and we'll have everything installed by the end of the month. In plenty of time for the beginning of the harvest. You'll stay for dinner, Edouard?"

"Thank you, but I'm sure you have plenty to discuss with Solange on her first evening home." Edouard finished his whiskey. "I'll hope to be invited back later in the week."

Solange opened the hall door and they stood together in the spot where he had kissed her. She wondered if he even remembered the incident. He was her father's partner now, and that was what he had really wanted.

"It sounds as though all is proceeding as planned."

"Nothing connected with the land is ever certain. But we've accomplished a great deal in the last week or so. And your father is everything I knew he would be – full of sound advice, with so much experience and knowledge to offer. I'm very fortunate."

"Good. I expect we'll see you soon."

"You'll see me tomorrow, and probably every other day as well." His expression was quizzical. "I hope you enjoyed your brief visit to Paris. You look tired actually. Even strained. Is Guy back in Montpellier?"

"Yes, I expect so. Well, no. No, he's still in Paris. He's busy at the law conference, so I thought I'd . . . And it's not very polite to tell a woman she looks strained and tired." She knew she sounded flustered.

He placed his hands lightly on her shoulders, his eyes searching her face. His voice was very soft. "It's none of my business, but if there's something wrong maybe I can help by listening."

"You're right. It's not your business. And there's nothing wrong. I just got tired, and Guy was at meetings all the time, and I came home."

He leaned towards her and kissed her gently on both cheeks, then put his fingers beneath her chin. "Ah well. Goodnight then."

Henri was waiting in the library. "So tell me what brings you home so early, my darling? Your travel plans are becoming rather changeable."

"Papa, I don't know quite how to explain this. Guy and I have broken off our engagement."

"What? We only just announced it!"

"Well, I don't know if it's broken off for ever, but we've postponed the wedding. It was Guy who made the decision." She began to cry, sobbing inconsolably. Henri was unsure what he should say.

"Solange, what has really happened? When did all this trouble begin, and what is the real root of the problem? Isn't it time you told me all about it?"

But she could not tell him. She could not tell him that he was not her father, and that her mother had deceived them. She could not tell him of her awful encounter with the Kirwans in Paris, or her worry that Eleanor might have come here in her absence. There was no way of explaining how she had hurt and misjudged Guy. And she could not tell him that she knew he was a hero of France.

"I'm just not ready to be married. I thought you'd be upset, disappointed, that you would think me foolish. So when I went away for a few days to think about it all, I didn't go to Spain, Papa. I went to see Cedric in England and talk to him."

Henri felt the shaft of hurt. She had not been able to confide in him. He was a failure as a father, blind to the language of her body, unaware of her deepest fears. "Darling, I don't want to trivialise this, but most people experience prenuptial nerves. I'm sure Guy is upset, but he'll wait this out."

"I don't know if we can ever get back together. I thought I loved him. He's kind and good and I feel guilty about hurting him. But he knew I wasn't ready."

In the morning she awoke to the cooing of wood pigeons, the frenzied song of the cicadas and the cool sound of splashing. She ran down the stairs to join Henri in the swimming pool that Celine had built for him below the stone terrace. Solange swam thirty lengths with him and they breakfasted together on the terrace.

"Do you want to talk about Guy, and your grandmother?"

"No, Papa, I don't. I need a few days to get it all clear in my mind. I'd rather catch up on what you've been doing here. On all the progress you've made."

Henri was both hurt and angered by her rebuff. But he did not feel that there was anything to be gained by pressing her, and he began to talk about the changes in the vineyards.

Solange kept busy in the weeks that followed, learning the details of the new project. She waited for some sign of reconciliation from Guy but heard nothing. In the newly repaired *cave* at Roucas Blancs the first stainless-steel tanks and new oak barrels were installed. When the masons and carpenters had completed their work she set up a small, partitioned office. She painted the walls and hung them with old prints, and one morning she arrived with a trailer bearing a large desk, several chairs, a small table and a comfortable sofa.

"What's this for?" Edouard threw himself down on the sofa. "Are you think of having tea parties?"

"It's for you," she said, laughing at him. "You're going to be sleeping here some nights, waiting for the last of the *vendange*, for telephone calls, for important analysts and oenophiles from Bordeaux, for . . ."

"All right, all right. I get the picture. In the meantime since we are the only important people here, do you want to try it out?" He was grinning at her, deliberately predatory.

354

"Try what out?"

"The sofa, Solange. The sofa."

"I don't need to try it out, thank you. It was in my playroom for years." She smiled at him sweetly and drove away, disturbed by the small jolt of excitement she had felt when he had laughingly pro-positioned her. There must be something wrong with her. It was only a month since she had broken up with her fiancé, and it couldn't be right to look at another man and experience – experience what, exactly? She pushed aside any attempt at deeper analysis. Any woman in her situation would want to feel attractive again, desired.

Edouard came and went daily, often dining with them in the evenings, sometimes bringing his father. They talked not only of vine-yards but of music and travel and books. During the blistering heat of late July Solange frequently packed a picnic and Edouard drove them up into the shady forests of the Haut Languedoc above their vineyards where they swam in the river and lay out on the flat rocks to dry themselves, and talk of the great vintages to come.

As the glare of the August sun continued unabated, they watched the skies and the weather reports, hoping for another week or two of dry weather. No one had any real faith in the official weather predictions and each additional day was a gamble. The grapes nestled beneath the cool canopy of their leaves, absorbing the full, wild character of the surrounding *garrigue*. They were thrilled and expec-tant, although none of them wanted to express it. With so much hope riding on this vital period they were afraid to put their feelings into words. And so they waited and tried as best they could to read the weather, and to keep their rising optimism in check.

"This is the last day of August." Henri finished his wine and pushed his chair back from the dining table. "I don't think we should wait much longer. Let's begin the harvest a week today. The grapes are ready. Are we agreed?"

They had dined together on the terrace. The air was filled with the perfume of lavender and roses and jasmine, and the smell of freshly cut grass. Edouard sat opposite his partner, and watched Solange. Her skin was a dark, honey colour, and the moonlight emphasised her cheekbones and her long neck, playing on the swell and curve of her breasts and her bare arms.

"I want to tell you, Henri, that your daughter is like a goddess this evening. I think I should try and describe her to you, sitting there in the moonlight." He had meant to speak playfully, but he could hear emotion in his voice.

"I think you're trying to embarrass me." Solange flushed and turned away.

Henri registered the sudden atmosphere, not altogether surprised by what it suggested. Edouard rose abruptly to take leave.

"I'll come to the door with you." Solange felt her pulse racing and hoped that it was not obvious to anyone other than herself.

"No Solange, stay there with Henri. The vision is too delightful to be disturbed. Goodnight."

She went up to her room and lay on her bed, unable to sleep. The air had become heavy and close. Finally she dozed uneasily, but some hours later she was woken by the sound of her shutters banging. Outside the sky was black. Then she heard the sound of the rain, soft at first, then drumming steadily on to the earth. It was too close to the harvest for rain. The grapes would absorb water, and the alcohol content would drop. Solange stood at the window, waiting for the shower to pass. After a while the wind came up, rushing through the plane trees, rattling and clattering in the stands of bamboo along the river, ruffling the cypresses so that they spread their branches like plumes in the angry air. Below her the river began to rise, turning its quiet song into a crescendo of roaring water. There was a flash of lightning followed by growling thunder. She put on her dressing gown and went downstairs to Henri's bedroom.

"We didn't need a rainstorm." He was standing by the window, gazing out into his visionless night.

"No, but the wind is strong, so it will probably blow over quickly. And we can delay the harvest for a few days and hope the sun will do its work again. There's time for that. We're only at the end of August."

Solange went to make them some hot chocolate. When she returned from the kitchen the rain had not eased but the wind had died. They froze as they heard the awful noise. At first it was a light pattering sound, but within moments it had increased in volume and speed so that they were barely able to hear one another. The hailstones battered the roof and the walls of the old house, and smashed across the terrace below them.

Henri stood at his window, seeing in his mind the damage to the protective leaves, the small, lethal pellets of water splitting the skins of the grapes, wrenching the bunches from their stems, tearing his dreams into shreds of blackened pulp. The telephone rang and Paul Ollivier told them that Edouard had gone out to try to assess the strength of the hail. They sat in silence, waiting. It was almost two hours before the storm began to die away and a sullen dawn crept over them.

Solange pulled on an old shirt and shorts, tied her hair under a felt hat and grabbed a waterproof jacket. Outside the rain had become a thin drizzle. All that remained of the tempest was the brooding grey of the sky and the strange, answering whiteness of the ground, which lay blanketed by the beautiful, crushing burden of the hail. On the western ridge she found Joel and his son, standing mute with fatigue and dismay.

"Where is he?"

"Over in the last of the new vineyards, near the *cave*."

Edouard was silhouetted in the growing light, standing in the midst of the destruction. Solange watched him for a moment and then she began to run through the last of the ruined vineyards, choking in the foggy air, her legs torn and cut by the broken stumps of twisted vines. Once she tripped and fell over the sad, fragmented remains of their grapes, gashing her arm. She picked herself up, brushed the mud and leaves from her skin and continued to run until she reached him.

He turned his head and she saw that his face was streaked with mud and his clothes were wet and ripped. There was a sorrow in his expression, so intense, so ferocious that she could not look at him. He held out his arms to her, and they stood holding each other, silent in their grief. She took him by the hand and led him to the *cave*. They lay down amongst the barrels of oak that were to have held the content of his dreams, and made love in a desperate search for consolation. Afterwards they lay together and he held her, his eyes shut, his breath uneven. She raised her face to him, and he kissed her, tasting the earth on her skin, the salt of her tears. He unfastened her torn shirt and pressed his face against her body. He caressed her for the first time, tracing the curved lines of her, stroking the creamy surface of her belly and the soft inside of her thighs. She held him and cradled him and murmured to him. When he entered her again she did not know whether her tears were for the destruction of his dreams, or for her own joy at his desire and need for her. She held him tightly, willing him to feel her compassion and solace.

At last he rose and found their abandoned clothes. He dressed her tenderly, smoothing her hair, wrapping her jacket around her, stopping several times to kiss her and hold her close to him. When she was ready, he placed his arm around her waist and they opened the doors of the *cave* and stepped out into their ruined world.

Chapter 44

St Joseph de Caune, 1970

The rain continued for two days, soaking the vineyards from a pewter sky. Solange tramped through the mud with Edouard and Joel, examining the grapes that had been split asunder by the deadly bullets of hail. On the second morning they sat down to assess the disaster, each of them fighting despair. Solange was troubled by Henri's response to the storm. He seemed unable to recognise the enormity of what had befallen them. When she thought about Edouard she felt herself drifting helplessly away from the safe course of her original plans. But he did not attempt to make love to her again, or even to find a time when they could be alone together. She wondered if he had needed her only for comfort in his moment of bitter disappointment.

Paul Ollivier treated them with a rough, protective kindness, offering to pool the proceeds of his own damaged harvest with theirs, to diminish their loss. The bank manager called, sympathetic, but cautious. On the third day the rain stopped and patches of sunlight struck the sodden hillsides.

"We can only pray, my dear, that we'll get a good north wind to dry all this out." Henri lifted his face to the weak sun. "Then we might avoid rot in the remaining grapes."

But the wind crept in, soft and slow from the south, its warm breath bringing further destruction. The bank called to set up a formal meeting early in the following week. Henri's face became drawn with apprehension. Edouard came for dinner, displaying a determination that created a force and energy of its own. For a few, brief hours they allowed themselves to believe in a solution that would not ruin them. At the end of the evening Edouard rose from his chair. Solange stood up, her heart making a thudding sound in her own ears.

"I'll see Edouard out, and then I think I'll go up to bed. I don't think I can last any longer without an early night." She put music on the stereo for Henri and left him, closing the door that led out into the hall. In the mirror she saw Edouard waiting for her. When she turned he took her into his embrace with such force she found herself gasping. He kissed her mouth, her cheeks, the hollow of her throat, lifting the heavy strands of her hair from her neck. He was murmuring into her skin, his breath in her ear. She began to tremble and put her arms up around his neck to stop herself from falling. She guided his hands to her breasts, sighing and unfastening her shirt. He touched her and stroked her, his caresses travelling slowly down to her stomach. He gave a small groan and she leaned back, delighted at the strength of her effect on him.

"Not now, Solange. Not here, with Henri so destroyed. We can't do this here."

"Of course, you're right. Goodnight, Edouard." She stepped away from him, filled with doubt, belittled by his rejection, unable to understand why he could not consider her needs as well as those of Henri.

"Don't be angry, please. I want you very much." He reached for her and saw the defiance, the smile that was too bright, flashing a warning. He took her hands and gently wrapped her arms around his waist. "Goodnight. I'll see you tomorrow."

She lay awake wrestling with her thoughts. Why could she no longer see anything in a clear, logical manner? Edouard cared only about the vineyards. She had known that from the first evening he had come to see Henri. She had simply been there at a moment when he needed to assuage his sorrow. He was too volatile, too unlike Guy whose steady assurance she had relied upon without ever realising it.

The past months returned to haunt her and she turned over, twisting her sheet and blanket in frustration and despair. Her inheritance would go a long way towards saving the entire enterprise. Thinking about Richard Kirwan she felt the old resentment stirring. Even her grandmother had found his last gesture incomprehensible. If guilt had motivated him, why hadn't he left her a sum of money in a numbered account that her grandmother could administer? But Richard Kirwan's money could keep them all afloat. It would allow her father and Edouard to wait out this disastrous harvest, and to expand the planting of new vineyards for next year. She flung aside the bed covers and sat by the window, listening to the river churning below her, with its cargo of mud and debris from the battered fields.

"I need someone to talk to, I need advice," she realised. "But I can't go rushing off to Paris or to see Cedric again. I've got to stay here now with my father, in the vineyards."

She had no idea how the transfer of her inheritance could be arranged with anonymity. It was not feasible to approach the local bank manager, or Henri's lawyer in the village. She did not want them to know her mother's secret. Her agitation grew as the dilemma spun in her mind, creating wider ripples of anxiety until the solution came to her like a spearhead of lightning. She returned to bed and fell asleep at once, knowing that she had found a way.

After breakfast she made a telephone call, and set a time for a meeting. She felt nervous, and although she did not have to be in Montpellier until the afternoon she left early for the city. She sat down at a café in Place de Comédie for a solitary lunch, giving herself time to think out what she would say. She was at his office a few minutes early.

"Monsieur St Jorre will see you now."

Solange opened the door and went in to him. Guy stood up and came towards her. She had almost forgotten the athletic strength of his body, the touch of green in the hazel eyes, the feeling of reassurance he gave her.

"I didn't want to telephone or contact you. I thought you might need some time, and I didn't know how long to stay away. I thought you would perhaps let me know when you felt . . . Well, anyway, are you all right?"

She saw the slight twitch at the corner of his mouth that betrayed his outward calm. It gave her a sense of relief, a rush of tenderness, and gratitude that she could trust him with her predicament. "You've heard about the hailstorm in St Joseph de Caune."

"I read how badly the area was hit. I've been thinking of nothing else for the last three days, thinking of Henri – wondering if there was some way I could be of help. But I wasn't sure what had happened between him and Edouard Ollivier – whether they'd ever finalised a partnership."

"They did. They formed their company, and went ahead with investing in a new *cave* and all kinds of equipment for the *vendange*. And they've ordered thousands of new vines for planting after the harvest. This could ruin them both financially." Her hands were trembling, and her heart was beating so fast that she could not speak clearly. "I've inherited a great deal of money from Richard Kirwan, the man who was my father. And I want to give it to them, to Papa and Edouard. Invest it in their company, so that we can save the whole project. Expand it, even. But I can't let Papa know where the money is coming from." She tried to smile at him. "I don't know if you've forgiven me, Guy. It was wrong of me not to have told you the whole, miserable story as soon as you came home from Guadeloupe. I'm sorry."

He came to sit beside her. "Neither one of us has handled this well. I was hurt that you couldn't trust me. But I should have stayed beside you, seen you through all this."

"No. That's not what this is about. I haven't come about our engagement, our relationship. Not at all." She drew back and closed her eyes, hearing the way he caught his breath, waiting for a moment to compose herself. "This is about my inheritance, about Papa and the vineyards. I can't give the money to my Papa, you see. I don't think he knew about Richard Kirwan. So I want you to help me work out a way to give it to Edouard, make him take the money instead. I want you to arrange it so that he can make Papa believe that he's found another investor."

"Are you telling me that you haven't discussed this with Edouard Ollivier? That you're just going to hand him this sum of money and hope he spends it wisely?"

She could hear the chill in his words, but she continued in desperation. "Of course I haven't talked to Edouard! I'd have to explain where I got the money. Why I couldn't give it to Papa myself. I don't want to discuss that with him. And I don't think he would accept money from me. He's so proud, so independent." She tailed off.

But he knew her too well, recognised something in her voice. "Solange, are you asking me to arrange for this man to have your money, not only to help Henri, but because there's something between you?"

She felt his pain and jealousy. But the only way to obtain his help was to lay the facts before him, ugly and stark though they might be. "I don't know what I feel. That's the truth. I haven't known what to feel about anything since that first letter from Eleanor Kirwan. Nothing is familiar. Not my own emotions, not these people who've invaded my life. James Kirwan, the brother, tried to see my grandmother in Paris. But she wouldn't receive him without my being there, and God knows I never want to set eyes on him again. I came back here because I was terrified Eleanor Kirwan had come down here to look for me."

There were tears in her eyes, and she was furious at herself for breaking down in front of him. His anger exploded like a fireball, and she saw the muscles of his neck stand out in knots of rage.

"How dare you ask me to do this for you! Have you ever considered how I feel? How much hurt I've experienced in these past weeks without you, when you never phoned, never wrote, never thought to explain what happened that night? Do you have any understanding of the hell I've been living in? Or would that be too much to expect?"

Solange stared at him. I don't know him, she thought. I never really knew him at all. And until recently I knew nothing about myself, either.

"First you disappear. Next you have a series of tantrums and you withdraw from me. You accuse me of having done something exceptionally stupid and cruel. And then, before the wounds are even closed, you set out again on the same track, deceiving another man!"

He was pacing the room, his body taut. She saw that he was trying to contain himself, to return to some kind of calm. "You were going to be my wife, my partner for life. But you couldn't trust me with the only important crisis you've ever experienced. What kind of basis for a marriage is that?"

"I'm sorry. I'm truly sorry, Guy. I was so unprepared. Can't you understand how I hated discovering all this? I don't want to know about their past, and yet it won't let go of me. Why should I be scarred by their affair?" She had begun to cry. "Anyway, I tried to explain to you in Paris, that morning when you came back. After we met the Kirwans."

"But your reaction was so immature, so unreasonable. You're not the only person ever to have discovered a secret in your parents' past. I tiptoed around you, wanting to help, not knowing what troubled you. But you never thought of me at all. And you probably haven't thought of me since I left you in Paris. Until now, when you want me to devise some way of handing over your money to your new boyfriend."

"It isn't like that at all! It's for my father. You know it's for my father that I'm doing this!"

"I don't know anything, Solange. Except that the way you've been behaving is totally incomprehensible to me."

"Stop preaching at me! You're right, I behaved badly and I'm sorry. How many times do you want me to say it?"

He drew up a chair and sat very close to her. "I will help you to set up an investment fund, from which you can transfer money into the vineyard. I can organise it so that Henri would find it difficult to unravel. But I will do so only if you promise me that you will go back to St Joseph now, today, and tell Edouard Ollivier the truth about the money. About where it came from. And about Celine de Valnay and Richard Kirwan. I will do this because I love you, and I cannot see you rush into a terrible mistake with some arrogant, ambitious man you barely know."

"You can't dictate to me, Guy!"

"That's the deal, Solange. I can give you the name of another lawyer, of course. But if you want me to do this for you and for Henri, those are my terms."

Guy waited while she sat with her head down, anger stiffening her body. Then she slowly nodded her agreement.

A sense of fierce exhilaration coursed through him because he knew that Ollivier would jump at the chance to use her inheritance. And then she would realise that his vineyards were all that really mattered to him.

Chapter 45

St Joseph de Caune, 1970

Over the next two days Solange worked with Aunt Jeanette, drawing up a revised set of dismal figures. She knew she was procrastinating, but she continued to concentrate feverishly on the report, avoiding any confrontation with Edouard. She was checking a line of figures when the telephone rang.

"Hello, Solange, it's Guy. I wondered how things were coming along? How is Henri doing?"

A twinge of guilt assailed her. "I've been working on an assessment report for the bank. Papa and Edouard have a meeting there the day after tomorrow. They need to be well armed and I've been very busy."

"So you haven't spoken to Edouard about your plan?" The silence lengthened, stretching out along the line. Then his voice came again. "I've talked to your law firm in Paris, and I've worked out a way to transfer these funds anonymously into the company Henri and Edouard have set up."

"There'll be total anonymity?" She kept her voice low, acutely conscious of Aunt Jeanette.

"Yes. But we have an agreement, remember? I suggest that you finalise your part, so we can get the paperwork completed. Then I would like to come and visit Henri. And I'd like to see you too. I'd especially like to spend some time with you."

She did not respond directly to his last remark, telling him only that she would telephone him within the next day or two. As she hung up, Edouard appeared in the doorway. "Good afternoon." He sounded cheerful. "Has either of you noticed the sunshine? I gather we may now expect a week of good weather. I've just come from the co-operative, and they've agreed to take the old grapes from the Roucas Blancs vineyards first, so we'll start picking those tomorrow."

"What about the new vineyards?" Solange did not look at him.

"We'll harvest those towards the end of next week. That will give the surviving grapes the maximum amount of time to recover. If the weather holds they'll absorb some extra sunshine, and the alcohol content will go back up again. We'll see. Come outside with me, I want to take you up to the top vineyard for a look."

She went out reluctantly into the hot afternoon. They drove together to the hill overlooking Domaine St Joseph. The sun was high in a canopy of blue sky. Below them the vines spread out their leaves, greedily sucking the afternoon heat from the damp earth. He turned off the ignition and they sat together in silence. Solange was anxious, irritated by her own reticence, at pains to disguise her agitation.

"I want to make love to you." He traced a line along her cheek and leaned towards her, his mouth seeking her response.

"No. I have to talk to you. There are things you don't know, Edouard. I want to talk to you about the vineyards – about the whole disaster. About how I'm a disaster myself. I have to talk to you about my father."

Her tone was aggressive, and he moved away from her to try and gauge her mood.

"Solange, it wasn't right the other evening, somehow, with your father so worried nearby, and no place for us to be alone. But now it's just you and me, here in our vineyards."

"He's not my father." The words sounded lifeless and dull, making the statement more shocking.

"What? What are you saying?"

"Henri de Valnay isn't my father. I'm a mistake, an accident – the result of a liaison between my mother and an Irishman she met during the war. They had an affair and she got pregnant."

"I don't know what this is all about, but Solange you're beautiful. You could never be a mistake – you're a deliberate miracle of creation."

"No, you aren't listening. I must explain to you. He's dead, you see, the man who was my father. And I never knew he existed until recently, and Papa doesn't know I'm not his child. At least I don't think so. I don't believe she ever told him."

The story came pouring out, and he listened in silence until she was done. Then he opened the door of the car, reached for her hand and took her out into the evening light. "I can understand the shock, the burden of keeping this to yourself, of trying to carry on as normal with Henri. But look around you Solange. You've been given all of this. You and Henri and I are the fortunate ones who have inherited the gift of this beautiful earth. It doesn't matter who we are or how we came here. What matters is that we're meant to be here now, together, all of us."

He put his arm around her shoulders and drew her in close, unaccustomed to this protective feeling, unused to the swell of tenderness that filled him as he stood holding her, stroking her hair, smoothing it back from her face. "God knows how we are going to do it, but we will find a way to save all this. For ourselves and for our children and their children. I know we'll find a way to do it. That's our destiny. As for Henri – you are the daughter he has always loved. And you are yourself."

"No, there's more. Richard Kirwan left me money. I have enough money to keep up the payments with the bank, to keep us going.

Enough even to cover the expansion of the new vines, the next phase of replanting. I want to put the money into the company you've created with Papa."

"Henri will never allow it."

"He doesn't know, for God's sake. Haven't you been listening to anything I've said? But I can help to continue what you've started." Her voice was flat. "I can do it anonymously. He'll never know where the money came from. And that's what is really important to you, isn't it? To have the money to go on?"

"Yes, it's important. Of course it is. But we can make it through with the bank. I think we can persuade them to re-negotiate the loan. I don't believe they'll pull the rug from under us because of one setback." He moved away from her but he was still holding her hand tightly. "Something can be worked out, I'm sure. I've thought of nothing else for the last four days. I'm the one who is responsible for Henri sinking all this money into the vineyards. And I won't allow you to use your inheritance in this way."

"And I won't have him live through years of worry!" She interrupted him impatiently. "I want him to enjoy this new project, but with security. You're thinking only of yourself and your vineyards. You don't care if you sail too close to the wind for a while. But I'm thinking of Papa and his peace of mind. I'm going to have my inheritance transferred into your company account. And you will tell my father that you've found a silent investor who will lend you the funds to keep going and to expand."

"That's ridiculous and I won't do it." He let go of her hand. "You're suggesting I have no interest in Henri's wellbeing – that my motives are purely to keep the vineyards going for my own sake. Well you're wrong. You're wrong and what you're saying is an insult. You don't understand me at all. I will not take this money of yours and lie about it. I won't do this."

She moved further away from him. Her hands were in her pockets and he could see the outline of her clenched fists and her feet planted firmly on the soil they both loved. He reached to take her again in his arms but she pushed him aside.

"Yes you will do this! You'll do it for Papa! To refuse would be unspeakably selfish – motivated only by your pride, by your stupid ego! You will agree to do this, so that he doesn't have to worry about re-negotiating loans. And you'll agree to it now."

He tried another tack. "Henri will never believe in some silent partner who can't be identified. He'll never swallow something so unlikely!"

"Guy has found a way to make it work. He told me so this afternoon –"

"Guy St Jorre?" Edouard swung round in disbelief. "Guy St Jorre is involved in this? Henri told me you'd broken off your engagement to him." Solange absorbed this information in silence. Surely her father would not have confided this news to anyone? They had agreed not to mention it. He had not kept his word. "Guy heard the story from my grandmother in Paris, and from the Kirwan family."

"Is that why you haven't seen him? He didn't want to go on because of your parents?"

"No – of course not. He's far too honourable for that. He was just upset because I hadn't trusted him enough to tell him."

"But you were able to tell me all this? You felt you could talk to me about it?"

"Guy insisted that I tell you. It was part of the deal." She knew the words were wrong before she had spoken them.

"So I'm just the working part of a deal between you and Guy St Jorre, to save your father." His laugh was derisive and loud. "That's very clever of Guy. And if I don't agree, you'll consider that I don't care enough about Henri – that I'm not worthy of being his partner. I never thought I was so expendable."

"It isn't like that."

"Oh yes it is like that between you and your clever, resourceful lawyer. What a bloody fool I've been. What an idiot!"

She wanted to touch his hand, to caress him and lead him away from this disagreement, to draw him down on to the earth and wrap her limbs around him. She lifted her face up to him, offering her mouth, placing her hands tentatively on his chest.

He kissed her violently, hurting her lips, pulling her towards him so roughly that her back arched in pain. She tried to soften him, to stroke his face, to make him touch her gently, but he let go of her abruptly and climbed back into the car. They drove in silence to the house. Then he turned to her, his expression grim and closed. "I can see that you're set on the whole idea that Guy St Jorre sold you and that you've neatly worked out my role. Neither of you gives a damn about how I might feel, of course. About my integrity. In fact it's plain that you assumed I didn't have any integrity. So when do we meet your lawyer friend to discuss the details of this blackmail?"

"Perhaps after the meeting with the bank, or the following morning. It will be before the weekend anyway."

"Tell Henri I'll phone later." He drove off without another word.

The meeting in the bank was friendly but tense. The bank manager remained courteous and concerned, but non-committal. All agricultural loan reviews came from the bank's regional headquarters, it was not a decision that he could make personally. They nodded in polite, disappointed understanding.

Lunch was a less than cheerful affair. In the afternoon Henri retired to rest, his forced good humour contrasting with the pinched look of his face. As soon as he left the room Solange turned to Edouard. "We can go into Montpellier tomorrow morning. Guy has everything ready."

Afterwards Solange wondered how she had survived the antagonism of that meeting. Guy was polite but left no room for doubt or dissent. Edouard became more antagonistic at what he saw as a patronising attitude to his opinion. "The whole thing is dishonest. Deception results only in more deception. Eventually it collapses in on itself and destroys everything around it. We're building a partnership on quicksand. I prefer more solid ground. But I suppose that means nothing to a clever lawyer."

"It's Solange's choice and you're perfectly well aware of that." Guy's voice was steely and he made no further attempt at civility. "It will save Henri a great deal of worry. I think she's right, in this case the means justify the end."

"Lawyers have a wonderful way of bending the truth when it's convenient. I have another interpretation of integrity it seems. But I'm only a farmer so my objections don't count for much."

There was a further half-hour of fruitless discussion before Guy was able to produce the transfer documents and the agreement he had drawn up, for Edouard's signature.

Henri was openly disbelieving. "Who in God's name would want to invest in these vineyards right now? Can't you tell me anything about the investor?"

"I'm sworn to secrecy Henri. As for the reason, it could be a tax break of some kind. At any rate, you're satisfied with the structure of the agreement?"

"Yes, of course I am! I don't know how you managed to negotiate something so reasonable. He must know that he has the advantage over us."

Edouard would not stay for a glass of champagne or for dinner. Later in the evening Solange sat in the library with Henri.

"You know, I've been trying to work out Edouard's rescue package," he said slowly. "I think he persuaded his mother to give him the funds. She's very wealthy, but even if she were willing to back her son, she wouldn't want Paul to know she was putting money into the vineyards. Hence the secrecy. What do you think, Solange?"

Her heart sang out with relief and when she went to bed she fell asleep instantly, her mind clear and untroubled.

The *vendange* began on a morning when the sun had gently warmed the grapes and the dew had vanished from the black, glistening fruit. Solange left Joel in charge of the harvesting close to Domaine de Valnay, and joined Edouard in the new vineyards where he had started to handpick the remaining grapes. All day he moved tirelessly through the rows of vines with the pickers, plucking and snipping the fruit, lifting the protective canopy of foliage to expose small, hidden bunches of grapes clinging to the trunks. She slipped easily into the rhythm of the picking, bending forward and back, teasing the leaves aside, joining with pleasure in the songs from Occitanie, from Spain and from the dusty hillsides of North Africa. At noon she shared the workers' bread and cheese, olives and saucisson, helping Lorette to pour the wine and hand out heavy baskets of peaches and figs from their orchards.

In the evenings Henri joined the dinners for the pickers, discussing the length of the fermentation with Edouard and Joel, listening to Paul Ollivier's jokes and anecdotes and to stories of other harvests. The nights were filled with starlight and soft air and song, and Solange found herself in a welcome limbo of physical effort. She rose early, filled with purpose, taking pleasure in moving through the orderly days. At night she sank with a rewarding sense of lassitude into the welcoming depths of her bed.

On the last day of the harvest a haze of scorching rays spread across the vineyards and the work pace slowed a little in the breathless air. At noon Solange took her bread and cheese and some lemonade, and left the group of harvesters sitting at their trestle table under the umbrella pines. She had always loved the long, straight stretch of river between her home and the Ollivier land. The bank was high above the shimmer of the water and she could hear the thunderous sound of the waterfall increasing as she drew nearer. She scrambled down the bank to put her feet into the rushing water and feel the exhilaration of its cold current. She pulled her shirt over her head, and stepped out of her shorts, discarding them on a log before plunging into the deep pool beneath the fall, gasping with the thrill. The dust and heat of the vineyards flowed away from her and she lay there floating for a moment.

"You're a water nymph, magical and beautiful. I always knew you weren't quite real."

She had not heard him or sensed that anyone had been watching her. She felt a light fluttering in her stomach. "It's wonderful. Come in, if you're brave enough to stand the temperature."

He had unfastened his shirt when they heard Lorette.

"Solange! Where are you?" The urgency of the voice registered at once. She rose from the river and pulled on her clothes. Lorette was running towards them, with Joel behind her.

"You must get home quickly! Joel has come for you with the car! It's your father, he's sick. Dr Michel has just arrived from the village. I think your poor Papa has had a heart attack!"

There was a roaring sound in her ears as she stumbled up the bank and she heard herself screaming. "No! Oh God, not Papa. Please don't take away my Papa."

Chapter 46

Paris, 1945–1947

Celine had always known this day would come. She had pictured Richard taking her hand, telling her that he must leave, but the image hadn't progressed beyond the moment when they put their arms around one another, unable to let go. At the end of a humid, frustrating afternoon she came off the wards to find an urgent message from her mother. She sat in Charlotte's office, listening to the large Irishman across from her. She had steeled herself to believe she could one day accept Richard's obligation to return to Ireland, to his wife. But she had never thought she would have to share this deeply private agony with a total stranger.

"It's been very hard for him Dr O'Riordan." Celine willed herself to sound professional as she described Richard's condition when he had arrived in Paris, bearing the scars, physical and mental, of the brutal circumstances under which he had lived for nearly three years. He was a doctor, this rugged Irishman and he would hear the whole story soon enough, recognise the wounds, see the toll they had taken.

"He is recovering steadily. Love and patience are the main medicines he needs now."

"It's going to be very difficult for him to adjust," Seamus said. "He'll need a great deal of help, I understand that. And perhaps, in other circumstances, it would be better if he stayed on here for the time being. But he has a family he doesn't even know about, Dr de Savoie. In his absence Helena has borne him twins. And her need of him, their need of him, may be what finally brings him back to a full recovery."

Seamus's voice held a note of defeat. "I don't know how to proceed," he said. "My appearance will be a shock for which he'll have to be prepared. I think you should talk to him first, Dr de Savoie. Tell him I'm here."

It was decided that they would return to Avenue Mozart so that Charlotte and Celine could break the news to Richard. Then Seamus would come to see him later in the evening. Celine sat listening to their voices through a haze of grief, praying that she would be able to carry out her part with dignity. She glanced up, dazed with pain, and in that moment Seamus realised what he had stumbled upon. He looked with compassion at the courageous woman who had saved the life of his brother-in-law and friend, seeing her desperation, her love and her loss. He thought of the other search that had brought him here, and to the finality of the black letters on the page he had been shown only yesterday. Leah Svenssen, listed as having died on a forced march from Bergen-Belsen.

On that last evening Richard and Celine stood in a silent embrace, holding one another in dumb grief. He took her face in his hands, kissing her over and over, touching each adored, familiar part of her, unable to hold back his tears.

"I can't do this – I can't go back." His words were barely audible. "I can't leave you. Help me darling, please help me. I can't be without you, and she won't be able to cope. It's too cruel, too late to go back. It's all different. I'm not the same man that she knew, that she wanted."

At last she gently removed his arms from her waist and stood back from him, her face swollen with weeping. "Tell me you'll never forget me, Richard. That you'll always love me, no matter how far apart we might be."

"I love you. I'll always love you, always, no matter where you are. You are my life, you gave me my life. I love you Celine."

She opened the door still weeping, pushed him gently out on to the landing and watched him descend the staircase into the bare hall where Charlotte and Seamus were waiting. Then she turned and closed the bedroom door, doubling over with the terrible agony of his leaving her, clasping her arms across her stomach to try and stem the sorrow. She walked over to the bed she had shared with Richard Kirwan and lay down, trying to calm herself and to slow her breathing. Then she placed her hands gently on to her stomach in a band of comfort, so that the child growing inside her might somehow be protected from her pain.

When his letter arrived she sat alone in her room and opened the envelope, her hands shaking. He was safely home in Dublin. His reunion with Helena had been difficult, but she was brave. He had not known when he left Ireland with Seamus, on that fateful day in 1942, that his wife had been pregnant. In his absence she had borne him twins, a boy and a girl now three years old. Helena had waited for him to return to her and to their children, often in a state of total despair. He could not describe all this in detail – it was too hard, he said, the hurt too immediate. He could not express how much he loved Celine, longed for her. In the cruel complexity of their situation he could not think of any immediate way to resolve the torment in their lives. He could not simply turn away, destroy his wife, abandon his children. In his anguish and torment he was punished by days of black desolation and dreams he could not escape. Seamus planned to take him down to Connemara soon to rest. He repeated again and again that he loved her, and that he would always love her, that he would return one day, no matter what the cost.

377

Celine knew that she would not tell him she was carrying his child. There was enough heartbreak in all their lives and perhaps, through the care of his brother-in-law and his wife, he would be made whole again. She had no idea, no fixed plan as to what she would do as her pregnancy advanced. She stroked her stomach at dozens of intervals throughout the day, whispering words of love to Richard's child.

One evening she gave in to Charlotte's urging and accepted a dinner invitation with family friends. The large brasserie was crowded and it was not until she rose to find the ladies' room that she saw Henri de Valnay. He was dining with a young woman, dark-haired and slim. She sat opposite him in a sequined dress and a small, feathered hat, her hand over his on the table. He looked up and when he saw Celine he pushed back his chair and stood, swaying slightly, to greet her. She realised that he was drunk.

"Celine, my dear. Long time. I'm sure you're busy, too busy for the telephone. Too busy for months now. But maybe you have a moment to meet Florence." His voice was slurred. He staggered a little and sat down, grasping the hand of his companion whilst still looking up at Celine.

"Henri, I'm so sorry I haven't been in touch."

"How have you been? And Charlotte? I must drop in on you both one day." He reached for his glass but knocked it over, so that the contents spilled red across the white cloth, causing the young woman to rise to her feet and a waiter to come hurrying with a napkin. Celine was embarrassed and disturbed by his manner, and his obvious inebriation. Several other diners had turned to look at his table. She answered him as lightly as she could, smiled politely at his companion and left them.

A few days later she met Dr Brossard, the eye specialist, as she came out of the children's ward. "I'm sorry about your friend's eyesight," he said. "It's very sad."

"My friend?"

"Henri de Valnay. Nice man. Quite a hero too, I understand, although he's far too modest to have told me that himself. It's very tough to face the prospect of losing your eyesight so young."

"I haven't seen him for a while. I didn't know. This is too awful. Is that a final diagnosis?"

"Well, we've done all the tests that can be done here. I don't know where else I could send him that would be any more advanced. He sustained a heavy blow to the head sometime last year. The head wound healed of course, but it wasn't properly treated at the time. It's left him with one eye already badly impaired and the other one likely to follow. I'll be seeing him again next week."

Celine left the hospital immediately and took a taxi to Henri's apartment on the Ile St Louis, the memory of the night she had fled there after Richard's arrest vivid in her mind. When he opened the door she saw that he had been drinking. His breath smelled strongly of alcohol and his eyes were glazed as he looked at her, unsmiling.

"Dr Brossard told me about your eyesight. May I come in?"

He did not answer but stood aside to let her in. The apartment was in disarray. There were books and magazines all over the floor, and his clothing was scattered across the backs of chairs. In the kitchen she discovered a sink full of sticky glasses and several empty bottles.

"You've been having yourself quite a party, I see."

"It's good to have a drink to nurse while you're reading." His rejoining laugh was bitter. "I have to read you know. I have to read every book there is, and I'm in a great hurry. You remember how I love to read, don't you? Not much time. And you've come to tell me you feel sorry for me, I suppose. Scold me and pep me up."

She brought him some coffee and sat down on the sofa, pushing aside a crumpled jacket and a pile of newspapers. He flung himself into an armchair opposite her. "Well, how do I look for a blind man? How do you think I'll look with a white stick, tapping my way along

379

the river bank? Will you stop to help me across the road, Celine, before some bastard runs me over?"

"The diagnosis isn't absolutely final. It may be that there's something that can be done through a specialist outside France. There's so much to find out."

He cut in angrily, waving his hand in scornful dismissal. "Oh for God's sake! I'm going blind. I'm thirty-five years old and I'll soon be useless, and all I can be for the next thirty years is even more useless. How's your favourite patient, your boyfriend, by the way? Have you made him feel any better with a few similar little speeches?" Henri saw the pain flash across her face as though he had slapped her and felt at last an unselfish pang of regret.

"Richard has gone. He went back to Ireland to complete his recovery. With his wife and children."

He knew instinctively not to ask more. In truth he was so grateful to see her that he hardly dared speak, afraid she might suddenly leave him there alone in the sinking sands of his misery, floundering in his well of self-pity.

"It's been very hard, Celine," he said at last. "I haven't taken it well. I'm not one of those stoical souls who can find the strength to be cheerful and go on fighting. I felt sorrow at first, then rage. Now I just feel hopeless. And resentful."

"I'm going to help you, Henri. We'll do everything that can be done. And if the loss of your sight is inevitable, then we'll find every single aid that exists and I'll help you to use them all, so that your life will still be full of interest and meaning. I promise I'll be here to help you. All the way."

When she persuaded him to dine at Avenue Mozart he was moved by Charlotte's welcome and her honest understanding and support. He and Celine took up their evenings of companionship again, sharing the consolation of common memories, playing an occasional game of bridge, dining out in the burgeoning number of restaurants in the city. Her gratitude for his constant protection and care during the hardships of the war, and his need of her now, formed a solid base for their growing affection.

She dropped in to his apartment late one evening to find him sitting in the half-dark, alone and depressed.

"I don't think I can drive any more, Celine. I didn't expect things to deteriorate so quickly. I thought I would have months, even a year or two maybe, before my daily life was affected."

She sat down beside him and took his hand. He grasped her fingers, hesitated, and then plunged in. "I'm still in love with you Celine. I understand your grief at losing Richard Kirwan. Because I grieved too, when I thought I had lost you." He stood up and offered her a whiskey, pouring himself an extra-large measure. "It would be selfish of me to ask you to marry me now. But God, I do want to marry you."

"Dear, wonderful Henri, you're not selfish at all. You'll make someone a wonderful husband. But it can't be me." She was filled with sadness for him, and she did not stop him when he drew her towards him and kissed her.

"Marry me, Celine. I've loved you for so long. And if you can cope with my terrible problems, then I can cope with them too."

"There's a reason I can't marry you, Henri. It's the most important thing that has ever happened to me. I want to tell you what it is, so that you will see why I couldn't possibly . . ."

He placed his fingers on her lips, pressing them hard against her teeth so that her mouth hurt. "No, Celine."

"You have to hear this —"

"Listen to me." His tone was fierce. "Too many things have changed in too short a time. For both of us. I don't want to know what you're going to tell me. I don't want to hear the words. Do you understand?" He was shaking her slightly, holding her tight in his grip, his face drawn and his eyes never leaving her for a second. "I want you to say that you will be my wife. And from that moment we will begin our lives anew."

She began to shake her head, but he brought her closer and spoke with a slow intensity she could not mistake. "Celine, whatever has happened, I accept, as you accept my blindness. And I will love you always and for ever. Will you marry me? Darling, beloved Celine, will you?"

When she slowly nodded her head there were tears running down her cheeks, and he put his arms around her and buried his face in the softness he had always longed for.

At Avenue Mozart, Charlotte de Savoie felt, for the first time in her life, as though she might be getting old. Celine stood in front of her, full of vitality and life, her face serene, her voice confident.

"I don't know what to say, darling. Henri is the most admirable person, and he's been in love with you for a long time, probably from the moment you met. But it's so soon for you, after Richard and all your sadness. And I worry that it's not fair on Henri."

"We're going to be happy Mama. We've shared so much. And we can make a good life together, we both believe that fervently. Don't you believe it too?"

"Celine, I wouldn't be a good mother or friend if I didn't tell you that I think you're marrying him much too quickly." Charlotte looked at her daughter. In her mind was a vivid image of a night, only a short time ago. Richard had been sitting in this same room when a car had backfired in the street outside. When his legs began to tremble Celine had moved instantly to him, moulding her body against his, placing her hands firm and soothing on his thighs, leading him gently through his fear. Charlotte had seen his gratitude, his reliance on Celine's love and strength. It was all so recent.

"Richard may return one day, Celine. He may come back for you. And then what would happen to Henri who would have become so dependent on you?"

"Mother, I want you to be happy for me. I want you to put your confidence in my decision." Celine's tone had become angry. "Richard has a wife who couldn't survive without him, and two children. He wouldn't be able to handle all he has suffered, and carry the guilt of abandoning his family as well. We couldn't build our happiness on that. You'd be the first to say so, if I told you Richard was coming back."

"Such terrifying logic, Celine. It sounds right, of course it does. But you loved him so much. You must still love him, I know you must. And this seems so precipitous."

"I'm pregnant, Mama."

Charlotte sat down suddenly. "This is not Henri's child." It was not a question. "Oh my dear, this is simply not going to work. I don't know what to say. Have you told him? Have you and Henri . . . ?"

"I don't want to discuss this. We've made a decision, Henri and I, and I know it will be all right. We'll bring up this child together, and other children too. We are going to do this, and after all that's happened I want you to support me in my choice."

"Oh darling, are you really happy? Can either of you honestly, truly hope to find joy like this?" Charlotte's eyes were brimming with tears.

"We're going to take care of one another, now and for always."

Celine dried her mother's tears. Then they hugged each other, clinging together in the new, uncharted tide of events that was sweeping through their city and their own lives.

The day of the marriage was bright, the cloudless azure of the winter sky forming a canopy under which Charlotte de Savoie held the wedding reception for her daughter. The house at Avenue Mozart echoed with the sounds of celebration for the first time in many years. Afterwards Celine followed through with her plan to become a general practitioner, arranging to work only four days a week, so that she could spend time at home with Henri. They remained in his apartment on the Ile St Louis and slowly began to build their life together.

When the time came, Celine's labour was long, the birth difficult. Lying there, sweating and tired beyond belief from the constant exertion demanded of her by this diminutive creature, she fully understood the moment of birth, the desperate force of it, the pain and pride, the near-defeat of exhaustion, the ultimate triumph. She had advised so many women making their journey through this experience. Now she was ashamed by how little she had known, and humbled by her pain and her sense of victory. She closed her eyes and slept. When she awoke Henri was at her bedside. As he bent to kiss her, a nurse came to her room with the miracle that was her daughter, and she could hardly believe the perfection of the tiny form.

"She's beautiful," Henri said, and she saw the gleam of tears in his eyes. "She's tiny and beautiful and I love her. I love you, Celine. I love you both so very much."

Moments later Charlotte de Savoie arrived, and the three of them gazed down at the baby in her crib and fell hopelessly in love. Celine lay inert in the hospital bed, filled with joy and tragedy, with jubilation and guilt. Her longing for Richard was so intense that she was afraid it would overcome her ability to function as a mother and a wife, that it would threaten the brave new resolution of her life.

As Henri's sight deteriorated even further he began to drink heavily once more, returning to the apartment late at night having spent several hours in small bars and restaurants on the way. One evening he did not come home at all. Celine sat up until dawn the following morning, frantic with worry, anger rising within her. When she heard the taxi and listened to him stumbling on the stairs she knew, in a sudden flash of certainty, what she must do.

Henri's parents, close to retirement, were delighted with her plan to move to the South and take over the vineyards. Domaine de Valnay was large and comfortable but old-fashioned, and it needed renovation. Henri spent the weekdays in the vineyards and in the office with his father. Celine worked twice a week in the small practice in the village. Charlotte came to visit them and was appalled by the rustic conditions in which they were living. She insisted on taking Celine to Montpellier where she found an upholsterer and a furniture restorer, a good plumbing supplier, and a company that could install a central-heating system before the winter set in.

Solange began to crawl. Henri took on a young man named Joel from the village and began, with his father's help, to train him as a future manager of the vineyards. The days became ordered and secure, and Henri and Celine's carefully nurtured love grew steadily as the days and nights flew past them. By the end of the year they were both immersed in their new way of life.

When the telephone rang in the surgery one afternoon Celine picked it up, smiling at a departing patient. Within a few moments she felt the foundations of her existence, so painstakingly constructed, begin to disintegrate like quicksand beneath her feet.

Chapter 47

Paris, 1947

Afterwards she thought that there had been something particularly shrill about the sound of the telephone, that she had known before lifting the receiver that the news would shatter her peace. Charlotte de Savoie's voice sounded strained, uncertain. "I don't know how to tell you this. Richard is returning to France. He's going to be here next week. It's taken a long time to unravel the war records and to discover that an Irishman under a French name contributed so much. He's been awarded the Croix de Guerre. For his actions during the war, as a foreign national who gave outstanding assistance to France. He would like us both to be there when he accepts his medal. He says it really belongs to us. And he desperately wants to see you."

Celine's stomach lurched and the safe surroundings of her small consulting room began to spin. "I can't do this. I can't see him. I just can't."

"I understand, darling. I know it's a terrible shock. But he made me promise to tell you. He knows you married Henri, and that you're no longer living in Paris. But as for the rest – you have to make the decision and I have no intention of influencing you. It will be very painful either way."

As she sat in Henri's study two days later her words filled her with shame, but she did not have the will to avoid the lie she told him.

"Mother called today, Henri. She sounded unusually down. Lonely I think. I'd like to go and visit her for a few days. She's longing to see how Solange has grown, and it would be fun to spend a few days in Paris. Would you consider coming too?"

But her heart was thumping loudly and her face was flushed, because she did not want him to come to Paris with her, and she had not told him the truth. On the train journey north she cradled Solange in her lap, whispering to the baby as guilt and elation chased one another in her mind. But she knew that above all else she had to see Richard Kirwan, and that nothing would stop her. At Avenue Mozart she was weak with relief to find that he was staying in a hotel. Charlotte poured them a drink and took stock of her daughter, noting the new quality of placid, almost solemn beauty that she wore, wondering inwardly at the damage this encounter might cause.

"I saw Richard yesterday, Celine. He looks stronger, not so painfully thin. But there is such sadness in him. He came here, and we spent the afternoon and evening together. The most extraordinary thing has happened, and we talked about it for a long time. Do you remember the cleaner I helped to go away to Switzerland? Jeanne Revere was her name. She was a refugee from the camps and she had no memory. You treated her and I got her papers and arranged for her train journey to Geneva."

Celine nodded, recalling a young woman with large eyes.

"I had a letter from her about two weeks ago. I was skimming through it and trying to place her, when I suddenly saw Richard's name. It jumped out at me from the page."

"She knew Richard? Where?"

"It seems that she and her brother were university friends of Helena Kirwan. Her name was Leah Nazarre. She's Jewish as we thought. But she didn't remember anything about her life before the war, because she'd been close to death. It was Leah and her husband Stefan that Richard came here to find."

"That can't be!"

"Of course, Richard was captured and ended up with us, and Leah was sent to Auschwitz in 1942. When she got to Switzerland last year, she discovered her husband there, in a clinic. He's very disabled, both physically and mentally. She wrote to me for advice. She wanted to care for him herself, and she was wondering if they would be better off in France."

"I can't begin to believe such a coincidence. It's a miracle that such a thing should happen." Celine was gripped by the strangeness of the situation. "A chance in a million. What did Richard say about it?"

"Well, he's going to change his plan. Instead of going directly back to Ireland he's going to Geneva at the weekend. To visit Leah and her husband and see how he can help them."

The ceremony was formal and dignified, the moment of award brief but moving. They stood close to the podium and watched as Richard received his medal, the red and green stripes of the ribbon and the distinctive cross shining brightly in the morning light. Then he was descending the steps, walking towards them, his face filled with uncertainty as he took Celine's hands. They drove in silence to Avenue Mozart where Charlotte de Savoie left them on a vague pretext that they did not even hear.

They stood facing one another, the loneliness and longing and passion held in check, but stretching taut and quivering between them. He spoke at last, his voice husky. "Are you all right, Celine?"

She tried to answer him but the words would not come. She nodded her head.

"Oh God, Celine." He had wrapped her in his arms and he said her name over and over as he kissed her forehead, her hands, her eyelids and the hot salt of her tears, and then her mouth. She saw herself from far away, watched her limbs giving way to her weight, saw herself crushed against him. She broke from him first, and he led her to a sofa where they sat down and with trembling fingers explored each other's features, rediscovering the lines they loved and knew and remembered.

"Are you well? The dreams? The tiredness?"

He nodded. "I'm improving. I've spent a lot of time with Seamus."

"And Helena?" The name cut like a sharp instrument.

"It's very hard. She's trying and she's very brave. But I can't explain to her how it was there. It's not possible to speak to her of those things. And I can't bridge the space, that awful space." He could not continue.

They were still for a time, looking into one another's faces. Then he took a deep breath, holding her hands very tightly. "You have a daughter."

He saw her bowed head, looked at the pale gold of her hair, and his heart was hammering when he spoke again, his voice thick and slow. "Is she our child?"

She looked up at him and he saw her smile for the first time, saw the brilliant light appear in her eyes. "Yes, my darling, she is our daughter. She's so beautiful and she is the child that we made."

"And Henri?"

"He is the kindest and best of husbands and he loves her very much." She put up a hand to wipe the tears away.

"Could I see her?"

Celine stood up and walked out into the hall, calling for Louise to bring Solange. Charlotte appeared at the top of the staircase with the little girl in her arms, coming slowly down the steps to where Richard was waiting to meet his daughter. He touched her cheek and his face was full of wonder. He marvelled at the texture of her skin, staring in amazement at the small, round face of his child who looked back at him with a grave curiosity. He moved his scarred hand towards her and she coiled small fingers around his thumb, continuing to regard him with great seriousness. His eyes were shining with joy when he turned to Celine.

"Could we spend the day together? Will you join us Charlotte?"

They chose to pass their precious hours just outside Paris. In the grounds of Marly le Roi where the kings of France had once whiled away their leisure hours, they spread out a picnic rug on the grass and set Solange down on the soft, green carpet. They held her so that her feet could paddle in the lake and they laughed at her delight when she saw the swans glide past her in the water. Richard lay back on the rug and watched Celine with their daughter, revelling in the gentle, curving shape of her, in the new fullness of her breasts as she bent to lift the baby.

Watching them, Charlotte took in the awful complexity of their pleasure and the anguish that was to come. As the afternoon drew to its inevitable close, she kissed them both and took the baby home, leaving them alone. For a time they stayed close together, holding one another. Then, without speaking, they packed the remains of their picnic and returned to Richard's hotel.

They lay on the bed with their limbs entwined, whispering their adoration, their lips almost touching, burning with their longing and their joy. His hands stroked her, touched her, found the places she wanted him to caress. She undressed him very slowly, touching each scar, each precisely remembered inch of his body. They ordered a light supper but never ate it. They made love again and lay with hands lightly clasped, her head resting on his chest, breathing in the scent of his skin, holding him. They talked of their lives and the needs of their partners. He told her of Seamus's great kindness, of the months in Connemara where the wild, clear air and Helena's tender patience had brought him some modicum of peace. She talked of Henri's blindness, of their life in the South and her growing medical practice in the village, of her happiness and love for their beautiful child. For a short while they slept, cradling one another, until Richard woke her to make love to her again, and to whisper to her and caress her, until the insistent, oncoming dawn crept into their stolen hours. Celine lay beside him in the grey light and closed her eyes as he traced his messages of love across her face, her neck, on to her breasts and her stomach and her soft, opening thighs. She lifted herself on to one elbow, her hand stroking his face. Her eyes were closed and she pressed her lips together and swallowed hard before she was able to say the words to him. "We can never see each other again, Richard. You know that we cannot, because it would always be like this."

"I know, darling. I know." His eyes were glittering with tears. "I love you. And nothing will ever alter that."

She rose at last and bathed and allowed him to dress her, and then she came and stood very close to him. He turned from her suddenly and walked over to the small desk by the window, taking up the box that held his Croix de Guerre.

"This is for you, my darling, and for Charlotte. This is all I can give you, for the life and the love you have given me. You are my life, Celine. You will always be my life, and I will always love you."

He was weeping helplessly. She knew that she must leave him immediately, that they must not speak or touch one another again or they would not be strong enough to do what was required of them. "I'm going to walk away from here now, Richard, and we will remember this day and night together, and being with our daughter, for all of our lives."

When she reached Avenue Mozart she was glad to find that Charlotte had taken the baby out to the Bois de Boulogne. She sat alone in the garden, her mind filled with the image of him, feeling his beloved body becoming more and more distant, until she thought her heart would be torn out of her body. And in some rational part of her brain she knew that she would never see him again.

Chapter 48

The remains of their supper lay on the tray, with another bottle of wine and a pot of fresh coffee. Stefan lay asleep on his makeshift bed, moaning occasionally or flinching in some uncontrollable spasm. Night seemed to enclose them in a world outside time as Eleanor listened to the rest of Leah's story.

On an autumn day in 1946, she stepped from the train in Geneva as Madame Jeanne Revere. She took a bus to Thonon les Bains and found herself a small *pension* not far from the clinic. Dread hung over her as she approached the sombre building, set back from the road in a gravel courtyard behind high walls and iron gates. She decided to say she was a family friend on this first visit, and see what developed. The spectre of fear stirred sluggishly in the recesses of her mind and she knew there were things she did not want to remember. It seemed as though she was crouching in the shadow of a beast that she must turn and face, knowing it would devour her.

The sound of the doorbell echoed inside the building. A porter admitted her, leading her to a reception desk in the entrance hall. A nun was seated behind the table, with a crisp white veil and starched collar over a black serge habit. Leah tried to hide the discomfort she felt under her gaze.

"I've come to visit Mr Stefan Svenssen," she said. "His mother,

Countess Svenssen, suggested that I might call."

"Are you related, Madame?" The nun was polite but guarded.

Leah hesitated. Perhaps she would not be allowed to see him if she were not a relative. "We were in France together for a number of years. And later during the war in Paris. His mother wrote to me and asked me to visit him." She looked at the calm face before her and finished lamely. "We were very close."

Tears threatened to gather, and she frowned in concentration, trying to force them away. The nun relented and smiled. "Just a moment, Madame. I will have to check. I don't know if Mr Svenssen is well enough today for a visitor. Please wait here." She indicated a row of seats in the large, bare hall. "What name shall I give, Madame?"

The name on her papers was meaningless and she could not as yet lay claim to her married name. "I am Leah Nazarre," she said in a low tone. The name reverberated in the empty hall, resounding in her own ears like a drum roll of doom. It was the first time she had said it aloud since seeing it written on the marriage certificate and now she knew it to be the truth. She felt faint.

"Sit down, Madame Nazarre, please." The sister was looking at her with concern. "I will be back directly."

Leah sat very still, trying to appear composed. Finally the nun returned with the matron, a large woman in a starched blue and white uniform. Leah stood up nervously.

"Madame Nazarre?" The matron inclined her head to one side in enquiry and Leah nodded stiffly. "It is a little unusual for Stefan Svenssen to receive visitors."

Leah attempted another explanation, but the matron interrupted her. "It is not that you cannot visit him, Madame Nazarre, but he becomes agitated with the few who do come. And I must warn you that his appearance may come as a shock." Her smile was brief but kind as she spread her hands in a gesture of helplessness. "Well, you'll see for yourself."

A sick feeling rose in her, but Leah nodded and set off with the matron, walking swiftly down the long corridor and up a flight of stone stairs, to arrive in an airy ward with a high ceiling. At the end of the long room was a cubicle, glassed in on two sides with a panelled door facing on to the corridor.

"I think I should stay with you, until we see how he reacts."

The man lay in a white hospital bed, with high metal frames around it to prevent him from falling out, and he seemed to be in a kind of straitjacket. He was huge and he shook continuously. Occasionally his legs jerked up. His head was turned away towards the barred window and Leah could see only his profile.

"Stefan?" The nurse's voice was bright. "I've brought someone to see you. An old friend."

She indicated that Leah should step forward and with dread she moved towards the bed, her legs like lead. What could she say?

"Stefan." She spoke softly.

The great head turned. Crimson scars covered the skin, one eye was drooping, the mouth twisted downwards on one side. He regarded her with total blankness. Pity and memory stirred in her heart and she suddenly saw herself with this man, only he was standing upright and strong. She was playing a violin, and he was dancing to her music, and laughing. She saw candles burning and rich, red draperies, others joining in the music. She clung to the metal frame until her knuckles were white. Now she was seeing Stefan again, this time somewhere high up, under the statue of an angel. He was lying on a stone staircase, his face pale, his head supported by another man whose face remained a blur. The scene began to disintegrate and then she saw herself running with Stefan, in wet, slick darkness, running and running with danger and destruction all around them. And suddenly she saw her brother, Daniel, lying in a red pool on the street and she was holding him, and Stefan was shouting something.

She sank to her knees. Stefan was thrashing and shouting. What was he trying to say? Leah struggled to her feet and moved close in to the bed, pulling at the side frame to lower it. The nurse was calling out for help, trying to pull her away. The frame gave way suddenly, slamming down, and she leaned in and gathered the distraught man into her arms, loosening the restraints that kept his hands tied around his chest. In a heaving spasm he clung to her and she could see the tears stream down his face as he tried to form the word.

"Leah," he was saying, over and over.

She held him against her, rocking him, whispering softly. "It's all right Stefan. It's all right my poor, dear friend. I'm here now, I'm here."

A doctor appeared and stood at the door with the nurse and two orderlies, silent, awed. After some minutes Stefan sank into a heavy sleep, quiet as a child, his arms still round her tightly. The nurse whispered to Leah, looking at her with eyes full of compassion.

"Madame Nazarre?"

Leah looked up at her. A great weariness prevented her from denying what she now knew was the truth. "No sister, I'm Madame Svenssen," she said. "This man is my husband."

Dazed and drained of energy, she was ushered by the doctor into his bright, comfortable office where she began, as best she could, to explain her situation. When she had finished her story, the doctor spoke to her gently. "Madame Svenssen, Stefan's parents are now living in South America, and they do not expect to return. They made financial arrangements with us so that we would continue to care for him. Stefan suffered serious head and spinal injuries after his arrest in France. His mother told me they had great difficulty getting him released from Gestapo headquarters. She said the Germans suspected him of being involved with the resistance."

He folded his hands together. "The countess said that when Stefan was finally returned to them in Paris little hope was held out for his survival. He is receiving the best treatment he can get here, but it's doubtful that he will ever be able to live outside a hospital."

He explained to Leah that her husband would be subject to serious physical problems for the rest of his life, and there was no likelihood of major improvement in his mental state. Today's dramatic episode was the first time the medical staff had seen him respond positively to anyone. He paused, visibly moved by the condition of the ruined man, and the tragic story related by his wife. Their future, joint or separate, would be bleak.

"He must have loved you very much, Madame."

Guilt washed over Leah as she recognised fully the cost of Stefan's gallant action. Half of her screamed to be allowed to leave this nightmare place and the man upstairs. She wanted to escape from him, return to France, try to put some sort of life together. After all, what could she do for him now? The other half of her recalled the pitiful pleading in Stefan's ravaged face when she had taken him into her arms. She heard again his dreadful sobs, felt the frighteningly strong grip of his misshapen hands. He had come to this because of her. He had been abandoned here and she could not run away from him now. There was no one else to care for him.

"What can I do for him?"

The doctor was kind but practical. "You have been through as much trauma as your husband. I know you want to help him, but you must help yourself first. You need to build up your own strength."

Leah's head was lowered, her face set and the doctor took this as a sign that she agreed with him.

"It would be impossible even to consider letting him out of hospital into your care, unless there was a considerable change in your circumstances. Switzerland is an expensive country to live in, and it's hard to find work and accommodation. It would be too much for you." His words were sympathetic but final.

Leah leaned back in her chair and closed her eyes. Scenes from her past flashed across her mind, in no particular order. The doctor was right. She could not help Stefan without first finding herself employment and a home. At least she had something she could do. She knew now that she could play the violin. That might bring her a livelihood. She returned to her *pension*, sat on her bed, and counted the money Countess Svenssen had left. If she found a job as a waitress or a cleaner somewhere, to pay for her lodgings, she could use the rest of the money to buy a violin. She could practise, eventually look for work as a teacher. There must be a Conservatoire in Geneva.

In the house at Le Coppet there was silence for some time. Leah stared out at the water, her memories too painful to articulate. Eleanor remained motionless in her chair, listening to the lap of the lake against the stone terrace. She could so easily have left him there, she thought. In his condition, and with her own precarious circumstances, she had the perfect reason, the perfect, blameless excuse to walk away. She was about to speak when Leah took up her story once again.

Each week she took the bus to the clinic and sat with Stefan, talking to him, holding him by the hand, coaxing him to respond to her. At the end of each visit she had to brace herself for the harrowing sounds when she left him and walked away, his pleadings echoing down the long corridors in her wake. At last she managed to obtain an appointment as a part-time teacher at the Conservatoire in Geneva, but she was no nearer finding a larger place to live or solving the problem of Stefan's ongoing care. He began to fail, fretting constantly when she was not with him. His total dependence on her was like a slow suffocation, but she felt she must give him back something for the life he had lost on her account.

Finally, unable to find a solution to her problems, she wrote in desperation to Charlotte de Savoie. There was a chance that this kind woman, or her daughter the doctor, would be able to advise her. Perhaps there was some possibility of taking Stefan to Paris, some way that would allow her to find a more lucrative job for herself and provide him with a home. Dr de Savoie might know a specialist who could help. She was unprepared for the result of that one letter, written in despair on a lonely summer evening. Four weeks after she sent it, Richard Kirwan stood at the door of her *pension*, his face looking older, his smile bringing her the first thrill of pure joy she had experienced since the war had ended. They laughed aloud and wept at the same time, marvelling at the miracle that Charlotte de Savoie had been the link between them. They sat for hours in Leah's dreary little room, drinking coffee, talking of the happy days in Paris, speaking about the suffering they had undergone and witnessed in the camps. Then he had told her about Helena and the twins, and of Seamus and his kindness. Finally he told her about Celine and what she meant to him, all that she had done for him. He spoke in wonder and pain about the discovery of his little daughter, Solange.

"What did he say about Seamus?" Eleanor could not prevent herself from asking the question.

"He told me about the return from Brittany. How he was brought to the boat unconscious, how Helena nursed him when he got home. How she was almost demented by grief and loss after Richard's disappearance. She was expecting twins, her husband was possibly dead, and her brother was in a deep depression, consumed with guilt at having come back without Richard, or Stefan or me. It was Helena, Richard said, who made Seamus fight for his sanity. It was her begging him to be strong for her that brought him back to life."

Eleanor heard the transparent loneliness in Leah's voice, recognised the same anguish and wrenching sadness that she had heard on the beach in Connemara, when Seamus had first told her about his love. It seemed senseless that these two innocent, courageous people had been subjected to such an unjust separation.

"He loved you, Leah, to distraction. He still does. He never married. Why did you not allow him to help you? It's what he would have wanted, more than anything else."

Leah covered her face with her hands.

"Do you not understand, Eleanor? I destroyed one man, allowed him to marry me, in order to save myself. I never loved Stefan. That was what was so terrible. He was destroyed by his effort to save me, and I never loved him. I loved only one man in all of my life, and that was Seamus."

"Then why?" Eleanor protested, but Leah cut in.

"How could I tell him? You know what he would have done! He would have come straight here, to take care of me and of Stefan. He would have tried to bring us to Ireland – he was that kind of man. How could I have endured that? Tied to my poor, broken husband, yearning for another man, torturing Seamus and destroying his life as well as ours?" She was silent for a moment. "In the end it was decided for me. I brought Richard to visit Stefan at the clinic. I thought it would help him to know that Richard had survived." She shuddered. "Stefan's reaction was appalling. He became totally hysterical, screaming, covering his head with his arms. He fell into a series of convulsions that nearly killed him. They had to sedate him for days afterwards."

"Why should Father's visit do that to him?"

Eleanor glanced over her shoulder at the recumbent figure on the floor. Stefan seemed to be deeply asleep.

"After the ambush on Ile de Groix, Stefan was arrested. They took him to Gestapo headquarters in Paris," Leah said. "It has taken me a long time to piece this together and I will never know the whole story. I have to be so careful in case I upset him. But his mind is sometimes clear and I understand a lot of what he says." She poured more wine and curled up in the armchair, warming the glass with her hands. "Count Svenssen was a Nazi sympathiser. He had contacts with the Germans in Paris. When he discovered Stefan was a prisoner, he came to an agreement with them. They let Stefan go, but they followed him and he led them unwittingly to the resistance group that had tried to get us out of France, the cell that sheltered Richard."

With a tremor in her voice, Leah described Stefan's horror when he realised what he had done. "He had been interrogated too, and brutally beaten. But it was the fact that he had betrayed his friends that shattered his sanity. He tried to commit suicide by throwing himself down a flight of stairs, and that was when he received the worst of his injuries."

"Poor, poor Stefan! What bravery, what sacrifice! It's hard for someone of my generation, my sheltered existence, to take it all in."

"Stefan never recovered," Leah said. She placed her hand on Eleanor's arm. "He couldn't forgive himself for the role he played in the capture of his friends. The sight of Richard at the clinic that day sent him straight back to hell. We couldn't convince him that Richard was alive and that he didn't blame Stefan for what had happened. He thought your father was a ghost, come back to haunt him. Richard was never able to approach him again." Leah drained her glass, her voice slurring a little with the wine and fatigue. "I knew then that I couldn't let Seamus see him. There was no future for us. I couldn't abandon Stefan and I couldn't ask Seamus to ruin his life on my account. There had been enough sacrifices."

She closed her eyes. Eleanor wondered how Leah could have brought herself to tell her story with such dignity and restraint.

"Richard told me how Seamus searched for me after the war. How that woman reported that I had died in her arms on a forced march. What was the point then in resurrecting Leah Nazarre? I made Richard swear he would never tell Seamus or Helena that he had found me. It was cruel, I know. But I was already dead to them, and Helena could never have kept it from Seamus if Richard had told her."

"So you just disappeared?"

"It was the right thing to do. I know it was. I hoped that in time

400

Seamus would forget, be free to find someone else."

"But he never forgot! We wondered why he never married but now I know it's because he never loved anyone else. I'm sure of it."

"I couldn't have endured having him love me, having him close, when I had to stay with Stefan," Leah said. "As it was, your father took care of us with all the goodness that made him the extraordinary man he was. He bought this house for us, arranged with the clinic to use the monthly fees to send nurses here. I've never been able to earn the kind of money that could provide Stefan with everything he needs. I agreed to accept Richard's help only if he kept the secret. Not for myself, but for Stefan. I've tried to give him some quality of life. But without Richard it could never have happened."

Eleanor rose and put her glass and plate on the tray in front of her. She realised that they had drunk almost two bottles of wine.

"Leah," she said softly.

But Leah was asleep. Eleanor looked round for a rug to cover her. As she turned, a tremor ran through her.

Stefan's eyes were wide open and he was watching her every move intently. How long had he been awake? She saw him trying to raise himself and ran to him, knelt at his side, taking one of his crippled hands in hers.

"Stefan," she whispered. "Stefan, it's all right. Leah is sleeping. She needs to rest. Can I help you? I'm your friend and Leah's friend. I'm here to help you."

He was gripping her hard and she tried to push her fear away.

"Let me help you Stefan. If you lean on me, I can get you to bed, then you can go back to sleep."

She positioned her arms under his shoulders and lifted him towards her, still unsure what she would do if he became agitated. He was gesturing to her with his twisted fingers, bringing them towards his lips, and she realised that he was trying to move quietly without waking his wife. He leaned on her as he stood, then shuffled in a grotesque waltz towards his bed. When he was finally lying down his forehead was drenched with sweat and his arms were shaking, but he tried to smile. Then he closed his eyes, and Eleanor watched as a sort of peace settled over his contorted features. At last when she felt he was asleep, she tiptoed softly out of the room, leaving the door ajar.

Stefan lay in his bed, images of his captivity in the Gestapo head-quarters in Paris reeling before his closed eyes. He had always shied away from those visions of hell, but now he let them come. They had mocked him, and smashed his fingers with their truncheons, but he had endured the blows, the interrogations. Twice he was taken to an icy bath and chained to the side of it with his hands tied behind him. They pushed his head and shoulders under the water until he began to choke, flooding his lungs with water as he gasped for air. After he had lost consciousness they left him lying on the floor in the water he had vomited. But he had remained silent. Until the terrible moment when he had led them to his friends. Now he lay alone in the darkness and felt the weight of his useless body, the interminable pain of the years since that leap. Why could he not have died then? If only they had let him die there, on the stairs. Instead he was entombed in this paralysed hulk, tormented by his actions, and he had condemned Leah to a living hell. Lying in the soundless room, tears seeped from his eyes and traced their path down his face as he waited for the dawn of another endless day.

Chapter 49

Geneva, 1970

Slumped in an armchair Eleanor drifted in and out of a fitful sleep. Once she woke, disturbed by a strange noise, jolting upright in a rush of alarm. At first she could not remember where she was, but then Leah stirred in the chair opposite, and recollection flooded her mind. She listened intently in the darkness, but there was only the sound of the wind gusting across the black expanse of the lake. She sighed and tried to turn herself around in the confines of her chair, rubbing her aching neck and stiff limbs and dozed off once more.

Dawn seeped into Eleanor's consciousness. A steady drizzle had begun, and the waters of the lake lay sluggish beyond the terrace and the small expanse of lawn, a gunmetal grey under heavy clouds. There was a heavy thumping in her head and her mouth felt dry and stale. She looked around the dim room, remembering the sound that had disturbed her during the night. Perhaps a branch had fallen in the rising wind. But she was filled with a sense of unease. She glanced towards Stefan's room and saw that the door was shut. Eleanor frowned. She had deliberately left it ajar last night, after helping him into bed. Should she wake Leah? No, she would look in on Stefan herself. She went softly into his room.

Stefan was not in his bed. Eleanor ran around to the other side of the bed, afraid that she would find him lying on the floor, but he wasn't there. The covers had been pulled to one side but Stefan was nowhere to be seen. She looked into the bathroom. It was empty. In rising panic she turned towards the doors leading on to the terrace. They were half-open, and a chill, damp air was blowing into the room. The curtain was hanging at a strange angle, pulled off its rail on one side. The geraniums in the planter outside had been crushed, as though someone had fallen against them. Surely he couldn't have gone out on to the terrace in the dark and the rain? A terrible feeling of dread invaded her. She began to pray as she ran down the steps to the lawn. With sick certainty she saw churned clods of grass and wet, flattened tracks trailing down to the water's edge. She could see the top of the narrow slipway leading into the lake.

At the water's edge Eleanor saw the body face-down in the water. Sobbing out loud she waded out into the cold lake, oblivious to her sodden skirt and the drizzle plastering her hair to her neck. She took Stefan by the arms and began to pull frantically. The huge body moved slowly and sluggishly as she dragged him towards the shore, crouching down at last to haul him on to the slipway below the terrace.

He lay half out of the lake, his blue-white face contorted but strangely peaceful, his eyes blank and staring up at the skies. Eleanor attempted to resuscitate him, hurling her whole weight down on to him, pressing her mouth to his unmoving lips, in a vain attempt to pump air into his lungs. But he had been in the lake too long for her to help him.

She did not see Leah coming towards her, did not realise she was there, until she felt herself being pulled away from the drowned man's body. Leah's eyes were huge and dark as she grasped Stefan by the shoulders and pulled him up out of the wet mud and slime. Then she knelt beside him, using the hem of her skirt to wipe the water from his face, moving her hands to smooth his clothing, straightening his legs, caressing his cold feet, holding each one on her knees as she carefully dried them on her dress.

"Stefan, we must get you dry," she was saying. "You've lost your shoes, dear. You must have shoes. You'll get frostbite if you don't have shoes."

Her movements were deliberate, her voice a whisper. She did not seem to see Eleanor at all. She stood up at last and went inside. Eleanor was torn between the desire to follow her and a reluctance to leave Stefan on the slipway, lying out in the cold drizzle, his feet white against the dark, wet stone. Inside she heard the sound of a violin. Leah was playing a brisk, mad march, repeating the same two phrases again and again. Eleanor was shaking now, afraid to move, afraid to stay where she was. She forced herself to stand up. She must call a doctor, get medical help of some kind, as much for Leah as for her poor, ruined husband. Eleanor turned from Stefan's body and ran inside. Leah, her eyes blank, stood in the corner beside the piano. Her fingers gripped the bow, her violin dug into her cheek. She stood perfectly straight, only her bow arm moving, her fingers on the strings.

Eleanor fled through the sitting room to the telephone in the hall. Riffling through the pages of the phone book she found the emergency services. She should ask for an ambulance, notify the police. But she did not know how she could possibly deal with it all, explain the night's events to the authorities. Behind her the frenzied playing wailed on. An image of Gareth's solid calm flashed through her mind. He would know what to do. It seemed an eternity before she heard his voice, blurred with sleep. Then he was wide awake, alert, promising he would be there straight away. She leaned against the wall and tried to calm herself. Leah was still playing, the music slower now, more poignant. Eleanor began to go through the assorted notebooks and papers on the telephone table and she found a small address book. Skimming through it she saw the name and address of a local doctor. She dialled the number. He was immediately understanding. He was on his way, he said. He would telephone the authorities and request an ambulance.

Long moments drifted by, each one drawing out the nightmarish quality of the grey morning. It was Gareth who arrived first and she flung her arms gratefully around him and drew him inside. Moments later Dr Koenig was there, reassuring, explaining that he had been Stefan's doctor for more than twenty years. It took time for them to get the stricken Leah to her room. When the doctor opened his medical bag the violin crashed to the floor and she backed away from him into a corner of the room, her hands raised over her head in a defensive gesture. At last Eleanor led her gently to the bedroom, and Dr Koenig gave her a sedative. The local police and the ambulance arrived to remove Stefan's body and Dr Koenig wrote out the death certificate confirming the death as accidental. When the police and the ambulance had gone, the doctor sat down in the living room to talk. He examined Eleanor's pale, pinched face.

"You have had a bad shock yourself, Mademoiselle."

"I'm fine, Doctor. It's just that it was all so sudden. Leah is an old friend of my father's, whom we had never met until yesterday. What will happen now?"

Dr Koenig shook his head, his plump, kindly face full of sympathy. "She has gone through a great deal over the years. Her husband's condition had deteriorated considerably in the past few months. I don't think he would have lived much longer."

"But what's to be done about Leah now?" Eleanor asked. "I'd hate to see her taken off to hospital."

"This could last for just a few hours, or for days. But it could be more serious and long-term." His eyes were compassionate behind the thick spectacles. "It would be best to keep her in her own familiar environment, but she will need medical supervision until such time as recovery begins, or it becomes clear that hospitalisation is necessary."

Eleanor stood up suddenly.

"Are you saying, Dr Koenig, that if there was someone she loved and trusted here to take care of her, she could stay at home until she recovers?"

"If her problem is purely a short-term reaction to shock, then yes. That would be best for her – with proper nursing care, of course."

"Leah does have someone who could take care of her. My uncle, Seamus O'Riordan. They were very close many years ago. They would probably have married if the war had not separated them. And Seamus is a doctor. If he was willing to come to Geneva, do you think it might help her?"

"This is a very delicate situation, Eleanor," Gareth said, frowning. "We don't really know Leah. And we can't say what her feelings might be. It sounds a wonderful plan, to be sure. But what happened between them was almost thirty years ago."

"Seamus told me only last week about Leah and how he has always loved her. And I've just spent the whole evening here with her. She said herself, last night, that she never loved anyone but him."

Gareth took Eleanor by the hand. "Maybe she would rather Seamus remembered her as she was. It would be tragic if the dream of her that he has carried for so long was destroyed now."

"Oh Gareth, I'm sure Father gave me that letter to deliver because he knew they needed one another and he hoped they would find each other again. I'm certain of it! And of course it's a gamble! But love can heal, above all, love heals." She turned to Dr Koenig. "What do you think, Doctor? Would it be all right if I phoned my uncle?"

Dr Koenig paused, removed his spectacles, polished them, and replaced them, blinking slightly, perhaps hoping to gain a clearer vision of the situation. Then he slowly nodded his agreement. Eleanor lifted the receiver and dialled the operator.

Seamus was woken by the insistent ringing of the telephone downstairs. It seemed to him that he had only just found his way to bed. James and Elizabeth had arrived home from Paris the previous evening, and were astonished to find that their sister was in Geneva. Seamus had driven Helena back from Connemara to be with them, and had told them what little he knew about Eleanor's mission. When

407

James had finished describing their encounter with Solange and the discovery of the details of their father's Croix de Guerre, Helena had sat staring into the fire. Then she looked up at her children. "I want you to know that I've done some terrible things that I deeply regret," she said. "But I also want you to know that I do love you all very much."

"Mother . . ." James had found it hard to acknowledge the pain in her voice.

"When your father died, I just went away into my own private world." Helena did not seem to have heard him. "I didn't think of you at all. It was unfair. Cruel, in fact. And not what your father would have wanted."

"It was natural," Lizzie had said. "It was a normal reaction."

"No," Helena said. "It was self-indulgence. I didn't want to live without him, and I didn't even see the needs of the rest of you, and I'm sorry for that. But I'm sorriest of all about Eleanor. She tried to take me out of my self-absorbed grief and I hurt her. I wish she was here."

"Please, Mother, don't." James's voice was quiet. "We've all come to realise it's not that simple."

"I'm very tired now. I'm going to bed." Helena had stood up. "When Eleanor returns from Geneva I need to sit down with you all and tell you a number of things you should know. But not until she gets here. This is for all of us together." She had kissed them lightly, touched her brother's cheek and left the room.

Seamus had remained downstairs for several hours, talking to James and Elizabeth, describing his first voyage to France and the events that had led to their father's capture. At last he had insisted on going to bed.

When the telephone began to ring he sat up and checked his watch. It was barely seven in the morning and for a moment he thought that he was on call at home in Connemara. He heard James answer the telephone but could not make out what was being said. Then there were footsteps running up the stairs, and a knock on his door.

"Seamus," James called out. "It's Eleanor. I think something is wrong."

Seamus threw on his dressing gown as he ran downstairs.

"Eleanor?" He could hear her uneven breathing at the other end of the line. "All right, two deep breaths before you speak, girl, to get yourself calm."

Eleanor looked at Gareth, who gave her a smile of encouragement. But how could she even begin to find the words?

In the study in Killiney, James saw his uncle stagger and helped him into a chair. Seamus's face was grey with shock. Helena appeared and ran across the room to her brother and he clung to her like a small boy.

"Leah is there? Richard did this? And Stefan is dead?" He repeated his questions again. "I can't believe this! I can't take it in. For God's sake, Eleanor, say it all again!"

Helena's arms were around him, her face pressed against the receiver as she strained to hear what Eleanor was telling him. Seamus leant against her slight body, listening to Eleanor, his eyes closed, his face ashen. "Of course I'll come. I'll be on the first available plane. I'm sure the doctor is right, her own surroundings are best. I'm leaving immediately. I'll be with you sometime today."

He could not even begin to discuss the details with Helena, far less explain anything to James. Elizabeth, woken by the uproar, came downstairs to the kitchen. She could make no sense of the scene. Her rock-steady uncle was crying on her mother's shoulder. It was frightening. Helena made coffee and plied Seamus with toast. James followed instructions and phoned the airport to book a flight. Elizabeth sat down, ignored, bewildered by what she was seeing.

Finally, Seamus was at the door, a small valise packed by Helena in his hand, James outside revving the engine. Elizabeth, still mystified, stood on the steps with her mother as the car accelerated away.

"Lizzie," Helena's face was luminous. "Come inside with me. I want to tell you a love story."

Chapter 50

Geneva, 1970

The journey seemed interminable. Seamus went over Eleanor's story endlessly, frustrated that in the initial shock he had forgotten to ask questions, things he desperately needed to know. In a maelstrom of hope, fear and impatience he sat and stared out over the clouds below him, willing the plane to go faster. Gareth met him at the airport and drove swiftly away from the city and along the lake shore, explaining what had happened over the past two days. At the door of Leah's house, Seamus stood paralysed on the steps until he felt Gareth's hand under his elbow, steering him into the hall. He was reminded of Richard's support all those years ago when he had stood in the cottage in Brittany on that last, terrible day, staring at Leah with her platinum hair, as she told him she was married. Eleanor's embrace was fierce and loving, full of encouragement.

"Seamus, this is Dr Koenig. I asked him to come and have a word with you. Leah is sleeping. She's still confused, but I think she knows me."

Seamus gazed at his niece, recognising the insanely romantic notion that had led her to summon him. The legacy of his earlier failure to save the woman he loved rose to taunt him. He wanted to turn back, to say "I can't do this. It's not for me. It's all too late," and then walk away.

Eleanor could see that he was adrift. "You mustn't feel like this Seamus. You can't," she whispered, putting her hands on his shoulders. "You are the best of men, everything that anyone could need. She will get well, and you will be the one to restore her." She shook him hard, smiling in relief as she saw him gather every reserve of strength and faith he had and straighten up.

"Just pray for me, Eleanor," he said.

He went into the drawing room, shook hands with Dr Koenig and began to discuss Leah's condition. The Swiss doctor was impressed by the quiet wisdom of this big man with the soft voice. He explained Leah's medical history, her occasional periods of exhaustion, her tenacity, her determination to make Stefan's life endurable, regardless of the cost to herself. Seamus turned at last to his niece. "I'll go in and see her now. Will you take me?"

Eleanor opened the door of the bedroom. Leah's eyes were closed, the lashes dark and thick. Her hair was raven against the pillow and her face was hollowed, marked with suffering. But dear God, she was beautiful. The vision of the nineteen-year-old girl blurred and merged with the face of the sleeping woman as if the years between had never been. He knew her, she was the same. He could bring her back, he would spend the rest of his life trying to do it. In great humility, Seamus knelt down beside her bed and thanked God that he had been allowed to find her again. He had been given another chance to help her, love her, as he had promised to do so many years ago.

Eleanor stood watching him. She wondered at first whether to stay, in case Leah should wake and become frightened at the sight of a stranger. Now she knew her presence was unnecessary. Quietly she went out and shut the door.

Seamus drew up the armchair and sat down beside the bed to study the sleeping figure, reliving all the years since their parting. Had he really found her again, this woman who was the love of his life?

They had spent only a few short weeks together. And yet it was real, enduring, the love they had discovered. Seamus had given his heart to her within hours of their first meeting. He had known, even then, that there would be problems to surmount: religion, language, culture, her youth. He was convinced that they could deal with all these obstacles, given time. But time was the one luxury they had never been allowed.

Seamus had set up his practice in Roundstone, dedicating long hours to his patients, spending all his leisure time with Richard and Helena and the children. They became his anchor, his reason for living, and he shied away from all other attachments. With the passage of time the pain dulled, but his emotions were hedged about with signs that kept people at a distance. There had been several romances down through the years as his youth ebbed away, and ten years had passed when he began to see Ciara Davitt. Helena watched with delight and relief as their relationship deepened. At last Seamus made up his mind to marry the girl, pushing away all doubts.

He took her to a concert in Galway one evening, and decided that he would propose to her over dinner afterwards. As the last chords of the Beethoven symphony sounded, the audience rose as one to call for an encore. Seamus froze as the first notes of the Wieniawski Romance filled the auditorium. Tendrils of the poignant air reached his long-buried memories, like wisps of smoke heralding a fire. He gasped. The music transported him instantly to the drawing room of the Nazarre house on that last evening in Paris. Seamus closed his eyes. Tears ran down his face as he listened to the same melody that Leah had played for him then, her face flushed in the candlelight, her long fingers pressing down on the strings of her violin, her arm trembling a little as she raised her bow. He saw her eyes gazing across the room seeking him out, dark and brimming with love. In the small Galway theatre, the music tore at his soul, destroying his defences against the past. As the last bars hovered in the air around the spellbound audience, he lurched to his feet and rushed out of the theatre with Ciara hurrying after him.

The hurt and rejection she experienced filled him with guilt, and he vowed that he would never again create such pain in another human being. From that moment onwards he knew that he could not contemplate sharing his life with anyone else.

His friends thought of him as a confirmed bachelor who preferred to enjoy the charms of a variety of attractive women. The reality was that his vision of Leah was enshrined in his innermost self, and no one could replace her.

Now Seamus sat in the half-dark beside her bed, trying to assimilate the knowledge that all this time she had been alive, a kind of prisoner, caring for a living corpse. How would she look upon him now? A man who had not suffered any of the terrors she had undergone. Perhaps he would be a stranger to her, unable to comprehend or share her past or reach her on any level. She might not ever feel again the passion she had once known with him. She would leave him, or be taken from him again. And what would his life be then?

The slow hours ticked away. He turned off the lamp, worried it might disturb her, and sat quietly in the dim light beside her, not touching her. She hardly stirred. Several times he leaned closer to assure himself that she was still breathing. At last she turned in her sleep and her hand slid down at the side of the bed. He took it in his and laid it gently back where it had been, beneath her cheek, but her fingers closed over his, and for the remainder of the night he felt the even warmth of her breathing against his palm.

In the early morning she woke, climbing to consciousness through a heavy mist of medication. For a second, in the pale filtering light, she felt a jolt of dread as she made out the bulk of a man beside her. Fear poured through her veins like molten lead so that she could not move or scream. Her thoughts tumbled between the certainty that she was back in Auschwitz where some new torture awaited her, and a vague sense of calm that was unexplainable.

"I must lie still," she told herself. "I must not show any sign of fear or consciousness. If I don't move he will think I am dead."

The outline in the dark was familiar in some way. Part of her was aware that someone was holding her hand. Leah willed herself to let go of the dream, the warmth, the clean sheets, a pillow, a mattress, the smell of furniture polish and flowers, and above all the sense of healing that came to her from the warm hand. Seamus, in a half-doze, felt her sudden movement. He sat still, aware that he could damage her fragile peace irreparably if he frightened her now. Her fingers were twitching in anxiety, pressing his hand. He wanted to take her gently into his arms and comfort her, but he dared not move. Leah opened her eyes wide. The room seemed to be the same. Yes, it was the same. She was in her bedroom, her own bed. She turned her head for a first, conscious look at the man who sat in the chair, his hand covering hers. In the pale light she could make out the blue eyes, the lines of his features, the complexion of a man of the outdoors. This was a man who had sun and wind on his face, a man of the sea.

"Leah." The voice was very low, not much more than a faint whisper. It was like an echo across a wide ocean, an echo she had imagined so many times in the past. She closed her eyes.

"When I open them, he will be gone. He is just another dream. I am having another dream." A wave of indescribable sadness rose in her. Perhaps he was dead. Like poor Stefan was dead, lying there in the cold water with his feet white and bare. Stefan was dead, that was why she was dreaming. Everything was over, she had nothing left now, no one to care for. The first sobs, as they came, tore from her throat and shook her from head to foot. Then someone was holding her, strong arms had lifted her into an embrace. She could hear a voice saying something to her.

"There, there now, Leah. I'm here, I've come to take care of you. You'll never be hurt again. Just hold on to me. Hold on to me. It's all right my love. It's going to be all right."

She did not know when she started to say his name. She had not allowed herself even to think it, for so long. She clung to him, let him rock her, and she whispered it over and over. Until she was sure he was not a dream. He was real. He was here.

Chapter 51

St Joseph de Caune, 1970

At the hospital in Montpellier the cardiologist and the nurses came and went, their starchy kindness leaving Solange in a confused state of optimism and helplessness. Henri was receiving the best available care, but in the unfamiliar surroundings of the hospital his blindness had become a prison, and he was obliged to lie powerless in his white metal bed. The specialist took Solange into his consulting room and put his arm around the frightened young woman.

"I think the best thing is to send him home as soon as we can, to the place he knows, so that he can slowly regain his strength. He's getting depressed and uneasy in here. He must get plenty of rest, but he can start to exercise a little."

"But will he be all right now, Dr Laurent? Will he be well again?"

"His heart has suffered a great deal of damage. He will never be very well again, I'm afraid, and he will have to be patient. He'll need a great deal of rest and we will have to watch him very carefully. I would be lying if I said he was out of danger entirely."

"You mean he could have another heart attack?"

"It's possible, yes."

Solange had telephoned her grandmother as soon as Henri had been settled in the hospital, her voice broken and afraid. Charlotte had been deeply distressed.

"I shall come down tomorrow, darling. You can't deal with this on your own. I'll keep you company and infuriate Aunt Jeanette. That will make your father laugh, when he's well enough to enjoy it!"

On that first terrifying afternoon, Edouard had driven to Montpellier behind the ambulance. In the waiting room he found a comfortable chair for Solange and brought her coffee and later, something to eat. Since then he had come to the hospital each day, bringing her food and drinks to supplement the grim hospital fare, and books and magazines to fill the long hours of her vigil.

Charlotte was at her most imperious when Edouard was presented to her. She wasted no time in grilling him about his family background and his education.

"Extremely intelligent, very focused and intense. Much too intense in fact – bordering on obsessive," she said to Solange. "Attractive in a dark, impassioned sort of way. There's a wicked sense of humour under the surface that saves him from being a bore. I don't know yet if all that makes for a worthwhile person. He has character and determination, though, and a genuine respect and affection for Henri. But I'm sure I'll be seeing a great deal more of him in the next few days."

Her assumption proved correct. With the *vendange* at an end, Edouard had more time to visit Henri at the hospital, keeping him abreast of the complex process of vinification that their harvest was now undergoing. Each evening Henri waited impatiently for Edouard's arrival, listening intently to the young man's summary of the day's tastings that would transform their grapes into the beginnings of a fine wine. Now that Henri's condition was no longer life-threatening, Edouard turned his attention to Solange.

"Are you coming to the *fête des vendanges* tomorrow night, Solange?" His tone was so lacking in optimism, that Henri gave a great hoot of laughter, startling them all with its strength.

"My God! Put him out of his agony, for heaven's sake." Henri was not prepared to listen to any argument. "You have to represent me, Solange, and I'm tired of seeing you hanging around here day and night. You and Charlotte must both be at the fête. I'm much, much better and you can leave me to the tender mercies of the young nurse with the soft voice. I think I'll do very well."

The *fête des vendanges* took place on a gold and azure September evening. The light seemed to soothe away all the anxiety Solange had felt over the past few weeks. Preparations had been going on for two days and Madame Prunier's kitchen was filled with bubbling pots of pungent tagine of lamb, and great pans of vegetables melding the sweetness of their juices to form a fragrant compote. Outside on the terrace long trestle tables with starched cloths and bowls of flowers had been set up. Candles were lit and coloured lights hung from the trees.

Solange stood with Edouard looking down into the brightness of the late-summer garden. She stepped back, creating a small distance between them, recalling how she had stood in this same place only months ago, as her father had announced her engagement to Guy. Now she was standing here without her fiancé, her heart seemingly captivated by another man. How could she have felt such affection for one man and yet been so instantly attracted to another? Was this how her mother had felt about her Irish lover and her husband? Seven months had passed since the first letter from Eleanor Kirwan, and still Solange felt that her life had not regained its balance. Her uneasy train of thought was interrupted by the appearance of Joel and the first workers, followed by her grandmother and Paul Ollivier. Edouard vanished into the melee of his pickers. The musicians began to play and Lorette brought a tray crowded with glasses of golden muscat.

After dinner Solange went inside to telephone the hospital and check on Henri. When she returned to take her place beside her grandmother, she saw Edouard in the midst of the workers, dancing wildly with the rising tempo of the music, his face filled with delight, his head thrown back, eyes black and flashing as he whirled and leaped. She felt a little push and turned to register Charlotte's half-smile and raised eyebrows. Then she was in the throng and he reached out and pulled her close to him. She felt the current of music flowing through them and found that they were spinning faster and faster but in perfect step, so that their bodies seemed to be welded together in a whirling wave of movement. At last they came to a dizzy halt, elated and laughing, and in front of all the assembly he kissed her on the lips as she struggled for breath.

The dancing began again, this time sweeping up Charlotte so that she was passed from one strong arm to another in a circle of young men. It was after three in the morning when the last songs had been sung and even the most energetic dancers admitted defeat. Edouard and Paul drove away with the harvesters, and Solange collapsed beside her grandmother in the cool air.

"That was the most wonderful fête we've ever had. Oh how I wish Papa had been here. He would have loved it."

"Yes, he would," Charlotte said. "But I was glad to see that you were able to enjoy a carefree evening. Now tell me about Edouard Ollivier. That's a very wild, passionate young man you have there, my dear. What are you going to do about him? He's certainly madly in love with you."

"I don't know – I've been trying not to think about it."

"Are you lovers?"

The bluntness of the question took Solange by surprise and she needed a few moments before she was able to answer. "On the day of the hail storm, I went to him. All that he and Papa had hoped for had been torn apart by the hailstones. So I went to him. And then – and then we were lovers." Charlotte made no comment and Solange heard herself stumbling on. "But we've had a disagreement. I wanted to give him my inheritance, so he could put it into the company he and my father formed together. I asked Guy to arrange it so that

Papa wouldn't know where the money had come from. And Guy made me promise that I would explain the whole situation to Edouard."

She heard her grandmother give a small exclamation. "You hadn't planned to tell Edouard where the funds were coming from? Oh Solange, my dear, didn't you learn anything from your experience with poor Guy? And how did he feel about being asked to do this?"

"I didn't think it all out properly. I just wanted to get the money into the vineyard account. I could see how worried Papa was."

"But darling, the bank wouldn't have pulled out on him overnight."

"I'd never been in a situation like that before and I panicked." Solange knew how foolish she sounded with hindsight. "Edouard was angry because I hadn't trusted him, and because it was Guy who had made me tell him the whole story. So I didn't see him after that. And then Papa got sick."

"Darling, secrets like that never work because they eat away at the foundations of trust, like rot in a building. If you love Edouard you must be able to trust him, otherwise there's no basis on which to build your relationship."

"He's so intense, fiery. Like a volcano. I love what he says, how he looks, the smell of him." Solange was laughing now, and felt self-conscious as she tried to bring her emotions out into the open for the first time. "But I'm scared too."

Charlotte made no comment but sat as if waiting for the next verse of some unfinished ballad. Now that she had begun, Solange did not want to hold anything back. It was a relief to be able to say aloud the words that she had kept in dark suppression.

"After all that's happened, I'm not sure of anything any more. Before I learned about Richard Kirwan I knew who I was. I knew where I came from and I had everything planned. It was all so simple and straightforward and honest, like the vineyards and their seasons. Now I feel guilty and unbalanced. And there's Guy. He's kind and loving, and I thought I was going to marry him. So how could I feel like this, all of a sudden, about Edouard? Maybe this is all some sort of insane phase I'm going through – a consequence of the shock I had."

"You don't really think that."

"I don't know what I think. I could live with Guy, I'm sure I could. He's good and reliable and funny and clever. And I never wanted to hurt him. But now I'm not sure that we want the same things in life."

"Darling, when you make a lifelong decision about a man, you have to ask yourself not whether you could live with him, but whether you could ever live without him. If you can answer that question truthfully, then you won't have many regrets."

"Is that how you felt about Grandfather?"

"Yes, that is how I felt about him. I knew I could never live without him. And that's the way it was."

"But what about Mama? How could she have loved Richard Kirwan and then married Papa and come down here?"

"Your mother never allowed her life to be filled with regret for what might have been. She made her days, Henri's days and yours, full of joy and meaning, and she lived them to the full."

She rose from her chair a little stiffly and held out her hand to Solange. "I'm up too late for an old lady and it's getting chilly. Reach down into your soul, Solange, and don't be afraid. Because the answers to your questions are there waiting for you."

Henri returned home two days later, excited as a small child at the beginning of a long-anticipated holiday but exhausted by the short car journey.

"Ah, the countryside! Thank God for that wonderful smell and for the feel of the air. I wasn't made to be cooped up in a hospital. I don't think I ever want to see the inside of another one, no matter what my condition. If I'm going to die I want to die here, darling, in the place where I'm happy and comfortable."

Solange hugged him fiercely, feeling how much weight he had lost in that brief time, hearing the shortness of his breath as he returned her embrace.

"You're not going to die, and you're not going back to the hospital either. Now, I want you to rest, because this evening Edouard is coming to see you and he'll stay for dinner."

It was an evening of quiet contentment. Charlotte described her first visit to the house twenty-four years earlier, making them laugh at her exaggerated horror of the old plumbing and the numerous crawling and buzzing creatures that had invaded her spartan bedroom. They talked of the harvest for the region as a whole, and of the plans they had for the coming year.

"I'd like to come and walk around the vineyards a little," Henri said to Edouard.

"Perhaps tomorrow in the late afternoon we could visit some of the new areas with Joel and you can explain to me which grapes you have planned for each section. And I'd like to be there for the tasting."

On the following afternoon, however, their excursion had to be postponed by the arrival of Guy St Jorre. Henri's face lit up with pleasure as he greeted the young man. Charlotte linked her arm through his as they moved towards the terrace to join Henri in the September sunshine. Guy seemed cheerful, his tone betraying no hint of his feelings about Solange from whom he had heard nothing since his visits to Henri in the hospital. She looked at him now, as if for the first time, laughing at something Charlotte had said, his eyes flecked with green, his body relaxed and loose-limbed. He was so attractive, so consistent, so easy to love and to like. But watching him, she remembered her grandmother's words, and she knew that she could live without him. When he rose and took his leave of them, she went with him to the door.

"Well Solange, your plan has worked out just as you had hoped. And Henri tells me he thinks Edouard's mother might be the anonymous investor. None of us would have dreamed that up, no matter how hard we'd tried! I'm so relieved to see him at home and improving." He looked at her for a long moment. "You know where to find me when you need me."

"It would be easy to let you believe that I'll change again, that things will return to what they were before. I'd like to believe it myself. But I can't do that Guy."

She was so overwhelmed by sympathy and affection that she could not prevent herself from reaching up and kissing him softly. The old feeling flared in her suddenly as her lips touched his, but she knew with sadness that the flame would die. He did not turn when he reached his car, or raise his hand to wave, but stepped in, closed the door and drove away and out of her heart.

Chapter 52

Geneva, 1970

Four days had passed since Seamus's arrival, and Leah was making gradual progress. He made her rest, kept everything around her calm, helped Eleanor to prepare their food. In the evenings he settled down to read to Leah, to play the music of her choice, and to make himself endless cups of tea. He slept on the sofa and was awake at the slightest sound from his patient at night, padding softly to her bedside to sit close to her until she slept again. Now, while she was resting, Seamus sat on the terrace in the sunshine, talking to Eleanor and Gareth.

"What will happen now, Seamus?" Eleanor asked.

"I want to bring her home with me, but I haven't dared to broach that with her yet. I'll have to ask Jim if he'd take care of the practice for longer, or find another doctor to fill in for a while."

"Suppose Leah never feels able to leave this place?" Gareth looked at Seamus sombrely. "What will you do then?"

"I'll have to think of some way I can stay close to her," Seamus answered without hesitation. "Maybe I'd have to retire from medicine. I've made a promise that I'll never leave her, and I'll hold to it."

"Oh Seamus, you must think this out more carefully! To leave Connemara and everything you love there. Have you really counted the cost of an action like that?" Eleanor could not disguise her concern.

424

"Now that I've found her after all these years of desolation, now that I know she's alive, nothing I have would be worth a grain of sand if she wasn't with me." He had seen her doubts. "That's not just romantic talk, my dear. It's something I've always known, from the first time I met her."

"But she's been so badly hurt, so damaged. She's beautiful still, and an extraordinary human being with such courage and grace. But can you be sure? Can you really be sure after so long?"

"My dear, love can be experienced in different ways. But for me it has been possible to love just one woman for all those years, and no other. And I think we can make a life together that will be filled with love, in spite of all that's happened. It won't be the same kind of love that we might have shared had we been together since we first met. I realise that. But we'll come to it with a deep gratitude that we have a chance after all."

Seamus leaned over to kiss his niece on the cheek, and then left them to walk down to the lake and along the shore. Gareth stood with Eleanor beside him, wondering if she would ever feel that kind of love for him. He longed to touch her, to tell her again how he felt about her. But he was afraid that she would reject him, and then their situation would become impossible.

"I'll have to go slowly and carefully," he thought. "I'll just have to be patient and try to win her with all the skill that I can muster. But will she ever love me like that?"

Eleanor turned towards him and looked up into his face intently. "Yes, I will," she said.

"You will what?"

Eleanor glanced at her uncle's retreating figure, and then up at Gareth again. She slid her arms round his neck. "Yes, I will love you like that, if you'll let me."

Her mouth was close to his. He could feel her breath and he inhaled the sweet fragrance of her, and felt dizzy. "Can you read my mind as well?" he asked, staring into her blue eyes.

"Only when you're thinking the same thing as me," she replied. "We can love each other like that, can't we? Because I do love you, Gareth Duggan, and I can't fathom how I never knew. And I want you to love me, and hold me, and never let go of me."

Gareth put his arms around her and kissed her. "Will you marry me? Marry me, beautiful, sweet, wonderful creature. Let me love you with my body and my mind, my soul and my spirit." She relaxed into his strength and smiled up at him.

"Could you marry me very quickly, do you think? Because now that I've found you, I don't want ever to be separated from you." Then she said suddenly, "What about the children? Oh God, what will they think?"

He laughed, and answered her without hesitation. "My dearest girl! You know they adore you. And they'll be pretty impressed that their mouldy old Dad has managed to snare such a prize!"

Eleanor was studying every detail of his familiar face as he spoke – the lines of laughter round his eyes, the strong nose and full mouth, the way his hair rose with a life of its own away from the high forehead, and the little tracks of sadness that had etched their path across his expression.

"How could I not have realised before now what a devastatingly attractive fellow you are!" She was laughing as she covered his face with kisses, her fingers touching his features.

He murmured her name, drank in the miracle of her closeness as they stood holding one another, swaying gently. Seamus, looking back suddenly, saw the two figures and was thankful, even as he prayed that Leah and himself might be given the same joy.

"Oh God, I have to leave tomorrow," Gareth exclaimed in dismay. "When can you come back, Eleanor darling? How long must I do without you?"

She shook her head, covering his mouth with her fingers to stop him saying it, wanting to shut out any other day, to immerse herself in the moment.

He took her hand away gently. "The Kirwan Press will go down the tubes, if one of us doesn't do some work soon!" He was still breathless, half-laughing.

"Oh damn! Why did I have to fall in love with a responsible man?" She kissed him lightly, tempting him away from reality, back to the exhilaration and gladness of their discovery. But she was laughing too as she went inside, calling back to him. "Leah should be waking up soon from her siesta. I'm going to make her some tea. Then if Seamus doesn't mind, how about taking your fiancée out to dinner tonight?"

After Gareth had left the following morning, Eleanor sat on the terrace and wrote to Solange de Valnay. Her thoughts had been increasingly with her half-sister and she felt strongly that Solange should share in the discovery that both her father and mother had been brave, unselfish people who had given so much to others, and sacrificed so much themselves. She picked up her pen and began to write all that she had learned.

On the day of Stefan's funeral, the sun shone in a cloudless sky. He was buried in a small cemetery overlooking the lake. Several of Leah's colleagues from the Conservatoire were there, together with Dr Koenig and his wife, Stefan's nurses, and some of the staff from the clinic. The members of Leah's quartet played a tribute to his life, and his grave was a carpet of flowers set down in the midst of the surrounding fields. Leah had written to Countess Svenssen but there had been no acknowledgement of her letter. Walking away from the fresh, damp earth of the new grave, Eleanor knew that she must now return to Dublin.

Her uncle had been delighted by the announcement that she and Gareth had made, certain that she had found the ideal partner. Eleanor realised that his future, with or without Leah was something he had to work out for himself. They did not need her now, and she wanted so badly to go home. She wanted to feel the texture of Gareth's face, touch his hair, and have the strength of his arms around her.

On the morning after the funeral she said goodbye to them. As she went up the steps to the taxi, Leah called out her name and ran out to hug her, holding her close.

"I don't know how to thank you, Eleanor. You truly are your father's child. Here, take these. I want to give them to you." She handed Eleanor a bundle of letters, tied with ribbon. "They are Richard's letters to me. I want you to have them, and I want Helena to see them. So that she will know. She needs to know. And give that man of yours the very best of yourself," she said. "Hold nothing back. He loves you. It is a gift beyond price, to be able to love like that."

Eleanor got into the taxi, holding the letters close to her, resolving not to read them until she could do so with her mother. She turned around to wave to Leah and saw her slight figure walk down the steps and into the small house by the lake where Seamus was waiting for her.

Chapter 53

Dublin, 1970

Gareth was waiting at Dublin Airport. Eleanor ran into his embrace, laughing with excitement. He held her, kissed her, gazed at her.

"What are you looking at?" She smiled up at him.

"I can't believe that you haven't changed your mind!"

"Never!" she whispered. "You will never get rid of me now."

As they drove towards Killiney she turned and put a hand on his arm. "Could we go to the cemetery first? There's something I want to do."

"Of course." He glanced at her, concerned, but her face told him nothing.

At the graveside, Eleanor knelt down, her lips moving silently. He thought of the evening he had found her here, at the edge of the cliff. Looking at her bowed head, he vowed that she would never again have to face such things alone, not while he was alive to care for her.

She took a piece of paper from her pocket and smoothed it out. Without looking up, she said quietly, "Gareth, you said to me before he died that I should write to him. Do you remember?"

He remembered all too well seeing her crouched on the steps, overwhelmed with misery because she could not ease her father's suffering.

"I didn't do it then," she said. "But I should have. He might have been able to tell me if I had. It might have made it easier for him."

She turned her face away. Flashes of Richard's last days appeared in her mind. She saw herself spooning liquid between his cracked lips, singing to him all the old tunes they used to sing together on car journeys, or gathered round the fire in Seamus's house in Connemara.

They had all been with him at the end. Helena sat beside him, stroking the lank hair back from his forehead, whispering words of comfort. Lizzie, tears spilling from desperate eyes, clung to his other hand where it lay on the coverlet. James stood by the side of the bed, his hand on Helena's shoulder. Eleanor was acutely aware of the terrible battle raging inside her father. She willed him to let go, to slip away. No one should have to suffer like this. Then his eyes were open, for one brief second. A light and sweetness suffused his face and he smiled. His fingers closed on Helena's hand one last time and she leaned down to hear him murmur his last words. Then he was gone.

Eleanor dug gently into the soil, laid the page down, and covered it over so that the flowers surrounded her last testimony to her father. Silence surrounded them in a moment of peace. Richard was very near. Eleanor looked up at Gareth.

"He knows now, doesn't he?"

"Of course he does, my love."

Gareth bent and took her hands in his own, gently brushing away the crumbs of earth. Then she rose and walked away, her head against his shoulder.

Helena came from her studio when she heard the car draw up in Killiney. She had a smudge of paint on her nose, and Eleanor felt a surge of relief. She looked good. The dreadful strain and tension had eased.

"Coffee, we must have coffee," she said.

They followed her inside. Eleanor stopped at the door of the drawing room with an exclamation of surprise. The picture on the wall behind the sofa was new. A large canvas, full of Helena's magical talent with light and water, it showed the sweep of Gurteen Bay, with the Twelve Bens in the background, as though from the eyes of a hovering bird. There was an atmosphere of weightlessness about it, as if the viewer soared on wings above the landscape. In the water, when she looked closely, Eleanor saw that there was writing, melting into the waves. On the rocks were two large seals, and a standing figure. As she moved closer, Eleanor saw herself, surrounded by a mystical light, depicted with a beauty she never dreamed she possessed. Words caught in her throat.

Helena was standing beside her. She said quietly, "It's for you. It's what I see, when I look at you, Eleanor. I can't say it very well. But I thought maybe if I painted it, you would understand. I was always better with a brush."

She hugged her mother's small form and whirled her round suddenly. "I can't believe you've painted this for me! And Mother, I have to tell you something extraordinary and wonderful."

Helena's face lit up. "Thank God, you did it at last, Gareth. I began to despair of you."

Eleanor was looking at her in amazement. "How did you know? Oh Gareth, you promised!"

"I never said anything, I swear! Your mother is a witch." Gareth was laughing in protest. "She knows too much!"

He drew Eleanor close to him to hold her again, lingering in the happiness of their reunion. "Helena, thank you for the coffee. I must get back to work but I'll leave my prize in your care."

"Come for dinner, Gareth. James will want to see if he approves of the match." Helena was smiling, her voice teasing and light with happiness.

Helena and Eleanor stood for a few moments looking at the picture, then went to the kitchen. The percolator hissed and gurgled and the smell of fresh coffee filled the air. It was good to be home. As they sat over their coffee Eleanor took out the letters that Leah had given her.

"Mother, there's so much to talk about. But first I have something to show you. Leah wanted you to read these," she said. "She gave them to me for all of us, but especially for you."

Helena took the letters, and slowly untied the ribbon. They were old, some of them going back to 1948, the pages yellowing, all in Richard's spidery hand. He had held his pen with a strange grip because of the injury to his hands. Sitting very close together they began to read the testament to his love. Amusing, sad, funny, the letters of a man who knew that the person he was writing to had no family, and so he offered his own so that Leah might feel she belonged. They laughed at incidents Richard had described, remembering moments of childhood, disaster, triumphs and failures. There was no doubting his deep love and admiration for his wife, his desire to encourage her burgeoning talent. The mentions he made of the past and of his years of imprisonment were without self-pity, though many were marked by profound sadness. He was writing to someone who knew what he had experienced.

The account of his journey to Paris to receive the Croix de Guerre, the first and only time he had seen his daughter, Solange, and said goodbye for the last time to Celine, came very late in the letters. Eleanor realised that he must have written it shortly after he had learned of Celine's death and when his own terminal illness had been diagnosed.

I cannot believe that she is gone. I still remember every moment of that stolen time. I suppose it should never have happened, but I think providence intervened, so that I might have that one brief day with my little daughter, and with Celine, to carry with me for the rest of my life. Rightly or wrongly, I have always been so grateful for that.

When the letter came with the news of the Croix de Guerre I was going to tell Helena. I felt I couldn't live with the secret any more. But somehow I couldn't find the way to begin. So I told her I

432

was going to Paris on university business, and asked her to come with me. I thought there would be an opportunity to explain it there. Helena was full of plans. We hadn't been in Paris since the war began. She wanted to go back to all the old places we'd known. The more she talked about it, the harder it became.

And then my mother had a stroke. I decided I would get someone to accept the decoration on my behalf. I had already insisted I did not want any publicity. So I told Helena I could go to Paris some other time. In the back of my mind there was relief that I would not have to tell her, that maybe there would be a better opportunity later. How very weak and cowardly I was. But Helena insisted that I go to Paris as planned. She would take care of my mother, she said, and we would go together one day soon.

I was so ashamed, and so elated at the same time, because it meant I could write to Charlotte, and ask if she could arrange for me to see Celine. Imagine my joy at finding my little daughter Solange as well, so beautiful, so full of life. It made the pain of parting that last time just a little easier, to know that we had one perfect thing that we could always share, out of all our loss.

I wanted so desperately to take Celine away with me that day. I had never fully understood, even in all the years in the camps, that pain could be so pure and so full of desolation. I was completely torn. I cannot describe to you, even now, how I feel about her. She gave me back my life, and I left a part of it with her. And yet I loved my wife. I loved Helena so much, and my other children. When I went home, I left the decoration with Celine. It belonged to her and to Charlotte, far more than to me. I never saw them again, neither Celine nor my daughter. And I never told my beautiful, generous wife that I, the most abject of cowards, had received a decoration for bravery that I did not deserve, and that I had left it with the real heroine whose story I could not share.

But it's not right, Leah. It's still not right. The truth is best,

433

bitter though it may be at first. I did them all a disservice — Celine and little Solange, Helena, James, Eleanor and Elizabeth. And now I don't know how to mend it. I only know that Celine is gone. She was my spiritual anchor and my light, and I never acknowledged to my family the debt of love that I owed to her, and to my child. Instead, with each moment that has gone by, I have dug myself a grave of silence.

Don't let it come to this for you Leah. I made you a promise, just as Celine and I made each other a promise. But it is killing me as slowly and inexorably as the cancer that is eating into my bones. Forgive my dark thoughts, my dear, but I love you as I would my own sister, and I love Seamus as my dearest friend. You should tell him, Leah. You should tell him before, like me, you find it is all too late.

Your loving friend,
Richard.

Helena and Eleanor sat staring at the letter. This was the one Eleanor had brought to Leah in Switzerland, his last lines to his treasured friend and confidante. James had come in and was standing in the doorway, watching them. He smiled at his sister and she took the letters from her mother's hands, and gave them to him. He sat down quietly and began to read. For a long time there was silence. When Helena spoke at last they could barely hear her words.

"He loved me."

James moved to sit close beside her. "Of course he did. Anyone could see that."

"You don't understand it at all, do you?" Helena's voice was sharp suddenly. She searched out one of the letters and gave it to him. "This is the only time he ever speaks of her, anywhere in all this correspondence. After she had died."

434

James took the letter and read it again. He looked into his mother's face as he finished and spoke very gently. "Yes, he loved her. But it didn't diminish his love for you. You were worth more to him than any other kind of happiness he could seek." He looked again at the last lines. "And this goes some way to explaining why he did it."

"Did what?" Eleanor asked.

"Made that incredible will," James answered. "It's always puzzled me. He must have known what anguish it would cause, how it would hurt us all. And Solange, too. Even now, I ask myself why he would choose to make the bequest in such a bizarre way."

"He didn't," Helena said.

James looked up. "What do you mean?"

"He didn't choose to do it that way." Helena clasped her hands together and looked at them both for a long time.

"I did it," she said.

Eleanor gazed at her mother, aghast.

"He was right," Helena said. "It's better to tell the truth. That's what he said to me, the night he told me the whole story about his relationship with Celine, about Solange, everything. Except Leah." She made a high, bitter sound that might have been a sigh or an attempt at a laugh. "He knew he was going to die. There wasn't much time left. He said that he hadn't told me about Celine before, because he didn't want to hurt me. That he hadn't been able to talk about anything that had happened during the war. It was too raw, too horrible."

She used her knuckles to banish the tears. Her voice rose, harsh and angry. "I saw, only, that he was referring to the pain of parting with her. It seemed to me he had made a sham of our marriage, living a lie with me, all the time longing for another woman. I knew from the way he told me she had died that he had really loved her, that he still loved her." She poured herself another cup of coffee with shaking hands. "I found him in the study with a letter from a friend of hers in England, telling him she was dead. Her mother had written too.

435

He was weeping. And suddenly my life was a pile of ashes, reduced to nothing, because he believed I would never be able to understand how it could have happened. And now, years afterwards, he was telling me that he had loved another woman all the time, and had a child by her, and he was weeping because she was dead."

The bleakness in Helena's face was frightening.

"What did you do?" James asked.

"Do?" Helena's laugh ended with a small sob. "I did what I always did, whenever he was in distress. I comforted him. Took him in my arms. Said it was all in the past, over and done with. But it wasn't over and done with at all. Not for me. She was dead, and I was left to compete with her memory, and the daughter she had left behind."

She gathered up the letters that Leah had sent. "That was the truth as I saw it that day," she said. "He was right, you see. I didn't understand." She touched Richard's final letter to Leah and said softly, "I never understood until today. But on that night I told him he must acknowledge his daughter in France, tell the whole family." She sighed again. "I didn't realise, of course, that Seamus already knew. Richard couldn't decide what to do. He was so sick, so vulnerable. I knew he was struggling. But I was determined in my rage, in my perception of what he had done to me. I told him to write an additional clause into his will acknowledging her, and that I would take care of the explanations and the execution of his bequest."

"You were to have told us? Before the will was read?" James could not hide his amazement.

"He trusted me. Why should he not?" Helena put her head in her hands. "I had never let him down, in all the years we were together. Yet only weeks after he left to go to France, he had betrayed me. That's what I chose to believe when he told me about her. I felt he had turned his back on me and made the rest of our lives together a lie."

"You drafted that codicil?" Eleanor was staring at her.

"Yes." Helena clenched her fists. "I had it written. And yes, I brought it to him to sign, and had it witnessed. He kept asking me should he not write to her grandmother, to ensure discretion for her, and protect her privacy. But I could only think of how he had deceived me over that trip to France, when he met her again and saw his child."

"But did he know what was in the codicil he signed?" Eleanor was pale with shock.

"Yes, of course he knew. He signed it. Because I promised I would explain everything to you before the will was read, insisted it would be better coming from me. I was in the grip of some kind of madness, discovering first that I was losing him, then finding that I'd never really had him at all. The more he voiced his concern for the feelings of his daughter in France, and for his children here, the more I wanted to make him admit what he had done."

"Regardless of the consequences?" Eleanor could not disguise her horror.

"I was in such turmoil! I was vindictive, perverse in my anger and in my love for him. But during those last few days, I realised I couldn't tell you what I'd made him do – destroy that poor girl and her relatives. I wished Seamus was here. I prayed he would come quickly and fix things. But he didn't and we couldn't contact him."

"Jesus!" James could not look at his mother directly.

"Even then, in those final moments, Richard wasn't with me."

"But Mother," James said, "I heard him whisper your name. He was looking at you with such love, and he said 'Helena'."

"No, James." Helena's voice quavered. "He wasn't looking at me. And he didn't say 'Helena'. He said 'Celine'.

"I don't remember much more about that day, or any of the others that followed. I don't remember the funeral at all." She looked up at her son and daughter, her face grey and drained. "On that last day, I fully intended to tell you everything, and then arrange for Solange's inheritance to go through her grandmother, so that Madame de Savoie could do whatever she thought would be right for Richard's child."

437

James took Eleanor by the hand as Helena tried to finish her story. "In the end I was sure that it was Celine he saw, just before he died." She put her elbows on the table and covered her face. "I didn't want to remember anything, feel anything, ever again."

"And what now?" Eleanor asked at last.

Helena straightened up, and squared her shoulders. "Now I shall paint, and rebuild. The disguises and deceits are over. And I shall have to see to Seamus and Leah. Seamus has lived alone for far too long. I should go down there and start getting the place ready for them. I'm certain she will come."

"Mother, what an extraordinary person you are!" James said, his mind still reeling.

"Have you only just realised that? What's going on here?" Elizabeth had just come in. Her coat and bag landed on the armchair. Then she noticed Eleanor and flew to hug her sister in silent apology. A car door slammed. Eleanor glanced up at the clock.

"That will be Gareth," she said, jumping up. Helena caught James's eye and he smiled at her broadly.

"James, Lizzie," Eleanor began. Gareth had appeared in the doorway behind Elizabeth. "Gareth and I have something to tell you."

Chapter 54

Geneva, 1970

In the drawing room overlooking the lake, Leah took off her jacket and sank on to the sofa. She smiled at Seamus, her dark eyes shining, her face flushed with pleasure. "The food was wonderful and your choice of wine was inspired. And your French is almost fluent. A perfect, relaxed, beautiful evening."

His heart was singing, brimming with hope. Could he tell her now how much he loved her — could he take her into his arms and kiss her and hold her?

"There's something we need to talk about, Seamus." He made a small gesture of protest, but she reached out and touched his hand gently. "You need to get back to your work. You need to go home."

Seamus ran his fingers through his sandy hair, trying to hide his sudden agitation.

"I'll be all right now. I'm strong again. I can cope."

Seamus nodded, dumb with dismay and dread.

"You must not stay any longer. I have to learn to get on by myself." She continued in a rush, refusing to let him speak. "Please don't make this harder for me. It's painful enough already. I'm not the girl you fell in love with. That was thirty years ago. I've seen too much, known too much."

"I cannot even begin to imagine the horror of what happened to

439

you." He took her hands and lightly traced the numbers of the tattoo on her bare arm. "But that hasn't made you less of a person. One day, perhaps, you will talk to me about it all, and I will be ready to hear whatever you have to tell me, however terrible it may be. I will be with you and I will help you."

Leah stared at him, knowing she must say everything now, make him walk away before his dream destroyed him. "In the camp they made us play marches while thousands of us stood shivering in the snow, falling from exhaustion and being beaten to death or torn to pieces by the dogs as they lay there. The guards took a special satisfaction in making us watch that." Her voice was unemotional and distant. "One day an officer ordered me to come to his house. I had to take my violin and go there in the evenings to play for him. In exchange for a little food, to be warm for an hour or two. And I could wash myself sometimes, get rid of the filth. He wanted me to look clean in his house, for his guests. One evening he took the violin from me."

Seamus looked directly at her, holding her hand tightly, making no attempt to prevent her from continuing the story she had chosen to tell.

"Horrible, degrading things he made me do. For a piece of bread, a cold potato, a moment in a real bathroom with water and soap. I hated him, but there was no refusing."

She paused again. Still Seamus held her hand, waiting for her to continue.

"I was lucky," she said at last. "He was transferred to the Russian front and I never heard of him again. But for years I felt dirty – used and soiled. I tried to tell myself I'd had no choice. But in my heart of hearts, I felt I had sold out for a crust of bread, a little warmth, because I was too cowardly to refuse, too afraid to die."

There was a long silence. Seamus did not dare to speak. Instead he stroked the skin on her arm, and lifted her hands to his lips to kiss them. After a while she spoke again. "When I'd been at the

Conservatoire for a while I joined a chamber music group. The other violinist was very talented. A brilliant and inspired performer and a fine man. He fell in love with me and we began an affair. I used him, Seamus, because I wanted to see whether I could allow a man to touch me again. I wanted to see if I could still be a normal woman."

She stood up abruptly and moved away to the doors looking out over the lake. "It lasted for two years. He wanted me to go away with him, to put Stefan back in the hospital. But I would go home to my husband who would cling to me and mumble my name and I would think of the day I found him in the clinic and I knew I could never do that to him. Eventually I told that poor man that I didn't love him, that I never had loved him, and I could never love anyone again."

"Leah, all these things that have happened in our lives, they were steps in a journey that has brought us back to each other. But even the most painful experiences can teach us to love and help one another now."

"I couldn't bear your pity, Seamus," she said. "It would destroy both of us."

He walked across the room to where she stood and put his hands on her shoulders, gripping her hard. "I didn't come out of pity. I came because you are the missing part of myself, of my life. I love you, Leah and I cannot be whole without you."

She broke from his grip and went to huddle in her chair, afraid of what she might feel if she let him come too close. She began to recount all the fear and cruelty she had known, to tell him of her efforts to absorb all the humiliation that had been hurled at her, and hold on to her human dignity. She spoke of the days when her body had been crawling with lice, of the dark, freezing mornings when they had marched out to yet another hell, and her comrades had gradually been taken from her in the insistent nightmare of death and execution. She described how hope had deserted her, and she had lain down in the snow, and waited for death.

Seamus sat quietly as she poured out the ugly litany. He listened to every dreadful detail until at last she was silent. Then he went to kneel beside her.

"I have never known hurt like yours, Leah," he said finally. "Except in Richard. And he was blessed with people around him who loved and cared for him when he came back after the camps. I'm humbled by the extraordinary spirit that brought you through it all." His words were tender and hopeful. "I never suffered the way you did, but I never gave up hope either. I prayed for some miracle that would restore you to me. And now the miracle has happened."

She put her hands on his head almost like a blessing. He reached up and touched her cheek with the back of his hand as he had done, so many years ago, when he had begged her to come with him the first time. Now he was watching for some sign that she might be willing to let him look after her.

"Come with me to Connemara, Leah! I want to love and care for you. I want to show you it is possible for us to find happiness now, together."

She stared at him for a long time. His voice was so desperate. She closed her eyes and sighed.

"Please, Seamus. I can't think. I'm just so tired."

"I'm sorry, I'm being selfish." He stood up, angry with himself.

"I think I'll just go to bed. Goodnight."

In the chill hours of early morning he woke to see her standing at her bedroom door. He slid off the couch and touched her gently. "You're frozen. Let me take you back to bed and get you warm."

She made no gesture of resistance, and he helped her into bed and covered her. Then he sat down beside her and rubbed her cold hands, stroked her hair.

"Seamus please hold me. I'm so cold. I've had a bad dream. I'd like you just to hold me."

She was awake now, her eyes wide and desolate. In one sheltering movement he climbed in beside her and drew her close to him, warming her with his body, speaking to her as he would to a child. "Just lie still and soon you'll be warm."

Her trembling ceased and soon her breathing became slow and regular. He lay beside her sleeping form, his arms around her, every part of him alive to her closeness. When she stirred he felt the involuntary tensing of her body and then she moved into his embrace. In a sort of shock he pulled away to look at her, saw her smile, felt her arms come around him. She offered her mouth for his kiss. Her fingers wound in his hair and she drew his head down towards her. In delight and wonder he touched her, saw her eyes close at his caress. He began slowly, carefully, as though she was made of porcelain, touching her, kissing her with tenderness, murmuring all the words of love he had stored up for her in his dreams. She drew him down to her, whispered to him, clasped him and arched up under his weight. Her responses were passionate and she moved urgently against him until at last they reached a fusion of joy and release. Then she lay quiet in his arms, her face turned towards him, and he saw the love still alive in her.

When he woke the sun was shining. In warm remembrance he reached for her but she was gone. He sat up. Through the open window he saw her standing on the jetty where they had found Stefan's body. He went outside to stand beside her, touching the prominent bones at the back of her neck. She did not turn around.

"Would you like breakfast?" he asked, smiling. "I'm pretty good at doing breakfast."

She shook her head and moved out of his reach. Puzzled, he dropped his hand to his side and waited, unsure what to do. At last he went inside, bathed, shaved and dressed. Then he went to the kitchen to make coffee. This is natural, he told himself. It will pass, if I just give her time. He felt her presence before he turned around. She was standing in the doorway, watching him. He poured two cups of coffee and offered her one. At last she spoke.

"Nothing has changed, Seamus. I can't come with you. The girl you fell in love with is gone. And I don't think I can ever take on responsibility for another person's happiness. Especially someone as precious as you."

"Leah, don't you love me?"

"I cannot love you," she said. "I cannot accept your love. I don't know what love is any more. I only know how to survive and that is not enough, not for you." She stood with her eyes closed, beyond tears. "Go back to Ireland, Seamus. Go back to your work and your friends and your family. I need to be alone. Don't be afraid that I'll do something stupid, take my life. I'm a survivor. That is all I am. I don't want you here – I can't bear it." She gave him a twisted smile and then turned her face to the wall.

In the raw silence that followed Seamus left the kitchen. Leah did not move. Before he went back to Ireland he wrote her a letter and propped it up on the hall mirror.

Leah
You are my love, my life. There is nothing without you. You know where I am.

He left for Ireland that afternoon. He told no one that he was coming home. Two weeks passed before he felt able to contact his sister. When she heard the desolation in his voice, she went immediately to Connemara.

For a time he hoped that he would hear from Leah, but the weeks that passed brought no word from her. Eleanor came down to Roundstone with Gareth, their joy creating a gladness and a wretchedness that Seamus tried to hide. He rode with Helena, sailed with his brothers, tried to create days that did not feel hollow and aimless. Autumn brought sweeping rain and a flu virus that filled the surgery.

Seamus worked round the clock, always on call. He trudged out to isolated cottages to visit the elderly at home, spent hours dispensing medicines and advice, soothed crying children and concerned mothers. Late on a rain-soaked Friday he saw his last patient out and went back to his office to wait for Helena.

He began to clean up, filling the steriliser, locking the drugs cupboard, finishing his reports. He heard the door of the surgery open and called out. "I'm just finished, Helena. Come on through." He was gathering up the last of his patients' records as the door of his small consulting room opened. "I hope you didn't get drenched out there. That's quite a downpour."

"Helena told me I'd find you here." She was standing stiffly in the doorway. Rain ran off her face and hair, dripped from her coat and scarf. She lifted one hand slightly and then stopped.

"Leah."

"What I said to you, when I told you to leave." She was speaking with difficulty and he saw that her fists were clenched. "I hurt you Seamus, but I was hurting myself too. A punishment."

He was afraid to move towards her or to speak.

"You'll have to be so patient with me," she whispered.

"I left you a letter Leah. I meant what I said."

"Yes."

"You shall have all the time you need."

She stepped closer to him and stared into his face, searching for the slightest sign of hesitation. Then she held out her hand. "I'd like you to take me home with you now, Seamus. I'd like you to show me your home."

Chapter 55

St Joseph de Caune, 1970

"Solange, how about driving us over to Roucas Blancs to see what's happening with the fermentation? And I'd like to visit the new vineyards. Last night's dinner made me realise that I'm back in the swing of things at last."

Solange was tempted to object, fearing that the excursion would be too much, but Dr Laurent had said it would be good for her father to live as normally as possible, and he was so enthusiastic at the idea of leaving the house that she did not have the heart to refuse him. She went to find her grandmother who was immediately keen to join them. They drove past the freshly ploughed earth, and the soft furrows of the fields that were waiting for planting.

Edouard and Joel set off with Henri for a short walk, while Solange and Charlotte watched their progress from the shade of a fig tree. They returned sooner than expected, their steps slow and careful. Solange saw at once that Henri was tired and a little breathless.

"Perhaps we should go home now, Papa? And you could come back tomorrow for the tasting?"

But he was determined to visit the *chai* to touch the tanks, to feel the temperature and taste the wine. When they arrived home his face was grey and bathed in perspiration. He did not want any lunch and Solange helped him upstairs to bed. When she had settled him in his bedroom and gently sponged his forehead and hands with a damp face towel, she went downstairs to telephone Dr Laurent.

She returned to the bedroom to find him lying with his eyes closed. His breathing was quick and shallow.

"Solange?" His voice sounded so feeble to her that she put her hands up to cover her mouth, lest she should let out a cry of distress.

"Yes Papa, I'm here."

"Will you read to me, darling? I'm very weary and I might fall asleep, but I'd love you to read to me."

Her eyes stung with tears and she went to stand by the window and compose herself before beginning to read, for she did not want him to detect the catch in her throat. Then she drew up a chair beside the bed. She was turning the pages to make her choice when he reached out to touch her.

After a few moments he seemed to have fallen asleep and his breathing sounded more normal. Solange ran out of the bedroom and went to look for her grandmother, flinging herself into Charlotte's arms. "He's so weak. Will you phone Dr Laurent again while I go back upstairs and stay with him?"

She returned to his bedside and after a little while Charlotte came to join her, sitting quietly in a large wing chair beside the window. Henri slept on, his breathing even, his face pale but without any hint of strain. Solange sat quietly, grateful for her grandmother's presence. When Dr Laurent arrived Lorette showed him upstairs, her face white with alarm.

"He seems fairly stable now. I'm going to give him an injection that will let him rest peacefully and calmly. He should really be in the hospital, but I know he'd hate it, and the move might do him more harm than good in his present condition. I'll be back tomorrow morning, but you know you can telephone me any time. Get some rest."

They dined together downstairs, neither of them with any appetite, and then returned to the library.

447

"I can't bear for him to be like this, just when everything is falling into place for him. It's so unfair, so undeserved. He's been my loving, steady guide since Mama died. Always so patient, so strong. He never seemed to lose his balance." Solange was speaking half to herself. "And although I know now how it all happened, how Mama became involved with Richard Kirwan, it still seems so unfair on Papa, somehow, because he wasn't ever at fault."

"Solange, it's hard to believe that after all you've learned about these three people, you could come up with such a shallow judgement of them. Or any judgement at all, in fact." Charlotte made no attempt to hide her anger and disappointment. "There's no such thing as a blameless life, you know."

"But there was no blame attached to Papa! It was Richard Kirwan who caused all this turmoil! He was to blame for their having to come down here. She married Papa and came South because she couldn't have stayed in Paris, unmarried and with a child, without disgracing our family. Wasn't that it?" Solange's voice was full of bitterness.

Charlotte did not answer for a moment, and when she turned towards Solange her gaze was coldly direct, her face stern. It was the wrong time perhaps, but she knew that she must tell the remainder of the story. She explained, plainly and accurately, the circumstances of Henri and Celine's move to the Languedoc. She did not omit her own doubts at the time about the wisdom of Celine's plan, or the reasoning behind it. She knew that Solange would find it both hurtful and incredible to think of Henri as a man on his way to alcoholism, but she felt it was too late to spare the girl any part of the truth of her parents' tangled story.

"She came down here for father's sake? Because he was becoming a drunk?" Solange was incredulous.

"You know, Solange, I loved all three of these people very much – and I mean all three of them. Your mother was my adored daughter. And Henri was both our friend and our protector, long before he married your mother. As for Richard Kirwan, he was a man of the most astonishing courage and bravery. He saved my life, just as surely as your mother saved his. And I loved and admired him to the end of his days."

Solange still could not grasp how Richard Kirwan could have genuinely and sincerely loved two women. Her grandmother began again, choosing her words carefully, holding her granddaughter's hand.

"It was my feeling," she said, "that with Helena, Richard had always felt strong, in control, protective towards her. He was glad to play that role. But with Celine he simply felt blessed. With her he could bare all his vulnerability, talk to her about experiences that were too frightful to share with anyone else. She had seen the wounds to his mind and his body, and she had no fear of them. It was Celine who lived with him all through his physical and mental tortures, who watched over his excruciatingly slow recovery. He knew she accepted every part of him as he was, that no one would ever know his most terrifying secrets except for her. He was as captivated by her strength as he was by Helena's frailty."

"But couldn't he have recovered without making Mama fall in love with him?"

"He never needed to seduce your mother, Solange," Charlotte said firmly. "It was a singularly beautiful, unselfish love they had for one another and it never, never died."

"You make me feel very small and foolish, Grandmama."

"Richard continued to visit me for many years. He felt that he had been responsible for my losing all my family heirlooms, my furniture, to the Germans. For years he sent me gifts for the house, to replace the treasures I had lost. They will all be yours one day, my dear. And so will the house in Avenue Mozart. He bought it from me years ago and put it in your name, with the understanding that I would remain there for my lifetime. No, don't say anything, darling. Because your father – your natural father – was a great man, and I can only hope that one day you will come to understand that and accept it, as your mother and I knew and accepted it."

There was a sound from upstairs. Solange jumped up from her chair and rushed from the room, taking the stairs two at a time. Henri was awake, and struggling to sit upright in his bed.

"What is it Papa? What can I do for you?" She was beside him, listening to his breathing, hearing the effort he was making to gather enough strength to speak.

"You were always my darling little girl, Solange, and I was always your loving Papa. I was your father, your Papa, and I loved you, and that was so good, wasn't it?"

"Oh Papa, yes it was good. And it is good, darling Papa. And there are so many things we're going to do together still."

He was very quiet for a while and Solange leaned back a little in fear, seeing that there was no movement behind his closed eyelids. Charlotte had come quietly into the room and was standing beside the bed. She took Henri's hand and he looked towards her and smiled.

"Ah, dear Charlotte. What precious friendship and great adventures we've shared. And what days of happiness and affection! I wouldn't have missed any one of them."

"Nor I, Henri. Not one." Charlotte kissed his forehead.

His eyes were still closed. Solange smoothed his pillows, moving him gently into a more comfortable position. He opened his eyes suddenly and looked up at her and he was smiling.

"Solange. You've grown into such a beautiful young woman. I never realised how beautiful you'd become!" He did not say anything more then, and as she bent to kiss him he sighed and she was overcome with terrible apprehension.

"No, Papa no! Don't leave me now! It's too soon. I need you Papa and it's too soon."

There was a smile on Henri de Valnay's face but she knew that her adored Papa had gone, and that she would never be able to smile with him again. She sat beside him sobbing quietly. Charlotte rose and came to put her hands on Solange's shoulders, and she too wept for the loss of a deeply loved son and a brave and honourable friend.

In the days that followed, Solange moved in a daze through the preparations for the funeral. She telephoned Cedric Swann with her devastating news and although his health would no longer permit him to travel, she knew that his spirit was beside her, sharing her sorrow. It seemed that all of the Languedoc was there as she walked, dumb with grief behind Henri's coffin and listened to the prayers for eternal rest and peace. At the cemetery, she watched as the coffin was lowered into the ground, listened to the sound of weeping that she thought might be her own, and heard the first clod of his beloved earth as it hit the wooden casket in which he lay. All around her the cypress trees seemed black and lonely against the dome of endless sky.

Afterwards there were people in the house, touching her with sympathy, taking her arm, murmuring to her. As if from very far away she saw Guy, felt his arms around her, recognised the sorrow and compassion that flowed from his body to hers. As he held her for those brief moments, she experienced a wrenching regret and affection for him, and for all that they had shared. He looked at her for a long moment. Then he spoke her name and the word was a question. Solange reached up and touched his face with her fingers. Then she slowly shook her head and her heart was heavy with sadness as he turned and walked away.

She knew now what was meant by never, that death was never, that she would never see her father again. Charlotte remained with her for a week and tried to persuade her to come to Paris, rather than to stay alone in the house, but she refused. One morning, in a wasteland of days later, she awoke to a stream of sunlight gilding her bedroom, so that she blinked against its invasive brightness and rose to close her shutters. When Lorette appeared with a tray of coffee she saw the letter. She turned it over several times, looking back at all the pain that this same hand had brought to her and she was tempted to tear it in several pieces and never learn its contents. But simple, human curiosity overcame her other emotions and she opened the envelope and sat down at the window. After she had read the letter several times, Solange put it away carefully in her desk and went downstairs.

An hour later, she was still in the library with Henri's keys, opening the cabinet in which he had always kept his personal papers. There were three drawers of documents and reports, letters and photographs, and she pored over them. At last she came to the files concerning his health. Slowly she read through the reports that had come in over the years, from the many specialists he had visited in Paris and London. She read the last of the opinions, written almost fifteen years ago, regretful but definite with regard to the finality of the prognosis. The clear, hard words told him that he would become totally blind. Amongst the many letters she found a small, buff envelope with the name of a laboratory on the outside. It was addressed to Henri's doctor in Montpellier and marked private and confidential. The paper was yellowing with age, and the text was short and precise. It confirmed that the results of the recent tests undertaken by Monsieur Henri de Valnay had shown that he was sterile and would never be able to provide his wife with a child.

Solange sat motionless. He had known, then. He had always known she was not his natural child, but he had loved her with all his wonderful heart and spirit, and without reserve.

On the following afternoon she was sitting at the desk in the library, beginning the task of replying to the hundreds of letters of condolence she had received, when she heard Lorette open the hall door. Edouard came into the library and stood looking down at her. He held out his hand to her and she took it and rose to her feet. She felt her love for him flare in her and she placed herself in the circle of his arms and raised her hands, her fingers touching his mouth.

"Is there something I can do to make it more bearable?" he asked. "Can I tell you how much I love you, how much I want you? Can I ask you now, at this terrible moment, if you will marry me, Solange, and we'll make children that Henri will be proud to see growing up in his vineyards. Will you marry me, Solange?"

She did not answer him and turned away to the window. Without looking back at him she said, "I'm going away for a little while, Edouard. Away from here."

"Will you go to your grandmother in Paris?"

She spun round to look at him directly and then he saw her smile at him.

"No, I'm not going to Paris. But I am going to travel with my grandmother. We're going to make a journey together. It's a kind of pilgrimage I suppose and she is the only one who can guide me through it. I want to go to Ireland, Edouard, and she has agreed to come with me."

"And then?"

"And then, in a while, when the grief is not so piercing, so over-whelming, then we will plant the new vineyards together. For you and me and Papa. And for our children."

Epilogue

Le Monde, Paris
30th September 1970

GUN-BLASTS SHATTER CHARITY DINNER AS GUESTS WITNESS SHOCKING SOCIETY MURDER

Buenos Aires, Argentina

The Swedish Industrialist, Count Carl Svenssen was shot dead at a glittering charity dinner last night. Countess Aneka Svenssen, one of the city's most wealthy and influential socialites, was married to the count for more than fifty years. Eye-witnesses described how she rose to her feet and took a small revolver from her evening bag, shooting her husband twice in the chest. Countess Svenssen then turned to the assembled guests and said, "This was for my son."

The count was pronounced dead on arrival at the Buenos Aires City Hospital. Countess Svenssen was arrested and is under a suicide watch in Buenos Aires prison. Count and Countess Svenssen were resident in Paris from 1937 to 1943 before moving to Argentina.